Sarah Bartrum grew up in the Nortu ~
south to study Education at Exeter University. She ...
extensively around the world and worked in a variety of locations
and employments. She now lives in Devon with her husband and
two children.

www.sarahbartrum.com

Tracks

by
Sarah Bartrum

Mason
Publishing

Prologue

Some recent academic work suggests that radicalisation occurs as people search for identity, meaning and community. It has been argued in particular that some second or third generation Muslims in Europe, facing apparent or real discrimination and socio-economic disadvantage, can find in terrorism a 'value system', a community and an apparently just cause.[1] We note that organisations working on Prevent have also found evidence to support the theory that identity and community are essential factors in radicalisation.

[1] Dalgaard-Nielsen, A. (2010), Violent Radicalisation in Europe: What We Know and What we Do Not Know. Studies in Conflict and Terrorism. 33 (9) pp. 797-814

On previous page:
Extract 5.22 from the Prevent Strategy, HM Government June 2011. Contains public sector information licensed under the Open Government Licence v3.0

Saturday 23rd May 2014

It was a regular Saturday, like any other in London. Ralph, a paramedic, had started his shift at eight as usual. Halima was on her way home with the shopping. Austin was doing overtime on a project that was behind schedule. Adam Rasheed had just played his last game of football. Ever.

Adam set the pace along the pavement, his football boots loud against the tarmac. He wanted to get back in time to watch West Ham play on their home ground.

'I still can't believe we beat them.' Johnny said, trying to keep up.

'You betcha. We were on fire today.'

'Well you were.'

'Can't believe they want me to go for the try outs. Johnny, just think, this could be my way in, a few years and I could be playing for England.' Adam leaped into the air and thrust his fist towards the sky as they approached the station.

Adam scanned the electronic departure screen.

'Platform one. Quick.' He beeped through the barriers and charged up the stairs. The train was waiting, its doors open wide. He leapt into the carriage, dropped his kitbag and turned around, breathing hard. Johnny had just made it to the top of the stairs and slowed down, looking left and right.

Adam waved, 'Over here!'

Johnny spotted him and sprinted forwards but the doors were closing. They shut tight with a clomp and Johnny slapped the glass with his palm.

Adam laughed at his friend through the window. Poor bugger, he would have to catch the next one. Still, they'd meet up again at the Boleyn ground. He waved cheerily to his best mate.

The train lurched forward, gathering speed towards Clapham Junction.

A few miles away, just before Battersea bridge crosses the Thames stands a tall mirrored building belonging to Thyredata Enterprises. Inside on the fifth floor, in an almost empty open-plan office, Austin was sitting at his computer with his colleague Tim hovering by his shoulder. They were analysing the results of the first upload of Transport Rail's data into the new test system.

'So what do you think?' Tim said.

'Rather more problems than I expected.' Eight hundred thousand and sixty four to be exact but maybe that wasn't unreasonable at this early stage of the project.

'We're going to be here all day.'

'Yeah I know, I'm not giving up my Sunday too. I promised Matt we'd get out of London for a change.'

Tim nodded at the photo on Austin's desk of a smartly dressed young man with dark hair. He was laughing at something off camera.

'Nice photo. How long has it been?'

'Three years pretty much.' Austin pulled the photograph closer.

Tim whistled, 'Must be true love.'

Close by, in the Lidl car park, an ambulance was standing with its back doors open. Ralph and Emma were two hours into their shift and had delivered only one casualty to A&E so far.

An elderly gentleman was sitting on the bed in the back while Ralph finished applying a dressing to his knee. Ralph encouraged him to ring his wife while a supermarket employee arrived and handed the gentleman a bottle of orange juice.

The man put his phone away. 'We only live around the corner. My wife's coming to get me.'

'How are you feeling now?' Ralph asked as he carefully lowered the man's leg back to the floor.

'Yes, better. I think I'll be fine.'

Ralph touched the old man's shoulder gently. He suspected there were bruises from the fall but nothing serious. It amazed him how some old people were so resilient. Just like his kids, putting a brave face on it, brushing the dirt off and getting on with it. Ralph smiled.

'We'll wait with you until she arrives.'

Beyond the car park was the train line and beyond that, on Falcon Road, Halima was carrying two bags. She had a variety of fruit and vegetables from the Battersea market which was even cheaper than Lidl. The bags were heavy and Halima paused to put them down. She was wearing a scarf pinned around her lined face and covering her hair. It helped to keep out the brisk wind that chased a polystyrene burger box across her path. Halima rubbed her hands together where the plastic handles had left deep clefts. Ahead loomed the low tunnel under the train tracks. It was lit at regular intervals but the lights did very little to repel the oppressive dark. The sound of cars got louder as the brick walls closed in around her. She took a breath and held it, to keep out the smell of urine. She wouldn't stop in the tunnel, she'd keep going to the far side before she took another break from her load.

A bus came thundering past, the number forty-nine glowing orange. She should have taken it, saved her aching limbs, but the money from her cleaning job didn't stretch far. Halima clamped her lips together and stayed focused on the bright daylight at the far end. Some things simply had to be endured, and this was just one of many.

Adam didn't make it home, nor did he ever see that West Ham match.

Austin had a growing sense of doom. On Sunday he stayed home. Alone.

Ralph had the longest and busiest shift of his life.

Halima reached the end of the tunnel. Just. But without her shopping.

It started with a screech. One that didn't stop but kept increasing so that those waiting on the platform had to clamp their hands over their ears. Metal shearing against metal. Of course, it was joined by other sounds: the crumpling of the concrete platform, the screams of the people, the smashing of the roof as it toppled forwards onto the stricken train.

A group of tourists embarking at Putney pier looked behind them down the river Thames. One of them pointed at a gull assuming the screech had been from the swooping bird.

In Thyredata Enterprises, Austin glanced at the large windows. The building had shuddered as if a large lorry had rumbled past.

Those that were closer were under no illusions. Traffic stopped, pedestrians looked around them in fear. The vegetable seller at Battersea market, who had sold Halima five kilos of best British spuds, shut his mouth suddenly after the words 'Get your-'.

Ralph had his hand on the door handle of the ambulance. He looked towards the terrifying noise, his hand squeezing tighter and tighter until the metal left a groove on his palm.

Halima fell to the ground.

For a brief second before Adam lost consciousness, he wondered why his kitbag was rising off the train seat like some kind of levitating miracle.

The people on platform ten stepped back as the train carriage slid past on its side. The undercarriage was facing them, displaying all its pipes and wires. The wheels were still spinning as if gaining traction against the air, aiding its forward momentum. Sparks slashed the scene making one child wonder if there were fireworks. The smell of burning was acrid in his nose. A lady heading up the stairs to platform ten holding the hand of her two year old stopped and clung to the vibrating handrail. She scooped her child up, turned around and started walking back down again on shaking legs.

The carriage came to a stop leaning awkwardly across the end of platform nine. The screeching ceased, leaving the air smoky. Tiles and bricks rained down on to the carriage as it lay on its side like some huge felled beast. The objects bounced and clanged as if thrown by angry residents determined to keep on fighting, despite the monster being dead.

Soon even that noise stopped and the harsh reality of silence deafened those that could still see.

Part 1

2 ½ years later

1

Adam - Playing to win

Adam Rasheed pulled the strap tighter that bound his dead legs together. Returning his hands to the rims of the wheelchair, he gripped the smooth metal firmly. He was ready to give Stumpy what for. The whistle blew and Sophie had the ball. Adam made a sweeping turn towards the basket right around his opponent. The wheels glided smoothly over the sports hall floor. Pushing through a gap between two others he beckoned for the ball.

'Soph.'

She sat small in her chair, the basketball oversized in her hands but still she launched it high. Adam watched it arc away from him, her aim was pathetic, but then Stumpy slid up, leaning far to the side, and grabbed the ball after the first bounce. Adam shoved his wheels hard coming up close on Stumpy's flank. He put on a spurt of speed hoping to cut in front but there was a great clang as they crashed together.

'Watch the chair,' Stumpy shouted at him.

Adam didn't care. He pulled back but Stumpy was already reaching up, lifting partly out of his seat as he launched the perfect basket. It was all right for him, he wasn't carrying around heavy dead legs. In fact Stumpy had left his prosthetic ones leaning against the wall by the benches. Adam glared at the nonchalant way they stood there, one still wearing the trousers Stumpy had arrived in, the other looking thin and naked gleaming in the harsh lights of the sports hall.

Their coach Mikael retrieved the ball and said, 'Great shot Stumpy. Shorter, faster passes Sophie. Adam, don't forget this is not a contact sport.' He put the whistle back in his mouth and blew it long and hard. 'Right that's it, good game everyone.'

Adam looked away. His hands were stinging and he checked to see if he'd broken the skin. There were a couple of blisters on his right hand and another on his left. Maybe he should try wearing gloves again like Sophie. He turned and started heading towards the benches where his friend Vijay sat grinning at him in that quirky way of his. Behind and to the right, he recognised Stumpy's girlfriend. Lucky bastard, another reason to hate him. As Adam's chair rolled past the prosthetic legs, he swerved slightly and one of them clattered to the floor.

'Oops sorry,' he said loudly without turning around. Adam drew up next to Vijay. 'Have you been videoing it?'

'You could be a bit nicer out there, it's only a friendly match.'

'I'm not going to make the team by being nice am I?'

'Have you considered you might not make the team at all?' Vijay stared.

'That's not an option. I don't belong here with this lousy lot, I need to be with other professionals. Real athletes. It's who I am.'

'Hey Kiddo.' It was Cara, Vijay's carer, teeth shining through bright painted lips. 'I'm gonna get Vijay to design you some bull bars to go on the front.' She cackled loudly nudging Stumpy's girlfriend who giggled on cue. Adam's face grew hotter.

'So the videos?' he said to Vijay.

'I think we've got enough footage don't you? Besides I've already programmed in an analysis and categorised your moves.'

'What does that mean?' Adam leant forwards to pick up his sweatshirt and bag that he'd left on the bench.

'It's all about statistics, we see where your trends are, patterns of failure, patterns of success, that kind of thing. For example I have a category called 'left turn' and it sequences all the shots of you making a left turn.'

Adam slung the bag through one arm and over his head so the strap lay diagonally across his chest then looked at Vijay.

'What - like all the left turns in all the games that you've videoed?'

'Yes. And I have to say it looks like you have a stronger right turn than left.'

'Really?' Adam stared at Vijay. For someone who spent his life in an electric wheelchair with only minimal movement in his left arm and hand, Adam was amazed at what this guy could do.

'Ready to go boys?' Cara stood looking at them both with her hands on her hips. 'Good game Kiddo?'

'I'm not a kid.'

Adam turned his wheelchair and headed for the exit. Why did Cara always make him so irritated?

'Oh dear, teenage angst.' Cara's voice was particularly loud, as usual, echoing around the sports hall.

Stumpy called across the room, 'Better luck next week.'

Adam banged the footplate into the sports hall door, making it swing open.

He could hear the whir of Vijay's electric wheelchair behind him and the clip clip of Cara's high heels.

'Actually I am an adult,' Adam said between his teeth.

'Still a teenager,' said Cara.

'Only for a few more months.'

'Well you still need bull bars.'

'No I don't.'

'Actually I also have a category called 'crash' which is quite interesting to watch,' added Vijay.

'Will you two get off my case. You're supposed to be helping me make the team. The national coach is coming in a couple of weeks. How else will I ever become an Olympic champion?'

'More skill,' said Cara.

'More practice at your weak areas, my analysis program should help.'

'Be more like Stumpy,' Cara grinned.

Adam wanted to bite back but he held his tongue. He was grateful to Vijay; he just wished sometimes he wasn't encumbered by his annoying carer.

The cold air was brutal, the wind rushing over Adam's bare arms.

'I'll get the car,' Cara disappeared across the tarmac.

'So are we going back to your place so I can watch this amazing program of yours?'

'Fraid not,' Vijay gave one of his crooked half smiles, 'I've got a date.'

'What?'

'Don't look so surprised. I'm not just a brainbox in a chair.'

13

Adam studied his friend, his old style wool jumper, loose jogging bottoms hiding his withered legs. Vijay's head was permanently cocked to one side where it leaned against the head rest. The built-up chair fitted around his body snuggly with controls built into the left arm rest where he could grasp a joystick with his hand. Vijay's hair was combed with a side parting and looked like something his uncle would be proud of. Vijay was quite a lot older than Adam, he must be at least thirty if not more. Who in their right mind would want a date with Vijay?

Suddenly Adam felt embarrassed, he looked down at his dead legs. Who in their right mind would want to date Adam?

Adam zoomed along the pavement. A pretty Asian girl was walking towards him wrapped up against the cold but she didn't meet his eye. He wondered about who Vijay's date was and pushed the wheels harder. All he wanted was to be home. He shot past a man dawdling and almost caught his Jack Russell under the wheels.

'Hey, watch it!'

Adam snarled in reply.

'Stupid Paki,' the guy called after him. The comment bounced off Adam, his arms pumping to make it to the junction at the top of the hill. His muscles were beginning to burn and he slowed down, turning the wheels in a longer, slower rhythm. At least the exercise had warmed him up against the winter wind. There was a bunch of people waiting to cross at the lights but Adam knew that they'd likely move out the way so he didn't slow his pace. It was a group of young men chattering loudly together. However, Adam was forced to come to a sharp stop, his hands sliding on the rims. He felt his blisters smart with the friction. Adam was ready to give these guys a piece of his mind for blocking the pavement when he realised they were all wearing football kit, mud splattered on their legs, sweatshirts and bags slung carelessly on shoulders.

'Hey Adam.' The traffic lights changed and the group moved as one into the road, all except the guy that had spoken. Adam steeled himself.

'Johnny.'

Adam watched Johnny glance at his mates and then back down at Adam, sitting in his chair with his hands stinging.

'How's it going?' Johnny nodded in a vague way indicating Adam's useless legs.

'Fine,' he lied.

'Great.'

There was an uncomfortable pause as they both averted their eyes from his dumb limbs. 'How about you?'

'Yeah good, we just played Dartford, can't believe we won, they're way above our league. It was a great game. We've got a new...' and then his voice tailed away and Adam followed his gaze across to the group. Adam could still recognize most of the team; he searched the familiar backs and heads. There was a blond lad he didn't recognise. Was that him? Was that their new striker?

Adam nodded, not wanting to look up into Johnny's face, instead he kept staring at the lads who had reached the other side and were meandering en masse down the hill towards town.

'We're going to get something to eat,' Johnny paused, 'wanna join us?'

Adam gripped the rims really tight. 'No.'

'Right.'

Adam glanced up to see Johnny shrugging his shoulders and looking towards the team.

'I'm...' Adam felt the rush of emotion, the anger, the embarrassment. He searched for a lie, 'I'm meeting a friend.'

'OK, sure.' Johnny was visibly relieved. 'I'll see you around.'

'Fine.'

Johnny leapt into the road just as the lights turned green and a horn blared as he darted across and ran to catch up with the rest. Johnny's muddy legs moved fast and confidently. Him and Johnny, that's how it had been before. Team mates, buddy athletes. But that was then. Adam watched him get absorbed back into the group as it neared the bottom of the hill. A new striker. Of course they had a new striker. What else were they supposed to do?

Adam swung his chair back on course grimacing as he felt the tears teasing at the corners of his eyes. It wasn't fair, it was a disaster. That should have been him, trotting down the hill on healthy legs, jesting with his team mates. Their hands slapping his back, congratulating him on the fabulous goal he'd scored. That was what it had been like, before the accident. But not now. He blinked, forcing the tears aside, pushing hard on the wheels to get some distance between him and the football team. At St Martin's Avenue the tears were almost winning and his vision blurred. He refused to pause to wipe his face but kept on, even faster. The lamp post took him by surprise, he misjudged the turn and it caught his left wheel which bit into his hand and swung the chair a quarter turn to the side. Pain ripped up his arm.

'Are you all right mate?' A man in an overcoat came hurrying towards him.

'I'm fine!' Adam bellowed as the pain hit him again like another kick in the teeth. He reversed, manoeuvred, blinked several times and set off at a renewed pace, the skin on the back of his left hand raw and cool as the air passed over it. It was all shit. As he hit the curb of Creighton Avenue, he didn't stop to look, just ploughed straight across. What did it matter anyway? There was a screech of tyres loud in his ear but Adam paid no heed. The pain in his hand and the hurt in his heart were far louder.

By the time he reached the newsagent on the corner, he had worked off a good deal of his frustration and his hand was only throbbing. He slowed right down, realising how hungry and thirsty he was. At least his mum would be home to feed him. Tired after the game, he forced his arms to keep going. If only it had been a normal Saturday, Cara would have given him a lift back to Vijay's. Her noisy chatter and Vijay's optimism would distract him from his failure. They could watch that program Vijay had created. Work out his best and worst moves. There were only two weeks left before the national coach would be coming. Adam needed to be ready. He needed to convince the coach that he, Adam, was the best player and deserved a place in that team.

'Hey mate, your hand's bleeding.' A youth was stood leaning against a wall next to his friend.

Adam was about to give a sarcastic rebuke when he recognised the wall was part of the mosque. He couldn't risk offending the guy. His mother's relations permeated every street around here. He slowed to a stop and looked at his hand.

'Yeah, only a scratch.'

'Looks like more than that to me,' he moved forwards off the wall and leant towards Adam intently.

'It'll be all right.' Adam swallowed and managed a smile.

'There might be a first aid kit inside,' the young man offered gesturing to the building behind. His eyes didn't follow his hand, instead they stared at Adam, taking him in, studying his lifeless legs, the chair. There was no shame in his gaze but a thoughtful intensity.

'Yeah, there's one in the kitchen. Mustafa used it when he burnt his hand on the kettle,' the friend chimed in.

'It's all right, really,' Adam put his hand back to the wheel.

'Are you Nadiyah Rasheed's kid?'

At the mention of his mother's name, Adam inwardly sighed. It wasn't a sad feeling, more of a longing, a wish to be home, to be free of all the pain and difficulties. She was so good at soothing away the turmoil with her tea and Jalebi.

Adam looked up, they must be a similar age to him, maybe a little older. They were waiting for a response.

'Yeah.'

'I'm Faizal, my mum's related to your uncle's second cousin or something like that.' He shrugged and held out his hand.

Adam shook it.

'And I'm Tariq,' the other man said.

'Adam,' they all nodded together and then were silent as a small group of elderly men came out of the mosque, turned away from them and continued muttering together down the street. Now that he'd started thinking about his mother and the attention to his hand, Adam could see how awful it looked. Bits of skin had peeled back leaving a raw surface that was bleeding and trickling down his fingers. It was a mess. If he went home looking like this, it would give his mother more reason to worry. She had done enough worrying for a lifetime since the accident. Adam felt his chest tighten at the thought of his mother's tears.

'Why don't you come in?' It was Faizal, watching Adam study his hand. A huge smile suddenly swept across Faizal's face. It was such an open unabashed grin that Adam felt like he had to agree.

'OK.'

There was a small step up from the pavement through the door which was easy enough to negotiate. They led him to a disabled toilet where Adam rinsed his hand. When he came out, Faizal applied a dressing and one of the men inside the mosque expertly bandaged it. They offered nothing but kindness which only made Adam feel even more guilty. He never came to the mosque, rarely prayed even, but fortunately they didn't ask questions. When they'd finished, Adam thanked them and was about to leave but turned back.

'My hand,' he said, then paused staring at Tariq and Faizal. He couldn't ask them to lie, not after their kindness, but maybe they could at least say nothing. 'It was an accident- at the basketball court.' Adam swallowed. 'I wouldn't want my mum to worry.'

The boys said nothing, only nodded and then Faizal was holding open the door for Adam, their eyes locked together, his gaze overly long.

'Thought you might have been in a scrap or something. Parents don't need to know everything. Only Allah knows all. You should come to the mosque sometime,' he said.

Adam nodded, suddenly awkward.

'Here, take my number,' Faizal had pulled a mobile from his back pocket. 'We're family after all, us guys should stick together.' Another of those huge grins made Adam smile back.

2

Adam – Patterns of failure

Adam and Vijay were sitting side by side in their wheelchairs staring at the three monitors on Vijay's desk. A video of a basketball game was playing showing Adam swerving to the left. The video jumped to another game where Adam was closer to the camera and again turning left but this time with the ball on his lap.

Vijay paused the sequence. 'See what I mean, your body looks stiff, I don't think you're leaning far enough.'

'Wait, play them again,' Adam leaned forwards studying intently.

Vijay twiddled the controls and repeated the sequence. 'Here, I'll show you a comparison with a right turn.'

'Pause it.' Adam almost shouted. 'You're right,' the image froze. 'Look how fluid I am there.' He pointed to himself on the screen, his body leaning over to the right, almost tipping the wheelchair.

'When am I ever wrong?' Vijay said.

'This is so cool mate, I don't know how you do it. Play it again.'

'Simple really. Once I'd classified the clips, it was easy to rearrange and sort into similar sequences.'

'Did you see that? What a cool spin.'

'It's your weaknesses we're supposed to be analysing remember?'

'Yeah, yeah, all right.' Adam waved his hand at the screen. 'Again.'

Vijay sighed and hit the repeat. Adam couldn't take his eyes off the monitors, it was clear that he was definitely using much more of his body during the right hand turns than his left. Adam drew his head back and leaned experimentally to his left side away from Vijay.

Vijay looked at him. 'Have you got more nerve damage on one side than the other?' He used the joystick to manoeuvre his electric chair so he was facing Adam.

'I don't think so. It's just the bottom of the spine, nothing up top is wrong.'

'Hmmm.' Vijay gave that thoughtful expression of his. 'Face me square on.'

Adam turned his chair and tried to sit normally so his friend could study him. 'Well?'

'You look even.'

Adam pulled up his shirt to try and get a look at his stomach and side muscles. 'Am I more developed on the right?'

Cara suddenly appeared in the doorway. 'Ooh, is that for my benefit, Mr Hunky?' she said, staring at Adam's bare chest.

Adam yanked his shirt down. Vijay smirked at his friend and then turned his chair to face Cara.

'Is it that time already?' Vijay said.

'Fraid so, we need to get those limbs of yours moving.'

'Give us ten more minutes,' Vijay said.

'All right, but no more, you know how stiff and painful it'll be if you leave it too long.' Cara had her hands on her hips, then she pointed at Adam with a red fingernail. 'He's been working for hours on that stuff for you, don't you go making him suffer.'

Adam frowned and glanced at Vijay's lopsided grin, then she was gone.

'Why do you let her tell you what to do?'

Vijay raised his eyebrows. 'I employ her for exactly that reason.'

Adam shrugged, he didn't get it. Surely once you'd left home and finally got rid of your parents telling you what to do all the time you wouldn't want to stick someone else in their place.

'Without her, I wouldn't have any freedom. I wouldn't even be able to do my job.' Vijay stared pointedly at Adam.

Feeling uncomfortable, Adam looked back at the screen. It was all right for him, working as his father's finance director for a chain of hotels. Adam didn't have that luxury. It was true he envied Vijay's apartment, his lifestyle, even his brains, but he wouldn't want to be him. Vijay could never be completely independent, but Adam could. In fact, maybe sooner rather than later. His luck was about to change big time.

'Shall I put this stuff on a memory stick for you?' Vijay said.

'Yeah, that would be great. Thanks Vijay, you're a star.' Adam grinned at the frozen image of himself leaning to the right. Getting into the national wheelchair basketball team was going to be his ticket into a new life. One where he could be independent, maybe even afford a place of his own, nothing quite as grand as this, but still. He'd be a professional athlete. A man, instead of a disabled teenager living with his parents. Adam stared at the screen as Vijay copied files.

'There's more to life than basketball,' Vijay said.

'Not for me there isn't. Basketball *is* my life.'

'That's the problem.'

'You don't understand what it's like.' Adam indicated the electric chair and Vijay's withered body. 'To be a professional sportsman you have to live and breathe it. You didn't know me when I was playing football, seriously, my whole life was about the game, it has to be if you want to succeed. Basketball's no different. I need to train every day, and this recording stuff you've done, it's great. I can target my practice even more. I am so going to get this.'

'Maybe.'

'There's no maybe about it. This is it, Adam Rasheed is heading for gold.' He struck his fist into the air. 'I haven't been this good since we beat Sutton. I was on fire and I'm going to be like that again. Two more weeks of training, I'm going to nail this.'

Vijay glanced sideways at Adam. 'And look what happened after that game.'

'Come on, it's not like I'm going to be in another train wreck. What's up with you?'

'Do you ever gamble?'

'No. Why?'

'Just as well.' Vijay glanced away from Adam.

'What's that supposed to mean?'

'You're the kind of person to put all his money on a horse running at thirteen to one.'

'Are you trying to say I'm unlucky? That was a once in a lifetime event. Listen, it's all about the skill and the training, and I've got it, we've seen on the videos, all I need to do is get that lean improved on my left side. Everything else is top notch. I'm heading for victory and you're just jealous.'

Vijay sighed and turned the electric wheelchair. 'You need to pull out the memory stick down there. Put a new one in for me, they're in the second desk drawer.'

'No probs.'

'And unplug me too.'

'Sure thing,' Adam disconnected everything and followed Vijay's electric chair as it whirred out of the office. 'Fancy coming to watch me at the next Olympic games?' Adam called out.

*

Adam rolled the wheelchair in a neat figure of eight over the tarmac, then swung left, aimed and shot. Perfect, he was definitely improving on his left side. He went over to collect the ball passing it from right to left and back again, faster and faster, then bounced it on the ground on his left side while pushing the rim of the wheel with his right. He headed to the far end.

'Adam!'

He stopped, scooping the ball onto his lap and noticed a figure hunched against the cold. It was his dad. A sudden burst of pride set Adam moving again, he made straight for the hoop at the opposite end, swishing past his father and launching the ball even before he'd come to a complete stop.

'Pretty good huh?' Adam collected the ball and went to join him.

'Your mother has been calling your mobile. You're late for dinner.' His gruff voice was loud across the empty court.

'Yeah but did you see that shot?'

'How can you even play in this gloom?'

Adam shrugged, his good feeling beginning to dissipate. He

hadn't really noticed the light fading. He looked up at the dark sky, an orange sheen across it. Of course it never got really dark in London, not with all those lights.

His father began walking back towards the road and Adam pulled alongside him.

'Don't you think I've improved? Vijay's got this cool set of videos and he's worked out some formula or something so he can put the same moves all together, like all my successful baskets or all my misses so I can see where I'm going wrong.'

'I'll tell you where you're going wrong. Staying out here all day and night instead of helping your mother or getting a job.'

Adam slowed down to a stop.

'You didn't come here to see me play, did you? You just came to have another go at me.'

'You're not a child any more Adam. This is just a game. You need to get serious.'

'You don't get it do you? I *am* serious.' Adam pulled up his sweatshirt then stretched it outwards over the ball so that he wouldn't drop it on the way home.

His father had also stopped a few yards ahead. He turned around to face Adam, rubbing at the edge of his ear where the cartilage was flattened into a small disc. It was a habit of his father's pulling at the edge of his ear when he was considering something. Adam had that strange anomaly on his own ear too, round and flattened like a small coin but he resisted the urge to touch it. An inherited trait from his father just like he had his eyes and the shape of his nose. Sometimes Adam wished he looked more like his mother, like his older brother Sully did. Suddenly his father stopped rubbing and pushed his hands deep into the pockets of his coat.

'You have to start thinking about your future.'

'I am.'

'How can you be? What will happen when you're too old for this, when you get to thirty, which isn't old at all. What then?'

Adam set off again past his father. The air was freezing.

'Just leave me alone.'

23

He went into the kitchen where his mum was dishing out dinner. It smelt good.

'How was your practice?' his mum asked.

'Too short.'

'But you've been out there hours. What happened to your mobile?'

Adam dipped his finger into the Nihari and tasted it, enjoying the surge of saliva as the spices ignited in his mouth.

'More coriander.'

'Really?' She shrugged and tore some leaves from the plant on the windowsill. 'What have you done with your father?'

'He was too slow.'

The front door banged shut and Adam felt his shoulders tense.

'I think we should speak to your cousins, get this child some proper work,' his father declared skirting around Adam's chair and giving his wife a kiss on the cheek.

'Oh Rafi, give him a break, it's hard.'

'A break? Spending all day playing basketball? Is that what Sully's had, a break? If you want to get ahead in this country, you need to work hard. And if you want a decent job, you need a decent education.' His father picked up a roti which was swiftly yanked out of his hand and placed back on the plate.

Adam locked eyes with his father who loomed over the wheelchair. Adam gripped the wheel rims tight and refused to look away. With a sick feeling, Adam knew this would never have happened if he still had the use of his legs. Before the accident, Adam had been growing fast, his long lean body about to surpass his father's, although not yet as tall as his brother, Sully. And after two and a half years he was surely taller than them both, yet nobody could tell. Not with him stuck in this dumb chair. Now his father had all the power and Adam had none. Unable to bear the forceful figure any longer, Adam reversed his wheelchair and went into the dining room.

They started to eat. Adam was starving and heaped in mouthfuls. The steam rose up from the food taking the aroma around the room. It was delicious. He ignored the silence and the irritation emanating from his father and let the taste of the ingredients fill his mind. She'd used fresh ginger. If he'd been here to help he would have added more garlic.

They all heard the front door open and slam. It would be Sully.

'Smells good,' he smiled around the door, his white teeth shining. Then he disappeared into the kitchen and Adam heard him washing his hands at the sink. Sully walked in with a glass of water and sat next to Adam.

'Been working hard?' He clapped a hand on Adam's back and then laughed.

'It is not a laughing matter Sully. You and I understand the value of hard work, but it seems that Adam here does not. Playing games is all he wants to do.'

'They're selecting for the British team next week,' Adam growled.

'And what's your plan B?'

Adam hunched his shoulders, scraping at the last of the curry on his plate.

'He doesn't need a plan B Dad, he's going to be a world famous wheelchair basketball player. Aren't you little brother?'

Adam hated it when Sully called him little.

'How can you be so sure?' His father frowned.

'Aw, come on Dad,' Sully continued, 'there are loads of famous wheelchair basketball players, you've seen them on TV, in the newspapers. They earn shed loads, like pop stars aren't they?' Sully gave Adam a punch on his shoulder and roared with laughter.

'Exactly, a fairy tale, that's what it is. You need to get out of that dream world of yours and start living in reality.' Adam's father clanged his fork onto his plate.

'You think I don't know what reality is, in this thing?' Adam pushed his chair back hard so that it hit the wall.

There was silence for a moment. Then his mother pulled her scarf over her face to hide the tears and muttered, 'There's more roti.'

'That's your excuse for everything,' Sully said quietly.

'Shut up.'

'Why should I? Dad's right, they've been pandering to you ever since you came home from the hospital. You need to start pulling your weight.'

'Shut up!'

'Or go to college or something.'

'Shut the fuck up.'

His mother made a sharp intake of breath.

'Adam. That's enough, go to your room.' His father's voice was low.

'I'm not a child. And I'm going to my room because I want to get away from you lot.' Adam shoved his wheelchair against Sully. 'Move.'

Sully stood up and pushed his chair under the table as Adam barged his way out of the stifling room.

'Cheer up Dad.' He could still hear Sully. 'At least he's not one of those religious terrorists, have you seen today's news?'

*

Above the sports hall doors was a large clock. There were only ten minutes left. Not enough time for Adam's team to score enough points to win, but maybe that didn't matter. Adam needed to show the national coach how good he was. The game was not about winning but showing off his talent; making it clear that he was way ahead of the rest of this stupid bunch. He glanced quickly over to the seating area, it was busier than normal. Parents and friends, Vijay and Cara were there and the national coach was sitting with a clipboard, talking to Stumpy's girlfriend.

Adam wiped sweat from his hands, he didn't want them to slip on the rims, and prepared himself. He couldn't help that feeling, that excitement of getting the ball and shooting. He wanted to score, really wanted to prove his ability, to show these slow cripples what he was made of.

Within seconds, he had the ball in his lap and charged towards the net. He could see the opposition racing in towards him but he was not stopping, the chairs collided and his opponent was thrust out of the way leaving him a clear shot.

In.

Yes.

Fists to the sky, he congratulated himself.

The national coach was watching too.

'Yes!' Adam shouted.

Mikael blew his whistle and walked over. He stared at Adam shaking his head.

'What?' Adam demanded. 'That was a great shot, straight in the hoop.'

Mikael addressed both teams. 'Right, that's it. Time's up.'

Adam stared across at the clock. 'We've still got five minutes.'

'I don't think you'll change his mind in the next five minutes Adam.' Mikael gestured at the national coach who was standing up and stretching.

Relief washed over Adam and a huge sense of triumph.

'Yes,' he said again, as his hands gripped the wheels and thrust the chair around in a three-sixty spin, then he waited for the coach to come over, his hands flexing and releasing.

The other players were heading towards the benches or the changing rooms and Mikael turned away from Adam to meet the coach on court. Adam stayed put. He wanted to go over, to start that incredible conversation about contracts and start dates. He noticed his hands trembling with the anticipation and smelled his own sweat.

Adam licked his lips.

Taking a deep breath, he wheeled himself confidently towards the national coach just as Mikael turned and shouted, 'Stumpy, can you come over here for a minute?'

Adam stopped.

Frozen to the spot, he could only stare as Stumpy rolled over and smiled, shaking hands with the UK wheelchair basketball coach. Adam couldn't move. It was as if he was watching a scene on TV. People talked, gestured, he wasn't a part of that scene, only a viewer in a remote location. Far, far away from the conversation that would surely change Stumpy's life forever.

Adam felt the universe shift, as if on the head of a pin, the bright future ahead of him swung away and aligned with Stumpy's wheelchair instead. Sound faded and he could no longer feel his body in the chair.

Through his blurred vision he recognised Vijay whirring across the court towards him. Behind Vijay, Cara hurriedly grabbed her coat and handbag. Adam wondered if anyone else had noticed his life crumbling into dust.

He was nothing and nobody.

3

Halima - Cracking open the shutters

It was raining. It was always raining.

Rain on her coat, rain in her shoes, rain dripping off her nose. God, what an awful country. Halima kicked at a squashed beer can. It skittered into a puddle. Cars added more water to the pools on the pavement that filled her shoes. Ahead she could see the garden wall, the holly hedge hanging over with a plastic bag wrapped amongst the prickles. She stopped.

'Watch out!' a woman behind her yelled and Halima lurched out of the way, narrowly missing being struck by a buggy and an angry teenager.

'What the fuck you stopping in the middle of the way for?'

The buggy wheel splashed into a puddle and Halima hid her face.

Across the road, a peeling poster in the bus stop told her to 'Sleep Eeeeazzzzy'. Down towards the junction, the noise of rain on streets, engines, windscreen wipers. Together it all made a general mush of sound. She turned back towards home and the waving supermarket bag beckoned her. Wasn't home supposed to be where you wanted to go? Wasn't it supposed to be your castle, the place you felt warm and safe? Not that Halima didn't feel safe; it was just that....

The rain seeped through to her scalp, another trickle down her face following the creases and rolling past her lips. She slid out her tongue and licked it. Fresh cold rain. She turned her face up to the bleakness above and shut her eyes. She could feel the drips running past her scar, taking detours on her scalp where the raised tissue made a crooked line.

Was that when she'd stopped feeling like this was home? When the accident happened?

A man in a raincoat with a large umbrella swished past, his coat flapping. A spoke narrowly missed her ear.

No, it was before then, long before the train crash. Perhaps home had never been home, at least not one you'd talk about with friends, not one you'd invite people to come and stay. Not this home anyway, the one she'd lived in since she was fourteen. She was about to turn fifty-seven in a couple more weeks. Had she really lived here for over forty years? In this house that didn't feel like home? Halima wondered if that said more about her than it did about the bricks and mortar she lived in. Squinting through the rain up at the sky was making her back ache.

A shiver got her moving again. There was the flicker of the TV showing through the net curtains behind the rain-streaked windows. Halima rummaged in her handbag for her key with the yellow heart fob. The lock was stiff, had been for years, but Halima knew the right way to wiggle and get that satisfying click. The door opened into the grey hallway. Resigning herself, Halima stepped inside, at least it was dry.

'That you?' shouted a voice.

'No, it's a burglar come to rape and pillage,' she yelled back.

Silence. Halima took off her coat and scarf, slipped off her shoes. There was a tide line on her socks. She took them off too. Then, barefoot, she walked into the kitchen. She filled the kettle, noticing the corroded plastic edge as the tap water flushed into the spout. She opened the cupboard door with its mismatched knob and pulled out the old tin. Two tea-bags, two stained mugs, one with a chip, the other with a crack.

In the lounge her mother was sitting in the armchair, a blanket over her knees, her prayer beads nestled in the centre of her lap. She was watching the news channel.

'What's up with you then? It's only a bit of rain.'

Halima handed her the chipped mug.

'Well, been struck dumb have you?'

'Shut up. It's got nothing to do with the rain.'

'What hasn't?'

Halima sighed and stared at her mother. The grey hair, tangled and forlorn, her faded salwaar kameeze covered by a misshapen cardigan on a bloated body collapsed into the chair.

'What you staring at? Finally decided that job's no good then have you? Or have you been sacked? Yeah, that's more like it with a face like that. Told you it was no good, not that you can do any better. And where's my biscuit? Sometimes I think you've only got half a brain.'

Halima watched her mother's lips, thin purple lines moving over her old yellow teeth. The filth that came from that mouth. Sprayed across the years, injected into her soul, eating her life away.

That was the problem with home – her mother. Halima scratched at the scar and then sipped the scalding tea. She slid onto the sofa and stared at the newsreader standing in front of a picture of flooding in Bangladesh; his face stared grimly out of the screen but Halima wasn't really listening. She was thinking about her mother. Thinking about what it would take to make this Halima's home.

'You should be grateful we're not over there. Their homes destroyed, washed away. Can you believe it? Dreadful. There's no point being sad about a bit of rain when those poor people have nothing.' Her mother gestured at the TV with her prayer beads, the sleeve of her cardigan swinging gently. 'Well, have you been struck dumb or something? Can't you get an old woman her biscuit or do I have to do everything myself? Talk to me.'

Halima frowned, got up, went to the kitchen and took a biscuit from the tin. She had an urge to spit on it, but didn't. Instead, her wet hair did the job with a large drop square in the middle. She got herself some toast and layered it thickly with jam. Then another slice, and she decided that after all the work she'd done she deserved a third.

'Can I smell toast?'

Halima bit into her third slice. She added a fourth to the toaster for her mother and made a second cup of tea. There was a 'phlat' sound behind her on the tiles. Halima turned around to see two white envelopes tossed into the hallway. She turned back to the toast; it wouldn't be anything interesting. There were already three letters on the kitchen windowsill awaiting her payment. Halima spread the toast with a double layer of butter, then the jam spread more thinly. She put it on her mother's favourite rose plate beside the damp biscuit and took it through.

'What's in the post?'

'Dunno.'

'Well can't you be bothered to pick it up? Could be something important from my doctor, or from that nice man I met at the station.'

Halima rolled her eyes. When was she going to give up on that 'nice man at the station'?

'They're only more bill reminders.'

'Well if you hadn't lost your job there wouldn't be a problem, would there?'

'I haven't lost my job, I'm just tired all right, it's pouring with rain, the place was a terrible mess this morning, why can't you just button it?'

'Don't talk to your mother like that, you always had a bad mouth on you Halima Shah. It's never got you nowhere, if those are red letters then you better get off your lazy bottom and get them paid. Money doesn't grow on trees and if you don't want your old mother turned out into the street then you'd better get working my girl.'

Halima looked down at her cold feet, she turned one of them over and grimaced at the dark brown sole. This place was disgusting compared to the office she had cleaned all morning. She flexed her toes, wondering for a moment what it might be like to walk barefoot across the blue office carpet. There certainly wouldn't be this sandy sensation she got here, or any damp patches.

'Ow.' She grabbed her foot, it had cramp. The house was cold, she was wet and she'd begun to shiver. She rubbed hard along the sole of her foot while her mother munched noisily on the toast. Maybe she should have a hot bath despite her mum's complaints about there not being enough hot water for the heating. It wasn't Halima's fault it had been raining so hard and besides, it was she that paid the bills.

They slurped on soup from the rose patterned bowls in front of the one o'clock news. Someone in Dalston had been murdered. The cost of fuel was up and the MP for Dover was facing charges of sexual assault. Mother sucked loudly at the last bit of soup from her spoon.

'What you looking at me like that for? Think you're superior do you? Been working at that fancy office too long is what I think. Anyway, you've got another bill and you need to read this one. It's probably something important from my doctor.' She waved a white letter at Halima. 'I bet he wants me in for tests. I knew this chest was going to be the death of me.' Her mother paused to give one of her hacking coughs and thrust the white paper at Halima again.

'It's not from your doctor,' Halima said as she began to read. Her eyes widened as she took in the information.

'Well tell me then,' her mother demanded, 'are they turfing us out?' Her voice took on a shrill tone.

'No. It's an invitation.'

'From that nice man at the station, I told you he liked me.' Her mother's face suddenly brightened.

Halima sighed. 'No Mum, it's for me.'

'What?' Her mother snatched it back and squinted at the print as if she could decipher the secret information it held. 'Who's inviting you to things? Have you got a new boyfriend?'

Halima shook her head and scratched at the scar. 'It's for the memorial event at Clapham Junction.'

'What's that got to do with you? You don't go on trains anywhere.'

'I got hit on the head remember?'

'Well that was your story. Another one of your lies no doubt.'

'It was not a lie. How do you think I got this then?' Halima stopped scratching and bowed her head forwards pointing at the scar so her mother could see.

'I've no idea. Probably your boyfriend. Some men can be horribly violent. Your own fault for running off with him.'

Halima gripped her empty soup bowl. 'There was no boyfriend.'

'How come you didn't come home that night then?'

'I told you, I was in hospital.'

'Then why didn't they call me? I'm your mother.' She waved the letter angrily.

'It was busy, loads of people were injured Mum. They probably didn't have time.'

'Well anyway, you won't need this.'

Her mother waved her hand holding the paper as if wafting an annoying fly away. Halima tried to grab her mother's arm to get the letter back but instead she upset the soup bowl and sent it crashing and spinning across the floor. Her mother winced, crossed her hands over her head and howled.

'How can you? How can you break our best bowls? Your poor mother who never did you no wrong. Who gave up her life to save yours. Can't leave the house, can hardly breathe and now you're chucking bowls at me, I can't bear it. I've nowhere to go and my own daughter is attacking me.' Great sobs made her wheezing sound awful.

Halima glanced at the faded prayer in its beaten frame on the wall. She shut her eyes for a moment attempting to breathe in some peace before picking up the broken pieces and walking silently out.

*

Halima walked a little slower today, her back was giving her pain and she hadn't slept well. It would be at least another hour before the sun made its pathetic winter appearance but already the traffic was noisy. She huddled into her coat as an icy wind whipped across her. Ahead she could see flashing lights and lots

33

of cones. Not more work on the bridge, surely? Red signs for 'Road Closed' and yellow diversions but Halima thought the pavement would still be usable.

'Sorry love, we won't be open till six.' A burly man in a reflective jacket and hard hat stood solidly in her way.

Halima looked past him, there didn't seem to be much activity going on.

'You'll have to use Plough Road or the A whatsit. Where you going love?'

Halima pulled her scarf tighter around her face. She couldn't wait till six, she would have to detour. She hurried back the way she had come, she would have to cut down Falcon Lane and along the footpath by Asda.

Halima broke into a trot trying to catch the pedestrian crossing but she was too late and the white van driver didn't even look at her. She waited, pressing the button several times just to be sure. A brief swirl of wind caught at her headscarf and blasted cold air into her ear. The lights changed, Halima crossed to the other side, past the boarded-up shops and along to the large office just before the road headed out over the Thames. Halima paused briefly to push open the door of Thyredata Enterprises into the bright reception area. Vincent, the security guard, was behind the desk as usual.

He doffed his cap, 'Morning Miss Shah. Bit nippy out there today, looks like you're well wrapped up though.' He beamed at her.

Halima nodded and went to push the button for the lift. Vincent was still smiling broadly at her and she felt compelled to say something.

'I hate winter.'

'Me too. Trouble is I don't know no different. Spent me whole life in this country, I guess we get used to it.' His black face shone in the bright electric light. 'My day's brightened by the likes of you Miss Shah and your pretty smile.'

Halima could feel her ears getting hot. The lift was taking forever.

Vincent was still smiling at her. She liked the way his brown eyes twinkled when he smiled. She looked away embarrassed and glanced up at the clock.

He nodded solemnly. 'She's up there already.'

Halima sighed. It wasn't the best way to start her morning, still, she couldn't turn back time. She took the lift up to the fifth floor, turned left down a corridor and saw the cleaner's room was wide open, with her boss Cheryl Phipps inside.

'You're late.'

'Sorry,' Halima mumbled. She wasn't normally late. In fact she could remember a couple of times when Cheryl had arrived when Halima was almost half way through her routine. She could feel Cheryl's eyes watching her as she gathered the cleaning solutions from the cupboard and prepared her trolley with a fresh bucket of water.

'Nothing to say then?' Cheryl stood with her nose in the air. She was a dumpy lady, about six inches shorter than Halima, but she made up for it with her snooty arrogance. 'Lateness won't be tolerated Halima. Consider this your verbal warning. This is a place of work, not a hostel for the homeless to loaf about in when they fancy.'

Halima paused with the bucket in her hand. 'I'm not homeless.'

'No.' Cheryl pursed her lips as if about to say more, her eyes pausing at the top of Halima's head. Halima waited, wondering if this horrible woman would say something about her head scarf. Instead Cheryl sneered, turned on her heel and marched out. Halima sighed and gripped the handle of her trolley and began pushing it out into the open plan office. She noted her pale knuckles as she squeezed the smooth metal, thinking of all the injustices that were inflicted upon her. It wasn't her fault she'd been late.

There was no one in the office as Halima set to work with a duster on the first desk. She moved a couple of pens, dusted the phone, wiped the computer screen, then moved on to the next. She soon found her rhythm, emptying bins, wiping, patting, doing a little tidying along the way. She had her favourite desks of course. The one more or less in the middle was the untidiest and yet she liked it, obviously belonged to a chaotic man. Sometimes there would be a tie hung over the back of the chair, papers strewn about, computer often left on with the standby light glowing and the computer humming gently. Today it wasn't too bad, but she noted that he'd scribbled very forcefully around a date and time for yesterday. She hoped he hadn't forgotten the meeting - whatever it was. There was a small photo of a baby stuck beside the computer which she always stopped to look at. So cute. Halima could feel that familiar hard stone of shame roll around her stomach even after all these years. Halima supposed the discomfort would be with her until she died. Sighing, she left the photo of the baby and concentrated on scrubbing at a stubborn pen mark.

In contrast, the desk nearest the manager's office was always incredibly neat and today was no exception. There was one pen of each colour lined up next to a pencil. Beside them were a calculator, a ruler and a rubber. The monitor was switched off and the mouse stood exactly in the centre of the mouse mat. Underneath the desk was one of those foot stools and the chair was different to the others in the office, this one had more levers and padding. Halima imagined a small tight-lipped woman with high heels who was extremely efficient. Miss Hoity Toity. Despite this being the easiest desk to clean, she didn't like it at all.

Gradually Halima made her way down the long office. There were thirty desks in all grouped in banks of four or six. Her favourite one was by the window at the end. She had named it Jessica's desk. She paused, leaning over to straighten the phone, move some papers to the side, and set the photo holder straight. It showed a charming young man with dark hair. Halima stared at the photograph, imagining the young man holding out his hand to her. The girl who sat here was very lucky. The pink pencil with its fluffy feather on the top was partly hidden behind a folder. Halima moved it back to the pen pot. There was a doodle of love hearts on one of the papers and some suggestive shapes next to them. On the bottom of the monitor was a sticker which read:

"Don't forget you're loved!"

Halima thought it was the sweetest thing, full of hope for Jessica's romance with the young man in the photo. She pulled the bin out from under the desk and emptied the papers into the bag on the side of her trolley. One missed and tumbled onto the floor. She reached down and as she did so, her hand brushed against the blue carpet. Halima stood up and looked across the open plan office. There was still no one in yet. She slipped off her shoes, and then peeled off her socks. The carpet felt rather flat and hard, it wasn't particularly coarse, or hairy, just sort of ticklish. She walked about a bit, staring down at her feet. It was warm, they heated these offices so hot that it was a far cry from her own cold gritty floor at home. An odd feeling really, she couldn't remember having felt a texture quite like that before under her feet. Enjoying the weird sensation of freedom, she continued down the last bank of desks.

As she emptied the final bin, she spotted something on the floor, far beneath the desk. Crouching down, she reached in and pulled it out. It was a Visa card for a Mr T Ryder. She turned it over in her hand; it was still in date and had the man's signature on the back. Halima looked around her, still no one here yet. On the other side of the thin divider was the chaotic man's desk, it was probably his. Quickly Halima marched round and put it on top of the messy paperwork. Troubled, she thought it might get lost again and instead looked around her for a more suitable spot. Of course, Miss Hoity Toity would deal with it in her efficient manner and hand it to T Ryder herself with a reprimand for being so disorganised. Halima stood looking at the perfect desk and frowned. No, Halima considered, maybe Miss Hoity Toity would be too severe. She surveyed the room. Of course; Jessica's desk. She placed the card directly in the middle of the desk where Jessica was sure to find it and return the card to its rightful owner in a kind motherly manner. Halima reviewed the room, satisfied that all was well.

'Umm, excuse me.' A young man with blond hair stood behind her in a smart pink shirt.

Halima blushed deeply, she looked down horrified at her toes splayed against the blue carpet.

He looked down too and asked, 'Sore feet?' He smiled kindly.

Halima nodded and yanked her shoes off the trolley, slipped

her feet into them and scooped the socks into her pocket. She wanted to melt away, wanted him to disappear. Couldn't he just go back to his desk? Halima stared at her shoes waiting for him to leave but he didn't. She looked up nervously and he gestured at the desk.

Halima followed his hand and her eyes stuck on the pink fluffy pencil.

'This is my desk.'

'Oh?' Halima pushed the trolley quickly away not stopping until she reached the end by the huge window. Behind her she saw him sitting down on the blue chair and switching on the monitor. Why was he sitting at Jessica's desk?

Halima pushed the trolley back towards the cleaner's room. Of course, she had made up the name Jessica, but it seemed to fit, and she was pretty sure that the man in the photo was Matt, she had seen the name doodled so often. Perhaps Jessica was out and that man was sitting in for her. But then he'd said *my desk*. Halima shrugged, it didn't mean anything, in a big company it was probably normal to have temporary staff coming in now and then. Maybe Jessica had gone on maternity leave. Perhaps she and Matt were going to have a baby? Halima smiled to herself, how lovely. If only she'd- . No this wasn't the time to be thinking about the what ifs and the if onlys. She'd had no choice all those years ago and that thought had no business running around her head. She squashed the thought with all her might and hurried through the door of the cleaner's room.

*

The doorbell jangled noisily. Halima looked at her mother, as if she would know who was calling.

'Well answer it then! But if it's the bailiffs, don't let them in. I'm not being turfed out of my own home. In fact, don't answer it. Drink your tea,' her mother ordered.

Halima balanced her mug on the arm of the sofa and got up. She opened the door ignoring the envelopes as they slid across the floor to rest against the skirting board. There was a kindly lady with a briefcase standing on the doormat. She thrust out her hand.

'Good afternoon, I'm Mrs Thurston from the Elderly Care at Home charity.'

Halima shook her head, 'I don't give on the doorstep.'

'Oh,' the lady laughed lightly, tipping her head back so that Halima noted the stringy neck. Despite the smart clothes she was probably a similar age to herself.

'I'm not collecting, I'm here to see Mrs Kaneez Shah.'

'What for?' said Halima. Mum hadn't said anything.

'Mrs Shah's your mother? Of course. When you opened the door, I did wonder, is it Halima?' Her eyes travelled up and down, pausing at Halima's worn slippers.

Halima shifted her weight, curling her toes in, wishing she still had her shoes on, at least they were fairly smart. She looked at the woman a little more closely, did they know each other?

'Wow, isn't this amazing?' The woman gave a nervous laugh. 'It's me, Veronica.' She paused, 'Um, Veronica Thurston from Somerville Primary.'

'Veronica?' Halima stared hard at the shape of her face, the eyes, those slightly heavy eyebrows. Yes, she could see her now, the girl with the mousey hair. A girl she had played with at some point through primary school and even into secondary. Hadn't she been the one with the Sindy doll that they all envied?

'Veronica,' Halima said it again, confirming the fact. 'Veronica Pease.' They stood silently. Veronica's smile faltered a little.

'Ah-ha,' she kind of laughed and then cleared her throat. 'Thurston's my married name. Well I'm here to see your mother. We have a special program, some volunteers. I wondered if your mother could benefit?'

Halima wasn't sure what to say. If it had been a stranger she would have made excuses and shut the door, but this was Veronica Pease, a face from a lifetime ago, and it seemed rude not to invite her in, so Halima did so.

'Would you like a cup of tea?'

'That would be lovely, thank you Halima. I can call you Halima?'

'Er, yes, of course. My mother's through there.' She pointed towards the lounge and hurried down to the kitchen. Halima threw open the cupboard looking for a clean mug that didn't have any chips knocked out of it. There was an old brown one at the back, but there was something green at the bottom. Halima thrust it back, picked up one of the regular ones they used and gave it a thorough rinse. She wasn't used to this, having people in the house. They didn't have guests, didn't have people who rang the doorbell and expected tea. Halima added milk and two sugars, the same as she and Mum had it.

When Halima went into the lounge she was taken aback by the heavy flowery scent that pervaded the room and even more so by the bright poppy-red skirt sitting primly against the drab beige of the armchair. Even Veronica's animated face looked out of place in the grey room.

Veronica took the mug, nodding her thanks, and continued talking to her mother. Halima took the opportunity to study Veronica a little more closely. She wore brown leather boots with buttons up the sides. The skirt appeared to be made of a heavy wool and lay perfectly on her knees revealing snag-free tights. Although her neck was creased and folded, it was decorated by large felt beads in green and red. Her coat was a darker green yet still so bright in their dingy lounge. It was like seeing the Wizard of Oz, all black and white on the farm with Dorothy to begin with and then being transported to the splendid technicolour world of Oz.

'So, it's really about giving you something a little special, a bit of personal attention. We vet all the students who work with us, and they receive training too. Is there a day and time that would suit best?'

Halima saw Mum was studying Veronica and the clipboard she had perched on her knee.

'Why do you think I need personal care?' her mother demanded.

'Well, we all like a little treat occasionally don't we?' Veronica looked at Halima as if for support, but Halima didn't have a clue what sort of treat she meant. They had chocolate in the house, and that was a treat for her. Sometimes she bought Mum's favourite from the baker's: millionaire's shortbread.

Veronica glanced around the room and changed tack. 'Is it just the two of you living here?'

Halima nodded while her mother scowled. Veronica turned her attention to Halima and aimed her next question at her: 'So you are the sole carer Halima?'

But Halima didn't get a chance to reply.

'Carer? Halima couldn't even look after a simple mouse. I have to do it myself, useless daughter leaving me all day long to fend for myself, always worrying about the bailiffs coming to take everything away. She's got red letters piling up on the windowsill in the kitchen, it won't be long. When she was young, I bought her a pet mouse, and do you know how long it lasted? Two months, two months and then it died. No, Halima's no good for caring.'

Halima scowled, it had been a gerbil not a mouse. It was going cheap, probably already sickening, but Halima said nothing. She wasn't sure how to begin. Veronica's smile was flickering on and off like an ancient black and white movie. Halima hadn't really thought about being Mum's carer. They lived together, they always had, and it was true that now Mum rarely ventured out of the house. It had been a slow process of gradually doing more and more, and her mother doing less and less. In fact, the last time they had left the house together, had been to attend a doctor's appointment in an expensive taxi.

'It's not quite like that. I work, but only in the mornings.' Halima tried to assert herself. After all, this was Veronica Pease and Halima must prove something to the woman who'd had all the latest clothes for her Sindy doll.

'I see.' Veronica's face softened. She sipped her tea and then her eyes opened wider as she stared into the cup for a moment. Recovering her composure, she put the mug back on the floor.

'Call that work? She's useless, never amounted to anything that girl. Knew she wouldn't, not with that father of hers. Runs in the family, at least hers.'

'Is Halima not your daughter then?' Veronica asked.

Halima smiled, that shut her up. Mum looked annoyed and started a long and wheezing cough.

Halima took the opportunity to ask, 'What are you going to do?'

'We run a program of volunteers that come to see elderly people. They might do any number of things, perhaps cut toenails, wash and set hair, maybe just sit and talk. It depends on the elderly person really.'

'I see.' Halima already did those things for her mother. It seemed odd to have a stranger come in and do them.

'It would give you a break,' she paused, 'being the sole carer.'

Mum stopped coughing. 'Halima doesn't need no break, she's lazy. Doesn't pick up the mail, forgets the bins, doesn't pay the bills. A break is the last thing she needs, besides, what about me? Stuck here all day.' Mum was leaning forwards as if trying to block Halima's view of Veronica sitting in the other chair.

'Yes Mrs Shah, it would give you both a break. Well, how about next Monday then? I can have someone come round at about nine.'

'Who's coming round?' Mum shouted.

'I'm afraid I'll be at work at that time,' explained Halima.

'Perfect timing then,' nodded Veronica and she winked at Halima. This was odd, Veronica seemed to be taking her side. This woman, who had suddenly appeared from the past, was suggesting she could help Mum, and yet, Halima realised, that Veronica might actually be looking to help her.

Halima went to the hall with Veronica to let her out. On the doorstep the red skirt swished around to face Halima.

'It must be hard for you,' she paused, 'I'm sure you look after your mother brilliantly but it must be tiring.'

Halima didn't know what to say, she nodded ever so slightly but even that made her guilty. You weren't supposed to complain about looking after your mother. It was expected, an unmarried woman like herself did not leave her parents' house. After all, Mum was the only person she had. Veronica was staring at her with a sympathetic look, and then she smiled widely.

'I'll be in touch. You and I will have to catch up some time, just the two of us, a coffee perhaps?' She held out her hand and Halima tentatively shook it thinking how strange it was to hold Veronica's warm fingers in her own. How oddly intimate to be touching someone else's skin who wasn't her mother. It would be nice to see Veronica again and she nodded at those pretty red and green felt beads.

Once the door was shut, Halima went to the kitchen. Staring blankly out of the window remembering Veronica with pigtails and her tinkly laugh. Then she saw a movement under the hedge and a grey furry animal appeared.

'Oi!' She hammered on the window. The soggy thing slunk along the bottom of the hedge. Halima unlocked the back door, slipped on her shoes and went out.

'Go on, get lost!' She waved her arm and the grey thing disappeared.

'We'll never get warm with you dancing around with the back door wide open.' Her mother stood wheezing at the sink. She plonked the almost full mug onto the draining board.

'She didn't touch it, that's no way to treat people. Rude, that's what it is. I don't trust that woman, someone who doesn't eat and drink when you invite them in. You should have never opened the door.' She coughed for at least ten seconds, then spat a gob of phlegm into the sink. The wheezing lessened and she shuffled out.

Halima sighed and shut the back door, locked it and went to the sink. A shiver ran through her. It was still bitterly cold, she was desperate for some warmer weather and lighter mornings. A faint whiff of Veronica's perfume still hung in the air and Halima picked up the mug, noticing the bright red imprint of her lip on the edge. For a moment it seemed to get even brighter and then Halima saw a shaft of sunlight had suddenly split the clouds, lighting the drips hanging from the washing line. They winked and shone like fairy lights strung across the garden. Halima couldn't work out how come the drips kept changing colour, green, yellow and even pink – where could that colour be reflecting from? It made her think of flowers and the need to have something pretty became a dull ache in her chest. Like the bright red skirt that Veronica had been wearing and those red and green beads. Halima felt uneasy, as if something buried deep inside had cracked open.

4

Adam - Burnt ends

'He can't sleep his life away,' his father roared.

Adam tried hard to hear his mother's response through the wall, but it seemed the more his father shouted, the quieter his mother's voice became. They were in the kitchen. Adam was in his room staring at the ceiling above his bed with the door shut.

'He should be going back to college, get some qualifications. I told you he needed a plan B. Basketball. I always said it was just a game. I cannot have him wasting his life. We are Rasheeds, and I will not have any son of mine dropping out.'

There was a bang which Adam thought might have been a chair falling over or his father thumping the table. Then there was silence and Adam lifted his head from the pillow and looked towards the door. They hadn't come to blows had they? But then a low murmur and his father's footsteps marching past towards the front door. Adam flopped his head back and turned it to the side facing the wall; the blank wall.

This had been the lounge, but ever since the accident it had become his temporary bedroom. Adam sighed. Two and a half years wasn't really temporary any more and yet he still hadn't decorated it. When he'd come home from hospital, his mother had transferred his football posters from his bedroom onto these walls. He had asked her to take them down and then he had ripped up every one of them into tiny pieces and shed them all over the floor like confetti. They had never been replaced.

Time had stretched long and thin since those early days, he'd been forgiven everything. But not any more. It would seem the holiday period was over. Not that it had ever felt like a holiday, more of a nightmare. The trouble was the nightmare kept getting worse.

The front door slammed.

It had been humiliating on the basketball court a few weeks ago. In fact nothing at all had mattered since that day.

Adam waited, staring at the blank wall and then closed his eyes. After five minutes, there was a tap at the door and his mother came in.

'I brought you some breakfast.' The smell of warm toast made Adam open his eyes again.

'Thanks,' he mumbled.

'It's your day for the job centre,' she paused and Adam could hear her breathing and smell her fragranced skin. It was comforting but not enough to shift the hollowness in his chest.

'Do you want any help getting dressed?'

'No.'

'Shall I get your clothes out?'

'No.'

She moved away but Adam could tell she hadn't left the room yet, he stayed staring at the wallpaper, willing her to leave. She didn't. The silence began to press against Adam's chest and the smell of toast had evaporated. It would be getting cold.

'What?' he shouted, immediately regretting the outburst.

The door closed with a click and he was alone again.

Adam took the bus into town. He didn't care that he was half an hour late for his interview. He was told to wait on the second floor. Eventually a young woman with an over-bright smile came across.

'We're just over here, if you'd like to follow me.' She had a large mouth with so many teeth that Adam wondered if she'd had extra put in to fill it up. She led him to a desk at the far end and removed the chair to one side so he could roll up close.

'I just need to take a look at these for a minute and then we can get started,' her teeth said.

Adam scowled at the papers she picked up. There was no doubt they were about him.

'So, it says here you have Maths and Food Preparation and Nutrition GCSE, is that right?'

Adam nodded.

She frowned. 'Do you have any other qualifications?'

Adam clenched his jaw wondering if his father had been talking to Miss Teeth.

'No.'

'OK fine, I just wanted to be sure we hadn't missed anything. So it seems you were absent quite a bit from school.'

'And you wouldn't have been?' Adam spat out.

She frowned again, this time her lips closed tight, and then she said, 'I'm sorry?'

'It doesn't matter.'

'Well, it seems to me that an apprenticeship might be just up your street. There are a few currently being offered in partnership with the local college.' She looked at Adam with her head on one side.

'So?'

Her lips were closed again and she watched him unblinking. 'What would you like to do Adam?'

Stupid cow, what was that supposed to mean? He had wanted to be a famous footballer ever since he'd first kicked a ball in the park as a small boy, only that was out of the question since his bloody legs had stopped working. And even his dream of becoming a national wheelchair basketball player had been screwed. What did she expect from him? He couldn't do anything else. The job interviews he'd been for had been a total waste of time. It seemed he wasn't even good enough to work on the checkout at his local supermarket. Who would want a crippled Paki anyway? He was completely useless, just like his father said.

'It can be a difficult time of life, you're not the only one to find themselves in that awkward spot between school and work. But these apprenticeships are a great way of bridging that gap.' She was talking with a narrow mouth which made her look awkward as if she was trying to keep her teeth hidden from view. On the desk she placed a brochure from the college.

'I've marked three that still have places and that I think might work for you.' She opened the brochure where a yellow sticky was poking out. 'This one is with Transport Rail, it is office-based and you'd get day release on a Thursday.'

Adam stared at a photograph of a man in an orange overall standing next to a rail track. Did she really think that after what he'd been through he'd want to do anything remotely to do with trains?

'There's also this one,' she flicked through to the next yellow marker, 'this is with the council working here in the job centre.'

Adam couldn't think of anything worse than working with the unemployed. Imagine trying to motivate people like his uncle who'd been made redundant or the disinterested youths hovering outside smoking and swearing? It would be too depressing.

'And the other one is here,' she flicked again, 'apprentice nursery assistant working with young pre-school children. It's in the new day care centre off the Barking road. A brand new facility.' She glanced up from the page of children painting.

Adam sat still not wanting to meet her gaze. A room full of screaming toddlers racing around trying to climb on his wheelchair or push him along. What a disaster that would be.

Finally he said, 'I'll think about it.'

She closed the brochure and pushed it further towards him.

'That's fine. I'll make an appointment for two weeks' time so you can update me on your applications.'

Adam stopped staring at the closed brochure and stared instead at her blue eyes. She opened that gaping mouth of hers again.

'You will need to apply for a minimum of two jobs or further education courses by the time we meet.' She smiled broadly and her teeth flashed brightly at him as she stood up; the interview was over.

Adam glared. 'What if I don't?'

'You'll lose your benefits. I suppose you could ask your parents or a friend if they would be willing to look after you, if you don't intend to look after yourself.' She closed her mouth tight.

For the first time, he noticed she was wearing pink lipstick.

'Good day, Mr Rasheed.' She picked the brochure off the desk where Adam had left it and thrust it towards him. Adam snatched it from her and headed quickly towards the lift.

Vijay's apartment block was a huge glass building with a poncey concierge sitting behind a desk. Adam ignored him and went to the lifts and travelled up to the third floor. Vijay's front door was almost opposite the lift. He looked for a bell, realising he had only ever been here before accompanying Cara and Vijay and certainly never unannounced. But he hadn't wanted to go home. A few weeks back he would have gone to the Sports Centre, thrown a few hoops. But now there was no point. There wasn't a point to anything at all. Suddenly Vijay's front door flew open and a tall woman appeared.

'Oh, hello ducky, didn't see you there,' she said in a deep voice. She paused, giving him a careful once over.

Adam swallowed, he didn't think he'd met a woman as tall as her before, she towered over him in a short dress and high heels. Her face was heavily made up, a long winter coat draped over one arm. Adam backed up his chair as she moved forwards. She reached out a hand, Adam leant back, but the hand kept coming and stroked his chin. An electrical thrill whizzed straight down his neck and landed in his groin.

'Cute,' she whispered. 'Maybe next time.' She gave an exaggerated wink and then called back over her shoulder.

'Visitor. See you next time.' She passed Adam's chair and he noted her strong muscular legs as she headed for the lift. Adam couldn't help staring. Just before she disappeared from view she turned and gave him a little wave. 'Toodle oo cutey.'

Adam felt himself burning.

'Hi Kiddo, come on in. I just need to make Vijay presentable, but make yourself at 'ome. You know where stuff is.' It was Cara with the door opened wide. Adam wheeled himself into the hallway and through to the comfortable lounge where large windows looked over towards Canary Wharf.

'Who was that?' Adam asked as Cara was about to disappear into the bedroom.

48

'Oh pfft.' Cara waved his question away.

Adam wondered if his face was noticeably red, he certainly felt hot and wasn't sure it was the heating. He stroked his own chin where the deep-voiced woman had touched him. Adam decided to get himself a cold drink and went into the kitchen. Here the counters were designed for a wheelchair user, in fact the entire flat had been kitted out to suit a disabled person. He found the glasses and was able to turn the tap and fill it with ease. Wouldn't it be nice to live in his own place like this and be totally independent? He looked at the drawers and cupboards, the low counter and the inbuilt cooker. He'd even be able to cook for himself, make his own curries instead of relying on his mum to do most of the work. He opened the fridge and stared at the food, then he started rooting in the cupboards. There was a distinct lack of spices but some good pans and bowls and some basic ingredients.

'What are you doing?' It was Vijay in his electric chair in the doorway.

'I was just making some chapatis.' Adam had his hands covered in flour shaping the dough.

'Because?'

'Well I…' Adam slapped the dough onto the floured surface. He shrugged, the pan was beginning to smoke on the hob, there seemed little point in stopping. He dipped his finger in the pot of water and flicked it into the pan giving that satisfying hiss.

'Be about five minutes.'

'Because you've got nothing better to do?'

Adam clenched his jaw. 'Who was that woman?' he shot back.

'What woman?'

Adam glared at Vijay.

'Oh, you met Karen.' He did that annoying smirk of his.

'Who is she?' Adam couldn't help himself. He could feel that heat coming back as he remembered the way she stroked his chin. Adam flipped the chapati over.

'I don't think you really want the details do you?'

Adam turned to see Vijay reversing out of the kitchen with a smug grin on his face.

'You're disgusting.'

Vijay stopped and the smile disappeared.

'Why are you in my kitchen cooking?'

'I was just trying to be nice,' Adam threw the tongs onto the counter where they slid and hit the toaster with a clang.

'By throwing insults,' Vijay said. 'Perhaps you should be blowing off steam on the basketball court.'

'Oh very funny, that's right, rub it in why don't you?'

'Doesn't mean you have to give it up completely. You enjoy wheelchair basketball, you're even quite good at it. It could still be a hobby.'

'You don't get it.' Adam wanted to push past him but it was impossible with Vijay's large electric chair blocking the kitchen doorway. 'I failed. I didn't make the team.'

'Sometimes people like you and me need to look at our strengths, believe me, looking at my weaknesses could last all day.'

'But that's just it. I don't have any fucking strengths.'

'Really? So what are you going to do then?'

'Why is everyone on my case? Can't you just leave me alone?'

'You came here, remember?'

'Fine, and now I'm leaving.' Adam pushed his chair forwards. He could smell the chapati beginning to burn.

Vijay stared at him and then reversed.

'Hey, wait up!' It was Cara having raced the lift down the stairs. ''Ere.' She was breathing hard.

Adam ignored her, leant forwards and yanked the door open onto the street.

''Ee did want me to throw it at you, but 'ey you're both angry, I'll slip it in the side pocket.' Cara leaned closer and pushed something down the side of his chair. 'Cheer up, whatever it is will blow over.'

Adam wheeled himself outside and didn't look back. Blow over, that showed how little she understood. Why was this world full of fucking idiots? He was meant to be a sportsman. A footballer, or at the very least a wheelchair basketball champion, but he was nothing. How on earth was the reality of his insignificance supposed to blow over?

Adam thrust the wheels forwards to the end of the street, around the corner to the pedestrian crossing. As he waited for the lights to change he pulled out the object that Cara had shoved in the side pocket. It was the apprenticeship brochure he'd tossed onto the coffee table when he'd arrived. Something was stuffed in it that prevented it from closing properly. The booklet fell open to reveal a burnt chapati. Adam pulled the black bread out and then noticed the page 'Apprentice Chef'. Bastard.

5

Ralph – Pride before...

Ralph drove the ambulance steadily along Battersea Bridge Road across the Thames. Suddenly he pulled the wheel to the right and swerved, then slowed at the traffic lights.

'Take it easy, she's still stable,' Emma called from the back.

'Sure, sorry, it's the couriers on their bikes, blimmin' nightmare, darting out of nowhere.' The lights were red but Ralph negotiated around the waiting cars. The road ahead was clear and he picked up speed, braking only slightly at the T-junction as he turned.

'Have you ever thought of rally driving?'

Ralph chuckled as he slowed over the speed bumps and paused for the barrier at the back of the hospital. 'I'm not that bad.'

'Not sure Mrs Berkovich here would agree.'

Ralph could hear the smile in Emma's voice. It was always a better shift when he was partnered with her.

'OK, we're here.' Ralph jumped out and went to the back doors. He opened them up, pulled down the ramp and helped Emma guide the gurney out onto the wet tarmac. Ralph led the way and pushed open the doors; a doctor met them on the way in and guided them to a curtained cubicle. Emma was flicking through the paperwork and explaining to the doctor what they'd done to make Mrs Berkovich stable. Ralph smiled at the elderly lady on the bed, she was conscious and looking a little worried by all the talk between Emma and the doctor.

'Don't you worry dear, you'll be in great hands now.' He gave her hand a gentle squeeze.

She returned his smile and mouthed 'Thank you.'

Ralph placed her hand gently back onto her chest. Poor love, she was going to have a big bruise across the left side of her face but her milky eyes still twinkled at him. He thought about his own mother getting older; her skin becoming papery and translucent. She was already a lot thinner and her hands were covered in liver spots - he'd noticed when she'd given his son Cameron a high five the other day.

Once they'd left the cubicle, Emma said she'd check their supplies in case they needed to go back to the station while Ralph went down to the canteen to get two coffees, a latte for Emma and black for himself. When he returned, Emma was already in the cab finishing up her notes.

'All set?' Ralph passed her the latte.

'Thanks. Yep, ready to go. Thanks for letting me take the lead on that one.'

'No problem at all, the more practice you can get before those exams the better.'

'Yeah, thanks.'

Ralph pressed the button on the monitor to let control know they were green, good to go again. 'Let's see what's next, you never know we might get a chance to drink these coffees.'

Surprisingly there were no immediate call outs and they were given a location near which to wait. Ralph put the ambulance in gear and they bumped their way back over the humps onto the main road. Five minutes later and they were parked just off the crossroads.

'You know, I hate this spot, it's got to be one of the worst.' Ralph frowned at the windscreen as it started to spit with rain.

'It's not so bad,' Emma sipped her latte. 'The Farley junction is worse.'

'Well yes, nowhere is worse than Farley, but we always seem to get crap callouts from here, and it fries my nerves watching these drivers.' Ralph swallowed a mouthful of his black coffee. They watched a red Vauxhall jump the lights. A slow lorry that was still crossing had to stamp on its brakes. Ralph sucked in some air. The Vauxhall whistled past and swerved off down the A343.

'See! And then you get the joy of being called out to some rumpus on the estate.'

Emma smiled. 'Well, you certainly have to take the rough with the smooth in this job.' She finished her drink. 'Have you got plans tonight?' she asked.

'Shelly's got a late meeting and I'm taking Liam to his soccer club and then I need to get to the PTA meeting at about eight.'

'And Cameron?'

'I think he's at the crinklies till later.'

'The what?' Emma grinned at him.

'Whoops, that's a Cameronism. My mum and dad's.' Ralph shrugged, it was hard not to pick up the kids' language sometimes.

'The Crinklies, I kind of like it.' Emma was studying Ralph. 'Don't you ever just sit and watch TV?'

'Sure I do.' He thought about the last time he and Shelly had watched a whole film. The truth was, he couldn't remember. They might sit for half an hour eating dinner but after that, there was always something else to do. Like getting the kids to bed or doing homework, clearing the kitchen, catching up on paperwork. And then, of course, he liked to keep fit down at his local gym. It didn't leave much time for sitting doing nothing.

'Have you seen the new Game of Thrones series?' Emma looked at him expectantly.

'I think the kids have been watching it on the computer. Not really my cup of tea.'

The monitor suddenly came alive. Beeping loudly with a code red. The address appeared for the Winstanley Estate. Head injury.

Ralph gulped the last of his black coffee. He buckled his

seatbelt and switched on the engine. The windscreen wipers swished the droplets away and, with the siren on, they moved swiftly into the traffic. It didn't take long, but Ralph had to concentrate hard, the roads were very wet and the traffic heavy. At least it wasn't icy.

'OK next left then second on the right.'

'Got it. Hold on.' He swung the wheel and they charged past parked cars into the council estate.

'There look.' Ahead of them was a knot of people, a couple of youths with their hands shoved in their pockets and three adults under umbrellas, including a young mother with a buggy. They all looked up as Ralph brought the ambulance to a stop. They parted slightly and Ralph could see an older man sitting on the floor. Most likely drunk judging by his slumped posture.

'Here we go then,' he said.

An hour and a half later they had deposited the patient at the hospital and were back at the crossroads eating sandwiches that Emma had grabbed from the Tesco Metro on the corner.

'Don't you find people like that depressing?' Ralph said.

'What, you mean that last patient?'

'Yeah, I mean these drunken homeless people causing problems, he mentioned kids and his ex. How can they let their lives get so messed up?' Ralph shook his head, biting into the chicken and salad roll.

'It's different for different people. We don't know how come he's homeless or what went on between him and his ex. I think it's sad. Some people just need more help than others.'

Ralph chewed and thought about home with Shelly and the boys. What would it be like not living with them? Feeling so rubbish that you just wanted to drink your life away and then turning up and making a nuisance of yourself. It just didn't make sense to Ralph.

'When you have kids, you have responsibilities,' he said. 'You can't just go off the rails, you have to hold it together for your family. You have to be there for your kids. That's the problem with this society, people give up too easily.' Ralph lifted his head and smiled as he watched a young man pushing a pram with a toddler hanging onto the handle.

'Well that's the ideal but you can't really know what it's like till you're in it, don't you think?'

'I wouldn't give up,' Ralph asserted, thinking about how he and Shelly were a partnership, how they both raised their boys, Liam and Cameron. Working as a paramedic, helping people every day. Even his role in the PTA. It was all about responsibilities and facing up to them and doing what was right.

'Well, take Jacob for example,' Emma said.

'Jacob who?'

'The A and E doc with the cute eyes.'

Ralph looked across at Emma and laughed, 'Not sure about the cute, but I know who you mean.'

'He's left.'

'Stress?'

'Not specifically, from what I heard he'd gotten into gambling, run up a ton of debt. Just wasn't coping.'

Ralph shook his head. 'That sucks.'

'Yeah, apparently he left his wife, basically buggered off!'

'But didn't he have kids?' Ralph grimaced.

'Yep, twin girls, I think they're about two or maybe three years old.'

'Jeez, I'd never do that. Get myself in a situation and then walk out on your family, that's rubbish that is. See this is what I mean. Stand up to your responsibilities. Sure get help if you need it, but giving up, that sucks. I'd never-' Before he could continue the monitor blinked up with another callout.

6

Adam – End of the line

In the park, the court was deserted. The middle of a working day. He supposed most people were busy. An older guy in an overcoat was walking his dog slowly around the edge of the grass. The sky above was the colour of metal. Adam's hands were cold on the wheel rims, he should have worn gloves.

Adam pulled out his ball and bounced it on his left then right. He did a few turns and then headed down the court bouncing as he went, swerving to a stop and shooting. He missed.

After retrieving the ball, he did the same but in the other direction, this time bouncing on the left; his weaker side. Again he missed the hoop. His hands were still cold, so Adam blew on them and rubbed them on his thighs. It didn't really work. On his fourth attempt at a goal, he finally threw one home. A pin-prick of success. The ball bounced and rolled to the side where it stopped against the fence. What was he doing? What was the point? The national coach had said Adam might be ready next year. Adam hung his head. The fact he'd used the word *might* said it all. Another year of false hope. Adam had given his all and it wasn't good enough, just like he'd given his all at football. A possible star they'd called him. And he had been, about to hit the big time with that invite for the try outs, prove his worth; he would have succeeded. His whole childhood had been heading for victory until that day on the train.

Adam stared at the ball, it had come to rest against a sweet wrapper. It was like his life: washed up with the detritus. How had he got to this place where even scoring a smooth hoop was so utterly disappointing? What was the point of bouncing a piece of rubber around this tarmac and throwing it through a rusty ring? He was never going to be a sports superstar.

Two hands suddenly appeared around the ball. It was a boy no more than ten in a scrubby coat.

'Finders, keepers,' he said, tossing the ball into the air then catching it again. The boy bent his knees slightly keeping his feet apart, ready to sprint. Adam wondered why this kid was skipping school. At his age, Adam had been a model student, he was everybody's winner back then. But not any more.

'So is it yers or wot?' The boy had a glint in his eye.

'Keep it,' said Adam and turned away leaving the park for the last time.

At least the rain on his face would hide the tears that slid warm down his cheeks. He didn't have a direction, simply kept the wheels moving, anything so that he wouldn't stop and think. Think about his failed life, about how useless he had become. He pushed the wheels faster, hoping to generate some warmth against the icy damp. Ahead was the unmistakeable sign for the underground. At least he could get out of the cold.

When Adam disembarked at Clapham Junction with the help of a ramp, he tried to tell himself that it hadn't been deliberate, that it had simply been a coincidence, a desire to be warm, change lines, get on a train. A wish to leave it all behind him. The trouble was, it wasn't all behind him, here he was in his wheelchair and there was platform nine where it had all begun. Or perhaps that was where it had all ended. His dreams of being a world class football player crushed in the few seconds it took the train carriage to roll and crumple trapping his legs and damaging his spine. Adam sat on platform ten, looking across at the scaffolding on platform nine.

He couldn't remember much from that day. Pain, heat, a lot of people shouting and swearing. An intense smell of burning that made his nostrils sting. A man talking softly but earnestly close to his face. Promising that they'd get him out. Perhaps it would have been better if they'd left him. At least he would have died thinking he was a football legend, not some useless disabled teenager.

Another train arrived, this one heading towards Southampton, people got on and off. People with lives and purposes. Bags and laptops slung on shoulders. Phones in their hands or pressed to their ear. Everyone seemed to be caught up in a busy world that excluded him. They were stepping confidently along the treadmill of their lives from work to home and back again. A reason to get up in the morning, people to meet and expectations to be fulfilled. Adam felt like he'd fallen down the cracks of society. Left behind while the masses continued on their journey. Clapham Junction was not a destination for them but simply a place to pass through, to change tracks and continue on with their lives. Adam felt trapped in this time and place, like he'd lost his way, caught in the gap between boy and man. Derailed from his own track and unable to find his way back. Some people glanced his way, but he was irrelevant in their tight schedules, even less interesting than the adverts on the platform wall.

Adam contemplated the metal rails the train had left, perhaps this was how it should be. Slip his chair over the edge between the tracks. A closed loop bringing him back to where it had all ended.

7

Halima - New beginnings

It was another dark morning, like all the others. Halima stared despondently into the mirror as she brushed her hair. She thought about Veronica's neat hairstyle cut short into a bob and the red necklace that matched her bright skirt. In fact Veronica had been in her thoughts all week. Halima looked again at the text message, they would be meeting later today. A strange tingling sensation flittered around her stomach. She searched around in the little drawer and found some purple and black beads she hadn't worn for years. Perhaps she'd wear them today; Mum wouldn't be up until after she'd left. No one to mock her pathetic attempt. Halima fastened the beads around her neck.

In the kitchen she ate some chocolate and drank her mug of tea. As she went to put her mug in the sink, she was startled by a peculiar strangling sound. For a moment she thought her mother must have called out, but then she saw two big green eyes staring at her out of the blackness through the glass. She banged on the window and the grey creature disappeared. Pesky cat. Out of the window she tried to see where it had gone, but she could only see a mirror image of the kitchen in its harsh reflection.

In the hallway, Halima attached her scarf securely and then put on her heavy coat. She checked her bag for her keys and purse. As she stepped onto the pavement under the orange glow of the street light, Halima realised she'd forgotten the recycling again. The neighbours already had their black boxes out on the pavement. Checking her watch, Halima swore and hurried back to the front door. It took three times to get the damn thing unlocked, always the way when you were in a hurry. Their recycling box was outside the back door. Halima brought it in, opened the lid and shoved some tins and junk mail that had piled up on the kitchen counter into the box. As the rubbish cascaded in, she noted a white sheet of paper. Halima bent to take a closer look, moving some papers aside to pull it out.

It was the letter. The invitation to the Clapham Junction Memorial. Her mother must have put it in there. Halima flattened it out and read it again carefully:

Dear Friend

It is almost three years since the terrible disaster that affected us all. We feel it is time to honour those that died, to rejoice with those that survived and offer our thanks to all those that helped to make the suffering a little easier to bear.

The Clapham Rail Disaster Remembrance Trust would like to invite you to a special unveiling of a memorial at the re-opening of platform 9 at Clapham Junction on Tuesday 23rd May 2017 at 11am.

A frown brought Halima's dark eyebrows closer together. Her mother obviously decided that she shouldn't go but Halima wasn't so sure. She scratched at her scar and wondered what Veronica would do. Perhaps she could ask her when they met for coffee later. The thought pleased Halima and she folded the letter carefully and tucked it deep into her coat pocket. She banged the lid on top of the recycling box and carried it out to the pavement. She needed to get to work, and quick, she was late.

*

Halima thought about the impending meeting all through her shift in the office. She hadn't even seen Cheryl this morning, which was a blessing, but it also meant she had no distraction so her mind kept weighing up the coming rendezvous. She was both excited and worried. What would they talk about after so many years? Would they even have anything in common? Halima tried to remember what they'd done together at secondary school, hadn't they been on the netball team together for a while?

A movement caught her eye, a shadow behind the glass door of one of the side offices reserved for managers. They were normally empty at this time. Just as well she'd already been in to do her work, must be an early starter. Halima swept what looked like rubber shavings from Jessica's desk. She dusted the photograph, and put the pens away. Matt smiled at her from a garden somewhere. She wondered where it might be. Perhaps one of the London parks, or maybe it was from their own garden, him and Miss Jessica fluffy-pink-pen. She smiled back at the photograph and pushed her trolley towards the cleaner's room but as she got closer, she had the impression that someone was watching her. She spun around to see Cheryl just a couple of paces behind her.

'What?' Cheryl demanded. 'You look like you've seen a ghost. I've just come to get some more cleaning fluid.'

Halima could see the manager's door beyond Cheryl's back, it seemed rather more open that it had just now. Perhaps she'd been inspecting her work. In the cleaner's room Cheryl huffed loudly as she searched for another bottle and then suddenly she handed Halima an envelope.

'This is for you. Don't tell me I didn't warn you.' She held it out.

Halima waited until Cheryl had disappeared down the corridor before sliding her thumbnail under the flap. Inside was a typed letter. It explained that Halima was being given a formal warning for lateness and rudeness to senior staff. Currently she had one formal warning and only needed two more to be 'let go'. Halima gritted her teeth, she wanted to yell at the empty desks but it wouldn't do any good. That stupid snob-nosed cow. She crumpled up the letter and tossed it into the rubbish bag on the side of her trolley. It hadn't even been her fault, they'd shut the road that day, that was why she'd been late. That awful woman, she'd been trying to get rid of Halima ever since she got the job.

Halima thumped the bottles back onto the shelf, she refused to let Cheryl ruin her day.

*

It was already ten past ten. Halima was standing in front of the coffee shop, she peered through the window. It looked expensive. Maybe she should go home.

'Excuse me.' A man brushed past her carrying a bunch of red roses. The brilliant colour was like Veronica's dashing skirt. So bright and confident, utterly at odds with her own grey life. She wanted to see Veronica, wanted to be dazzled by her bright smile.

Halima spent a minute standing in the doorway trying to spot Veronica amongst the crowded tables. Finally she saw her sat at a low table in a soft armchair about halfway down the coffee shop, waving. Halima let the door shut behind her and made her way between the tables to the plain chair opposite Veronica. There was a cup already on the table, round and large filled with white froth.

'Sorry I'm late,' Halima mumbled.

'Oh don't be, I was early, it's fine.' Veronica smiled through perfect pink lipstick that matched the chiffon scarf at her neck. 'Do you want to grab a drink before you sit down? The cappuccino's good.'

'Yes. Right.' Halima clutched her bag and went to the counter. There were three people waiting. She read the board twice before it was her turn, and still didn't know what to order. She never went to coffee shops.

'Cappuccino please.'

'Thanks for coming to meet me.' Veronica grinned as Halima sat down with her bowl of coffee.

'Well you asked me,' said Halima.

'Yes, yes I did. Ah-ha.' The noise Veronica made was half-way between a laugh and an embarrassed cough. She took a sip from her smaller bowl and looked out of the window. 'Have you lived in Battersea long, Halima?'

61

'Yes. Seems like forever.' Thirty-six years was forever. 'How about you?'

'Oh no. Ah-ha.' Veronica had a hand on her throat as if it was silly to think she had lived here for many years.

Halima didn't think it was strange.

Veronica continued. 'Ian and I have lived all over. Let me see, Winchester, Edinburgh, Beaconsfield, Harrogate, some really lovely towns.'

'Is Ian your husband?'

'Yes, we met at college, gosh it seems so long ago and then he went to Sandhurst to become an officer in the army.'

Halima nodded, she couldn't imagine what it would be like, married to someone in the forces, moving house so often.

'And we have two boys,' Veronica went on, 'grown up of course. Andrew's up in Edinburgh, married a lovely girl Jasmine and they've got little Jack who's just turned one. He's so adorable. Do you have any grandchildren?'

Halima shook her head. She didn't want Veronica to start probing in that direction. 'What about your other son?'

'Oh that's Harry, he recently went out to Australia, he's working out there.' Veronica's voice faltered and she looked down into her coffee cup. 'They've both done so well, I just wish they were a bit nearer.'

'Couldn't you move to Scotland?'

'Well we came to London after Ian retired from the army. My mother's not been well, ever since Dad died actually.'

For a moment she looked away towards the huge plate glass window onto the street. When Veronica turned back she looked distinctly sad.

'I'm kind of like you, Halima. I've been helping to look after my mother, she's not well and it's not been easy.'

'No,' Halima nodded thinking about the article she'd read in the free newspaper the other day. Balham Sole Carers Taking the Brunt. Halima leaned back wondering if her new label sounded more professional than cleaner. She drank the luke-warm cappuccino.

'I don't know how you do it, my mum's in sheltered

accommodation. You might have heard of it, Ash Court on Broomwood road just near Clapham Common. Anyway, I go round most days, do some shopping, help her out.'

Halima shrugged. 'Why isn't she at home with you?'

'Oh crikey.' Veronica stared hard at Halima. 'Well, um, I guess we don't have the same kind of err, culture.'

'Culture?' Halima didn't really think she had a culture. It was just her and Mum. There hadn't been a culture since she was fourteen. 'Doesn't your mother get lonely?'

'Well I guess it sounds simple when you say it like that but I don't think her living with me would work. Obviously it's working for you and that's lovely.'

Halima frowned, it wasn't lovely at all. She was sick of living with her mother. 'How did you get her into a sheltered flat?'

'Oh, it wasn't me, she moved there a few years ago when she was feeling a bit anxious about living on her own, after Dad died. It's very nice and there's a resident manager who comes round and checks on them.'

Halima frowned and wondered how expensive it might be.

'How about your father? Is Mr Shah....?'

Halima pressed her lips together, maybe this had been a bad idea. She didn't want to tell Veronica about her father or anything that had happened back then. She should never have agreed to come. Halima grabbed the bowl of cool coffee and finished it.

Veronica was watching her, her eyebrows raised in expectation. 'I went round,' she said suddenly, 'After you disappeared. Your father opened the door.'

Halima didn't want to hear any more. 'He died,' she said and scratched the scar on her head.

'Oh, I'm sorry.' Veronica's pale cheeks went a little pink but then she smiled and said, 'We're more similar than I thought. How funny that we should both end up in London with our ailing mothers.'

Halima squirmed on her seat, she wasn't similar to Veronica. She hadn't mothered two boys to adulthood and there was no grandson. They were not alike at all. Not with her shiny handbag and smart rain jacket. The gold earrings that dangled from her ears and her soft jumper that looked like one of those really expensive wools, angora was it? Or lambswool perhaps. No, they were not similar, spending money on expensive coffees in cafés. It just wasn't what Halima did and besides she was struggling to push the memories back into their box. Next Veronica would be asking about why she'd left Washwood Heath Comprehensive so suddenly. The coffee rolled around in her stomach.

'Do you have children?' Veronica raised her perfectly-plucked eyebrows. Halima felt that stone inside roll uncomfortably. She should have had tea instead of coffee.

'No.'

'What a shame, I'm sure you would have been a fabulous mum.'

Halima wondered if she might be sick, it felt like she'd swallowed some pebbles. She needed to divert the conversation away and suddenly thought about the invitation.

'I received this the other day,' Halima said reaching deep into her pocket and passing the folded letter across to Veronica.

'Should I read it?'

'Go ahead.'

Veronica opened it out and read slowly. Halima could see her hand gripping tighter causing the letter to crease. Veronica's lips pursed. Halima reached across to try and get the letter back but Veronica clung on. She stared straight at Halima.

'Why did they send you this? Were you there?'

'Well sort of,' Halima pulled her hand back and scratched at her scar, 'I was under the bridge when it happened.' She didn't want to go into detail about that day, just wanted to talk about the memorial, that was all. Veronica was analysing the letter again, her eyes narrowed, her whole face pinched as if focusing on a point of pain.

'Were *you* there?' Halima said.

'No, no.' Veronica pulled on the chiffon scarf and dropped the letter back onto the table, she wiggled her shoulders, a sigh escaping her lips. 'Ian was trying to get home that day, he was delayed for hours and hours.' She stared into her coffee cup and then out of the window.

'I think I *will* go,' Halima said, quietly taking the letter and folding it carefully. 'To the event I mean.'

Veronica just nodded and then she said, 'To tell you the truth, it's been hard moving here. I don't know anyone and-,' she suddenly covered her mouth with one hand while the other searched hurriedly in her handbag.

'But you have your mother,' Halima corrected, feeling confused, 'and your husband.'

Veronica nodded. She'd found a tissue and blew her nose.

'And me.'

A small smile half-hidden behind the tissue.

'Oh Halima, it's so nice to have met you again. I have such fond memories of you and I.'

'I remember your Sindy doll.' Halima smiled. 'You had all the best outfits, I was really jealous.'

'Oh yes, I did. Do you remember when Matthew came over and ripped the ball dress? I was so upset.'

Halima frowned trying to remember.

'The blue one with the frill at the neck,' Veronica said.

Halima nodded, 'I took it home and Mum stitched it.'

'Oh my goodness yes. She did.'

Halima smiled. Her stomach had stopped feeling queasy. 'And didn't we play netball?'

Veronica laughed, 'Oh goodness, do you remember that match when we played against the grammar school girls?'

Halima suddenly recalled when they'd got their own back on a vicious posh girl in the changing rooms. Halima blushed and a giggle bubbled up and joined the sound of Veronica's tinkling laugh.

8

Austin – New opportunities

Austin had arrived early to counteract his nerves and the niggling annoyance that his company had sent him. He'd never had to teach customers before. His boss had sold it to him as a new opportunity to expand his skills. Austin reckoned he'd got the short straw. He loaded up his slides and set the welcome message to display on the board at the front. It read 'Rail Asset Management System – Report Writing'. He'd laid out four sets of exercises and checked the access and passwords worked. However, it was five past nine and he still had only one delegate in the room instead of four; a woman busy texting on her phone.

'Um, I think we should-' Austin began just as the door opened and a dark-haired man came striding in. The air whooshed with him and fluttered the papers from one of the desks. He was tall and broad in a blue shirt with his tie tossed over one shoulder as if he'd been running. The air stirred around Austin and he was sure he could smell a musky deodorant.

'Sorry, I got held up.' The man leant down to pick up the papers that had blown off. 'Sit anywhere is it?' His face was open and friendly under a long fringe which he swept to the side with a quick flick of his hand. Austin had to drag his eyes away down to the delegate list.

'Trust you to be late,' the woman at the front said.

Austin sent a smile across the room. 'It's fine, we hadn't started yet,' and then realised they were both sitting waiting for him. 'Right, so let me just see who's here.' Austin looked at the list again. 'Are you Melanie Stuart?'

'That's me,' the woman in the front row put up her hand and smiled widely. She had a neat brown bob and a grey blouse on.

Austin smiled back and ticked her name off.

'Neil Rawlings?'

'He's not coming,' the guy at the back said, leaning on his chair. Confidence and charm oozing out of him.

'OK, right, and I presume you're not Sinead McDougall.' Austin looked at the next name.

'Stick a wig on him and shrink him by ten sizes and he might just pass for Sinead,' Melanie said.

'I think she's off sick,' he said.

'She's always off. Don't know how she gets away with it frankly, you wouldn't find me skipping off with the slightest sniffle. Some of us have got more stamina.'

'OK.' Austin didn't want to involve himself in their office politics. 'So you must be David Calder,' he said.

'Everyone calls him Dave.'

'I haven't been called David since I was at school. Seems appropriate for today don't you think?' There was a sparkle in his eye which made Austin blush.

'Right, well we'll start by logging in, I've put some access details on the papers next to your computers. Then we'll get straight on to some simple reports so you can get a feel for the data.'

After the tricky start, the time whizzed by. Austin had to spend quite a while sitting next to Melanie explaining what the operators were and how to use them. He'd have preferred to help David but he seemed to get it straight away and was delving into the system quite happily. At coffee time, Melanie was only too pleased to take a break.

'I hope they've refilled the machine. There should be biscuits in the cupboard too.' She leapt out of her seat and began rummaging around at the back of the training room. Austin had never been here before, to the Transport Rail offices, so he was glad someone knew what to do.

David was still engrossed at his computer. Austin ran a hand through his short blond hair, pulling at the front spikes hoping it didn't look too flat and nerdy, and made his way over.

'Do you want to stop for a drink?' Austin asked.

'Yeah, all right.' David stood up and stretched, his shirt coming un-tucked from his trousers and giving a glimpse of fine dark hairs curled on his stomach. Austin swallowed and continued to the back of the room to see how the drinks machine worked.

'Do you always do this sort of stuff?' David asked, sitting on one of the desks holding a cup of coffee that Melanie had passed him.

'Er no, I'm from the testing group. But I've been helping with some of the coding and I know the reporting tool really well. I guess they thought I should teach it but I'm not sure I'm any good.'

'You're doing fine.' David smiled and threw a packet of custard creams across to Austin.

'I don't know why they sent me, I can't imagine I'm going to be using it much,' Melanie said handing an espresso to Austin in a brown plastic cup. It smelt good but tasted dreadful.

David nodded at Melanie. 'You're probably right but they're going to need someone to build these reports.'

'If they start adding any more to my job description, I tell you, I'm going straight to HR. They put this fancy new photocopier on our floor a couple of months ago and now it seems I'm the only one who knows how to use it so I'm doing everyone's,' Melanie said.

'That's because you do it so well.' David grinned.

'Cos you're all too bloody lazy to do your own.'

'Or too busy,' David added.

'Hmmm. You're not so bad, but some of the other managers, honestly they seem to think I'm employed to be their personal secretary. It's ridiculous.'

David gave Austin a sideways glance, raising his eyebrows so that Melanie couldn't see. It took Austin by surprise, he bit into a custard cream to hide his embarrassment.

Melanie indicated the clock on the wall. 'What time are we stopping? Because I haven't ordered a sandwich from the canteen yet and all the good stuff goes really early. The egg and cress is nice but they do a really good New Yorker too.'

It was only eleven. Austin had been told to provide a half-day's course and there were certainly plenty more exercises to do. 'Um, well I've got a few more different scenarios for you and then it's really about practising so you have the confidence to pull out the data you want.'

'I couldn't care less about the data. It's Neil that wants this stuff isn't it? Typical that he's not here to learn it himself.' Melanie went back to the coffee machine and pushed the buttons for another drink.

'Shall we get back to work then?' Austin said.

'Yes Sir!' David wiggled his eyebrows, 'It's not often I get a chance to be out of my office and back at school.' David nodded and went back to his seat.

Austin smiled to himself, he hadn't expected to like teaching others but he was very glad that David was one of his students.

At twelve o'clock Melanie was muttering about needing to get her sandwich and get some real work done. Austin knew there was nothing extra that he needed to share but he doubted if Melanie had mastered it.

David was still deep in concentration and Austin was secretly pleased when Melanie left the room leaving them alone together. He started to walk towards David's desk but then found himself pausing suddenly acutely aware that he fancied the pants off this guy. He hadn't felt like this since... Austin took a breath and let it out slowly. It was fine, nothing would happen. He wasn't ready for that, was he?

'Can I help? What are you working on?' Austin pulled a nearby chair a bit closer so he could see David's monitor.

'This is really interesting,' David put a finger on the screen and turned to Austin. But instead of carrying on with his explanation he stopped and they stared at each other. David broke their gaze by glancing towards the door and then he seemed to reset himself and was talking again about the report he was building.

'I was looking at rails between Clapham and Queenstown Road.'

'Where?' Austin felt himself tense.

'I was trying to find out if there'd been a failure or problem or something, whether you could run searches to see if there were any patterns.' David was looking earnestly between Austin and the screen.

Austin was sure David had said Clapham. Why did he have to go and say that? He really didn't want to be thinking about Matt just now. Austin fiddled with his watch.

'Erm, it's better to think of the database system as a preventative tool,' Austin hurried on, the words chasing over themselves, trying to cover up his awkwardness, 'that can manage maintenance schedules on all your rail assets and provide accurate forecasting for future expenditure on your capital assets.'

'Woah.' David frowned. 'Was that nerdy speak?'

Austin looked down, embarrassed. 'Sorry.'

'I'm sure Neil would love whatever it was you said but I was more interested in patterns of failure.'

'Oh.' Austin pulled absently at his short fringe. 'I could show you.'

David glanced at his watch. 'Damn, I can't stay any longer, I've got a meeting at half-past and then back-to-backs.' He stood up and Austin did too.

Standing this close, Austin could definitely smell that musky deodorant.

David held out his hand and Austin shook it. It was a warm firm shake. David's fingers longer and stronger than Austin's, wrapping around his hand. He stood taller and broader than Austin too.

'Do you have a feedback form?'

They dropped hands and Austin stepped back flustered.

'Er no, but you could um, write on this.' Austin grabbed a nearby sheet from one of the spare tables and turned it over to the blank side.

David picked up a pen and began scrawling and Austin hovered awkwardly.

'Here. You might want to keep this to yourself,' David thrust the sheet at Austin and a smile lit his blue eyes. Then he was gone with a whoosh out the door. More papers tumbled to the floor in his wake. Austin felt his whole body relax as if he'd been holding himself in for too long. He wasn't sure if he was relieved or disappointed. Austin looked at David's scrawl on the sheet in his hand. He hadn't written much, 'Thanks for a great course,' and then underneath, was his name and a mobile number.

9

Adam – A new tribe

Maybe this had been a bad idea after all. Adam wished he'd worn another layer; the cold wind was biting. He paused at the pedestrian crossing waiting for the lights. Ahead he could see the mosque and two men walking through the door. No sign of Faizal though. Traffic swished past on the wet road and Adam wondered if he should head back home. But Faizal's message that day by the track had probably saved his life. He couldn't turn back now.

At Clapham Junction, he'd been staring down at the tracks waiting for an announcement about standing back for a fast train. A message not of danger for Adam but of action. A final action so he could wipe the slate clean. Remove the mess that was his life once and for all. But while he waited, thoughts of his mother's tears made him feel guilty so he got out his phone to send her a final text, to tell her that he loved her. So she'd know it wasn't her fault. No farewells just a simple message of love so she wouldn't blame herself. But when the screen lit up, he discovered two new messages, one was from his mother asking if he wanted lamb or chicken for tea. The other was from Faizal. He'd sent a few since they'd met that time at the mosque. Adam had only replied to be polite. Sitting there on platform ten, he opened the new message.

Come to prayers Fri. Speaker after. Change your life. Inshallah. LMK

Adam read the message again. It was the thinnest of threads but it was enough to make him reconsider. He wondered what exactly made him pull back that day. Was it the word 'prayers'? Or the 'change your life' bit? He re-read it several times before tucking the phone back in his pocket. Perhaps it was the word 'Inshallah'. There was something hopeful and trusting about it. A familiar word within his community and extended family. Maybe that and Faizal's wide grin that came to mind whenever he received a message from him. It was a glimmer of hope and Adam had clung to that straw all the way home from Clapham Junction.

So here he was on Friday heading to the mosque. The traffic lights changed and the bleeping noise reminded him to cross. Still no sign of Faizal though. Adam slowed down a little, he didn't want to go inside on his own. The cold air made him shiver. Perhaps he could cruise past the front a couple of times. He rolled slowly, staring at the mottled glass in the top of the doors. A noise ahead diverted Adam's attention to two young men heading his way, talking loudly.

'I can't even get past level three, what did you do with the Rocky Rider?'

'That's easy, you have to use the ramp, jump and push him out of the way when you get to the canyon.'

Adam recognised Faizal and Tariq as they approached.

'Or you can throw a tack under his wheel,' Adam said.

'Hey Adam, As-Salam-u-Alaikum.' That huge grin of Faizal's reminding Adam why he'd liked him the first time they'd met.

'wa Alaikum Assalam,' Adam replied.

'Where do you get tacks from?' Tariq stared wide-eyed, he turned to Faizal: 'Have you found any tacks?'

Faizal shrugged and looked again at Adam, 'What level have you got to?'

'Eight.' Adam couldn't help smiling as they pushed open the mosque doors and held them for Adam to wheel inside. Warm air flooded around him, it was the right decision to come. He'd been playing the Xbox racing game almost solidly for the last two days. It was a diversion from his failed life. Maybe that time hadn't been completely wasted now that he was here with Faizal and Tariq.

'No way, you're going to have to show us, we'll meet up,' Tariq said taking off his black shoes and placing them on the rack.

'It's good to see you man, you won't regret coming, I promise,' Faizal said adding his trainers to the others. 'I guess you can leave yours on.' Faizal nodded at the Nikes that rested on the footplate of his chair. Adam nodded, it was too awkward to take them off, and too intimate to have someone else do it. Faizal seemed to accept this and led the way down the corridor.

The men's wash room was large with many places to sit, each opposite a tap. Tariq and another friend were already sat down, one washing his foot, the other his face. Faizal looked quizzically at Adam's chair and then went to a spot near the wall indicating that Adam should come beside him where there was room for the wheelchair.

'You've done this before right?' Faizal sat down.

'Yeah sure.' Adam swallowed, wondering if he would remember the sequence correctly. In truth he hadn't performed Wudu or been to Friday prayers since he was about nine. Adam watched Faizal out of the corner of his eye. He was sitting quietly, his hands on his knees, he shut his eyes and whispered.

'Bismillah.'

Adam didn't remember doing that bit, but when Faizal started with washing his left hand, it all came back. A routine he'd learned as a child from his father and seeing the other men at the mosque that his family attended. It was only when he tried to wash his nose that it went wrong and he ended up coughing and spluttering.

Faizal laughed out loud and then said, 'Been a while then?'

'Yeah, I guess so.'

When Faizal got to the foot washing part, Adam could only watch. It was difficult, even in his own disabled shower at home, to wash his feet. There was no way he could do it here. Adam wondered if it mattered and even that thought surprised him. After the accident he had dismissed Allah from his life but here in the mosque, the question of whether Allah would mind about unwashed feet seemed suddenly important.

In the prayer room, there were already about a dozen men in a line at the front. The red carpet silenced Adam's wheels as he followed Faizal to start a second row by the window. It was remarkably familiar and comforting to be there and Adam wondered why he suddenly felt so light.

Faizal stood with his hands clasped in front beside Adam waiting for the Imam to begin. When the others kneeled down and placed their heads on the floor, Adam simply leaned forwards letting his head touch his knees, it was as much as he could do. The cadence of the Imam washed over them, bringing a musical peace to Adam's mind. It was like being a child again, warm and safe. Nothing was being demanded of Adam, no hidden agendas or bubbling tension. Just the quiet prayers and the rustling of clothes as the men bowed in unison. Adam released his hands from the wheels and sighed deeply.

The prayers were over too soon and the men began to drift away and chat with each other. Adam felt the tension return to his shoulders and he gripped the wheels suddenly transported back into his disabled body and failed life.

'Come on upstairs, that's where the meeting is.' Faizal was hovering as if trying to contain an excess of nervous energy. Adam had momentarily forgotten there would be a speaker after prayers, at least it would delay his return home. Who on earth could make Faizal so excited?

There was an old battered lift at the end of the corridor. Adam wasn't sure if it would even make it to the next floor as it rattled and clanged its way upwards. Faizal took the stairs and was waiting wide-eyed to show him into the meeting room.

Adam baulked in the doorway. This had definitely been the wrong decision. What exactly was he getting himself into? The room was noisy with people, a lot of them young like himself. There were cakes and bowls of fruit. Teas and coffees were being served from one table and some canned drinks and squash on another. Tariq was stuffing some Jalebi into his mouth and giving him a thumbs up. Faizal went ahead shaking hands and chatting. But it wasn't the people or the refreshments that worried Adam, it was the large banner across the wall of the room. In huge orange letters it read: UMIA, and underneath in smaller text, United Muslims In Action. What was that supposed to mean? A young man with a traditional kufi, a prayer cap, on his head was standing in the corner just below the edge of the banner. He stared back at Adam. His eyes shifted away and then darted back again.

'Hi, you can go in, we don't bite,' said a female voice behind him.

'Er, I think I made a mistake,' Adam stared as the girl came around his chair. He wondered how best to make his escape, remembering his dad and Sully discussing the latest terrorist arrests in the paper.

She frowned at him. 'Don't you want ISIS to stop?'

'What?'

'I mean they're giving all us Muslims a bad name right? Well I want to do something about it, don't you prefer pluralism to fascism?'

Adam had no idea what pluralism was.

'Don't I know you?' She cocked her head to the side and studied him with her large brown eyes. They were a little too big for her face but she was still attractive in a slightly quirky way. 'Weren't you in Aisha's year at school? In fact aren't you the one that was in that train crash a few years ago? That's it, I knew I recognised you. Aisha's here somewhere, I'm sure she'd be thrilled to see you. Come on.' She beckoned him in and headed across the room.

Faizal suddenly appeared at his side and handed him a cake with chocolate icing on the top. He put a hand up to his face to whisper conspiratorially into Adam's ear. 'Aunty Aboud makes these, they're the best.'

More people flooded around him and Adam was compelled to move further into the room. He stopped and bit into the cake, it was light and delicious, the sponge melting on his tongue. That just-baked warm smell. Two women approached.

'This is my sister Aisha, I forgot to tell you mine, it's Noor.'

Adam gazed up at the tall willowy woman called Aisha. Was she really in his year at school? He stared astonished. Surely he'd remember someone with such beautiful eyes. Perfect brown almonds in her oval face. And yet not quite perfect. Bright flecks of green flashed as the overhead light caught them when she turned her head.

Adam swallowed quickly and wiped a free hand across his face. 'Sorry.'

'Good cakes?' Aisha smiled at him. 'Hello. Adam, isn't it?'

Noor was staring at him. 'Oh no, are they Aunty Aboud's? I bet they're all gone.' She dashed off.

'You don't remember me do you?' Aisha said.

'Sorry,' Adam was feeling too hot.

'It's fine, we all knew your name.'

'Oh?' Adam felt his sweat cool, some past failure that he couldn't remember?

'The wheelchair,' she gestured, 'there weren't a lot of disabled kids in our school.'

'Oh I see. Yeah of course.'

'In fact just you,' she smiled, not with embarrassment, instead it was like a warm glow shining down onto him.

Noor reappeared grinning widely holding two cakes, she passed one to her sister and then more people seemed to encircle Adam, introducing themselves and each other. Offering more refreshments. Everywhere he turned there were smiles and friendly laughter. It was like he'd walked into a huge family gathering, like he belonged. His earlier misgivings dissipated and Adam looked about trying to catch another glimpse of Aisha's beautiful face.

But there was someone else who seemed to be taking a keen interest in Aisha. The man with the kufi was still standing a bit apart from the rest and he kept looking over and shuffling his feet.

10

Halima - Blossom

'All done Miss Shah?' Vincent, the security guard, doffed his cap as she crossed the shiny floor of the reception area.

'Yes.' Halima smiled.

'Beautiful day out there. Have you got plans?'

Halima looked through the huge plate glass windows, the morning sun was shining down onto the street. As she moved closer, she could see blue sky beyond the tall building opposite. Vincent was right. It was like a clear summer's day.

He spoke again, 'Spring's me favourite time of year. Love all them growing things, flowers and the leaves comin' out on the trees. There's a 'ole bunch of snowdrops and crocuses down at the park.'

Halima didn't know which park he meant so she nodded politely.

'Perhaps you'd like to see them?' Vincent came out from behind his desk and went to open the door for her.

'Yes, I might.' Suddenly she felt self-conscious as Vincent stood there with his hand on the door, his smart navy uniform standing to attention and his glossy face smiling at her.

'I'm off meself in a few minutes.' He paused and then he said more quietly, 'I could show you if you like.'

Halima was half-way through the door, his warm breath brushed her cheek as she stepped past causing a tingling sensation in her thighs. The door remained open behind her and she could sense him waiting for her response.

Halima turned to see his face. He was no longer smiling; he lowered his eyes to his shoes, shiny black lace-ups.

'I.. I… I'm meeting a friend,' Halima said.

'Of course.' Vincent nodded vigorously, not meeting her eye. 'You 'ave a great day.'

'Thank you.'

He let the door ease shut.

Halima stood for a moment, a sudden release of wonder and possibility rising out of her chest as she stared upwards at that deep blue sky. Of course it wasn't a summer's day, the air was still quite cool but suddenly the world seemed filled with possibilities. Instead of turning left to head back home, she turned right, walking the length of the plate glass window. At the end, she stopped again and saw Vincent through the glass watching her. He dropped his gaze immediately and Halima felt suddenly sad, as if she'd done him a disservice. She placed her hand flat on the cold glass and Vincent glanced at her and then stared, a smile beginning to spread across his face and then he raised his hand in farewell.

She hadn't meant to come shopping, not at all, but now she was here, she was enjoying wandering past the windows of the boutiques. Spring blossom littered the pavement with pink petals while people rushed past on their way to work. Halima stopped beneath a tree and breathed in deeply, enjoying the fragrance, so rare in London. To her right was a small shop displaying a model in a striking navy suit and a bright red patterned scarf at the neck. Halima adjusted her focus to see her own reflection and automatically touched the side of her face. She, too, wore a scarf, but hers was tucked neatly around her face, pinned in place to stop it moving while she worked. It was black like most of her scarves, although she did own a beige one too and years ago she'd had a silvery grey one for a while. Halima gazed through the window again at the slim straight plastic legs, the tailored cut of the skirt and the shiny buttons on the lapels of the jacket. She thought about Veronica and her poppy-red skirt. Her eyes were drawn back to the red scarf at the top of the figure, how it lay knotted at the neck. No harm in going in to have a closer look.

'Would you like to try it, Madam?' A shop assistant approached even before the door had closed.

Halima felt caught. This wasn't a typical high street store. The lady smiled at her. 'I think it would suit you.' She gave a nod and walked smartly towards a rack of clothing. She selected a jacket and then swished around and stepped towards another rack where she pulled out a matching skirt.

'I'm afraid I'm guessing at your size, but you might want to try these first? Follow me.'

The lady walked determinedly towards the back of the shop where a thick curtain divided off a cubicle.

'Here you go.' She hung the jacket and skirt inside and then held the curtain back for Halima to step in.

Halima did so and the curtain swished shut, painted fingernails appeared around the edge as the lady pulled it in tight to the wall.

'Just let me know if you'd like to try a different size.'

Halima stood in the small blanketed space clutching her bag. Did she really want to try on the suit? She felt a bit silly standing there doing nothing facing the mirror. Halima stared at the loose black trousers she wore noticing there were shiny bits by her knees. On her feet were her scuffed black shoes and on top her dark grey winter coat with the furry edge around the hood. She took the suit jacket from off the hook and held it in front of her. Such a contrast. Halima sighed.

'Take your time, there's no hurry,' the assistant said.

Halima started to undress.

The assistant had been right about the jacket, it fit perfectly but the skirt was a bit tight. Halima struggled to do up the button at the back.

'How are you getting on?'

Halima swallowed, and then put a hand to her throat, she needed that red scarf. Cautiously she pulled back the edge of the curtain.

'I need a scarf.'

'Oh my goodness, look at you.' The assistant gently pulled the curtain back further. 'That looks lovely on you.' She beamed.

Halima felt awkward stood in just her pop socks and bare legs. The suit like some kind of foreign armour encasing her body.

'Here, come and stand back.' Gently the woman took Halima's shoulders and pulled her forwards and then around so she faced the mirror again.

Halima was acutely uncomfortable. It was kind of odd, like looking at her head stuck on someone else's body. She still had on her traditional black scarf tight around her face.

'You're right about a bit of colour, that will set it off just right, let me get you a couple to try.' The assistant marched off leaving Halima standing alone. There was no one else in the small shop so Halima turned to the side and saw how the jacket lay straight and then slightly in at her waist. She turned back to the front, the buttons shiny and new winking at her from the mirror. The square shoulders made her look official and she imagined herself as one of the managers who worked in the individual offices she cleaned.

'Here I've brought a couple.' The lady appeared with three scarves draped over her arm.

Halima's eyes alighted immediately onto the one she'd seen in the window.

'The red one,' she said.

'Certainly, let's see how that looks. The assistant put the others to the side, then stood behind Halima and expertly laid the scarf around her neck. It was a striking dash of colour but now that it was around her neck, it reminded her of fresh blood.

'Let's try the yellow, I think that would suit you better.'

The woman expertly whipped off the red one and replaced it with a pretty lemon one.

Halima gasped. It was stunning.

'My goodness, don't you look amazing?'

It was incredible, a smart navy suit and a lemon scarf, such simple items and yet the apparition in the mirror was nothing like Halima. It was somebody else entirely, all except the black scarf that still adorned her head. Halima struggled with the hair clips, removing them carefully and then pulled the drab scarf free.

'Liberating.' The assistant beamed again, stepping back allowing Halima full advantage of her reflection.

Halima gazed at her dark hair that tumbled partly over the new scarf around her neck. The bright yellow contrasted with both the navy suit and her mocha skin. Ignoring the pop socks at the bottom, and the too tight skirt, she really did look like a professional woman. The cut of the jacket emphasised her bust and narrowed her waist and that yellow, so crisp, it lifted her entire face.

*

Veronica was standing outside the coffee shop when Halima arrived.

'I thought it was too beautiful to be indoors,' Veronica grinned and took Halima's arm. 'Ooh, you've been shopping, do show me.'

Proud and guilty all at the same time, Halima pulled out the little package from the pretty cardboard bag. The assistant had wrapped the scarf in pink tissue paper, sealing it with a small sticker with the name of the shop on it. Carefully she peeled the sticker off and unrolled the scarf.

'Oh Halima it's such a pretty colour. Why don't you put it on?'

Halima frowned and took back the silk. She re-wrapped it.

'Of course, you're saving it for a special occasion.'

Halima returned her smile; if only she had a special occasion to wear it to.

With linked arms they started walking back across the river.

'I thought we'd walk through the park, we can always stop at the kiosk for a hot drink if we get too cold.'

'All right, Vincent said the flowers are out.'

'Vincent hmm? Is that who the scarf's for?'

Halima felt heat rush to her ears and stared at the pavement as it moved under their feet.

Veronica's arm was heavy and warm linked through her own. She wondered what Vincent's would feel like. The thought embarrassed her further so she pushed it away and concentrated on walking in time with Veronica. Halima didn't normally stand this close to people and certainly didn't link arms. But the touch was comforting and even though their bodies were barely touching it felt incredibly intimate. Halima checked to see if the other pedestrians thought it strange but no one seemed to be taking any notice at all.

They passed a large oak tree, its base surrounded by a variety of different coloured crocuses.

'I do love the purple ones, mine seem to have all died off and I've only got the yellow ones left. Do you like gardening?'

'No, we don't have much at the back, just weeds.'

'I tell you it's a constant battle but I find it very therapeutic. Especially when the flowers come out, it gives me a lift.'

Halima stared at the flower beds. She could do with a lift. Could she grow flowers?

'I never bothered before, MOD housing doesn't really lend

itself to gardening, as soon as you've made an effort you move on so I never really saw the point.'

'What things do you grow?' Halima said.

'Oh just a few small shrubs, tulips which I absolutely adore and the chrysanthemums did well last year. I've sprinkled some wild flower seeds on the funny patch by the fence so we'll see what happens.'

'Have you got a big garden?'

'Oh no, tiny. Prices in London and now that I'm…'

Halima felt Veronica's arm give hers a squeeze but she didn't say anything else and they carried on in silence for a couple of minutes.

'How's Mrs Pease? Does she still make those pink-iced cakes?'

Veronica gave that tinkling laugh of hers. 'How sweet of you to remember, but no, she gets meals on wheels and I often cook for her when I'm over. Actually I told her about you and she remembered. Called you that funny little brown girl that never stopped giggling.'

Halima suddenly stopped on the path.

'What is it?' Veronica's arm slipped out.

'Was I really that happy?'

'Oh yes, Mum used to say you had the giggle bug and that you'd given it to me.'

Halima couldn't help smiling and then she noticed her hand clutching the bag from the boutique and felt her cheeks stretch into an even wider smile.

'I'm really glad you came back Veronica.' Halima grabbed Veronica's arm and linked them in together again.

'Hey, it wasn't me that suddenly disappeared without saying goodbye.'

11

Adam - Popcorn and brimstone

'Right, well I'd better be off. Mine starts in five.' Cara waved her bag of Minstrels towards the poster for the latest romcom. She smiled broadly with her painted lips. 'It's good to see you both letting your 'air down for a change.' She paused and then laughed loudly. 'Hah, that's a good one, letting your 'air down,' she pointed at Adam's new goatee, 'and you 'ave been.' She cackled as she began walking away towards screen three. 'Slid down onto your chin. Ha ha ha.'

Adam gritted his teeth and turned to Vijay, 'Shall I get us a box of popcorn seeing as you bought the tickets?' he said.

'Sure, why not? Let's go crazy and get cokes too.' Vijay whirred towards the food counter.

'I thought Cara didn't let you have coke,' Adam said as he positioned himself in the queue.

'Exactly. See what a bad influence you are on me?'

Adam grinned.

Vijay smiled back. 'It's good to see you happy for a change. I thought maybe you'd gone into depressive hibernation.'

'Actually things are a lot better, I've been out loads recently.'

Vijay raised his eyebrows but it was Adam's turn at the counter to give his order. The attendant settled two cups and a large box of popcorn into a cardboard tray and then peered over the counter at them.

'Would you like me to carry this through for you?'

'No-'

'Yes.'

Adam gave Vijay a scowl. 'I've got this.' Carefully he took the tray and balanced it on his lap.

'Really?' Vijay sighed and whirred across towards the lift. 'It's not often that you get staff for free.'

'He's not your staff, besides I'm perfectly capable.' Adam

grabbed the tray as it suddenly lurched forwards when his wheels hit the bump onto the carpeted area.

Soon they were lined up in the disabled section opposite the large screen waiting for the latest James Bond to start.

'So what's been keeping you busy then? Got a job at last?' Vijay said.

'No, I've joined the UMIA. They're really nice, mega friendly and they haven't once mentioned my disability. And I've started doing my namaz.'

'Am I meant to understand these strange acronyms of your new underground society?'

Adam held the coke up so the straw could reach his friend's mouth. 'United Muslims In Action and it's not underground. They're totally cool, they're all about today's young Muslims, us British Muslims not like the old traditional stuff.'

'So you're getting up all hours of the night to pray to an invisible entity. Remind me not to invite you for a sleepover.'

Adam scowled. It wasn't like that. The daily prayers were reducing his stress and tension at home and it was giving him a new sense of peace and hope. But he didn't want to try and explain that to Vijay. It was too personal.

'It's not all night, only five times a day.' Adam said hotly.

'Well at least it will give you a routine. Haven't you always been a Muslim?'

'Yeah, but not properly, I mean this is different.'

The sound suddenly boomed around them as the Dolby advertisement came on.

Vijay looked at Adam out of the corner of his eye. 'Funny, I never took you to be one of the masses.'

'What's that supposed to mean?'

'Karl Marx,' he said. 'In fact prayer is simply a type of self-talk which when used correctly can be very productive. I've used it myself in the past.'

'That's not what prayers are about. You don't know anything about Islam.'

'Ooh touchy. You must be in deep.'

'Shh.' The movie was starting.

'At least you seem positive, maybe it's true what they say about opium.'

Adam grabbed another handful of popcorn and shoved it into Vijay's mouth.

*

'How does it look?' Faizal was holding the banner up for Adam to see.

'You'll need to hold it higher than that.'

'Yes but can you read it?'

They had used Adam's dad's car paint, and an old white sheet Faizal had found in the bottom of the airing cupboard. It was probably just as well his parents and Sully were out thought Adam, as he saw black marks on the table where they'd laid the sheet.

'Has your dad got any garden canes or something?'

'No.'

'We need two sticks, one at each side.'

'I know, but look at the time.' Adam glanced at the clock, they really ought to get going. 'Broom handles?' Adam said.

'Maybe.' Faizal threw the sheet at Adam and ran out the back. A couple of minutes later he returned with an old curtain rod and a retractable prop for the washing line.

'Perfect, grab the tape. There's a bus we can catch.'

'A bus?' Faizal picked up the parcel tape while Adam folded up the sheet. 'Won't the tube be quicker?'

'Not for me, not for where we're starting from, there's no disabled access out of the tube stations.'

Faizal scowled. 'Taxi?'

'Are you made of money?'

'No.'

'Right then, let's go.'

Once off the bus, it was just a couple of hundred yards to the meeting point and Adam was staggered at the size of the crowd as they rounded the corner. The hubbub of voices of what looked to be a few hundred people milled around the square. There were many policemen too, stood at intervals watching and a couple of police vans parked up around the edge.

'Blimey,' Faizal said.

'See anyone we recognize?'

'Yeah, like half the Muslims in London.'

They joined the throng and spent a while trying to work out the best way to hold up their banner.

'I have to use my hands on the wheels, I can't hold that as well,' Adam said.

'Yeah but I'm gonna be knackered holding it all by myself.'

'What about fixing it to my chair at the back?'

After a fair amount of experimentation and cross words when Faizal dug the curtain rail into Adam's back, it was finally in place, strapped tight to the metal frame and fluttering above Adam's head in the breeze.

'Hey it looks awesome, much better than some of these guys.' Faizal was standing back grinning at their masterpiece.

There was a whole host of posters and banners, some looking more home-made than others. They all said pretty much the same, *UMIA* or *United Muslims in Action*. One said *Muslim Brothers and Sisters Together*.

'Hey you two, most of us are over this way.' It was Tariq. 'Knew that was probably yours.' He pointed at the banner. 'Just got to get that smile in somewhere haven't you?'

Adam looked across at Faizal who was beaming as usual. When they'd been painting on the kitchen table, Faizal had turned the U of United into a smile with two eyes and a nose, much to Adam's annoyance.

They followed Tariq through the noisy crowd where the faces became more familiar.

'Hey Adam,' a voice spoke from his left. It was Noor. 'Isn't this exciting, I can't believe there are so many people. Just goes to show what grass roots can do.'

Adam looked around for her sister amongst the other women but couldn't see her.

'Is Aisha here?'

Just then a tall lady in a Niqab thrust a hand through the crowd and grabbed Noor's arm. 'I told you to stay with me,' the woman hissed. The Niqab covered her hair and face, only her eyes visible.

'All right, don't pull. Relax, it's a peaceful march.'

The woman's eyes alighted on Adam and immediately softened. It was Aisha.

'Hi,' Adam said, suddenly embarrassed that he hadn't recognised her and surprised to see her so covered.

'Hello again Adam.' She seemed slightly apologetic. 'We should keep further forwards.'

Noor butted in: 'What for? I don't know why you've gotten so bossy lately. Honestly you'd think she was the Queen of Sheba now she's decided to wear the veil. You wouldn't catch me in one. I think it just alienates us from the rest of the public. What do you think Adam?'

Adam stared at Aisha's figure in her flowing green fabric. For a moment he wondered if she could be naked beneath it and the thought brought heat suddenly to his cheeks. She was standing tall now, looking forwards and over the crowd. There was something strong and statuesque about her.

'I, I quite like it.'

Noor gave him a scornful look but Aisha turned back towards him and bent down, her eyes intensely on his. 'Come on, let's all move forwards.'

They did so, awkwardly excusing themselves as Aisha and Noor shuffled through the crowd with Adam close on their heels.

'Wow, this is amazing, I thought there'd be hardly anyone,' Noor said as they settled into a space alongside the barriers.

The buzz around him had taken on a new edge. Someone near the front was yelling into a loudspeaker.

'Looks like we're going to start moving.' Aisha stood on her toes and looked over the crowd.

Adam envied her height.

She turned back to him. 'Your banner really stands out.'

Pleased with himself, Adam could sense the excitement in the crowd. They were going to march to No.10 where a petition would be handed over requesting the government not to send forces into Syria. The UMIA wanted a completely different approach using its own members of the Muslim community to liaise both inside Syria and in the Western governments. It was an ambitious plan but maybe that's what made it worthwhile.

Adam had never been on a march before. He rolled his shoulders and stretched his neck. To be part of this, to be doing something meaningful felt good. He looked at Aisha standing next to her sister.

'You make a statement just like that.' Adam nodded at her Niqab. She seemed so arresting, standing tall and resolute.

'Thanks.'

And then the crowd started to shuffle forwards.

'I just hope there won't be any trouble,' Aisha said.

Trouble, what kind of trouble? Adam could only see the bodies of the Muslims around him, his line of sight confined to within the crowd. He would need to be careful not to knock the person's heels in front. Ahead a man passed the lid of a coffee flask to his friend. Over to his left he spotted Tariq and Faizal walking close together deep in conversation. And on his right, close enough to touch, was Aisha in her flowing clothes. Above him the clouds were parting, offering up patches of clear sky. He thanked Allah for his good fortune.

They had just turned into Whitehall when things changed. There seemed to be a commotion up ahead and then suddenly Aisha cried out and staggered into the barrier. Another Asian woman had grabbed at her Niqab and was pulling at it.

'Take it off!' the woman shouted. 'Stop the hypocrisy!'

Aisha's head was tipped back and Adam could see the pale skin of her neck. The fabric was coming away, the grips that held it to her hair pulling at the roots. Aisha cried out again and Noor tried to pull her back away from the barrier.

'Hey,' Adam yelled, turning his chair and driving it hard into the barrier. The footplate clanged against the metal. Another hand had joined the woman in pulling the Niqab free. Adam swung his fist over the barrier down onto the offending limbs.

'Leave her alone,' he yelled.

Before Adam could withdraw and try again there was a great bang behind him and a whumpf of hot air blasted across the top of his head. The onlookers suddenly scattered and the metal barrier fell to the ground. There were screams and people running, Aisha was on her knees, the torn fabric dangling from her fingers. Noor was holding her arm sobbing.

'We have to run Noor,' Aisha said, her eyes wide. She stood up, glanced at Adam and then they were scrambling over the fallen barrier and along the pavement. Adam turned his chair but all he could see was what looked like someone's coat burning on the ground and people running away from it. An empty space was opening up. The hot burning smell rooted Adam to the spot. He stared at the tarmac as if to reassure himself that this wasn't a train, that he wasn't at Clapham Junction. Adam had his hands gripped tight on the wheel rims. Sweat trickled down his neck. He looked up half-expecting to see the face of that paramedic, the one that had encouraged him to be brave, to hold on while his body remained trapped amongst the wreckage. But it wasn't a paramedic he saw. Across the other side of the flames was a man also staring. The one from the mosque. He was wearing his kufi. Adam stared until their eyes met, but the man shifted his gaze quickly and hurried off after the others.

12

Austin - Feast after famine

Two plates waited on the table and a candle glowed from the glass holder. Austin took a sip of Merlot and turned the oven down a notch. The smell of roasting meat would likely cling to the flat for days and Austin wondered if it was worth it. Raindrops slashed down the pane making it difficult to see the orange-washed street below. No one; not yet.

The digital clock on the cooker read 19:55. Not long. He hovered over the beans, wondering whether he should put them in the steamer yet. He straightened a fork on the table and then went over to the stereo, selecting Jack Johnson for that mellow mood. It would conceal the sound of the rain and traffic. He picked up a photo frame of Matt and thrust it in amongst the books on the shelf. The act made him feel guilty but that was silly.

Austin picked up his mobile from the coffee table, there were no messages. He threw it back down and checked his watch again. If his date was going to be much later, the beef would be spoiled. He went back to the oven and took the meat out. It would need to rest anyway.

Austin was surprised when the buzzer vibrated loudly; he'd allowed himself to get sucked into the X factor on the TV. He jumped up, switched it off and checked his watch. 20:30. The beef would be cold, he threw the beans into the steamer on top of the boiling potatoes, then back to the entry phone on the wall. It vibrated again just as he lifted it from its socket. He paused, feeling suddenly nervous.

'Hello?'

There was a deep chuckle in response.

'Who's there?' Austin continued.

'As if you weren't waiting for me,' came back the voice.

Austin could feel his toes twitching, 'I'm coming down.' He plonked the phone back on the wall, and trotted down the flight of stairs to the main entrance. He could see David's shadow through the knobbly glass at the top. Was he doing the right thing? They both knew what this evening would probably lead to. Was Austin ready for that? Opening the door just a crack, Austin peered out. The cold air whooshed in and filled the hallway. David stood grinning in the spitting rain. Austin pulled the door wider and David immediately stepped inside, making Austin stagger back as his visitor's wide shoulders filled the doorway.

'Hang on,' Austin cried. But it was too late, David had him pinned against the wall, his tongue reaching far into Austin's mouth. They'd kissed before, briefly in the club last week but this was different. He tried to fight back, but it was no use, he couldn't resist. Austin's arms wrapped around David's damp jacket feeling the strong muscles in his back. The door clicked shut, but he kept his eyes closed. When they finally broke apart, Austin gathered himself.

'You're late.'

David said nothing, just a glint in his eye and then bounded up the stairs ahead of Austin.

'I made dinner,' he called after.

'I know, I can smell it. Can it wait?' David's voice disappeared into the flat above. Austin checked the door was locked properly and hoped the residents in flat one were out instead of listening to the banging door and David's galumphing feet.

David had already found the wine and was draped across the sofa with a glass full.

'Nice place. Come sit with me.'

'No, I need to rescue dinner.'

'Aw come on, just a quick one, food can wait.'

Austin had spent ages on the internet finding the right recipe, then nipping out of the office at lunch to choose the beef from a nearby butcher's. Now it sat cold and shrivelled on the kitchen counter. He lifted the lid off the saucepan, removed the steamer bowl and then looked horrified at the watery mush below. The potatoes had disintegrated.

'Great.'

'Come here, it doesn't matter.' David's mellow voice called out.

'It does matter, I made a special effort and now it's ruined.' He clanged the pan into the kitchen sink, wondering how much solid potato could be saved. He strained it through the sieve and then slopped some on the two plates. There was no need to mash it. He could sense David's eyes on him, but he refused to turn around. The beef he left under the foil, simply moved it from the counter to the table. He laid the beans carefully in a criss-cross pattern on each plate. There was a snigger from the sofa which he decided to ignore. The peppercorn sauce would only take a minute to warm through in the microwave.

Finally, when everything was ready, Austin stood straight and looked at his dinner guest, but David had lost interest and was busy tapping a message into his phone.

'It's ready,' said Austin as he crossed his arms over his chest.

David looked up and smiled. He came to the table still tapping and only stopped once he'd pressed the send button.

'Hey, this looks nice. Shall I carve?'

Austin shrugged.

David expertly sliced the meat but to Austin's horror there was no succulent pink centre. The slices lay dark and dry on their plates.

David put down the knife and picked up his glass instead. 'Here's to dates that never go as planned. Cheers.'

Austin scowled. 'You were late.'

'You weren't that easy to find.'

David took a mouthful of meat and started to chew.

'I made a special effort,' Austin said starting on his own meal.

David didn't answer and when Austin looked up David was still chewing and trying to smile around the awkward mouthful.

'You can stop pretending, it's cold and chewy, spit it out.'

David got up and went to spit it in the bin. 'Thank God for that, I thought you'd make me eat the whole lot.'

Austin sighed. What a disaster.

'More wine?' David was back at the table sloshing the Merlot into their glasses. 'Here's to the chef.' He swung his glass at Austin and spilt more red wine on the beef.

'It's your fault for being late. It was just perfect at eight.'

David eyed him across the table until Austin had to drop his gaze.

'I'll tell you what's just perfect.' He slid around the table, his arm curling around the back of Austin's neck.

'Wait, the beans are good.' Austin tried to lean away.

'Yes the beans, so green and hard. So wonderfully long.' His mouth pressed into Austin, they tumbled back onto the floor. Arms and legs wrapping their bodies firmly together. Austin was melting, this was what he'd wanted wasn't it? David was strong and real, a presence that had been lacking for so long in Austin's life. Austin pulled him in tighter, as they rolled into the wall. The heat between them rising.

'Ouch.' Austin suddenly winced.

'You love a bit of rough,' David growled, wrestling to pull Austin's top over his shoulders. They wriggled a bit until it came free but then Austin's elbow caught David in the ribs, and his foot got wrapped in the strap from his laptop bag. Once they'd de-tangled themselves, David dragged Austin through the doorway and onto the bed. He yanked at Austin's jeans which wrinkled up and became stuck around his ankles.

'Do you have to wear them so tight?' David said as he pulled off a sock.

'Yes, they look sexy.'

'Maybe, but I need quick access ones.'

Austin laughed and leant forwards to release his heels and the offending denim.

'That's more like it.' David stood at the end of the bed staring down at Austin's naked body.

Austin pulled the edge of the quilt to cover himself and stared back at David's chest where the dark hairs curled around his nipples. He was so different to Matt and for a moment Austin felt scared as David stripped off his own jeans, stepped out of them and dropped his boxers. Austin couldn't help looking.

'My goodness,' Austin said.

David slid onto the bed and pulled the quilt from Austin's grasp. He slid his body along Austin's, their skin sliding together, David nibbled into Austin's neck. It was delicious, Austin could smell David's sweat part-masked by a spicy deodorant. There was no need to be scared. He wanted this, hadn't realised his own hunger. It felt like he'd suffered a long famine, but now it was time to feast.

Later, Austin went back to fetch their glasses and another bottle, he also brought back the beans on a plate.

David laughed. 'And now it's bean time?'

'They're still crunchy.' Austin grinned and bit into a long thin one. David took one, sucked it between his lips and swallowed it whole.

'How did you do that?'

'Practice.'

'You idiot, you could choke on it and die.'

'Yeah, I can just see the headlines: Gay lover killed by giant bean.' David mocked him, 'Detectives found the dead body next to a pile of green vegetables, still crunchy.'

'Stop it.' Austin gave him a playful thump.

David smacked him back.

'Alright, alright, don't eat them. I like them.'

'Of course you do, you look like one.'

'Thanks; I'm not that thin.'

'Hey, I like them stringy.' He nibbled Austin's neck and reached past him to grab his mobile. 'I need to get a pizza, vegetables just don't do it for me. Do you want any?'

'I don't know, what are you getting?' Austin pushed him off and went into the bathroom.

'Something spicy.'

'Not too hot, or I won't have any.'

'Hmmm.' David turned away and spoke into his mobile. Austin went to the loo and while he washed his hands, he stared at his face in the bathroom mirror. He had dark rings under his eyes and his cheekbones seemed a little higher than normal. He dropped his gaze down to his flat stomach and breathed in. You could only see a few ribs when he did that, he wasn't that thin was he? He turned sideways and then further around looking over his shoulder to see his reflection. Turning back, he ruffled his hair, trickled some water on his finger and drew it across each eyebrow. That was odd, he didn't remember sex with Matt ever making a mess of his eyebrows. And then he stopped, staring into the green eyes that were looking straight back at him. He blinked several times, decided to run some cold water and splash it on his face. He was OK, he didn't need to feel guilty or upset.

I'm moving on, he affirmed in the mirror.

Around the bathroom were his familiar things. The glass shelf gleaming clean with three bottles standing neatly together. The signs of Matt had long since been wiped away but Austin wasn't sure he was ready.

'What you looking so glum about gorgeous?' David gripped Austin's shoulders and kissed him on the ear. 'Move aside, I need a piss.'

Austin turned away and went back into the bedroom. 'What pizza did you order?'

'Meat feast with extra hot beef.'

'You're such a carnivore.' He eyed the vegetables on the bedside table and ate one. It was cold and despite the crunch seriously lacking in flavour. While David was still in the bathroom, he took the beans back to the kitchen and dumped them in the bin. Matt had always been a much better cook than he was. Austin searched the cupboards, found a packet of Doritos and took them back to bed. David bit into a large triangle and little bits sprayed everywhere.

'Maybe crisps was a bad idea.' Austin picked up a crumb from the duvet.

'No, they're great.' He grabbed two more and shoved them in his mouth. David had already switched on the TV and stared at the screen on Austin's chest of drawers. Matt would have carefully selected a romantic DVD, but not David. He was surfing the channels instead and stopped at a football game.

'Hey, that reminds me.' He leant over the side of the bed and picked up something from the floor. It was a picture of Matt in a football scarf. 'Who's this guy?'

Austin thought he'd hidden them all away. He bit down on his lip and snatched the photograph. 'Don't go rooting through my things.'

'I didn't. Just wanted to know what I was dealing with.' David's eyes flitted away and Austin could see him clench his jaw. Neither of them had discussed other partners, or any kind of expectations on this new relationship. Austin wasn't sure what to say, he didn't want to get emotional, didn't want to try and explain. Not now, not after the great sex they'd had.

'He's not around any more.'

'I see. Serious was it? How long?'

'Three years.' Austin felt himself hiccup.

'Lived here together?' David let his eyes rove around the

95

bedroom.

Austin nodded, not daring to say anything else in case the tears started.

'That figures.' David sighed and swung his legs off the bed. 'So do you want me to go?'

'No, no. I said. He's over. I mean, I'm over him.' It felt like a lie as Austin wrapped his arms around himself. Then he whispered, 'He's dead.'

'What?' David stood up, his eyes searching for his clothes.

'It wasn't AIDS or anything.'

'I never said it was.' David pulled on his boxers.

Austin wanted him to stay, wanted that fabulous feeling back when he'd surrendered his body to this man.

David had found his trousers now and was pulling them on.

'Stay. Please stay.'

'To fill a dead man's shoes?'

Austin felt the hurt sting his eyes. Then he said all in a rush, 'Matt died in a train crash two and a half years ago.'

There was silence.

Austin found he was scrunching up the quilt in his fists. He looked up at David who had stopped buckling his belt and was staring back at him.

Austin waited, then David sighed leaning back against the wall and ran a hand through his hair.

'Is this rented?' David said. 'Must be expensive.'

Austin nodded wondering what difference that made. But David was right, it was too expensive really, had been bleeding him dry since Matt had gone.

'Perhaps you should move.' said David. He sat down again on the edge of the bed, those blue eyes making Austin feel vulnerable. 'A new start.'

13

Adam – Moving out

'So I have some good news to share.' Adam's father beamed at the family then rubbed at the flattened cartilage on his ear. Adam bowed his head sighing. It would probably be something terribly dull like a big order at work or maybe some fifth cousin twice removed was getting married. Adam ate a forkful of rice.

'I have been talking to Mustafa Khan and he has agreed for Adam to come in and work at his factory.'

Adam looked up at his father and gasped. He was standing at the head of the table, his shoulders pushed back, his gaze steady. Rafiq Rasheed, head of the family. Adam tried to swallow but the rice had got stuck and he started coughing like mad to get it out of his windpipe. Sully smacked him on the back.

'That's great father, I'm sure Adam will quickly master how to use a sewing machine.'

Adam gulped some water from his glass.

'No, no, the sewing is done by the women, they are highly skilled. Adam will start with the folding and packing. Mustafa says he can get a higher table that should work out fine for Adam's wheelchair. And you will have plenty of time in the evenings to study for more qualifications.'

Adam stared at the half-eaten food on his plate.

There was silence around the table, even the scrape of cutlery had stopped. They were waiting for him. Adam stared at a piece of wilted spinach next to a chunk of lamb. The meal could have done with a touch more cumin and been a bit lighter on the onion.

Sully poked Adam in his side and said, 'Well father, I think that's great. You are always thinking of your family.'

'Very good dear,' his mother spoke softly.

Adam pushed the prongs of his fork deep into the meat, piercing the flesh and then put it in his mouth and chewed.

Nobody spoke.

What had seemed light and jovial when his father began had turned heavy and threatening. Sully pinched him this time, but Adam refused to react and succeeded in keeping still, despite the pain.

His father spoke again only this time his voice was low and breathy.

'You have nothing to say?'

His father's anger rippled the air between them.

Adam swallowed the lamb and put down his fork. He looked up at his father, could see his face set hard, his shoulders quivering. Adam clenched the rim of his right wheel. There was nowhere to go, nowhere to hide. He had to face this. Adam took a deep breath.

'What do you want me to say?'

'Why you insolent -' his father roared. A spoonful of rice came flying past Adam's head.

'I didn't ask you to interfere in my life.'

'You ungrateful little bastard.' A fork came sailing and Adam raised his arm deflecting the cutlery so it bounced off and crashed into a water glass.

'Dad.' Sully put his hand on his father's sleeve in an attempt to stop the flying objects.

'Rafiq, please.' His mother was on the edge of tears, her scarf scrunched up by her mouth.

His father stood up and glared at Adam. Sully stood too, his hand now sliding up to the top of his father's shoulder.

Adam said, 'I'm not going to work in a stupid bloody factory for Uncle Mustafa.'

Rafiq's face darkened as he leaned forwards. 'You are not going to waste your life under my roof. I've done everything for you. Why you-'

His arm came up, no weapon, just a fist which he waved at Adam.

'Dad, this won't help.' Sully squeezed his father's shoulder but he shrugged him off and stormed to the door.

'You don't care about anyone but yourself!' his father yelled.

Adam felt his upper back pressing into his chair. For a moment, everything was still, Dad looked uncertain, about to leave or ready to pounce on Adam. Sully was still standing ready to intervene if necessary. Adam gripped the wheel rims. Dad took a small step forwards but Sully was there, blocking his path. His brother and father glared at each other, two men in a stand off and then his father walked out. Part of Adam wanted his father to hit him, wanted that fight. To raise his fists and struggle physically with him.

He shouted after them, 'All you care about is the family name and what all our relatives think about you and your sons. You don't care about me, you don't ask *me* what I want or how I feel.' Adam wheeled his chair through the doorway, following his brother and father.

'You and your stupid sport – look where it's got you? Nowhere!' His father was shouting from the kitchen now, his frustration unable to vent itself in physical action, resorting instead to yelling. 'And now you've got yourself mixed up with some crazy fundamentalists. I don't want no son of mine turning into a terrorist.'

Adam wheeled his chair into the kitchen.

'I told you, that wasn't us, that was an ISIS infiltrator. The UMIA isn't a cult. You don't understand.'

Sully was still positioned between them, he spun his head around to Adam.

'You've said enough. Can't you just leave it?'

Adam could see sweat beading on Sully's forehead. His father had folded himself into a seat at the kitchen table, cradling his forehead in his hands. Adam swivelled around and pushed his chair down the hall and opened the front door.

'It was your sport that got you in that chair.' His father's voice carried down the hallway chasing Adam out of the front door. He zoomed down the ramp and onto the pavement, taking the corner tight. He didn't care when his wheel scraped the bumper of his father's parked car as he turned on the pavement. Tears blurred his vision as he raced along.

He'd thought his father had forgiven the fact that he'd been heading home from a football match when the train crashed. But it was clear he hadn't, and not only that, he blamed Adam for it. As if it was his own fault the train had crashed and ruined his legs. Bastard, Adam hated him.

A wheelie bin on the pavement was blocking his way so he crashed into it, knocking it over onto a car which set the alarm singing. Serves them right. He shoved against the bottom of the bin as it lay felled upon the pavement. It swivelled sideways and Adam continued on, the wheels running unimpeded towards the main road.

It had started to rain, Adam hunched his shoulders. He hadn't stopped for a coat, nor for his phone which he'd left charging in the kitchen. He couldn't even call anyone. Part of him wanted to go to Vijay's place but then he thought about the last time he'd turned up uninvited and that woman with the deep voice, Karen. Besides Vijay didn't get the whole UMIA thing either. And he'd probably tell Adam that working at Uncle Mustafa's was better than nothing. No, not Vijay.

He thought about his old friend Johnny, about how close they'd been. But then life had moved on, it wasn't like they were best mates any more, in fact Adam couldn't remember the last time they'd spent any time together.

A man walked past holding an umbrella and stared at him. Adam got moving, he couldn't stay here in the middle of the park in the pouring rain. After a few minutes he realised he was heading towards the mosque on autopilot, splashing through the puddles. He slowed down as he turned the corner into Barking Road. It was the one place that always felt welcoming. He was shivering now, the fabric of his sweatshirt sticking to his shoulders. Ahead, a group of people moved together and disappeared past the traffic lights. Beyond he could see the mosque entrance. Adam continued ahead drawing level with the building. The front door was open and he could hear voices inside. It was the only place he felt comfortable these days and it would be dry at least.

He pushed open the door with his footplate and went in. The

first thing he noted were the shoe racks, there were about twenty or so pairs of assorted footwear neatly lined up. Adam checked his watch, it must be Isha prayer time. He pushed himself towards the prayer room and sure enough there was a line of men ready to start. Rushing quickly to the wash room, Adam hurried through the sequence and then headed back to the large room where he could hear the Imam reciting the prayers. The soft carpet was difficult to roll on but kept his late entrance silent as he pushed himself to the end of the line. Closing his eyes, Adam gave silent thanks for being there, safe, dry and away from the conflict at home. This mosque truly was a haven of peace. Opening his eyes again, he joined in with the other men, leaning forwards, bowing his head and listening carefully to the Imam's voice as it swelled and retreated like warm waves on the shore of his soul.

The men began to drift out of the room. Adam stayed still pretending to pray. It was warm and quiet in here and he wasn't ready yet to leave. He heard a giggle and a woman's voice somewhere behind him and turned looking up at the screened gallery where the women prayed. Was Aisha up there? Had she seen him with those gorgeous eyes peering through the latticework? Adam looked back down at the carpet, he wasn't worthy of Aisha. He was nothing but a damp failed disabled teenager. What could she ever see in him?

Adam turned back to the window staring through at the dark wet paving slabs dreading having to go home now that prayers were finished.

'Hey brother, how's it going?' It was Faizal beaming as usual.

'Faizal.' Adam felt a soaring relief at seeing his friend.

'Are you praying five times?' His eyes were alight.

Adam lowered his gaze, no he hadn't quite managed it yet. He was still struggling with the early morning prayers. Five times a day seemed such a lot.

'Well, I was kind of passing.'

'Oh.' The light in Faizal's eyes dimmed ever so slightly.

'But I'm trying.'

'Great, it's one of the Five Pillars.'

'I know.'

'How come you're so wet?'

Adam glanced at his shoulder and realised his sweatshirt was soaked through. 'Forgot my coat.'

Faizal nodded with a frown.

'You heading home?'

Adam looked at his friend. 'I guess.'

Faizal seemed to be studying him which made Adam distinctly embarrassed so he set off towards the exit.

'Wanna come for dinner?'

'At yours?' Adam spun his chair around. He thought about the half-finished food he'd left on his plate at home.

'Sure, why not?'

They reached the hallway and Faizal went to find his shoes. The pleasure at seeing his friend and his open invitation soon vanished as the reality of Adam's life hit home.

'So are you coming?' Faizal stood holding the door open.

'I can't,' Adam pushed himself slowly through into the dark cold evening. At least the rain was only spitting now.

'How come? I'm sure Dad won't mind.'

Adam looked down at his lap. 'I probably wouldn't even fit through the door.' He sighed remembering being stuck outside Auntie Sana's house with its narrow doorway. Life in a wheelchair was a curse.

'Maybe not the front door but you would round the back.' Faizal was grinning again and motioned with his hand for Adam to follow.

'How come?' Adam was intrigued, any delay to going home was certainly welcome.

They were at the kitchen table each with a bowl of Cheerios. Faizal and his father had filled their bowls and passed the milk to Adam. It seemed an odd kind of dinner for a Tuesday evening. At least he wasn't particularly hungry, he'd managed half his dinner before the row earlier. Not wanting to appear impolite, Adam thanked them and poured some milk onto his own. The cereal crackled a little, the only sound in the kitchen.

'You can have seconds,' Faizal grinned through a mouthful.

His father scowled and said something in Punjabi.

'He's worried we'll have no milk left for breakfast.'

Feeling awkward, Adam said, 'I can go and get you some more.'

'No, it's fine.'

Faizal's father said something else, his tone angry.

'I'll get it after morning prayers.' Faizal responded.

They continued to eat in silence. Adam crunched on the cereal thinking about the half-eaten curry he'd left on his plate at home. At least he wasn't being attacked here. They finished the meal in silence, both Faizal and his father had a second bowlful, Adam politely refused professing to be full. Once the older man had left the room, Adam breathed a sigh of relief.

'Don't mind him, he's always grumpy when Mum's away.'

'Where's she gone?'

'Pakistan to stay with my Nan. My sister's gone too.'

Adam glanced behind him at the wide-entrance that led into the extension part.

'Your disabled Nan?'

'Yeah.' Faizal was washing up the bowls in the sink. 'You want some tea?'

'But I thought you said the extension had been built for her?'

'Yeah it was, two years ago. It's a sore point with Dad. They're always trying to persuade her to come and live here. Who knows, maybe she'll come back with them this time.'

'So she's never been here?' Adam twisted his chair around and headed back through into the extension, pausing at the open bedroom door. There was a single bed with a pink frilly duvet set, and a small chest of drawers. The next door opened into a blue bathroom with an open shower and a large handle on the wall next to the toilet. Beyond that was the back door through which they'd arrived over a low ramp. Faizal had followed him and stood leaning against the door jamb.

'Crazy huh? I tried to persuade Mum and Dad to let me have it, I mean it's just sitting here.' He shrugged.

'Faizal,' Adam thought about where to begin. He licked his lips. 'The thing is…'

14

Ralph – Disaster after effects

It was a bright day, for a change, as Ralph manoeuvred into a smart-looking neighbourhood. The house they were looking for, number thirty-nine, was a semi-detached, respectable with a BMW in the drive. Ralph stopped the ambulance and Emma leapt out first, grabbing equipment from the back. Ralph hurried to the front door which was shut and locked. He rang the doorbell but there didn't appear to be anyone home. Emma came to stand beside him and raised her eyebrows. Ralph shrugged, but then the door opened and a pale-faced man stood looking mildly surprised.

'You called 999?'

'Erm, yes, of course,' he moved back to let them enter but didn't appear to be in any kind of hurry or panic.

'Where is she?' Emma asked.

The man pointed upstairs.

Ralph ran ahead and Emma followed. The bathroom was empty, next was a child's bedroom with a poster of Rihanna on the wall. In the main bedroom lay a woman who appeared to be fast asleep. Ralph checked her responses, nothing. Her pulse was weak and rapid. Emma picked up the bottle on the bedside table.

'Diazepam,' she said.

Ralph held his cheek to the woman's blue lips, his hand still measuring her pulse. There was the faintest breath against his skin.

'Let's clear the airway and set the defibrillator to manual, I've got a pulse but we need to monitor it closely.' Together they moved the woman off the bed onto the floor, Ralph's elbow caught something on the bedside table and knocked it off. 'Can we put her at the end, there's more room.'

'Sure.' Emma had the woman's legs and manoeuvred around the space so they could lay her down between the bed and the chest of drawers. Emma already had the oxygen prepared and Ralph tipped the woman's head back so he could insert the OP into her mouth to keep her airway open. He connected the oxygen. Emma put a clip onto the woman's finger and now the machine was showing them the rapid heartbeat. Ralph looked up to see Mr Paleface looking even whiter, his eyes large dark circles against his pasty skin.

'Can you tell us what happened?' Ralph asked.

'I...' the man paused, staring as Ralph positioned the airbag correctly. 'She...'

'When did you find her?'

'I… I just got back.'

'What's her name?'

'Linda.'

Just then the machine beeped loudly, the woman's heartbeat was going mental.

'Right.' Ralph took a breath and turned to Mr Paleface, 'It might be better if you sit down or wait downstairs for the other paramedics.' The husband looked like he might become a casualty himself if he turned any whiter.

'Emma, Diazapam overdose, have you covered this yet?'

'Err yes, I think so.'

'What's likely to happen next?' Ralph hadn't taken his eye from the monitor watching the crazy heartbeat. He'd seen this before.

'Cardiac arrest?'

'Most likely yes. Get on the radio and find out where the others are.'

'Gotcha.' Emma took out her handset.

Ralph could see the husband was still hovering in the doorway. It was likely that things were about to get a whole lot worse. 'Sir, your wife is very poorly but we know exactly what to do, it would be helpful if you could go downstairs and look out for the other paramedics. We're going to need some space here.' Finally the pale man nodded and turned away.

The woman's heartbeat had slowed down a bit and was

looking less erratic. Maybe they'd get lucky. Ralph glanced away from the monitor to the picture frame he'd accidentally knocked off the bedside table. It lay face down on the carpet. He flipped it over. It was a photograph of a teenager smiling with a skateboard under his arm. That must have been his bedroom by the bathroom. Something about the eyes made Ralph lean in closer.

Just then the casualty flatlined. 'Oh shit.'

'The other team's only a couple of minutes away.'

'Just as well.'

Ralph changed position and immediately started chest compressions, pushing forcefully down between the woman's breasts. As he pumped, he found himself staring at the photograph. Ralph paused for a few seconds to let Emma do the airbag before his next set, he leaned across the woman's body and peered at the photo more closely. Ralph could feel beads of sweat on his forehead, suddenly his hands were clammy and he was holding his breath. He looked back at the unconscious woman on the floor and pumped more vigorously. Thirty compressions, two breaths. Thirty compressions, two breaths. The beeper on the machinery kept time but Ralph was going too fast. A noise in the doorway brought his attention to the new paramedics. Ralph nodded at his colleagues.

'So what have we got?' the senior paramedic said.

It seemed like forever as they tried to save Linda's life. Ralph was sweating profusely.

'Are you OK?' Emma was looking at him quizzically.

'Yeah, fine.' He swallowed but there seemed to be something stuck in his throat. He coughed but that didn't make it any better.

The senior paramedic sighed and sat back on his haunches. 'We've been here forty-five minutes now folks. I'm going to call it, is everyone agreed?'

Ralph wanted to say no. Almost blurted it out. They had to save this woman but he was a professional too. Forty-five minutes was a long time. They weren't going to get her back.

'Ralph?'

'A few more minutes?' But Ralph could see from their faces; even Emma disagreed. 'Damn.' He took his hands off the airbag and checked his watch. 'Life extinct at two fifteen.'

Routine took over then, paperwork needed to be filled in, equipment packed up, transport organised for the body and the police would be required to officially investigate the cause of death even though it was clear to Ralph.

Once outside again, the biting wind cooled the damp fabric under Ralph's arms. He shivered suddenly as he packed their equipment into the ambulance. The husband was still standing in the doorway, oblivious to the cold and everything else, as if not comprehending what had happened. Ralph could see the police car arriving and turned back towards Mr Paleface.

Emma was there kindly leading him back inside. Ralph returned upstairs to check they hadn't left anything. They had laid a sheet over the body and Ralph smoothed his hands across it, straightening out the cool clean cotton. He picked up the photograph from the bedside table, pulled out the little flap and set it upright. Those eyes, so crystal clear, so blue. The woman's son no doubt. His hands were beginning to shake. Emma came in and bustled around before pausing.

'OK, I think we've got everything, the police just want a quick word and then we're good to go,' she said, and squeezed his shoulder. 'I've never seen you like this.' She paused. 'Did you know her?'

'No,' Ralph said quietly, truthfully, he didn't. But he'd met her son. And wished he'd never had.

'Come on, you need some fresh air.' She pulled him out of the room.

*

'Dad, there you are.' Liam appeared in the hallway as soon as Ralph opened the door. His son was wearing his soccer outfit and his bag was ready by the hall table.

'Sorry mate, where's Cameron?'

'He's at the Crinklies.'

'I wish you wouldn't call them that, you'll have wrinkles when you're old.' Ralph dropped his keys on the table and went towards the kitchen.

'Where are you going? We're late.' Liam shouted.

'I just need something; you go on and get in the car.' Ralph stood in the kitchen wondering what it was he wanted. Actually a quick shot of whisky was probably what was required, something to calm his nerves. He was feeling better than he had earlier that afternoon, but far from relaxed. Liam had followed him in.

'Come on!'

Ralph knew he couldn't drink whisky, not with a thirteen-year-old teenager at his back, not at five to five on a Wednesday afternoon.

'Right.' He turned, took a breath and followed Liam back out to the car.

While Liam ran over a muddy pitch, Ralph sat cramped with the other parents in the tiny viewing shed. There were two benches and little else, with just enough roof to stop the next shower from dowsing them. He'd only thrown on a sweatshirt but was now regretting that he hadn't worn a coat. Liam had the ball and was running across the pitch; Ralph stared trying to absorb himself in the game, but it didn't work.

The memory kept surfacing; the boy lying by the track looking at Ralph. Those blue eyes set in a pallid face imploring him, questioning. So much time seemed to pass as he stood there, it was impossible to say how long. Ralph frozen to the spot watching a child's life ebb away. Dark red stains spreading from stone to stone. It was like watching one of those documentaries that speeds up the growth of a plant; the blood appearing like lichen spreading across the ground. And still he didn't move, standing as if this wasn't really happening, as if he was watching this death unfold on a TV screen. The child had dark hair, part of it lay against the cold metal track, a large chunk blown into a quiff against the gravel. But his eyes remained on Ralph, a cool blue, waiting, watching, dying. Why couldn't he move that day? What was it about the boy, about the crash, about himself that made him lose his way? It was inexcusable, a life lost, sliding away from him when he could so easily have reached out.

Done his job.

Properly.

'Hey Ralph, how are you?'

Ralph re-adjusted his focus onto the football field. He coughed self-consciously and wiped his sleeve across his face.

'Hi,' he glanced quickly at Natalie and then away again. She had slid along the end of the bench to sit next to him.

'So how's Liam doing, he's certainly got the moves today.' She nodded at the pitch.

'Er yes, good, yeah. He's been practising.' He blinked several times, hoping that Natalie wouldn't notice his distress.

'Troy's been asking me when Liam can come for a sleep-over. I don't know if this weekend would suit?'

Ralph braved another glance at her long narrow face. She was wearing a bright red waterproof and a fetching beret. Her face neatly made-up as usual with strong red lipstick that glistened.

'Sure, I think that would be fine.'

'Do you want to check with Shelly first? Say Saturday afternoon, and we can bring him back on Sunday.'

'Yep, sounds good, I'll get Shelly to give you a ring.' He leaned forward pretending to be fascinated by the muddy romp taking place before him.

Back at the car, Liam threw his kit in the boot and climbed in the front next to Ralph. They drove home along the wet streets. The radio warned about possible flooding in some areas and Ralph turned up the heating.

Through the windscreen Ralph noticed the lit shop-front of the off-licence as they drove past and wondered whether to stop. He could pick up some beers, something to quietly sip tonight. But then he thought better of it and kept driving; there was bound to be something in the house other than the whisky.

'Dad.'

'Uh-huh.'

'Jesus.' Liam turned away and stared out the window.

'What?' Suddenly Ralph realised that Liam had been uncharacteristically quiet since the game. Normally he wanted to analyse the moves, moan about the other team's tactics. He was refusing to look at Ralph.

'What's up?'

'Nothing.'

'Well what did you want to say?'

'It doesn't matter.'

Ralph negotiated the lights and pulled into their road. He cruised down the packed street looking for a space and then squeezed the car in behind a small white van.

Liam got out and slammed the door, not bothering with a thanks.

In the house Shelly was in the kitchen, warm smells and steam permeated the hall. He could hear Liam chattering to his mother.

'And then Troy passes me this great curve ball, and I got it right here, and Shen was almost on me, and I did this mega kick. Wow! Straight in. Dead clear shot, and right past Yaz.'

'Really? Even past Yaz, well that must have been a good one.'

'Yeah. Fucking A.'

'Liam don't swear. Are you going to get a shower? Dinner'll be ready soon.' Shelly was standing at the stove as Ralph watched from the doorway. So that was why Liam was cross with him, he hadn't even noticed him score the goal.

'Great kick mate.'

Liam gave him a scornful look and walked out. Ralph watched him head upstairs wondering what he could say to make amends.

'Hey,' he called after his son, 'I spoke to Troy's mum, you want to go for a sleep-over?'

'Maybe,' and Liam was gone into his bedroom.

'What's up with you two?' Shelly asked, stirring a pan of cheese sauce.

'I got distracted by Natalie.'

'Oh?'

Ralph smiled, and put his arms around her waist, kissing the side of her warm salty neck. 'Not like that. Will you call her about the sleep over?'

'Sure.'

Now that he was home with Shelly, Ralph felt better, but decided a beer with dinner wouldn't go amiss. He searched the fridge, then the cupboard under the stairs and found a Stella.

Cameron was back from his grandparents and the four of them sat down to eat. There wasn't much talk: the boys were starving and Ralph found his mind wandering again, this time to the colour of the quilt underneath the lifeless mother from that afternoon. It had been white with small sequin swirls in brown and purple.

'Aren't you going to the PTA meeting tonight?' Shelly was nodding at the bottle of beer that Ralph had just taken a swig from.

'Oh damn. I forgot.'

Shelly frowned.

'Well I didn't forget, I remembered earlier, but just well.' He looked at his drink, thought about the empty water glass at the side of the dead woman's bed. The PTA meeting would give him something different to think about. Ralph picked up the bottle and downed the luke-warm beer in one go.

'Ralph!'

'It's fine. I've just eaten, I'd better get going. Thanks for the dinner love.' He pecked her on the cheek and headed out hearing the boys arguing about which programme they were going to watch on the TV. As he picked up his keys, Ralph paused; what about the gym on the way back from the PTA meeting? It would be a good way to wind down. He ran upstairs to grab some clothes and a towel. Shelly was standing in the hall by the front door looking expectant.

'I'll go to the gym on the way back.'

She nodded without saying anything and held out a piece of paper. It was the poster he'd designed a couple of days ago for the school disco.

'Oh yeah, thanks. See you later.' They kissed and she closed the door behind him.

15

Adam - Committing to a greater purpose

Faizal studied the bus timetable, his hands shoved deep in his pockets.

'Should be only another few minutes.'

Adam nodded, twisting his chair to the side, attempting to allow others to get past on the narrow pavement.

'What did you say that dish was tonight?' Faizal asked.

'It was just a chicken curry, nothing special.'

'Not like one I've ever tasted, I like them spicy.'

'Yeah, I overdid the chillies a bit, it wasn't my best, could have done with more ginger.' Adam used his tongue to remove a small piece of chicken wedged in his back teeth.

'How do you know how to do all that stuff?'

Just then a lady with a long coat and a phone pinned to her ear joined them at the bus stop.

'My mum. I was at home a long time after the accident. There wasn't much else going on.' At the mention of his mother, Adam felt a pang of homesickness. He'd seen her a couple of times in the last few weeks, mostly just to get clothes and stuff. She cried and told him he should come home. He missed her gentle voice, missed the clean clothes put neatly away in his drawers. He even missed the way she would put her hand lightly on his head sometimes as if in some silent blessing.

'Has Dad paid you for the food?' Faizal said.

'Yeah, he gave me forty quid this morning. He's all right your dad.'

'You must be joking, he's a pain, but he seems to like you though. Do you know what he said to me?' Faizal leaned a bit closer. 'Reckons your cooking is better than Mum's.'

'Really?' Adam sat a little taller in his chair.

'Yeah, but don't tell him I told you.'

Adam couldn't help feeling pleased with himself. He'd worked hard to repay their kindness by cooking their evening meals. This new arrangement was working out just perfectly. He'd basically moved in with Faizal and his dad and Adam was revelling in the new freedom and independence it had given him. Of course it was only temporary until Faizal's mum and sister got back, possibly with their disabled Nan, but until then, Adam was free to do as he pleased, without hassle from anyone.

'Did you get a chance to look at those videos I showed you?'

'Yeah, it was horrific. I can't believe what's going on out there. I mean why would they torture Muslims?'

'Infidels.'

They both glanced briefly at the woman with the phone but she was immersed in a conversation about some meeting or other.

'Who's the speaker tonight, do you know?'

Faizal shook his head. He lowered his voice. 'They've started to be more careful, they only shared the venue via text message.'

'Yeah I got that too.'

Faizal continued in a hushed voice, 'Should be a good one. Tariq said someone was coming over from Syria to tell us the real story out there.'

'Wow, that will be cool.'

'Yeah exactly. We'll hear the truth instead of that crap they put in the media. They don't know anything about the new Caliphate and what ISIS is doing.'

They stopped speaking as the number 325 came hissing to a stop, the doors folded back and the bus lurched downwards slightly towards the pavement. Adam's wheelchair passed easily over the small gap and they were soon settled inside.

They were outside a large Georgian town house. White-washed with huge sash windows.

'This is it.'

'Looks posh.'

Faizal nodded.

'Who does it belong to?'

Faizal shrugged and pressed the doorbell. A long and

expensive chime played, echoing inside. The door was opened by a smartly dressed Arab in traditional robes. He neither smiled nor introduced himself.

'As-Salam-u-Alaikum,' Adam and Faizal said in unison.

'wa Alaikum Assalam.' He had an accent but Adam didn't know where from. 'Top of the stairs and turn right,' he added.

'Thanks.' Faizal wiped his shoes on the mat.

The Arab stared down at the ground. There were two steps up to the front door. Adam looked at them too, with a sigh and then beyond. He wasn't sure how he was supposed to get up the flight of stairs inside. Faizal was already half way up when the Arab coughed loudly.

'Your friend,' he said, pointing out the door at Adam.

'Oh. Sorry.' Faizal came galloping back down the stairs.

'I thought you could do small steps,' he hissed at Adam as he turned the chair around so he could tip it back.

'Only single ones.'

Inside the hallway Adam and Faizal stared up at the wide staircase with its elegant balustrade and cream carpet. 'I can't get you up there.'

Adam agreed. He could get out of the wheelchair and haul his own body up those stairs, sitting with his back to the stair and using his arms to push upwards one step at a time, his legs dragging behind. But it would take a while. Besides he wasn't sure what the Arab would make of it, to see a cripple sprawled across the carpet making slow progress up those grand stairs. It was demeaning. Adam noticed the chandelier hanging above his head.

'Have you got a lift?' Faizal asked.

The Arab was studying them both. Without a word he shook his head and disappeared down the hallway, opened a door and closed it behind him.

'Maybe you should go without me, I can get home alone.'

'Perhaps I can carry you.'

'Faizal, you're not exactly made of muscle.'

'Oh yeah?' Faizal grinned and threw back his shoulders. 'We'll see about that.'

First of all he arched backwards stretching out his back then he came close to Adam, his face contorted trying to work out the best method. Awkwardly he shoved an arm under Adam's thighs and then another around the top of his back.

'I don't think this will work, Faizal.'

At least the Arab wasn't there to watch. Adam resigned himself and wrapped his arms around Faizal's neck. With a loud grunt, Faizal heaved and to Adam's surprise, he felt the chair drop away beneath him. For a moment they swayed together and then Faizal staggered towards the bottom step.

'You weigh a ton.'

They mounted the first step, Faizal's muscles shuddering under the strain. The stairs reached upwards, it was a long way to go.

Faizal grunted again and made it two more steps. There was more swaying and Adam pulled forwards on Faizal's neck to stop him tipping backwards. The weight shift caused Faizal to stagger up another stair.

'Don't pull me over.' Faizal panted.

'You were going to fall backwards.'

'I'm fine.'

Faizal blew out through his mouth loudly straight down Adam's T-shirt. Adam shut his eyes. He hated this. Then suddenly they were pitching forwards and Adam released his hands to break their fall on the stairs. The cream carpet came rushing up to meet them and Adam's shoulder hit the stair. Faizal's face pressed into Adam's cheek while he struggled to find his feet.

'Idiot,' Adam said.

'Fat arse.' Faizal got back onto his feet.

The smell of wool from the rich carpet was strong in Adam's nose. He adjusted himself on the stair and looked down past Faizal's legs. At the bottom of the stairs stood three men. The Arab with arms folded watching. On his left was an enormous man with even darker skin. A huge beard trailed down to meet the V of his robes. He stood at least a foot taller than the others, must be almost seven feet. He was standing with his hands at his sides grinning. On the other side was a shorter man with white hair.

115

'OK, let's try again,' Faizal said, bending down; he hadn't seen the men at the bottom of the stairs. 'What?' He turned to see what Adam was staring at.

The Arab said something to the giant which Adam couldn't understand. Faizal immediately got out of the way and hurried up the stairs leaving Adam alone and prostrate. The giant came towards him two steps at a time and bore down on him. He plucked Adam off the carpet and carried him like a babe to the top. Below him the elderly man was whispering to the Arab who stared back at Adam, his dark eyes like two black pins. Why did they seem so interested in him?

Faizal stood with his back pressed against the wall, his eyes wide. The giant nodded at a door and Faizal dutifully opened it. Inside seemed suddenly full of people compared to the spacious hallway and stairs behind them. There must have been about fifteen men already seated in short rows of plastic folding chairs. Down the middle of the room were three moveable screens. Adam could only see the front row where the women sat. Perhaps Aisha was further back, he hoped so, he didn't want her to see him like this, a pathetic invalid in the arms of this giant. Around them, the walls were lined with cream and gold wallpaper. Large lamps on ornate side tables had been pushed back against the walls.

Adam nodded at a couple of faces he recognised from previous meetings. Somebody got up and gave a folded chair to Faizal who fiddled around trying to open it. There was nothing Adam could do to help, lying in the giant's arms. He waited, surveying the audience again and spotted the young man, who always wore his kufi, at the back. The one who'd been suspiciously close to the petrol bomb that day at the march. Adam stared at him but as soon as he caught his eye the man looked away.

With great delicacy, the giant lowered Adam onto the empty chair that Faizal had placed in the front row.

'Thank you.' Adam burned with embarrassment and busied himself adjusting his legs to make them stay in line, but it wasn't easy. This chair had little support and if he wasn't careful, his knees would flop to the side.

'Did you see that massive guy?' Faizal had grabbed another chair and set it up next to Adam.

'Hard not to when your face is buried in his beard.'

'I think you've broken my back.'

Adam's knees flopped and he pulled them back to an upright position. 'Faizal, I need my chair.'

'It'll be all right.'

At the front of the room, two men had set a table with a large screen behind it. Heavy gold drapes hung across the windows beyond. They were almost ready to start.

'Can I lean them against you?'

'Get off.'

Adam was uncomfortable; he had to set his legs with his feet a little apart so his knees would lean in against each other. It seemed the best way to stop them from sliding sideways.

The meeting started with the usual greetings. The speaker was the older man who'd been at the bottom of the stairs. He had a white beard and spoke in a thickly accented English. Sometimes he resorted to phrases in Arabic at which point Adam would look at Faizal hoping for a translation but he was too engrossed, nodding and agreeing with the speaker. The whole room felt like it was leaning forwards, especially when the old man's voice went quieter, it made the intensity within the room even stronger and Adam found himself gripped by the man's words. It was all so true, so right. He talked about each person's communion with Allah, of how regular prayers were a means to keep that openness between Allah and yourself maintained so that Allah could show you the way, so that you would know Allah's blessing. Adam shut his eyes for a moment, relaxing, feeling how good it was to be here, to be where he should be and to be doing what was right. The prayers and his growing faith were filling his life with purpose and meaning. These members of the UMIA surrounding him were his brothers and sisters, always so kind and understanding. Adam would stay true to Islam and in return, Allah would show him his path in this life.

'Adam, what are you...ow!'

Adam opened his eyes to find himself falling to the floor and pulling Faizal's arm with him. The plastic chair clattered down and Adam let go of Faizal's sleeve.

'We're so sorry, he doesn't have any legs, I mean, he can't help it.' Faizal explained to the room.

Then he whispered at Adam, 'How do I get you up?'

He was kneeling down trying to help Adam sit upright. The room was deathly silent. Adam wanted to disappear into the carpet. He knew he should have demanded that they bring his wheelchair upstairs. Did he lose concentration? Adam wasn't sure exactly what he'd done, probably one of his legs had slid out sideways pulling him off balance. Fortunately he was on the end of the row, so he hadn't collapsed onto anyone else, only stretched Faizal's sleeve.

The old man at the front had stopped talking and was watching the two of them. Nobody else spoke. The man behind put the plastic chair upright and with Faizal's help, they heaved Adam back onto the seat.

'OK, I'm fine, thank you,' Adam said then he hissed at Faizal, 'Let go.'

'You're a liability,' Faizal said out of the corner of his mouth as he sat back on his own chair.

Adam readjusted his legs and made sure he was sitting squarely, he wouldn't lose concentration this time. He looked up to find the speaker staring straight at him.

'Sorry.'

The speaker raised his hand, though whether in blessing or forgiveness Adam wasn't sure. But he didn't continue talking straight away, instead he stared at Adam a little longer. There was a softness to his eyes and intelligence. It was the kind of look Vijay gave him sometimes, assessing, considering options before giving Adam his verdict.

The speaker addressed the group as a whole and said it was time to bring their attention to more serious matters, to the petrol bomb at the recent peace march on Whitehall.

'We believe there are ISIS infiltrators attempting to tarnish the good works that we are doing. Their aim seems to be to create chaos and confusion.'

Adam glanced across at the screens that divided the room. He hadn't had a chance to speak to Aisha since that day, but he'd seen her at a couple of meetings. He'd been surprised that she was still so dedicated to the UMIA after that incident.

ISIS infiltrators. The term sounded ominous. Adam wanted to turn around to see that shifty young man in his kufi, the one who he'd seen staring into the flames.

The speaker at the front was in full flow, 'In some ways this is good news. It means that ISIS sees us as a threat to their organisation. However, it does mean we need to be vigilant. Fortunately nobody was seriously injured and those nearby acted quickly. If we are going to make a difference, we have to expect that there will be opposition. Only by acting together can we be strong.'

The door suddenly opened and the white-robed Arab who'd greeted them downstairs had a whispered discussion with the speaker. Then he turned, his face set in a grim line, his robes pristine. He gazed over the audience, taking his time on each face. When he got to Adam, he paused a little longer. Adam couldn't look away: his own eyes had become windows into which this stranger was analysing his soul. With no change in expression the Arab turned and said something to whoever was still out in the corridor. A whisper of voices started around the room and Faizal gave Adam's bicep a squeeze.

'What?'

This time, it was a black clad man who entered the room, again in formal robes but with the addition of a hood which he removed when he got to the front. There was a general gasp from the audience and the whispering stopped. Adam looked at Faizal but he was staring straight ahead. The man opened his mouth.

'As-Salam-u-Alaikum.'

'wa Alaikum Assalam.'

'Brothers and sisters, I come to you today far from my home land. It has been a long and tiring journey in which I have contemplated much. Not least the bodies of our dead brothers in

119

Syria that I myself have seen. Their blood lies drying in the sun while I go on living. What right do I have to life when so many have died?' His voice crescendoed and Adam's skin tingled.

'It's Ibrahim Muhammad Sharif,' whispered Faizal in the lull. The name meant nothing to Adam but he had a voice you couldn't help listening to.

'Many times I have prayed to Allah, that I am not worthy of this life. So many brothers and sisters more worthy than I have died. And yet here I still stand before you.

'When I stood on that battlefield and saw the bleeding bodies of our brothers and sisters, I prayed. I prayed that I would die too rather than bear this terrible sorrow.' He spoke softly and Adam leaned forwards in his chair, not wanting to miss a single word.

'My time is not yet. Our time is not yet brothers and sisters.' He opened his arms, the deep arm holes beckoning them in. 'We, who are still living, must take up the sword. For what right do we have to life if not to avenge the death of our brothers and sisters, if not to ensure that they did not die in vain? Their death is not a reason for us to give up, but to fight with renewed strength for Islam.' He raised a fist and shook it into the air.

Then out of his fist, came a finger that pointed directly at Adam. 'Allah has a purpose for each one of you.' He paused and Adam was drawn into the man's gaze. A thrill of excitement at being chosen by this commanding figure rippled through him.

'The British government are trying to control the situation with fire-power. They are preventing our European Muslim brothers and sisters from going to the aid of those that need it. More than that, in just three weeks time, the British government will meet to decide whether to send British troops into Syria.' He shook his finger and his head. 'They won't be going to stand alongside our dead brethren.'

He paused and took a breath. 'No! They will be going to slaughter Muslims. Do you think they'll know the difference between those ISIS fascists and our United brothers? Of course not.'

There was a collective murmur of unrest around the room.

'Is this right brothers and sisters?'

'No.' The room responded.

'Can we be true Muslims and faithful to Allah if we ignore this atrocity?'

'No!' The room was getting louder.

'We need to give the British government a strong message. We need to warn them to stay away so that our organisation can do its work. So that we can bring Muslims together, so that we can rid that land of the usurpers, of the godless people that assume the Caliphate.'

The audience agreed and Adam nodded.

The speaker put his arms up to the ceiling, 'Praise be to Allah.'

Adam responded amidst the voices around him, 'Praise be to Allah.'

The man in black folded his arms and smiled warmly at them. 'You may be wondering what you can do in your safe boring lives in London. When you go home tonight back to your comfortable homes where there is food on the table and fancy clothes on your backs.'

The man smirked and Adam wished he'd worn a plain T-shirt instead of his designer one.

'What have you ever done for Allah or for the Muslim faith, or for your Muslim brothers and sisters?' He surveyed them with an accusing look.

'But not any more.' The man thumped a fist into his open hand.

'You are Allah's chosen, together we can complete His plan and stop the British government from undoing much of our progress.' He opened his arms to encompass them.

'Who is with Allah?'

Adam put his arm in the air, he felt Faizal rising out of his seat. Looking around, he saw that every hand in the room was up. Beyond the screen where the women sat, Adam wondered if Aisha's hand was raised too.

At the end, there was clapping and lots of thank yous and Allah yusallmaks. The chairs were folded and stacked at the side during which Adam had to sit and wait. He couldn't move without his wheelchair. He turned to look behind him where the men were queueing to sign up at two tables at the back.

When Faizal returned, Adam said, 'What am I supposed to do?'

'Dunno. Maybe that huge guy will come back.'

'Can you find my chair?'

'OK.'

Faizal went out of the room along with a couple of other young people who had already signed up. In front of him the women were queuing to sign a sheet on the front table.

'I'm not too young at all. If you sign up then so am I.' A young woman's voice said crossly.

Adam could feel his fingers tingle with excitement as he recognised Noor's voice. Aisha must be nearby. Immediately he went to swivel his chair around to get closer to the line of women, but of course he couldn't. Twisting his head around, he gazed along the covered figures. He spotted her, wearing a Niqab like she'd been last time. Adam was beginning to get accustomed to her outline, her height and the pretty pink pumps she often wore on her feet. Aisha appeared to sigh as Adam watched her body language carefully as she stood next to her sister. At last the women's queue moved forwards close enough for a conversation.

'Hello,' Adam said.

'Hi Adam, we didn't see you.' Noor smiled brightly and let her hands drop to her sides. 'Have you signed up?' She motioned to the back of the room.

'I, err, Faizal's gone to get my chair.'

Aisha was staring at him and now she stepped forwards, 'I'm sorry we left you, at the march I mean, it's just that my parents would never forgive me if anything happened to Noor.'

Noor rolled her eyes. 'You have to stop treating me like a kid.'

'You are a kid.'

'I'm sixteen.'

Aisha's eyes twinkled at Adam. He wanted to say something witty, anything to hold those beautiful eyes but his mouth had gone dry.

He licked his lips and then said quickly, 'You were very brave that day.'

'Not as much as you,' Noor jumped in, 'you were amazing charging at the barrier like that.'

Aisha nodded.

'You're our knight in shining armour.' Noor grinned.

Adam looked away, embarrassed. He was glad the two girls had fled when they had. He remembered Aisha's face, the Niqab hanging in her hand, her rich dark hair tumbled around her face. She had been watchful as she grasped her little sister's arm. Determined rather than fearful, as she strode away, the fabric fluttering in her wake. Adam, on the other hand, remained rooted to the spot. The smell of burning brought back memories of the train crash. Terror had gripped him and he'd been unable to move until Faizal suddenly appeared at his side and broke the spell. Adam stared admiringly at Aisha's tall figure now as she moved forwards to take her turn at the table.

When they'd both finished writing, Noor picked up the papers and pen and offered them to Adam.

'You may as well sign this one or you'll be here all night,' she suggested, her eyes indicating the queue behind him.

'Thanks, I will.' Adam took them. Aisha had signed up. She was obviously committed to this cause. The incident at the march hadn't stopped her coming to these meetings. Adam gazed up at her eyes. The fabric across her face suddenly flattened against her lips and then fell away again as someone opened the door and left. Adam wondered what it would be like to hold her face and kiss those secret lips. If he had any chance at all with Aisha, he would have to prove himself worthy. Adam glanced down at the papers in his hand. Maybe he could do something more meaningful than parading with a banner for the UMIA.

'Come on, he's seen us.' Aisha's voice, urgent.

Adam looked up to see her grab Noor's hand. He turned to see the suspicious guy in his kufi heading towards them, his face set in a frown.

'Bye Sir Adam,' said Noor.

'See you later.' Aisha suddenly leant towards him and, to his surprise, gripped his hand and pressed a scrap of paper into it. She winked and then they were gone.

Adam watched the young man hurrying towards the exit after the two women. Immediately he put his hands to the rims of his wheels to intercept but nothing happened. He was still sitting on the foldable plastic chair. Instead, to Adam's relief, the white-haired speaker stepped into the doorway with his hand outstretched in greeting. The man had to stop his pursuit and acknowledge the kindly gentleman. Adam eyed him, wondering what he wanted with Aisha and Noor. Who was he?

'Are you finished with those?' Another woman was gesturing at the sign-up papers on Adam's lap.

'Oh sorry, not yet.' Adam stuffed the scrap of paper Aisha had thrust at him into his waistband and then studied the sheets. Aisha's looped handwriting provided her contact details. On another sheet that was entitled 'Ideas' Adam recognised the same loopy style. He read her suggestion:

> Join an NGO providing aid in Syria in order to spread information directly about UMIA.

Adam stared at the cursive script. Would she really be willing to enter the heart of ISIS? Put herself in a war zone just to spread the message of the UMIA? Adam swallowed. He should come up with his own suggestion.

16

Halima - Stepping out

Halima pulled her house key from her pocket and pushed it into the lock; for once she didn't feel the need to pause before opening the door. She had more exciting things on her mind. Inspired by her walks with Veronica in recent weeks she had bought some seed packets on her way home. Pulling them out of her bag, they showed huge bouquets of rainbow colours, bursting blooms of perfect petals. Maybe in a few months Halima could have a beautiful garden to show Veronica.

Mum was in her usual place in front of the TV; and instead of joining her Halima dutifully provided tea and a biscuit and then went straight into the garden.

Standing amidst the weeds and brambles, Halima surveyed the overgrown patch. There were nettles across one corner intermixed with some ivy that was creeping across the ground. Through it all brambles wove between the hedge and grass and trailed through the nettles. Along one side of the overgrown hedge were piles of this winter's brown leaves. In the corner stood the knackered shed, and behind that an old wooden fence with slats leaning at odd angles.

Halima's earlier enthusiasm drained downwards, leaking away into the dark wet soil beneath her shoes. She swung her foot at some nettles and as the sea of leaves parted a rotting tin can was revealed with a large black slug investigating the opening. Above her hung grey clouds, silent and heavy. What on earth had made her think she could have a beautiful flower garden here? She thought about Veronica beaming next to the crocuses in the park. Then of her red skirt against their drab furniture like a slash of a fairy-tale world ripped through the dull fabric of their house. Wind ruffled at Halima's scarf and she automatically scratched at the scar on her scalp, then thrust her hands into her pockets to keep out the chill. In amongst the scrunched tissue, crumbs and an odd button was the crisp new packet of seeds. Halima pulled it out and looked at the picture. Pink chrysanthemums blooming from a mythical garden. She rubbed her thumb over the picture, the roughness of her skin making a thin scratching sound. Her mother was right: she hadn't amounted to anything in her life. Why on earth did she think she could magic up a flower-filled garden? Halima began to scrunch up the packet of seeds in her hand when something rubbed against her leg and Halima jumped. The grey cat was back and it was staring up at her.

'Get away,' she said.

The cat arched its back, walked purposefully to the fence at the side and leapt easily on to the top. It stared back at her.

'What do you want?' she demanded.

The cat looked reproachful and walked carefully along the fence, never taking its eyes from Halima, and then it was gone. Halima rubbed the spot on her leg where the cat had touched her, she wouldn't be surprised if she'd caught fleas. Then she heard her phone. It buzzed loudly from the kitchen where she had left it on the side. She marched back, her shoes sliding on the dank mud; she wiped them on the mat and reached for the silent object.

There was a message: it was from Veronica. A tingle of happiness warmed Halima's stomach. She thumbed through, reading quickly. It was an invite to meet Mrs Pease and Veronica at the sheltered housing flat on Broomwood road. The warmth spread upwards through her chest. Halima texted back, of course she'd like to come and see Mrs Pease. Halima typed and after a moment's thought added that she would come even if there weren't any pink-iced cakes. Halima imagined Veronica's tinkling laugh as she read the text.

Putting the mobile on the kitchen counter, Halima looked again at the scrunched up seed packet, its flowers a bright promise of a beautiful future. She picked it up, smoothed it flat and went back outside. Taking a deep breath of the odour of damp soil, she plodded across to the shed.

Halima dug ferociously. Mud caked her shoes but she didn't care. By noon, she had cleared a square patch about three feet wide next to the shed. Behind it lay the detritus of her hard work – tufts of grass, nettles, brambles and two rusty cans. She had taken off her jumper and dropped it on to the bin lid by the back door.

Standing back to survey her work was not as pleasing as she'd hoped. Nine square feet, in a garden of at least five times that, was not a lot really. She was damp under her arms and the breeze felt cool on her skin. She wiped a hand across her forehead. It was a start, and for that she should be proud. She wasn't sure if March was too early or too late to set spring flowers in motion, knowing her luck they'd all die before April.

Straightening up, Halima could feel her back aching, perhaps this gardening whim would have to wait until tomorrow. She slung the spade back into the shed, spent five minutes trying to get the shed door to stay shut and bolted but eventually gave up. She was starving. Halima walked backwards towards the kitchen, admiring her handy work, and almost tripped over something on the step.

'Damn.'

The cat growled in response and stood up, giving itself a little shake. Instead of walking off, it sat down and licked a paw. Halima thought if she shooed it off, it would end up running through the narrow gap of the partly-open back door into the house. The last thing she wanted was to be hunting under her mother's bed looking for a cat while it pissed in a corner. Halima attempted to step to the side, hoping to get behind the cat to be able to kick it in the right direction. It yawned, turned its back and marched through the gap.

'Hey!' Halima rushed in after the moggy. Without a care, it leapt lightly onto the worktop where it sniffed at a mug, stuck its nose in and licked at the cold tea.

'Eaaahhh! Get out!' Halima made to swipe at the cat, but it was down and out the door before her hand was even close.

'What are you doing? It's freezing in here.' Mum stood in the doorway to the hall clutching her prayer beads to her chest.

'Nothing, damn cat.'

'I don't want no cats in here. You know I've got an allergy. Filthy animals, leave fur and fleas all over the place. If that thing comes in we'll end up with flea eggs in the carpets and them jumping up our legs. Halima, you know I hate cats.'

Halima ignored her, shut the door and poured the cold tea down the sink, but her mother hadn't finished.

'They're horrible sneaky things they are, hide in your house, then when you're asleep they'll lie on your face and suffocate you. Beastly things don't care about anyone 'cept themselves.'

Just like someone else I know, thought Halima. In fact, maybe she should let the cat in, suffocating her mother in the middle of the night might be just the cure Halima needed.

As she washed her muddy hands at the sink, the sun appeared

shining on the new bare patch of ground. Soon there would be flowers, something beautiful in her life, something to make it more like home.

'Why are you wasting your time? Nothing good ever grew in that garden, not with all the neighbours' cats doing their business in it. Soil's rotten, nothing but clay.' Her mother paused for her hacking cough. 'If you've got energy to be wasted on digging, you should be out getting a better job. Then you could pay them bills, and I wouldn't be worried sick every night wide awake waiting for them to come and take me away.'

Halima sighed; her mother snored every night before she herself was able to get to sleep. She turned to look at her, they stared at each other a moment and then her mother softened.

'You try Halima. You're a good girl, looking after your old mother, ain't no one else will do it. That father of yours never gave you a chance, no wonder you're only a cleaner.'

Halima turned away and went to look in the fridge. She was so tired of the same old words, the blame, the monotony of her mother's tirade. She pulled out some leftover chicken curry. But it was true, if Halima didn't look after her mother, no one else would, she'd be in a home for the elderly, a poor one at that; Halima certainly couldn't afford to keep her anywhere decent. It was hard enough covering the rent as it was. And yet, hadn't Veronica hinted at some other possibility?

'Go and sit down Mum, I'll make some lunch.'

Her mother tutted under her breath and turned the key in the back door then shuffled back to the lounge still grumbling.

As the curry began to bubble, and the rice fluffed up in the pan, Halima went to get the leaflets that Veronica had given her. She began to read.

Apparently there was a scheme where her mother could go into a kind of old person's holiday home just for a week or so to give carers a break. Halima was beginning to like this term 'sole carer': the more she read, the more she realised what kind and selfless people these sole carers were. And what was even more amazing was that she, Halima, was one of them. According to the information, she did all the things that a sole carer did, washed Mum's hair, cooked, cleaned, changed the bed sheets and towels, helped her mother get in the bath once a week, took her to the doctors. Mum could dress herself and move around the house fine, but everything else was down to Halima.

'I can smell burning,' her mother shouted from the other room.

Halima could smell it too, she grabbed a spoon and stirred the curry, watching the thick yellow liquid heave as another bubble burst through, she had to scrape the bottom where it had stuck to the pan. She tested the rice on the end of a fork and added a bit more water.

If her mother went away for a week, she could transform everything. She could paint the kitchen, clear away some of the old clutter. Throw out that rug, get some new curtains. The possibilities seemed huge with Mum out of the way.

Halima pulled the rose plates from the cupboard and served up their lunch.

'Why have you still got them stupid bits of paper? There ain't no way I'm going in to one of them old people's prisons. And can you imagine the food? It won't be Halal, they'll kill me off in less than a week. Bloody awful.'

Halima blinked, trying hard to swallow her rice and curry.

'Don't know why you're always wearing those either.' Her mother pointed at Halima with her spoon.

Halima automatically put a hand to her throat against the beads she'd taken to wearing.

'You're far too old. Nobody will look twice at you no matter how many pretty beads you sling around your neck.'

Even just a couple of days respite would be a relief. Maybe she should let the cat in after all, fur and fleas galore.

17

Austin – Moving on?

Austin awoke early. He was cold and pulled at the quilt but it didn't budge. There was someone else in the bed. The surprise constricted his throat and he suddenly had to gasp for air. Fear dissipated as he orientated himself into the present day. Of course it wasn't Matt, he didn't believe in ghosts, it hadn't been Matt for over two and half years. That terrible fact alone brought on a familiar crushing feeling. It was David beside him hogging the bed, Austin reassured himself. But that should make him feel better shouldn't it?

It had taken so long to get used to sleeping alone again after the accident. Nights of yearning for that familiar warmth, the love, the sex. Yet here he lay cold and utterly lost next to a warm body. Why did his life seem so topsy turvy? He swung his legs over the side of the bed and sat up. Perhaps he should wake David, seek out a warm embrace to soothe his mixed-up feelings.

Austin stared at the remains of their Chinese takeaway left on the side. Perhaps not. Instead Austin went into the bathroom, shut the door and put on the light. He stared at his toothbrush alone in its cup and a red one that David had left carelessly on the edge of the sink. Austin wiped a finger along the smooth surface of the glass shelf where Matt used to keep his shaving gel. That was why he'd woken early, why he was finding it difficult lately.

Moving on, literally. He'd started hunting for other flats on the internet, looking for somewhere cheaper that would be closer to work. But it wasn't easy.

Austin stared at his reflection, his eyes were puffy this morning. Behind him hung his silk dressing gown on the hook on the door. Lifeless, alone without Matt's blue fleecy one beside it. The shower cubicle stood in the corner, the screen folded neatly back, a few drops still in the basin at the bottom. How many times had they stood under the hot jets together? Steam filling the bathroom, soap and water making their bodies slippery to touch. Austin gripped the edge of the sink. Was he ready to give it up? This home that Austin had shared with Matt for three years.

Washed and dressed, Austin set about getting his breakfast. David still hadn't woken and Austin was taking pains to keep it that way. This was the third night he'd stayed over and Austin was relieved to have a morning when bacon and eggs weren't staining the air. He seemed to take up so much space. Austin took a mug out of the cupboard and poured his espresso while munching on a banana. A guttural snort from the other room punctured the still air. Austin gripped his cup tight and finished the last of his coffee. Was David the new love he needed or a rebound? He quietly rinsed his hands and mug and went back into the lounge. David's jacket lay strewn across the sofa. His huge shoes, lying at odd angles on the floor nowhere near the shoe rack. Austin tidied up and then pulled on his coat and grabbed his laptop bag. He didn't want to hang around any longer or David would be awake and come crashing through his emotions and stir everything up. Despite the early hour, he may as well take himself off to work. He had a long and arduous testing report to complete, a perfect document to occupy his concentration and keep his mind off the mess that was his personal life.

Austin had been engrossed for some time when the internal messenger beeped up on his screen. It was Becky from marketing, wondering if he fancied a coffee break. Austin grinned to himself and typed back. Grabbing his wallet he made his way to the stairs and down to the canteen.

'Hey soldier,' a female voice called behind him as he was sealing the lid on his cup.

'Becky, hello gorgeous.' They kissed each other briefly on each cheek. She was looking lovely as usual, her fiery hair piled on top of her head and wearing a cute red blouse with too many buttons undone.

'That will never do,' he carefully did up a button. 'Much better, chic but not too sexy.'

'You really ought to be a stylist Austin,' she laughed. 'Or maybe a model, you're certainly thin enough.'

'Hey, I need to keep in shape.' He pulled at the spikes of his fringe.

'Ah yes, how's it going with lover boy?'

'Well,' he shrugged, 'it's OK.' He slid into a seat at one of the empty tables. There were only two other people in there.

'It's bound to be difficult at first. I admire you Austin. It took me months to get back in the game after Ethan dumped me.'

Austin nodded and told her how he kept comparing David to Matt all the time even though he knew he shouldn't. That it wouldn't help. He told her about David putting on the pressure for him to move.

'You know, I think that would be a good thing, really. New beginning and all that. You always said it was costing you an arm and a leg.'

'I know.' Austin sighed. It was just that all these things sounded good in theory but the reality was much harder. They walked out of the canteen together.

'Change is always tricky but it opens up new possibilities, even if David isn't the one,' she wrapped her arm around his neck. 'Just do it Austin.'

'Is that your new marketing phrase?'

'No, it's my new Austin phrase. About time you got out of the doldrums.'

'Hey, I've not been that bad have I?'

Just then Austin's phone buzzed in his pocket and he pulled it out.

Becky raised her eyebrows. 'Another date with David?'

'No, actually Pat and John,' he read the text.

'Who?'

'Matt's parents, remember?'

'Really? You still see those guys?'

'Now and then.' Austin couldn't help feeling uncomfortable. He put his phone back in his pocket. 'They're good people.'

'Yeah of course, I didn't mean-' Becky shrugged. 'Anyway, I think moving's a good idea. I'll come help if you like, there's a good grocer near me that'll have boxes and stuff. I could bring them over and help you pack.'

'Alright, alright, I get the message.'

For a moment Austin wondered what Pat and John would think about him planning to move.

Just then Tim appeared out of the lift.

'There you are.' He looked relieved to see Austin. He pushed his glasses further up his nose. 'I need your help, the test I'm running in project Dyno has gone mental, the whole system is grinding to a halt.'

'Oh great.'

Becky put a hand on Austin's shoulder, 'Listen, I've got to go too, I'm presenting to the senior managers later. Fancy going for a drink after work?'

'Sure. And thanks Becky. Knock em dead you rouge fox you.'

Becky laughed and turned towards the sales and marketing department. Austin watched her go. As she opened the door, a wave of warm chatter washed out before the door shut again.

'So are you coming or what?' Tim strode back to the lift and pressed the button several times.

18

Adam – The inner circle.

Around the next corner and he would be there. Adam glanced into the shop window on his left, checking his reflection. He'd trimmed his new goatee into a neat shape. Yesterday he'd splashed out on a haircut and this morning he'd styled it with some gel. On his upper body he was wearing a new shirt his mum had bought and Faizal's leather jacket which had been hanging in the hall. Adam checked his watch, he was five minutes early. Perfect, he wouldn't want to keep Aisha waiting. His heart was beating fast.

Adam turned the corner carefully, not wanting to accidentally knock anyone and make a bad impression. There was Subway with a few chairs outside. Two guys were seated at one of the tables. She could be waiting inside. Adam licked his lips and rolled up to the door.

'Adam?' One of the guys stood up. The other was pushing his chair back.

Startled, Adam gripped the wheels tight. The two men came towards him. Shit, did they know about the note? That he intended to meet Aisha? Was this a trap?

'As-Salam-u-Alaikum,' the first one said and the other chimed in.

Adam swallowed and replied, 'wa Alaikum Assalam.'

They came closer, the first with his hand outstretched. 'I'm Jamaal and this is Hakeem.'

Adam cautiously turned towards them, they didn't look angry. Perhaps they were nothing to do with Aisha. Maybe they were UMIA members he didn't recognise.

'Hi.' They shook hands.

'Can we get you a coffee or something?' Hakeem said.

Adam glanced at the table where there were two cups. Had they been waiting for him? The door to the restaurant opened and a blond-haired man came out talking loudly closely followed by his larger friend. Adam tried to look past them into the restaurant.

'If you're looking for Aisha, she's not coming,' Hakeem said.

Adam's heart sank. So they did know.

'But don't worry, she's the one that recommended you.'

Adam looked up sharply at Jamaal, 'Recommended?'

'Why don't you pull up a chair?' He waved at their table. 'I mean join us.' Jamaal indicated that Hakeem should move the seats to make room for Adam's wheelchair.

'Drink?' Hakeem asked again.

Adam looked at the table and the two men. They didn't appear to be threatening but what would Aisha be recommending him for?

'I'll have a coke, thanks.'

'Aisha's spoken very highly of you,' Jamaal said, taking his seat again and drawing his cup closer.

Adam wheeled himself to the other side and pulled his leather jacket closed against the cool breeze.

'I understand you were quite the hero.'

Adam was surprised.

'At the march, she told us you tried to protect her from the crowd. Saved her from getting hurt and humiliated.' Jamaal smiled.

Did she really think that? Noor had called him their knight in shining armour but Aisha had been doing a good job of fighting back herself. Surely anyone would have done the same - helped a friend.

'I only...'

Jamaal raised his hand. 'Seriously, we were impressed. It's all very well for the UMIA to have a peaceful march but we need people like you to keep our members safe. Not only are there ISIS infiltrators but the police seem to think we're the bad guys. It's getting difficult to know who to trust.'

Adam nodded. That was true enough, he still wondered about that guy with the kufi. Maybe he should ask Jamaal about him. Were these guys heading up security within the UMIA?

Hakeem arrived with Adam's coke, scraping his chair loudly on the paving slabs as he sat down.

'Hakeem and I, and some others, we're part of an elite group.'

Adam eyed Hakeem in his hoodie and jeans. They didn't look particularly elite. And he couldn't remember ever having seen them before. Mind you the UMIA was a big organisation, growing all the time.

'Because of the difficulties in our communications getting tapped and the increased threat of ISIS, we've been putting together an inner team. People like you and Aisha.'

Him and Aisha? Did they really see him in the same league as Aisha? Could they work together for the UMIA? Adam leaned forwards, listening more intently.

'We're gathering people that we can trust, those that are truly committed and willing to take action, after all that's what the

UMIA is about right? Muslims in Action.'

'Sure, but what can I do?'

'We need people that can keep information to themselves, that don't splash everything on social media. Some of our plans will only work if we can keep them from getting into ISIS hands. By keeping information to just a few, we stand a better chance of succeeding.'

Adam was curious; his mouth had gone dry. Did they really think he could be one of the chosen few? He sipped his coke.

'I can keep secrets,' said Adam. 'You can trust me, but what kind of plans are you talking about?'

'We can't share that yet, there's a selection interview with one of the senior leaders that you'll have to get through first.'

'It's not difficult,' added Hakeem.

'We already know that you're committed and willing to take action. It's more of a formality.'

Jamaal leaned back in his seat, finishing the last of his drink. Hakeem was looking up and down the street.

Adam licked his lips again. 'I won't have to do anything illegal will I?'

Jamaal and Hakeem exchanged a look.

Adam suddenly felt incredibly childish, it was something his parents would say. What was he doing? 'I mean, it's not like we're going to be terrorists or anything is it?' Adam tried to laugh it off but the other two were gravely serious.

Hakeem adjusted his chair causing a sudden shriek of metal against metal as the chair grated against the table leg.

Jamaal leaned forwards. 'ISIS are the terrorists, not us. I thought you'd been to enough UMIA meetings to know that by now.'

Adam squeezed the rims of his wheels.

Hakeem was frowning at him. 'If that's what's on your mind, then maybe you're not the right guy for us.'

'No, no.' Adam was so stupid, he didn't want to blow this opportunity. 'I wasn't thinking. Of course I want to be involved. You said something about a formal interview?'

19

Ralph – Memories unleashed.

Orange street lights washed the patient in a dull glow. Shadows from curious bystanders added to the gloom. Ralph and Emma were kneeling on the ground next to a motionless body.

'Is he dead?' someone said.

Ralph ignored the question. 'Right. Are you ready?'

'Yep.' Emma held the man's arms by his sides. Ralph thrust the long needle deep into the man's heart. Hard and fast. There was a collective gasp from the surrounding audience. Ralph then gently squeezed the syringe down with his thumb. He pulled it out. There was nothing to do but wait; at first the guy remained static and then his eyes fluttered, he coughed, Emma let go. He rolled to the side.

'What do you all want? Get off me.' He was flailing his arms at them, getting up unsteadily. Ralph laid a gentle hand on his tattooed bicep.

'Take it easy. You've overdosed.'

'Gerroff!' He staggered a bit, stood upright and glared at the small crowd that had gathered. 'Where's my fucking shirt?'

'We had to cut it off. Please sir, it would be best if you came to the back of the ambulance.' Emma tried but the man was off.

Ralph followed but the patient turned aggressively. 'I said leave me alone.'

'Sir, you realise that what we've given you will wear off, you might collapse again.'

But the patient wasn't listening, he was intent on getting out of there.

'Doesn't he need to go to hospital or something?' An elderly man with worried eyes stood watching the casualty heading for the corner of the square.

'It would be a good idea, but we can't make him.' Ralph rolled his eyes at Emma, who smiled back. It was both frustrating and satisfying, a drug addict on the brink of death brought back to life only to disappear back into his life of substance abuse. Maybe next time, he wouldn't be so lucky. There was always the faint hope that the experience might make the person think twice about their addiction. If not, maybe next time the man would be on his own, lying under a bridge somewhere. Or crashed on a mate's sofa struggling for life with no one to help. Perhaps that was what he wanted, maybe his life was so messed up that it would be better to die. A choice like that woman the other day. The mother of the boy on the track.

'Hey.'

Ralph jumped.

'Let's get packed up,' Emma said.

Ralph zipped their bags, picked up the empty packet and the syringe and wrapped them carefully before retreating to the ambulance. The crowd was dispersing, the drama over.

'I never got to ask you.' Emma started.

'What?'

'Your funniest job, remember?'

'Oh yeah.' But Ralph's radio was already beeping for attention. Control wanted them free as soon as possible for another call out. They hadn't stopped, which was typical of a Saturday evening, still it was a bit early yet to be quite this busy.

Ralph radioed in to let them know they were just about sorted. Control wanted them to respond to a casualty from a fight. It wasn't far away; a young man was bleeding and unconscious.

Back at the hospital once more, having delivered their patient into the hands of the head injury unit, Emma and Ralph were starving. They stopped at the garage and got some sandwiches and sat in the cab eating quietly, hoping they would finish before the next call came in.

'Did you see, they're planning to have a memorial event for the train crash?'

'Really?'

'Yeah, there was something in the newsletter about it, wouldn't be surprised if you had a personal invite. Maybe they'll want you

138

to make a speech.' She grinned at him and took a large bite of chicken wrap.

Ralph shook his head. 'I doubt it.'

'Sure they will, what with your award and everything, they're bound to invite you. Our brave paramedic, it's not often our team gets recognised.'

A small muscle in Ralph's eyebrow had started to twitch annoyingly. He didn't want to be thinking about his award, or about the crash, or about the boy, or about the boy's mother. God. He stopped chewing. He didn't want to think about any of it, it should never have happened.

'Are you all right?'

'Fine, just a bit of gristle or something from the ham.' Ralph swallowed but found he didn't want to finish his sandwich. Emma was busy opening her packet of crisps. Ralph noted the side of her milky white neck, like that of the woman lying on the bed, smooth and curved like the sheet beneath. Ralph shook the thought away, but it refused to budge, those sequins on the quilt cover under her pale arm winking at him, laughing at him, at his failure, at the repercussions of that one event. Why couldn't he let it rest? It had been more than two years since that dreadful disaster. But here he was suffering the consequences years later, like ripples in a pond that never end. If only he hadn't let the boy die.

*

The award was stuffed in the drawer of the French dresser, beneath layers of mats and napkins, under the awful tablecloth that Shelly's mother had bought them years ago. Ralph pulled out the presentation box. He had put it there after the ceremony and hadn't touched it since. Ralph looked behind him guiltily. The house was dark and quiet, Shelly and the children asleep. Tonight, he had an urge to hold it. Turning the wooden box over in his hands, feeling the weight of it, the small brass hinges at the back and the little catch at the front. It still smelled new. He opened it and stared at the large golden disc with its ornate words engraved into the metal.

Ralph snapped the box shut. He didn't deserve it, he should throw it out. Give it to a charity shop. Maybe sell it to a jeweller to melt down into something more appropriate. Into something that wasn't a lie. Ralph ran a hand over his face, the rough stubble coarse. That twitch in his eyebrow was stronger. He raised his arm ready to throw the object with all his might across the room, but there was a movement in the corner, his arm hovered in the air, while his eyes readjusted to the figure in the doorway.

'What are you doing Dad?' Cameron stood in his pyjamas blinking in the light from the table lamp on the dresser.

'Hey little man.' Ralph lowered his arm and dropped the object back into the drawer, pushing it shut with his thigh. 'Let's get you up to bed.' He guided the groggy boy up the stairs where Cameron stopped.

'I'm thirsty.'

They deviated into the bathroom and Ralph turned the tap to run some water into the plastic beaker.

'Night Dad.' Cameron disappeared into his bedroom and Ralph stood on the landing staring after the shadow left behind where his son had stood. Was it fair that he still had two healthy young boys when that other family had nothing? Not even a family, just a lonely pale-faced man left alone in the world. The yearning deep within Ralph made him gasp. How could anyone endure such pain?

In the bathroom, the mirror reflected his frightened face, his eyes appearing sunken and there was that twitch, just visible if you looked really close. He touched it with his fingertip, feeling the muscle make its minute contractions. He should go to bed, but somehow he didn't think he'd be able to sleep. Instead he went downstairs and put the television on. In the kitchen he grabbed a tumbler of whiskey and went through to settle himself on the sofa in front of the TV.

20

Halima – Fallen petals

Halima stood uncertainly in the unfamiliar hallway, her coat in her hand. She was wearing the lemon scarf, which she had thought appropriate for such a visit.

'Halima. Do come on in, mother's in the lounge. You look lovely.' Veronica gave her a brief hug. 'Please, go through.' She took Halima's coat and ushered her into a flowery room that overlooked the communal gardens.

'Mum, this is Halima, the one I was telling you about.'

A frail lady with crinkled tissue-paper skin was sitting in an old-fashioned winged armchair opposite the window. Her head lifted and she smiled but her back remained hunched over.

'Welcome.' Her shrivelled hand beckoned to Halima.

'Hello.' Halima perched on the sofa, not wishing to intrude. 'It's nice to see you Mrs Pease.'

'Halima, come closer, I don't hear very well these days.' She waved her liver-spotted hand. Halima shuffled along the sofa.

'I said, it's nice to see you Mrs Pease.' Halima spoke louder.

The lady chuckled in reply. 'It's Mary, you're not a little girl of ten any more are you?'

Halima blushed as Veronica appeared with a tray complete with china teacups and a pretty tea-pot. There was milk in a jug and sugar cubes in a little bowl. A plate of fairy cakes completed the set up. Veronica poured the tea and offered the milk and sugar. Halima took two lumps and stirred them into the delicate cup.

'I was telling Mum what you said about my Sindy doll,' Veronica said.

Mrs Pease chuckled again. 'You know she even slept with that doll, loved it to bits. Had all the little outfits, she used to get her ready for bed and clean her teeth with a teensy little toothbrush.

Do you have children, Halima?'

'No, no I don't.'

'Shame, they're fun when they're small and useful when they're grown.' She put an affectionate hand out to her daughter.

'Mum said she thinks she remembers you in one of the school plays. Did you play a bear or something?'

'No, I was an eagle.' Halima hadn't thought about that in years, decades probably. 'I didn't make a very good one, my mum made my wings out of some old coat hangers and some brown tights.'

'That's what we did in those days, made do with what we had, none of this plastic ready-made rubbish they have these days.' Mrs Pease nodded to herself. 'How is Kaneez? Veronica told me she's in the scheme.'

Halima nodded. 'She's fine.' What could she say? That she was a permanent grey fixture in the house, like the mould around the bath, annoying and dark but accepted nonetheless.

'Has she mellowed with age?' Mrs Pease's lined face creased into a smile.

Mellowed probably wasn't a word that Halima would use, hardened perhaps, solidified like congealed fat sitting on top of a lamb curry. Mrs Pease was watching her.

'Same sharp tongue then?'

Halima was startled, did Mrs Pease remember Mum after all these years? Did they have coffee together when she and Veronica had been at school?

'The rest of us mothers used to keep clear of Kaneez Shah, she was certainly someone to be reckoned with, with that tongue of hers.'

Halima looked at Mrs Pease' sharp eyes. 'She, she protected me. She had to be strong.'

'Oh don't get me wrong, I respected Kaneez, you just wouldn't want to be the wrong side of her. How's your dad?'

Halima gulped and shook her head.

'Passed away?'

Halima kept still, the truth was she didn't know. Hadn't seen her father since that dreadful night when she was fourteen. Later they'd heard he had gone back to Pakistan. Maybe he was still there, maybe he'd married again and had a whole new family.

'Very traditional your father, I remember.' Mrs Pease shook her head sighing. 'Such a shame when traditions die and time marches on.' Mrs Pease shook her head again. Halima stared at the pot plant on the window sill, a couple of petals from a small red flower lay on the white surface like drops of blood, like the drops she found on the bathroom floor the day after her baby had been taken away. Drops of blood that her mother had missed when cleaning up after the birth. The only evidence that anything unusual had happened. Even her stomach wasn't that obvious under the salwaar kameeze her mother made her wear.

'Come on, let's not get maudlin. Would you like a cake Halima?' Veronica forced a jolly laugh and held out the dainty dish. Halima took a round fairy cake with pink icing. As she put it to her lips, she noticed her hand was shaking.

'I'm a cleaner!' she blurted out needing to remove the shakes, change the scene that was clawing at the back of her skull. Some crumbs escaped her mouth. Mary and Veronica stared at her outburst. She had to continue, 'That's my job, what I do. At a big office down on the Battersea Bridge Road. It's a good job, early mornings but it means I have the rest of the day.' Halima paused. 'To look after Mum,' she added.

'You're a good daughter Halima. She doesn't deserve you, but then when do any of us get what we deserve?' Mrs Pease chuckled again and bit into her second cake. Halima watched the crumbs gather at the corner of her mouth and was tempted to wipe them away. Is that what she would do for Mum as she got older and less able. Would she end up wiping the phlegm and food from the corners of her mouth? Halima shivered and concentrated on drinking her tea, carefully, from the thin china cup.

When Halima finally put her cup down on the saucer, she realised that Veronica had left the room, and Mrs Pease was studying her hard.

'Did they make you abort it?' Mrs Pease' eyes peered into the dark places of Halima's soul. 'Poor love.' She reached out and patted Halima's hand. The fingers were cold and hard and

Halima shrank back. 'Well it was all a long time ago. Teenagers will be teenagers the world over.'

Halima clamped her lips together, how could Mrs Pease know she'd been pregnant? She was pretty sure that Veronica didn't. Halima put her hands in her lap. They were shaking again. The scar hidden under her scarf was burning, and the desire to scratch it was almost irresistible. Veronica came back into the room holding the tea-pot. She looked from her mother to Halima with a crooked smile.

'More tea?'

'No, thanks, I really should be going, Mum will be wondering where I am.' Halima couldn't help glancing guiltily at Mrs Pease.

'Men can be tricky creatures, it's not just teenagers that cause problems. Sometimes even grown men can act like idiots, isn't that right Vie?'

Veronica looked embarrassed, 'I'm not sure I'd call Ian an idiot.'

'All right then, how about bastard then? That about sums him up. Can you imagine after all their years together, he takes off with another woman.'

Halima stared. This was news to her, she thought Veronica was living with Ian.

Veronica was on the verge of tears.

Halima said, 'Perhaps I should go.'

'Why don't you look around first. It's nice, nicer than you might think.' Mrs Pease smiled warmly at Halima as if this were a birthday tea. Halima wanted to leave, she glanced at the petals on the windowsill reminded again of those drops of blood. The weight of the past sucking her into the sofa cushions, pulling her under, suffocating all thoughts except those that swam in the dark shadows.

'Yes, let me show you around.' Veronica was standing ready to guide Halima.

'A change can be good,' Mrs Pease spoke. 'Your mother would like it here I'm sure.'

Halima stood up, keeping her eyes on Veronica's back, and tried hard to concentrate on what she was saying as they entered the kitchen.

After the tour of the flat, Veronica took Halima outside amongst the flower beds and wooden benches. Halima could feel herself relax, the tension easing out through her feet, down through the grass. The shake in her hands had stopped and her scalp felt numb. As they walked, Halima took special notice of the flowers, some were labelled and she bent to read the small stakes.

'I thought you didn't do gardening?' Veronica asked.

'And I thought you were married.'

They both stopped and stared at each other.

'I'm sorry,' Halima said as guilt and shame washed over her.

'No you're right, I should have said.' Veronica sighed, her voice trembling. 'I'm sorry I didn't say. It still hurts so much. You know that day you showed me the invite to the memorial?'

Halima nodded, recalling how Veronica had scrunched the letter tightly in her hand.

'I wanted to tell you then but we'd only just met and I didn't want to burden you with all my rubbish.'

They stopped by a bench and sat down. Halima could see the anguish etched on Veronica's face. She reached across and squeezed her friend's hand and Veronica squeezed back.

'Ian was on a train that day, had a connection at Clapham Junction. Not the one that crashed. Anyway, he got delayed for hours and hours. When he finally got home I was just so relieved he hadn't been involved. That it hadn't been his train.'

Halima's scar was itching again and she just had to scratch it through her scarf.

'Are you all right?' Veronica said.

'Yes, sorry.' Halima stopped scratching and clasped her hands in her lap. 'Do go on.'

'Well I later found out, six months later, that he'd met a woman that day on the train. Spent hours talking with her and then they'd started to meet up after that.' She sighed. 'I was doing the accounts and there were hotel and restaurant payments that he just dismissed as work, said they'd started a new system where they had to claim the money back rather than the company paying for it up front. Eventually I checked his phone and found...'

'I'm sorry.' Halima gave Veronica's shoulder a clumsy pat. Halima's own secrets were screaming now to be let out. Instead she said, 'It's a lovely garden.'

'Yes, yes it is.' Veronica dabbed at her eyes with a tissue. 'But you never did say why you have an invite to the memorial.'

'Me?' Halima felt trapped as if she was stuck in that tunnel on Falcon Road. She stared at the flowers not wanting to remember that day, trying hard not to scratch at the scar. Veronica was watching her with pale eyes and a soggy tissue bunched in her fingers. Halima rubbed her thighs with her hands and sighed, she'd only ever told her mum, what harm could it do?

'It was a Saturday so I'd got some things from Battersea market like I always do. They have a good fruit and vegetable stall, cheaper than the supermarkets. I probably had some milk and biscuits too, in fact, that's funny...' Halima let her voice trail away as she wondered what had happened to her shopping that day.

Halima had finished her cleaning on time and headed straight to the Battersea market to get her weekly vegetables. For once it hadn't been raining, just cloudy with that slate sky that hung above you making you hunch your shoulders. Heading home, she avoided an empty can of beer, her hands holding the heavy plastic bags. Halima scowled at the dark bridge looming ahead of her. She imagined it to be a tunnel, one that you could walk into that had no end. A tunnel that swallowed you whole. Before she entered, she paused, laying down the heavy bags and rubbing her hands together before swapping sides and continuing into the gloom. The number forty-nine bus came swishing past blowing up the litter. As she passed the half-way marker on the wall, a white line that someone had helpfully graffitied, she could hear a train approaching above. There was a squeal of wheels on the track that got louder, and even louder. Halima frowned up at the bridge above her head. It was shrieking in her ears, someone needed to oil something or sort the brakes out.

She hurried on along the tunnel but then the ground shook, or was it the bridge, or maybe it was *her* suddenly dizzy. The movement made her nauseous and the noise deafened her. Maybe this was the tunnel to hell. The walls appeared to be trembling. Halima went down on her knees and then cowered with her hands over her head. The ground was hard and cold beneath her. She lay down flat, the grit pressing into her cheek. She could feel the trembling through her face and a roaring metallic ripping sound above. Halima closed her eyes. There was a screech of cars and a crunch from nearby. With her eyes squeezed tight shut, only the sounds crashed about her. Her body still and cold against the pavement. Things dropped, big things that crumbled and sent a whoosh of air across her face. There was more trembling and then the ground was silent. Above and around there was a quietness as if the tunnel itself was taking a deep breath in, then out in a slow sigh that blew across the back of her head making her scarf ripple.

Then there was noise again, screaming, shouts. Car doors slamming, feet running hard that came so close and then away again. Tinkling of glass and crunching. More screams. The noises came in waves that crescendoed and then eased into the shallows before swelling again. A new sound of sirens added to the cacophony of vibrations bouncing around her head. Perhaps she was in hell. Is this where you ended up when your life had been a whole lot of nothing? Surely not.

Halima found that lying completely still with her eyes closed offered some kind of protection to whatever was happening. Perhaps it wasn't real, any of it, just noise, maybe she was dreaming. Except there was the hard ground beneath her and her knee was smarting for some reason. She tried opening one eye slightly. All she could see was a lot of dust and a small ant crawling away from her. No bright light leading her to heaven. The noise still washed over her in waves, sometimes frightening in its intensity. Halima closed her eyes and decided to wait for another lull. But each lull was quickly followed by more shouting, or banging, or sirens. Her knee was hurting more, and her cheek was uncomfortable pressed against the pavement. Halima opened her eyes again and stared at the wall of the bridge, some bricks had come loose and lay scattered. There was a large crack running upwards. No wondrous light anywhere, this was neither heaven nor hell. She was simply Halima Shah, lying on the ground under the rail bridge on Falcon road. There was nothing for it; she would have to get up.

It took a moment to steady herself, she reached out to the wall and looked down at her knee, a gaping hole in her trousers showed a bloody graze. Ahead was a car twisted sideways and folded against the corner of the bridge wall. There was debris all over the road and pavement. More shouting and people staring at her out on the street, but nobody approached, they kept looking up with stricken faces. Up towards the top of the bridge. A man with tattoos on his arms seemed to be beckoning her out. Halima made sure she had her handbag and keys. Around her feet were apples and potatoes that had spilled from her bags. She could even see the same ant was investigating one of the broken packets of biscuits. Ahead of her were more cars, people everywhere, many stood talking on mobile phones, others crying and hugging each other. Some were staring at her, perhaps they'd noticed her knee. It was only a graze though. Halima walked forwards stepping out from under the bridge where it was a shade of grey lighter. As she did so, a woman screamed and cut it short by a hand wrapped to her mouth. That was when the pain hit. A bolt of lightning was Halima's last thought, a bolt that struck her squarely on the top of her head.

'A bolt of lightning?' Veronica said.

'Well no, I mean.' Halima paused re-assessing where she was, here in the communal gardens where Mrs Pease lived. Now it was Veronica's turn to give her arm a reassuring squeeze.

'It felt like a bolt of lightning, that's what I meant.'

'Oh goodness. How frightening. Were you hurt?'

Later, Halima didn't know how much later, just that she had left the tunnel and was moving towards the light. This time she was warm and comfortable, she lay on something soft and there was definitely a bright light. Trouble was she could hear people walking around and a couple of beeps. And there was a terrible throbbing sensation from the top of her head. Halima opened her eyes into the glare of the fluorescent light above her. She touched her head where there was some sort of dressing stuck to her scalp and ouch, it was tender. She pulled her hand back under the blanket and looked about.

There were several beds, one with curtains all around. A nurse walked past carrying a small tray and smiled but she didn't stop. Halima wondered which hospital she was in. The Chelsea and Westminster or St George's. Not that it mattered much, either way, this certainly wasn't heaven. Halima lifted the blanket to get a look at her knee which had crusted over. She was wearing a hospital gown and she wondered what they'd done with her torn trousers. They weren't cheap those, she'd splashed out on a pair from M&S only a couple of weeks ago. She hoped they hadn't thrown them away, it might be possible to patch them.

Another nurse walked past and Halima called out, 'Excuse me.'

'Someone will be with you soon,' the nurse nodded and disappeared behind the curtain. There was more coming and going, a doctor appeared and then went again, but nobody stopped to see Halima. She was beginning to feel thirsty and she needed to pee. The next nurse that came past didn't even acknowledge her, let alone answer her question. Eventually Halima decided to get up and go and find the loo for herself. But no sooner was she on her feet than a nurse stopped and took notice.

'You can't get out of bed.' She came and pushed Halima back down, lifted her legs up and swung them under the blanket. 'That's a good girl.'

'But I need to go to the loo,' Halima protested.

'I'll get someone to come, just hold on, we're very busy.' The nurse tucked the blanket in and hurried off.

Halima waited. She'd wet the bed at this rate, and then it wouldn't be half as comfortable. Besides, the pain in her bladder was making the pain in her head worse.

'What a terrible time for you. I bet your mother was worried sick.'
Veronica had balled up the tissue in her hand.

'I had stitches on the top of my head, five of them. And they kept me in overnight.'

'Ah.' Veronica nodded gently. 'So that's why you rub your head.'

'Do I?'

'It's OK.'

Halima put her hands together in her lap. Yes it was OK sitting here in this beautiful garden next to her friend Veronica, sharing that awful time. Her scar had stopped itching. Perhaps one of these days she'd be able to tell Veronica why she'd had to leave Birmingham in the middle of the night.

*

'Where the hell have you been? I thought you were only going round for tea with that new friend of yours.'

Halima took off her shoes and hung her coat.

'You've been gone for hours, what about my tea? It's alright for you, but I don't eat much these days and if it's not regular, it messes up my system.'

Halima closed her eyes for a second. When she opened them, her mother was staring at her in the hallway. The prayer beads hanging from her fingers.

'What you wearing that for?'

Halima put a hand to her yellow scarf.

'Have you been meeting a man? I bet that's what it is. Sneaking off and shaming yourself. When are you going to learn? No good will come of it, catch yourself AIDS and a baby to boot. Then what'll you do eh?'

'Mum, I've been through the menopause.'

'Makes no difference these days, I watch the news, women having babies in their sixties, it's disgusting. Besides, what am I going to do if you go off with some good-for-nothing? You'll leave me all alone, move away to Brighton or something.'

Halima sighed. 'I've never even been to Brighton.'

Her mother's lips stretched into a thin purple line. 'Men are no good. You should know that!' She turned and stormed back into the lounge.

Halima's shoulders sagged as she went into the kitchen. Why could she never be forgiven? Must she really be punished for the rest of her life? She opened a cupboard and pulled out a tin of vegetable soup. The tears had started again. Back then her mother had saved her life. Given up everything to protect Halima. Perhaps she did deserve the punishment. After all, the reason her father was no longer with them was all her fault. The reason they'd had to move away from Birmingham was because of Halima. The reason her mother had to stop all contact with family and friends was because of her. Halima wondered if her life had been worth saving. What if they'd stayed? She supposed she would probably be dead, maybe her mother and father would have had another child. One that didn't disgrace the family, one that wouldn't fall in love with the wrong boy. If only she could have been that model child, her whole life would have been different. What if her mother hadn't suffered seven miscarriages before Halima came along? Would it have made a difference? Perhaps her mother wouldn't have been willing to give up everything if there had been siblings. Halima wiped the back of her hand across her eyes and opened the can, tipping the gloopy contents into the saucepan.

Suddenly the cat appeared on the other side of the glass; he had jumped onto the sill and stood rubbing himself against the edge of the window frame. Halima was about to bang on the window but the cat stared at her as if it could see the tears on her cheeks and then it made the faintest mournful whine and she suddenly realised they were not enemies, but two wretched souls together. She opened the door and the cat came in to wrap himself around her legs. Its tail hooked over at the top and slid against her calf. Finally Halima leaned down and stroked his arched back. His fur was soft and warm, it felt good. Perhaps having a life was better than none at all. Here was this soft warm animal purring against her skin and maybe he was full of fleas and would suffocate them in their sleep but right now that didn't matter. The grey cat trotted out the back door and Halima stood up straight and followed it. He strolled over to the fence, leapt up, turned to give her one last mournful look and disappeared.

Standing by the back door she looked across to see how her flowers were coming on. The green shoots had been so vibrant and new a few days ago. But there was something wrong. Halima slipped on her shoes and went out across the grass to the patch of mud. Some shoots had been pulled up, the delicate roots lying exposed on the soft earth. Others appeared to have been chewed. Halima crouched down running her hand over the damage.

'Halima! This soup is boiling over.'

21

Ralph - Trying to stay on track

'Again?' Shelly was pulling laundry out of the washing machine.

'What do you mean? You know I like to go a couple of times a week.' Ralph stood in the doorway with his gym bag.

'That's all very well, but this is the fourth time.'

'So? It keeps me healthy and helps me wind down.'

Shelly stood up and put her hands on her hips. 'You've been wound up for a while, something going on at work?'

'Nope,' Ralph searched for an excuse, 'just busy.' He left before she could say anything else.

At the gym Ralph worked himself hard, doing almost double his normal number of reps. Hopefully he'd be exhausted by the time he got home and then he'd be able to sleep. He was desperate for a good night's rest without those awful images keeping him awake and then invading his dreams.

Ralph pulled down the heavy weight, the lats in his back shuddering with the effort. He did eleven and tried to do another one, his arms and shoulders straining hard as if his body was freezing up. Ralph let the weight go and shook his head. He spotted Austin jogging on the running machine, earphones in and striding those skinny legs of his. As Ralph rubbed his shoulders, Austin slowed down and reverted to a walking pace. Perhaps he should go and say hi, anything was worth trying for a distraction from being inside his own head at the moment.

'How's it going?'

'Oh, hi.' Austin pulled out one of his earphones and stepped off the treadmill. 'Looks like you've been working hard.'

'Yeah.' Ralph used his towel to remove the sweat from his face.

'You were looking very relaxed on there.' Ralph wished he felt like smiling too.

'Did I?' Austin laughed. 'Yeah, actually I've been feeling pretty good lately.' He looked about him; the nearest two people were both engrossed in the video on the wall despite the loud thumping music.

'I've met someone, nothing serious yet.' Austin continued, shifting his feet. 'We met at a work thing.'

'Sweet.' Ralph attempted a smile. Poor bastard, he deserved a bit of luck.

'Do you think it's too soon?' Austin looked worried.

'Too soon?' It had been well over two years, of course, the same date as the boy on the track. The date on his award. Two years, ten months and three days. He looked at Austin's face, his bright eyes and flushed cheeks. Ralph remembered that day in the gym when Austin had collapsed, simply crumpled on the running machine. It had been the first time they'd really spoken. A delayed reaction to the shock and pain of losing his partner. Ralph thought about Austin's ashen face, the dark rings and the hopeless sobbing. He wondered if the woman on the sequinned bed had reacted to her son's death the same way. Collapsed from the emotional agony. Why did Austin appear to have recovered yet that woman...?

'Do you think I'm on the rebound?' Austin frowned. 'It's too soon isn't it?'

'No, no. It's good. You look great so you must be doing something right.'

'Really?'

Ralph remembered how broken Austin had been. His frail

body rolling off the end of the treadmill overcome with grief.

'Go for it.' Ralph gripped his pale arms. 'You deserve to be happy.'

'OK.'

Ralph let go. He wished that after two years, ten months and three days, that he could put the crash behind him and move on.

'Have you had a good weekend?'

Ralph shook his head. 'Work gets in the way sometimes.'

'Oh of course, you do shifts.'

'Yep, comes with the job.' Ralph glanced across at the leg press. The last thing he wanted was to talk shop, but Austin was still grinning at him.

'You must enjoy it.'

Ralph shrugged. 'It's a good job.' At least it always had been, but Ralph was beginning to doubt his calling. Not just that, he doubted his ability, his professionalism. Ralph rubbed at the twitch in his eyebrow.

'My work's much more boring. IT stuff for Thyredata Enterprises.'

Ralph had never heard of it.

'It's a big place on the Battersea Bridge Road.'

'I've probably driven past it a zillion times in the ambulance.'

'Yeah, you must know London really well.'

'Some of it, but I'm always discovering new places.' And new people he thought, like the boy's mother, now deceased. Ralph clenched his hand, he needed to work his body harder. Get rid of this stupid anxiety. 'I'm going to do some more reps. Good luck with your new guy.'

'Thanks.'

Ralph went over to the leg press, set the weight and sat down. He pushed hard with his legs, thrusting the annoying thoughts away. But they came none the less, flapping around like so many bats. The weight became heavier and clanged so he slowed down. He bit hard on his lip trying to concentrate on good technique instead of watching the images in his head.

Dead.

Dead. All dead.

His leg muscles burned. It was no good; he'd had enough. His body was tired, but he certainly wasn't any more relaxed than he had been when he left Shelly by the washing machine.

This was worse, now he had another body to think about. Austin's partner, lined up with the others. It was like a list of death row inmates, only the ones that have already received their penalty. But he'd tried hadn't he? Did he make a mistake? He couldn't remember if he had or hadn't. Did he even know who Austin's partner was? Doubt crept in editing his memories, making them fuzzy. But death was part of the job. Always had been, they were advised how to deal with it, accept that they couldn't be god. But still those blue eyes accused him from the track. Piercing right into Ralph's heart. He felt numb and realised he was staring intently at the large rubber foot pad of the leg press. He picked up his towel and headed off to the changing rooms. Austin gave him a cheerful wave as he passed.

*

'Did you go to a pub?' Shelly asked as Ralph curled into the bed.

'No.'

'You smell of beer.'

'I bought a can to wash down some chips on the way back.' He touched her smooth shoulder just visible above the edge of the duvet.

'You've been drinking a lot lately.'

'No I haven't, it was only a can of beer, that's hardly an issue.' Ralph felt her sigh under his hand. He kissed her neck gently.

'I'm tired.'

'Mmmm.' Ralph's mind was still busy and although his body was tired, he thought perhaps if they made love, it would help him to sleep. Besides her body felt so warm and soft after the hard mechanical machines in the gym. He kissed a gentle line up the edge of her neck, his hand sliding down her shoulder onto her left breast.

'Ralph.'

'Yes.'

She turned her head to face him. They kissed.

'I really am tired.'

'Me too.' He kissed her again, wrapping both arms around her.

'You smell like a brewery.'

'Mmm romantic.'

Shelly pulled her head back. 'No it's not, Ralph. Coming home and having dinner with me is romantic.'

Ralph stopped and got up on one elbow. 'We hadn't agreed to go out had we?'

'No. I just meant if you didn't spend so much time out of the house I might see you a bit more.'

Ralph relaxed again and continued to slide his hand across her nipple. 'Well, I'm here now.'

'Oh Ralph.'

And for a while, Ralph luxuriated in their bodies sliding together, the rhythm, the comforting smell of her, the sense that they were both very much alive. Her pliant flesh yielding to his desire. But once she'd turned away and the light was off, he was left staring into the dark.

His mind resisted all attempts at other thoughts, like it was attached to strong elastic pulling him back again and again to the movie by the tracks. The boy's eyes imploring, begging him. His leg twisted horribly. There had been a bird that stopped briefly down onto the ground near the boy's head, plucked something from between the stones and disappeared. Saving whatever had been there from the growing leak of life spreading over those stones.

Ralph turned over again and Shelly moaned slightly. He opened his eyes and stared at the shaft of streetlight that came from the window where the curtains didn't quite meet. Perhaps he should use the counselling service at work. He had used it briefly after the train crash but not needed it since. He had carefully locked away the part of that day that was so haunting. But it was as if the door had been broken open and the images spilled out like so many photographs from an over-stuffed album.

22

Adam – Moving back

Adam sat up and stretched, the alarm hadn't gone off yet, the light still dim. He checked his watch; only a few minutes to go. Funny how quickly his body had adjusted to the prayer timetable. He lay back down and switched on the bedside lamp. It lit the pale cream walls and the picture of flowers opposite. Adam smiled to himself and crossed his hands behind his head. Only the faintest sounds of London penetrated the extension at the back of Faizal's house. He'd even got used to the frilly duvet. Besides, only Faizal and his father knew he slept in a pink bed.

These last few weeks had been great. The freedom to do as he pleased without anyone telling him otherwise. The quiet of the house once Faizal had left for college and his father for work. The mosque was only around the corner and Adam was actually enjoying the new routine the prayers provided. Each day seemed brighter than the last, of course the fact that it was finally spring helped. But there was something more than that; maybe Allah was answering his prayers. It was as if his life was building up again, building for something amazing. He just wasn't sure what yet.

After prayers, while Faizal and his dad rolled up their mats, Adam put the kettle on and took out a pan for the boiled eggs. Faizal put some plates on the table and made them mugs of tea. How easily they had blended together in this new household. There were no questions about what Adam was going to do with his life. No complaints about how often he went to the mosque or the meetings. Here was only kindness and respect. A common worship of Islam and a sharing of their meals together. They were like three male friends sharing a house in harmony. Three men going about their lives.

Adam placed the boiled eggs on the table and caught Faizal and his father glaring at each other. Faizal averted his eyes immediately and grabbed a spoon. Nobody said a word and suddenly Adam realised there was an unspoken argument hanging in the air between father and son. It seemed at such odds with their normal morning routine that Adam had to ask.

'Is everything all right?'

'Perfectly fine. Thanks for the eggs Adam,' Faizal's father said.

Adam looked at Faizal but he was avoiding eye contact.

'I don't think it's fair,' Faizal suddenly said, his voice a whine.

'There isn't a choice,' said Faizal's father.

Adam brought the toast to the table where Faizal was staring at his plate. Adam put the toast down, he moved slowly as if someone had attached a huge weight to his chair.

'You know what your mother's like.'

'Yes,' Faizal sighed.

Adam paused as he was about to press down the lever on the toaster again. He was worried that the argument was about to ignite. Instead there was a grunt. Adam gathered some knives and the last pieces of toast and pushed his wheelchair up to the table to join them.

Faizal's father was studying him. Adam offered him the boiled eggs, hoping to deflect the scrutiny.

'You do know this is women's work?'

'Yes sir,' Adam swallowed. He thought back to that first morning when they'd eaten Cheerios, finishing the packet from the night before. Adam had asked if there was anything else. Faizal's father had laughed and said he'd have to make it himself if he wanted anything different.

By the evening of that first day, Adam had made a delicious beef curry with rice for when Faizal and his father got home. Just as a thank you and to delay the time at which he would have to go home himself. At first Faizal's dad had been annoyed to see Adam still there, but once he saw the food and begun tucking in, it was a different story. When they'd finished he'd said it would be fine if Adam stayed for a while. Since then, Adam had made virtually all the meals, much to Faizal and his father's delight. They had been only too pleased to have him do the 'women's work' up till now.

Adam spread butter slowly across his toast waiting to see what would come next.

'Javeria and Laila will be returning on Tuesday.'

'Oh, I see.' Adam looked between Faizal and his father. Neither of them looked at him. The women of the household would be back. There would no longer be a vacancy in the kitchen. They didn't want him there any more, that was clear. Adam gazed at the doorway leading into the extension.

'Is your Nan coming?'

Faizal and his father exchanged a look, and Adam felt the air frizzle with unsaid words.

'I'll-' Adam coughed, 'I'll make other arrangements.'

The older man grunted.

Faizal gave Adam a sheepish look and shrugged.

After Faizal and his father had left for the day, Adam tidied up and then mulled over his position. It had been a relief to be away from home, not having to face his father and his constant requirements to better himself. It had been good to avoid Sully too, not having to compare himself to the first son or have Sully's achievements thrust into his face all the time.

Of course, he'd known his stay here could only be temporary. Stupid that he hadn't even asked how long the rest of Faizal's family were staying in Pakistan. Adam admitted to himself that he'd deliberately avoided such questions. Absorbed by his prayers and educating himself on what was happening to his brothers in Syria and Iraq, Adam had begun to feel that he belonged here with Faizal and his father and especially within the new Muslim family he'd found.

But now it was clear the honeymoon was over.

Adam gazed around the tidy kitchen. The smell of toast still hung in the air. He supposed that Faizal's mother wouldn't take kindly to him being around the house most of the day and he doubted she'd want him in the kitchen. What was he supposed to do now?

23

Ralph – Keeping it together

'Hey Dad.'

'Hi Cameron, where's your brother?' They were standing by the school gates.

'There.' Cameron pointed to a group of youths lazily kicking a ball towards them. Taking their time, discussing who knew what.

'Hi Mr C.' Natalie's son gave him a nod.

'Hey Troy.'

Liam ignored Ralph, continuing to chat to the other two boys as they moved out of the gates towards the waiting cars.

'Liam,' Ralph said. The boys kept moving.

'Liam.' He spoke more sharply, 'LIAM.'

Liam glanced over his shoulder and rolled his eyes, then nudged his friend and kept walking.

'Bloody kid.'

Cameron looked up at Ralph. 'You swore Dad.'

'I know I bloody well swore, shut up and let's get in the car.' He led him to their vehicle which was parked on the double yellows.

Cameron scowled. 'It's not me who's been rude.'

'Fine, all right, I'm sorry, just get in the car will you?'

The two of them sat in the car for a minute and then the passenger door opened and Liam slid in.

Ralph was finding it difficult to keep his cool. 'What was that about?'

'What?' Liam shrugged, pulling on his seatbelt.

'The least you can do, is acknowledge me and not plain ignore me, you ignorant-'

'Daddy swore.' Cameron bleated from the back.

Ralph spun around. 'And you can shut up.'

They drove home in silence, and Ralph wondered what had happened to his great intentions of picking up the boys and going to the park together to have a kickabout. Was his son turning into one of those uncommunicative hoodies that hung out by the off-licence or was Ralph just over-reacting?

At home Ralph asked them if they wanted to watch the rugby match he'd recorded but they both said no and disappeared up to their rooms. Ralph sighed, decided to get himself a beer and watch it on his own. He was on his third can and the match was just finishing when Shelly got home.

'Have you been drinking all afternoon?'

'No. Just a couple to watch the match with.'

'Is tea ready?'

Ralph looked across at the clock, damn, it was almost six thirty already. 'I'll get it in just a tick, it's the last few minutes.'

'Fine.' The door shut.

Ralph gripped the edge of his chair, they had to make the final run, come on. He watched the ball hurtle and then number four had it and was belting across the pitch.

'Yes, come on.'

Number four made a run for it, side-stepped a tackle and headed for the line. Of course Ralph had already seen the outcome in the papers, but the anticipation of what was going to happen next was not dampened.

'YES!'

In the kitchen, Shelly was chopping broccoli.

'I said, I'd do it in a minute.' Ralph noted there were potatoes boiling on the hob and the oven was on.

'Well I'm hungry, and it looks like the boys have already raided the bread bin.'

'Have they?'

'Do you even know if they're in the house?'

'Of course I do, why have you got the hump?' First his rude son, and now his wife giving him a hard time just because he was slightly late getting dinner.

'I have not got the hump. I just think that it's about time we all ate something.'

'Well so do I, there's no need to get ratty about it.' Ralph laid the table, then he went upstairs to see what the boys were doing.

Liam's bedroom door was slightly open, and Ralph peered round not wishing to intrude or aggravate him further. The two boys were sitting at Liam's desk giggling at something on the computer.

'Found a good comedy boys?'

Liam slammed the lid shut. 'No. Nothing. Just, well just some private stuff.'

'What kind of private stuff?'

'Is dinner ready?' Cameron slid past him and ran downstairs.

'Liam, I think you should show me what you were doing.' He was keeping calm, he had this under control.

'Why?'

'Because, because I'm your father.'

'And?'

'There is no And. That's it, you're in my house, I want to know what you're doing.' This had gone far enough.

'I don't have to tell you everything, you're not MI5. Besides, it's *my* house too.'

'You don't pay the bills.'

'Fine, so take me out of school and send me to work.'

'That's not the point.' Ralph clenched his hands into fists.

'Then what is the point?'

Ralph lunged forwards to grab the laptop, but Liam was too quick, he threw his body in the way, grabbed it himself, spun away and jumped on the bed with the laptop underneath him.

'Liam. Hand it over.'

'No.'

Ralph tried to grab Liam to roll him over, but Ralph's foot slid on a text book lying on the floor and he tumbled partly onto the bed and partly onto the rug. His knee hit something sharp and Ralph automatically rolled away hugging it to his chest. Liam looked over the side of the bed at his dad.

'Give me the fucking laptop,' shouted Ralph as he lay on his back.

'What's going on?' Shelly stood in the doorway.

'Nothing.' Liam sat up still hugging his laptop. Ralph went to grab his sleeve, but Liam was already on his feet and slipping out the door past Shelly.

'What are you doing swearing at your son from the floor?' Shelly glared at him then raised her hand. 'Nope, don't even bother. You've been drinking.'

'Shelly, I'm not-' but she too had left the room. Ralph climbed onto the bed and rubbed his knee where he discovered the offensive weapon had been a small piece of lego on the floor. That twitch had started up again above his eye.

24

Halima – New life

There were definitely buds. Halima was peering at the mud patch crouching down on her haunches. Of the shoots that had survived, two had small oval buds at the top. It was working, she would get her spring flowers after all. She hadn't cleared the whole garden, perhaps half, well almost half. It was enough, enough to see if her experiment could work. Halima congratulated herself and shivered, she should have put on her coat, it was still cold out.

Sitting on the step expectantly was Smokey. He didn't have a collar, and she had no idea what his real name was, but it seemed to fit. This time he wandered in the kitchen like he knew the place, and Halima followed him. It had become a ritual, when she got home from work and after the tea was made. Some digging or weeding in the garden and then some milk for the cat. Mum didn't know of course, was too busy chanting her prayers at this time and so far Smokey hadn't ventured further into the house. Despite her concern about fleas, there hadn't been any sign, no tell-tale red bumps on her legs and no little black things jumping out of the carpet.

Smokey rubbed against her calf muscle and purred. She placed the bowl of milk down and stood watching his little pink tongue lapping it up. He was rather sweet really.

'Halima?'

She looked across at the lounge door which stood ajar.

'What?'

'Can I have another cuppa luv?' Mum called out, 'I'm a bit thirsty today.' Halima made one and took it through, the cups of tea consumed in this house were endless. She supposed it was better for them than coffee which they never drank.

'Thanks. Why don't you sit with me a while, we could chat.'

'About what?' Halima had noticed Mum was often a bit strange on Mondays. Of course she knew it was to do with Veronica's student who came while Halima was at work. But it seemed to leave her mother in a contemplative mood, and she often wanted to talk afterwards. Today she'd had her nails done. They were like a child's who'd played with her mother's things, the bright pink contrasting starkly with the dingy room and her mother's grey clothes.

'Do you remember when I used to take you to the fireworks at Ward End park?'

'Yes.' Halima picked at a hard lump on the side of the sofa.

'They were good shows, sticky toffee apples, and a huge fire, remember that year when Tommy Burns set it off too early? We all went running over at four in the afternoon.' Her mother was facing towards her but her eyes were focused on the past.

Halima nodded mutely, she didn't remember.

'Beautiful fireworks they were, lighting up the sky, you screamed you did, the first time me and your dad took you. Thought we were being attacked. You were so funny.'

Halima scowled, she didn't think it was particularly nice to laugh at a frightened child, even if she couldn't remember the event.

'So Dad came?'

'Once or twice. He had you on his shoulders so you could see the what-do-you-call-it on top of the bonfire.'

'Guy Fawkes.'

'No, I mean the dummy thing on the top.'

Halima sighed. She hadn't been to bonfire night in many years, not much point really, they could see various fireworks out of the lounge or kitchen window during the end of October and into November. The neighbourhood yobs let them off. She didn't much fancy standing out in the cold staring at the sky with a crowd of strangers.

'Your nails look nice Mum.'

Her mother looked at Halima as if realising she was in the room, then down at her shining nails. 'She's done a good job that girl.' She looked back at Halima and at Halima's hands, then at her clothes then back to her own nails. She didn't say anything. Halima felt self-conscious in her old black jumper with the hole by the hem and the slacks she used for gardening. Her hands were darker than usual where the mud had collected in the creases and under her nails. She could still smell the damp earth as it clung to her.

'I used to paint them.' Her mother's voice was faint. 'No point since you messed everything up. Even that nice man from the station hasn't been round.'

'No.' Halima sighed.

'All my pretty things left behind.' Mum's eyes sunk deeper into her lined face as she stared at Halima.

'We still have a few bits of crockery.' Halima could see her mother's good mood dissipating and wanted to hang on to it for a little longer.

'Ha. There's hardly anything and you broke one of them bowls the other day. Wouldn't be surprised if we have nothing soon with you hurling them at your old mother. They don't even make them any more.'

Halima was about to apologise but instead she pressed her lips together. She always apologised, always felt guilty. But today she wanted it to be different. Halima stood up.

'Nothing to say? I gave up everything for you, don't you dare be ungrateful. If I'd had a fraction of your opportunities and freedom-"

Halima left the room, ignoring the words that continued to spill forth, showering the air with blame.

Upstairs Halima rooted around her bedside drawer and pulled out one of the leaflets that Veronica had given her. She thumbed through it for the thousandth time. She hadn't dare do anything about contacting the home, or registering, but she wanted to. Veronica's mum was in one, not just for a holiday either, it was a permanent place, and Veronica didn't seem guilty about it. Halima scratched at her scar while looking at the picture of a smiling old lady being wheeled into a pretty garden by a nurse.

25

Adam - New track

Adam unlocked the front door. At least his dad was at work. The house seemed quiet and he breathed in the smell of home. But then he heard the chink of a cup on a saucer. Suddenly his mother appeared in the lounge doorway.

'Adam!' She clutched her scarf to her mouth.

Behind her two other faces appeared pushing each other to get a view.

'The return of the prodigal son.' It was Auntie Sana.

'There, told you he'd be back,' echoed Auntie Farida, one of his mother's friends.

Adam clenched his teeth.

'You've brought your bags,' his mother said tentatively as if she didn't quite believe it.

Adam sighed.

'Bring him in here,' another woman's voice commanded from inside the lounge.

Adam flinched, this was the last thing he wanted, to be interrogated by his mother's interfering friends and relatives.

'Well he looks all right.'

'I like the new beard, our Jamal grew one last month. Makes him look much older.'

'Let me see him,' came the insistent voice.

The ladies moved back. Adam wanted to push his wheelchair

166

straight past and on to his bedroom but his mother motioned for him to go in, nodding her head vigorously. It was old Mrs Ghaffari sat in a chair with a teacup in her hand.

'Is he still not out of that chair yet?' She frowned at him.

'It doesn't work like that, Mrs Ghaffari.'

'More prayer in this household is what you need Nadiyah,' she continued, 'Whatever you did to deserve a son like that, well, it's going to take some devotion to set things right again. And you -' she pointed her gnarled finger at Adam- 'get yourself a purpose, pray hard to Allah and he'll show you the way.'

'I think we should be going,' Aunt Sana said, attempting to remove the teacup from Mrs Ghaffari's hand.

'I haven't finished,' she shrieked.

'We'll get out of your way,' agreed Aunt Farida.

Adam backed his chair out of the room, the humiliation scorching his cheeks. The large kit bag that he'd slung across his back caught on the door frame and scraped loudly against the wall. He ignored it and continued straight to his bedroom where he slammed the door shut. Why was it they all treated him like some naughty little child? When would they recognise that he was a man? Sully didn't get this kind of treatment, they would never speak to him that way. Here was another reason why he needed to leave home.

A few moments later his mother walked past, the sound of the tray of cups tinkling through the wall. He heard her in the kitchen and then she knocked quietly on his door.

'Would you like some tea?'

Adam sighed.

'Adam?'

'Yes. I'll be out in a minute.' Adam took off his light jacket and slung it on the back of the chair by his desk. He ran a hand over his face and down the soft curls of his goatee. Turning his chair towards the door, he pulled it open and went to see his mother in the kitchen.

The guests had left and his mother came straight over to him and held his face in her two soft hands.

'Oh, Adam.'

Adam's anger slipped away and a great sadness welled up. He shook her hands off.

'I'm fine.'

'Are you hungry?'

'No.'

'Are you...' She paused and looked away from his gaze, instead fussing with the cups in the sink.

'I don't know,' Adam replied. It was true he didn't know if he was going to stay, but there didn't seem to be any other options. Where else could he go?

'Oh yes, some letters came for you.' She wiped her hands on a tea towel and reached into a top cupboard, pulling out the envelopes.

Adam could see one was his benefits letter, hopefully continuing his payments. The other two looked official, one a white envelope with a window showing his typed name and address, the other cream and expensive with a typed address on the envelope. He opened this one first. It was an invitation to the memorial and re-opening of platform nine. Adam threw it on the table in disgust and tore open the white one.

'I've got an interview,' he said out loud.

'Oh my goodness. Your father will be so happy.'

Adam read the letter more fully. Unbelievable, that stupid apprenticeship with Transport Rail. He tossed that letter onto the kitchen table too.

'I'm not going.'

'But why ever not? This is good news surely? Your father will be so proud, an interview.'

'For an apprenticeship?'

His mother picked up the letter and read it. 'Oh my goodness, it's today.'

'What?' Adam snatched it back. He read the date and then checked his watch, damn she was right, at two fifteen that afternoon. It was already midday.

'It doesn't matter, I'm not going.' Adam began to spin his wheelchair around.

'But Transport Rail is a big company. A good British company.

168

You could end up with a proper job.'

Adam shook his head. 'You don't really think I'd want to work in a rail company with this.' He pointed at his useless legs. 'Mind you, according to Mrs Ghaffari, it's your fault for not praying and nothing to do with the train crash.'

His mother pulled her scarf up close to her face again but Adam could already see her eyes beginning to water. He snatched the letter and went to his room. He wanted to rip it up, it was just all too hideously ironic that the only response he'd received was from a flipping rail company. Why was life just one kick in the teeth after another?

There was a gentle tap on his door.

'What?'

His mother's voice wavered uncertainly through the shut door, 'I just wondered, that maybe, um. If you don't go, won't the benefits people find out? They might stop your allowance.'

*

'Hi, I'm Stephanie from HR and you must be Adam Rasheed.' A tall woman in a smart jacket leant over to shake hands. She emanated efficiency and perfume.

Adam straightened up his body and grasped her hand. The fingers were long and soft but she gripped his firmly before releasing and then pointed down the hallway.

'We're in a room down here.' She checked her watch. 'Dave should be with us any moment.'

Stephanie led the way past three offices and then opened the door into a small meeting room. The smart but simple décor impressed Adam. These offices were new, a whole different environment to his old school. It seemed to be filled with smiling professional people in smart clothes. She moved a chair out of the way so he could roll up to the table.

A man had appeared in the doorway, tall with short cropped hair.

'Ah here you are, I thought we were in room two.'

'I did send you an email,' said Stephanie.

Ignoring her rebuke, the man came in and leaned down over Adam.

'Hi, I'm Dave Calder.'

Adam shook the proffered hand, it was large and warm. In fact his whole body was large and muscular in an open blue shirt. As he turned to take his place on the other side of the table, Adam noticed the taut pale chinos; he should have bought a bigger pair. Stephanie was already sitting down, her papers in a neat pile on the table.

'Shall we begin?'

'Sure.' Dave relaxed back into a chair with a closed paper folder in front of him. Adam felt a little uncomfortable under his gaze as if he were being assessed even before the interview had started.

'So, we have your CV here and I just wanted to ask you about your GCSEs.'

This would be the bit where he had to explain why there were so few, that the accident had interrupted his schooling. Adam sat up a little straighter and took a deep breath. He began, faltering a little to start but then finding that the words came out smoothly and for the first time he was able to tell his story without the emotion. Rather than mention the rail crash, he decided to keep it simple and just state that he was involved in an accident. That way, it seemed less personal, more abstract. Dave and Stephanie responded to him not like his parents or doctors. They were interested but not trying to heap on sympathy, or worse, remonstrating him for not achieving more. It was a refreshing change to be treated like an adult.

'That's quite something to overcome in such a short time,' said David. 'Tell me more about your position on the football team.'

Adam relaxed some more and told them about his club, where he'd been picked at only ten and was one of their youngest players. How he'd become their best striker and that he'd been playing in the under eighteens before the accident happened. That on that very day, a talent scout had invited him to a trial. Adam could feel the enormity of that loss welling up, so he hurried on and told them about his playing wheelchair basketball.

170

'What skills do you think you learned playing sport that could be transferred into the workplace?'

Adam paused for a moment. 'Well, sport teaches you discipline, you have to think quickly and make split-second decisions.' He thought about what the national coach had said to him, he'd burned with indignation at his failure to make the basketball team, but those words of advice came back to him.

'You need to work as a team, otherwise you won't win, you can't do it all alone and I think that's how it is at work too. I mean there may be some bits you can do on your own, but you have to work with other people, and get on together.'

Stephanie smiled and so did Dave. Adam was beginning to enjoy himself. For the first time in a long while he was being treated like a grown-up. These older people were listening and interested in what he had to say. It was a stark contrast to the gaggle of women that had greeted him at home earlier.

Adam had been talking for some time. He wanted to put his finger under the collar of his shirt to unstick it from his neck. It was one of Sully's that his mother had fetched for him.

'Adam, do you have any questions for us?'

'Um,' Adam tried to think quickly. They'd covered so much already including questions about simple maths, Excel spreadsheets, his school. Adam suddenly realised that he'd been performing rather well, what if they actually gave him the job? Would that be so bad? But then this was Transport Rail, could he really work for a train company after what had happened to his legs? A sudden moment of panic hit Adam and he wished he was back at school, back at home where his mother cooked and washed and did those things for him. Where he didn't have to worry about the big stuff. He wasn't ready for this yet. He thought about Faizal's father sitting at the breakfast table. Then a thought struck Adam; there was an easy way to get out of this. Faizal's father had told him that even at work he didn't miss his namaz five times a day. But he worked for a Muslim manager. No regular employer would allow that surely?

'Do you have a prayer room?'

'A prayer room?' Dave Calder frowned.

'I know what you mean,' Stephanie put up her hand to prevent Dave from saying any more. 'Actually we have a gentleman here who works in the post room. It's a private room so he uses that. It's in the basement and I'm sure he wouldn't mind if you joined him. Or,' she faltered as if not sure of herself, 'at least I assume you pray at the same times?'

'Is he a Muslim?'

Stephanie nodded.

Adam squeezed his hands together, well that hadn't gone the way he hoped. They were looking at him expectantly.

'Well as he's a Muslim, I'm sure we'll work something out. That's fine.' Adam shrugged. What an idiot he was. So much for trying to pull the religious card. He'd expected them to say no, an easy get out. They'd already covered the whole disabled thing; they had two lifts, ramps, toilets, the works.

Adam wondered if it would be so bad if he ended up here. It would get his dad off his back at least. Dave Calder would be his boss and he seemed OK. Adam would be working for him for the first few months before they moved him to a different department. The idea was for him to do admin work in three different departments over a period of twelve months. Perhaps he shouldn't worry. At least it would get him out of the house.

'Anything else?' Stephanie queried.

'Err.' He couldn't leave after that dumb question about being able to pray. He thought about what his mum had said. 'Would there be an opportunity for promotion after the twelve months or having a permanent job?'

Dave laughed warmly. 'Well he's got ambition, I'll give him that,' he nodded at Stephanie.

'You would have to get through the apprenticeship first,' she explained.

'It's a big company Adam, there are always opportunities.' He shrugged. 'For example, I've only been in the Communications and Data department for a little over six months. I was in IT before that.'

'Yes, but we can't promise anything,' Stephanie said.

Dave turned to Stephanie. 'The thing is, Adam's in a

wheelchair so he's going to need that extra gumption if he's going to get ahead.'

'I don't believe that's true in this company Dave, we promote our employees on merit. Perhaps we should leave it there if Adam doesn't have any other questions.'

'No, seriously,' Dave leaned forwards, 'I bet people look past you and ignore you all the time, don't they?'

Adam was surprised by Dave's bluntness, but it was true, they did. He remembered those first few months being out in public in his wheelchair, how people wouldn't meet his eye, how quickly they glanced away. It seemed safer to ignore him than to interact. Or worse, only speak to his parents as if he wasn't there. He hated it.

'Yes, it is a bit like that.'

'See.' Dave nodded satisfied. 'Good for you for aiming higher. I'm sure you could go a long way here.'

Stephanie gave Dave a stern look. 'I think we'll have to end the meeting there. As I said, we cannot guarantee anything and we have other candidates to see, don't we Dave.'

26

Halima - Rameses strides forth

Halima would never have thought to come to the British Museum on her own but with Veronica as her guide it was a real treat, a break from normality and her grey home and dull life. They were standing in front of an enormous stone gateway, carved into the shape of a mythical beast. At the top, a human head with a kind of turban headdress, lower down the body of a bull and huge wings which sprouted from its back. The entire thing was carved from solid stone, an immense and beautiful structure.

'Pretty impressive, wouldn't you say?'

'Amazing, it's just so huge.' Halima couldn't get over the fact there were two of these and that they'd been made about three thousand years ago.

'Do you remember when we came with school?' Veronica had a hand on Halima's shoulder. It felt nice.

Halima shook her head.

'You liked the Rameses head, I think it's over here, come and see.'

Halima followed Veronica to the other end of the hall where an immense bust of Rameses II looked down on them condescendingly.

They finished the Egyptian and Assyrian rooms and took time over the Acropolis. They even giggled together over the Greek bodies. Such curved and masculine charm captured in time. For a moment Halima was a young school girl again, sniggering over nudity with her best friend.

'Are you tired? Do you want to stop and get a drink?'

'No, I'm good thank you. Veronica, I'm so glad we came.'

'Hey, what are friends for?' With that she slid her arm through Halima's and led her towards the upstairs gallery.

They'd missed lunch and even though Halima was famished she'd declined Veronica's suggestion of eating in the museum café. It would be expensive and Halima was conscious of the amount of time she'd been out.

Veronica collected her coat from security and they left the building together, walking down the grand steps.

'We could probably find a bite to eat near here,' Veronica offered.

'No it's fine, really, I should be getting home, Mum will be worried, and hungry.'

'Oh what a shame, that was such fun.' They linked arms again heading towards the traffic along Great Russell street. 'It's a shame we missed all those years in between.'

'Mmm.' Halima would need to get the tube home, that would be quickest, she hoped she had enough money on her Oyster card.

'You never did say why you left Birmingham.'

They stopped on the pavement and Halima withdrew her arm

and scratched her scar. 'I have to go, sorry.'

'OK, bye then. Give me a call.'

Halima hurried quickly away across the street. She pulled a disintegrating tissue from her pocket, wiped her eyes and tried to re-orientate herself.

27

Adam – Unexpected opportunities

Adam wiped a hand along his top lip, it came away damp. He was pretty sure this was the place. They'd contacted him yesterday by mobile phone, given him a time and an address. After two tube rides, and a faff at the station because one of the lifts wasn't working, he sat outside No. 414. It was a typical tall terraced house in a better part of London. Fortunately for him, the path to the front door had just one step up from the pavement. He licked his lips, his heart was thumping away in his chest and it wasn't from the exercise. He was still amazed that they'd called him. Adam with the useless legs. Adam the failed basketball player. Adam the pathetic apprentice. This could be the start of a new Adam. Shown to him by the all merciful Allah, his true path in life. At last he might get a chance to wage jihad in the name of the United Muslims. He could prove to Aisha that she'd been right to recommend him; a worthy Muslim. Adam imagined those green flecked eyes drawing closer, the silk of her Niqab whispering against her secret lips. Grinning to himself, he tipped up the wheelchair to negotiate the step, then rolled towards the front door.

There was a bell within a brass disc setting off a distant chime. The door opened almost immediately. To his surprise it was the giant. Definitely the right house then. Adam took a deep breath, there was no going back.

'As-Salam-u-Alaikum.'

'wa Alaikum Assalam.' The large man's voice was deep but soft. He tipped his head ever so slightly as he opened the door wider and then made as if to step outside.

'It's fine, I've got this one,' Adam tipped back his chair, manoeuvred closer, the front wheels clearing the step and then he leaned forwards and pushed hard to get himself over.

The hallway was wooden with elegant rugs and a carved side table with a vase of flowers. He waited while the giant shut the door and then he walked ahead of Adam to another door at the end. He opened it and using his other hand gestured inside. Adam nodded and entered a smallish room with four chairs. Two of them were already occupied. There was a man of about thirty in a suit who looked up suddenly from his mobile phone, gave a curt nod and went back to his business. The other was younger, like himself in a T-shirt and jeans. His eyes flicked towards Adam as he came in and then away again, darting this way and that. The youth shuffled his bottom further into the chair.

'la natahaddath aintazar hna.' The giant barked at nobody and everybody and then shut the door. Adam felt awkward in his chair. He didn't have any idea what the giant had said, but he assumed he should simply wait like these others. Every now and then, Adam caught the youth looking at him but he wouldn't meet Adam's gaze. It was hot in here and there was a cloying smell of old sweat. Adam wanted to remove his hoodie but he felt too conspicuous. Probably best just to sit and wait.

After a few more minutes the man with the phone glanced up and Adam was compelled to say something.

'I'm Adam.'

The businessman frowned at him and shook his head briefly, glanced towards the door and then back to his phone. Adam felt the embarrassment hot in his face. How was he supposed to know what was expected? He wasn't even sure why he was here. What kind of interview was this? Did these men know something he didn't?

The door opened again and the giant reappeared, he gestured with a sharp thrust of his chin at Adam and held the door wide. Adam followed him into another room where there was an antique desk and two chairs, one on either side. The giant removed one of the chairs and motioned for Adam to set himself opposite the desk. After the giant had left, a different door opened and Adam recognised the white-robed Arab who had come to one of the meetings. The one where Ibrahim Muhammad Sharif had spoken to them. The Arab that had let them in with his penetrating stare. He turned it on Adam as he sat down opposite.

'As-Salam-u-Alaikum.'

'wa Alaikum Assalam.' Adam replied grateful that he could at least respond to a simple greeting.

'ldhlk 'ayuha alshshabb. Qul li limadha 'ant huna?'

Adam smiled back, hoping the man was just extending the Arabic greeting.

'limadha jit alyawm?'

Adam could feel the heat radiating off him, he wished he'd taken his sweatshirt off. The man was looking at him intently and it was clear he'd asked a question but Adam had no idea what. He was going to fail at the very first test.

'I'm sorry. I haven't studied Arabic.'

The man leaned back, his face giving nothing away.

'I see.' His eyes narrowed. 'And how long have you been a practising Muslim?'

His English was clear but accented.

Adam wanted to say all his life, that he had been brought up a Muslim, but that wasn't strictly true. His father and Sully tended to go to Friday prayers but they didn't pray all together at home, at least not regularly. He'd only really taken Islam seriously in the last few months. Adam could see that lying was out of the question. Those dark eyes didn't let up for a second.

'A few months.'

Again the man looked surprised.

'I mean properly for several months.'

'Who did you tell about coming here?'

The question shocked Adam, he'd been told not to share the information with anyone, told not even to write down the address but to commit it to memory.

'No one.'

'Your family?'

177

'No.'

'Your friend Faizal?'

'No, no one.' How did he know that he and Faizal were friends? The heat was beginning to make Adam a little sick. He really needed to take his jumper off.

'Why are you a practising Muslim?'

Again Adam was caught off-guard, this wasn't what he'd expected, and yet he hadn't known what to expect. How could he answer that question? Did Adam even understand why he'd become a true Muslim? Was it because Faizal had been kind to him that day? Planted a seed perhaps. Had Allah intervened to show Adam the way? Adam thought about his prayers, about the sense of peace and purpose they gave to his day. He pictured the Imam's back bending forwards and his warm words of 'Allahu Akbar'. How sometimes Adam felt a cleanness, a deep sense of well-being and righteousness when he spoke the words. That it felt as if Allah had come to warm his soul.

The man opposite was waiting for an answer.

'I, I don't know.' Adam swallowed. 'It just feels right.'

The room was incredibly quiet and Adam expected the giant to return and escort him out immediately. But the man wasn't finished yet; he gazed at Adam with renewed interest. There might even be a glimmer of warmth in the turn of those lips. Then he barked an order in Arabic.

Adam knew he'd blown it, he turned his chair towards the door.

'No, not you,' the man said.

The door opened and the giant appeared with a jug of water and a glass. He placed them next to Adam's interviewer and left. The man pushed the jug and glass towards Adam.

'Drink,' he said.

Adam picked up the jug and tipped it, the edge knocking against the glass as his hand trembled. He gulped the cold liquid, grateful for the cooling sensation down his throat and into his stomach.

The man was a little more relaxed; he had folded his hands on the desk.

'Why are you here, Adam?'

These were such strange questions. He thought they would tell him how he could help in Allah's plan. Give him a role in the United Muslims fight against ISIS or their work to promote a united Islam here in the UK. Instead this intense man was making him feel guilty for even coming.

'At the meeting,' he began, 'Ibrahim Muhammad Sharif asked-'

But the man waved the explanation away with his hand, a look of annoyance returning to his face. Wrong answer. Adam licked his lips, he wanted more water but it seemed rude to have a second glass. Should he mention Aisha? That she had recommended him and that he'd met with two other members of the elite group? But surely he must already know that. What did this man want from him? Why had Adam come?

He tried again. 'The talks, the faith, I've been inspired. No, more than that, like I belonged, that I might actually be able to do something with my life. Something worthwhile and in the name of Allah. It feels so right more than at any other time in my life.'

Adam pushed his hands down against the wheels, straightened his back and lifted his chin.

'I want to carry out Allah's plan. Obviously I'm in a wheelchair, but I have strong arms and I'm committed to doing what's right.' Adam suddenly felt like he was back in the apprenticeship interview. 'And I've helped with the UMIA website,' he finished lamely.

The man sighed and appeared uninterested. He clasped his hands together and Adam was worried he was going to end the interview. This was his chance to make a difference, he couldn't blow it now. He thought of Aisha, of her determination, her fearlessness.

Adam leant forwards and put his palms on the table. He locked eyes and spoke: 'I lost the use of my legs almost three years ago, but I think it was all in Allah's plan, He has a mission for me and I will not let Him down or my Muslim brothers and sisters. If you are the gateway to that plan, then open up and let me through, and if you're not, then let's end this now so I can stop wasting our time.'

The man broke his gaze first and for a second Adam felt triumphant, but then the man stood. Was it over?

'Take your jumper off, I'll be back.' He left.

Adam let out a breath in a big whoosh as soon as the door was closed. His shame and embarrassment had evaporated and instead excitement tingled down his arms. Briefly Adam closed his eyes and thanked Allah for His courage. Quickly he removed his hoodie and filled the glass again with water, downed it and filled it again. He wiped the sweat from his forehead and tried to relax.

It was some time before anyone came back into the room and Adam had finished the jug of water. This time the interviewer was accompanied by another man, a fair bit older with a scar on his cheekbone beneath his left eye. His skin was weathered and dark, creating a stark contrast with his clean white traditional robes. They arrived muttering in Arabic and Adam expected the new man to introduce himself and speak English, but neither of these things happened. They continued to talk in Arabic and came around the desk looking at Adam's chair. They gestured for him to move out from behind the desk. The new man got down on the floor and peered underneath, reaching his hand to feel the underside of the seat and the axle.

'I'm not bugged,' Adam said, 'it's my own chair, no one else uses it.'

They ignored him until finally they seemed to come to some agreement and then they left the room again. The original man was back almost immediately with a sheet of paper and a pen.

'There are things you need to know about our organization.'

Adam swallowed.

'For us to be successful in our plans, each individual must play their part. Each person must be committed to their task, to undertake it without discussion with anyone else. We need your absolute loyalty. Loyalty to Islam and to the UMIA. We need to be able to trust you absolutely.'

Adam felt as if he were on trial. He nodded.

'I assume you've heard about the RAF Marham operation?'

Adam was suddenly startled, RAF Marham? He couldn't remember exactly, there had been something in the news only yesterday, a protest on the airfield to stop additional Tornados heading out to the Middle East.

'That operation was one of ours,' he said. 'It was a success.'

Adam wasn't sure what they had been trying to achieve.

'Do you know why it was a success?'

Adam shook his head briefly.

'Because each individual followed their instructions to the letter. They did not discuss it with friends, involve a relative or doubt their purpose. If too many members know too much of the plan, information gets diluted, actions misdirected, important details leaked and so the plan fails.'

Adam was hardly daring to breathe. The man's eyes had turned to pinpoints of black, small shards digging into Adam's core. That phrase *ISIS infiltrator* swam into Adam's mind.

'And do you know why none of our members were hurt or injured during that operation?'

Adam made a tiny movement with his head.

'Because each individual followed their instructions to the letter. Am I making myself clear?'

Adam nodded vigorously, there was just one thing bothering him. Adam squeezed the rims of his wheels.

'Didn't they get arrested?' he said.

The Arab stared.

Adam shrank deeper into his wheelchair.

But then suddenly the Arab's eyes lightened and a smile touched the corners of his mouth. 'Yes, and today they were released. As expected.'

Adam's relief flooded through him. Of course they weren't terrorists. After all Aisha was a member, it was that kufi-wearer he needed to watch.

The Arab's smile widened. 'Peaceful protest you see. So you want to be a part of our special operations?' He pushed the paper towards Adam.

'Yes, I think so.'

The Arab paused with the pen in his hand, his eyes narrowing.

'Yes. I do. Definitely.'

'Fill this in then,' he said.

It was a form of some kind, address, age, contact details. Adam looked closer; it even wanted his Twitter and Facebook account details. They already had most of this through the UMIA membership. Perhaps they kept a separate list for those within this elite group.

The man barked and the giant appeared. He said something in Arabic, checked his watch and then spoke to Adam again.

'When you have finished, you must go.'

'But what happens next?'

'You will be contacted,' he said, 'assuming we can find a part for you in one of our operations.' He shrugged and headed towards the door leaving Adam with pen in hand, he pulled it open and then said. 'If not, you will hear nothing.' The door closed.

Somewhat deflated, Adam completed the form and handed it to the giant who stood waiting patiently by the desk. The man folded the paper carefully and then it disappeared inside his clothing.

Finally it was over and Adam could leave, it was only now that he noticed how desperate he was for a pee. He shouldn't have drunk a whole jug of water, especially when he had no idea where the nearest disabled toilet would be. The giant was heading towards the front door but Adam was grimacing in pain. The last thing he wanted was to wet himself on the way home. Now that the test was over, he felt bolder.

'I need the toilet,' he said.

The giant turned and stared blankly at him.

Adam gestured at his crotch and grimaced again.

The giant nodded and came back towards him. He went to the wall under the stairs and pushed the wooden panelling. To Adam's surprise a hidden door swung outwards to reveal a tiny bathroom. It was clearly too small. The giant looked down at him and then at the toilet and then back to Adam again. He seemed to consider something and then beckoned Adam to follow him.

The giant then pointed to himself and up the narrow stairs. There must be a bigger bathroom upstairs.

Adam considered the pressure in his bladder and the fact that he was in an unknown part of London. There really didn't seem to be a choice. Adam nodded at the giant.

Once again he lifted Adam and carried him up the stairs and into a large white bathroom.

When Adam had finished, he called out. There was silence, and Adam worried that he'd been left there, perched on a toilet in a stranger's house without his wheelchair.

'I'm done,' he said loudly.

This time the door opened and in walked the giant as if nothing was wrong. He scooped Adam up and turned around.

A skinny youth stood wide-eyed staring at them from the doorway. His skin shone dark brown, short black curls wove a mat across the top of his head. The giant gasped and then muttered in Arabic, Adam assumed it was an apology. The giant's beard came down onto Adam's chest as he bowed his head. Adam's own face burned with embarrassment. The youth backed out of the way. The giant, head still down by Adam's chest, strode out and then reversed along the corridor. Adam wondered why the youth, seemingly not more than a boy, was so revered. He wore ripped jeans and faded blue trainers. The laces were frayed and one had obviously broken and been tied in a knot halfway up the shoe. There was a hole in the boy's jeans just below his knee. Was he a member of the elite UMIA group? Adam looked at his face, the boy was staring back at him and then the youth lowered his eyes to the floor and stepped away into the bathroom. He said something in Arabic, but it wasn't like the interviewer's Arabic, this boy had a different accent, a rural region perhaps, far far away from London. The click of the lock re-activated the giant and he lifted his head, swung Adam around and down the stairs making Adam grip his large shoulders tight.

In the downstairs hallway next to his empty wheelchair was the interviewer again. He spoke in a low threatening voice as Adam was lowered back into his chair. He gestured at the stairs and beyond, the sleeves of his tunic waving wildly. The giant muttered a reply and silence fell thickly around them. It was clear that Adam shouldn't have been upstairs.

The front door opened.

'Goodbye Adam,' the interviewer said as Adam quickly wheeled his way down over the threshold and away.

*

The alarm vibrated and Adam threw out his hand, banging it against the lamp before finding the small clock and pressing the button. Thin blue light cut around the edge of the curtains providing enough illumination to see the shadows of furniture. Adam rubbed his eyes and cheeks, willing himself to be more awake. He sat up and heaved his sleeping legs over the side of the bed, pulled the wheelchair in close and hauled himself into it. After adjusting his legs, he rolled off towards the bathroom. The stark light was blinding so he closed his eyes, setting himself up under the shower by feel against the hard plastic fold-down seat and the cold tiles on the walls. Over the last two weeks he had tried hard to continue his namaz five times a day on his own at home. It had been easier at Faizal's house with the three of them praying together. However, at least the routine was becoming a habit now.

Dry, refreshed and clothed, Adam seated himself on the rug on the floor, his legs out straight in front of him. It was virtually impossible for him to kneel so adaptations had to be made. Allah would understand. Adam leaned forwards and began the prayers. Last night, he'd learned a new prayer and practised it from memory. This was a good way to start the day. The house stood squat and silent around him, the birds yet to awaken. It was the perfect time to commune with Allah. He gave thanks for the order that had entered his life, the prayers adding a routine to his days and the extra meetings with the UMIA, an added interest to his evenings. He gave thanks for the Muslim brothers and sisters that had entered his life; Aisha's tall willowy form coming unbidden. Thanks for their kindnesses and his growing sense of belonging. Even his father had backed off lately and been civil at

184

the dining table.

Adam bowed forwards along his lifeless legs murmuring the prayers one after another, each one helping his soul to lift higher, his heart to beat more soundly until the ritual was over. Then, with effort, he pulled his body up onto the bed, rolled over and readjusted his legs. He lay there staring at the ceiling waiting for the rest of the household to rise at a more sedate seven o'clock.

Today would be a good day, he was sure of it. Maybe he'd get a message about his first operation for the elite group of the UMIA. It was the next step on his path to righteousness. Adam had kept that scrap of paper Aisha had handed to him, as if it contained a secret message of love. Why had she recommended him if she didn't feel something for him? Was it only his growing faith she recognised or something more? His belief was deepening inside him, it was true, like a toning of the muscles. As if his whole body had been left fat and flaccid for too long but it was getting stronger, his very heart beating with a new firmness.

Adam was impatient for the next step. A chance to prove himself to the rest of the UMIA and in particular Aisha. What would they ask him to do? There seemed so many possibilities. Would it be an operation like that one at RAF Marham? Still, all would be made clear in good time, just as he was sure Allah would make clear his purpose given time. It seemed almost impossible to believe that Allah may have planned for Adam to be in a wheelchair, but now he wasn't so sure. What if Allah's plan necessitated the wheelchair? That first speaker, and the other ones, had helped him to think in new ways. It made so much sense, and his new friends were so welcoming.

And there was Aisha.

Adam closed his eyes, his heart beat assuredly in his chest, he would keep praying, asking Allah to show him the way. Maybe by following the truth he could get closer to her. After all, assuming he was chosen for the next elite operation, wouldn't he be working with Aisha and the other chosen ones? Adam smiled, he was sure she liked him, she often made a point of coming to talk to him before or after the meetings. She'd even befriended him on Facebook.

The first birds were beginning to sing in the bush outside his window. Yes, today was going to be a good day.

*

'Is it good news?' Adam's mother peered over his shoulder, her hands still wet from the sink where she'd been washing up the breakfast things.

'Mum.' He twisted his body so she couldn't see the letter he was reading. It was from Transport Rail about the apprenticeship. He'd got through. Adam lowered the letter, staring at the cupboard door.

'Well?'

'I'm not sure.' He thought about the interview, about Dave Calder and his refreshing honesty. About how they'd treated him like an adult and how smart and new the offices were. He also thought about his prayers. So this was it, perhaps this was what he was meant to do.

'Good news?'

'Yes,' he turned to his mother and grinned, 'yes Mum. I have been blessed. Mashallah.'

'Oh Adam.' She leant down to give him a hug, her soft cheek pressed against his.

'The apprenticeship at Transport Rail. I got it.'

'Oh, that's fantastic! I shall call your father right away.'

'Wait.' Adam caught her upper arm gently, he remembered his father's scathing comments about being a secretary. 'No, I'll tell him.'

'Adam it's so exciting, I shall make something special for this evening to celebrate. Will you help me?'

'I'm going out soon, sorry.'

'Where? Another meeting? With Faizal?'

'Leave it Mum. Don't you see that faith is helping me? You always wanted me to be a good Muslim boy.'

His mother nodded but the smile didn't quite make it to her eyes. He didn't mind, there were several members of the UMIA whose families were scathing about the United Muslims in

Action group. They didn't understand, stuck in their old ways, a culture from times and countries past. But Adam was a modern Muslim, part of the new age.

28

Ralph – Brief respite

Natalie opened the door. At first she looked tired, but then she opened the door wider and beamed at Ralph. 'Come in, come in.'

'Hi.' Ralph stepped into the large hallway with its Victorian staircase disappearing ahead.

'Why don't you come in the kitchen, the boys are out, I'm expecting them back at five.'

'Oh, well I could come back, Shelly said four.'

'No, no, don't be silly, come through and have a cup of tea.' She walked ahead into the vast kitchen with its six burner cooker and large dining table across the end of the room where the patio doors opened onto the garden. Ralph went to stand by the doors, looking out at the lawn. There was a neat vegetable patch at the far end, some flower beds on the right hand side. In front of him were four iron chairs around an ornate table on the stone flagging.

'Garden's looking good.'

'Yes, not me I'm afraid. Carl pays a gardener to come in once a week. Earl Grey or normal?'

'Normal please.' Ralph didn't have money to spend on gardeners, not that theirs needed it, it was less than half the size and scuffed to death by incessant football. He turned around and watched Natalie make the tea.

'Here you go, just a drop of milk.' Natalie passed him the blue mug. Ralph smiled, it always amused him when other people remembered how he liked it.

'Thanks.'

'Biscuit?' She reached for a tin of quality assortments.

Ralph took two.

'So how have you been?' she asked.

'Alright, busy you know?'

Natalie sighed. 'Not really.' She smiled weakly at him and sat at the breakfast bar. 'I thought I might get a job.'

'Really?' Natalie's status as a housewife with one child and various paid help had always been a discussion point for himself and Shelly. Her husband Carl was away a lot, often travelling abroad. Shelly was envious of their lifestyle and would often play the 'if only' game and complain about how difficult it was to fit everything in around their jobs, yet she would end the discussion by deciding that she would rather be using her brain at work than spending her whole day minding the house and doing the laundry. Natalie, on the other hand, had always seemed happy with her position. Involving herself in charity events, activities at the school, she also kept herself trim at the gym and Ralph couldn't help but admire her figure, today in a tight pullover with a short skirt that ended at her knee. Long boots stopped just below, giving a flattering glimpse of a small amount of flesh between boot and skirt.

Ralph realised he was staring. 'What does Carl say?'

'I'm not sure he's bothered what I do.'

'So have you got a job in mind?'

'I don't know, that's the hard part. I'm not like you and Shelly, I don't have a driving ambition to be anything exciting.'

'Mine was never an ambition, I just sort of fell into it really.'

'You're funny.' She smiled at him, her lipstick bright. Shelly hardly ever wore make-up these days. 'I'm not sure what I'm good at.'

'You're a great cook Natalie. You could use that.'

'Men!' She poked him playfully. 'Definitely the way to a man's heart.'

'No, but you could do proper cooking. I mean, be a chef in a restaurant or one of those arty cafés.'

'Hmmm.'

'You'd be good, in fact maybe you'd be better as, what's the person called who meets you at the door, at those posh places, takes you to your table.'

'A Maître d',' Natalie said.

'Yes that's it, in a really high-class place.' Ralph imagined Natalie in one of her party dresses, like that little black number with her high heels, shaking hands, giving that perfect smile of hers. 'Yes, that would really suit you.'

'Thanks.' She put her hand on his. The gentle warmth from her fingertips lay across the back of his hand. She looked at him with sorrowful eyes. 'You're a good friend Ralph.' He could see where the lipstick had worn off the middle of her lips, leaving them exposed and naked. Ralph dismissed the thought and drank his tea.

'And what about you?' she asked, her eyes searching him.

'Me?' He took his hand away, rubbing at his eyebrow.

'You seemed upset about something the other day. You can talk to me Ralph, if you want to that is.'

'Upset?'

'At the boys' football training.' She curled her painted nails around the blue mug.

'Oh, that.' Ralph swallowed. 'It was nothing really, just...'

She smiled sweetly at him, nodding ever so slightly. The house was quiet, just the murmur from the huge fridge freezer. Ralph realised his eyebrow had stopped twitching. He let out a sigh.

'Sometimes, work isn't all its cracked up to be, that's all. It can be hard.'

'Of course, especially with your work. You poor thing.' Her hand was back, soothing, caressing the tendons and knuckles, her painted nails drawing circles. 'You can call me any time, I'd understand. It must be hard on Shelly too, and I'm sure you don't want to worry her, or put more pressure on, she has her own stresses and strains to bear.'

Ralph was drawn into her brown eyes, which stared at him brightly, long black lashes curled forwards emphasising the wide-eyed look. It was true, Shelly did have her own stress from work, but she rarely brought it home. It wasn't fair for him to unload everything on her.

'Do you want something to eat? I was going to put some sausages on for when the boys get back.'

189

'No, don't worry on my account. I'm sure Shelly's got plans.'

'Oh, I don't think a sausage will fill you up. Not a man of your stature.' She playfully poked him and he automatically sucked in his stomach. She giggled. 'You're not fat Ralph, just strong.' She gripped his upper arm and gave it a squeeze. 'Big men need their calories. Besides, when's your next shift?'

'I'm on at eight.' He checked his watch. 'Oh go on then, you've twisted my arm.'

She laughed again, a light feathery sound, and busied herself in an unhurried manner about the kitchen. Her body moved gracefully between frying pan, drawer, fridge. Even the way she unwrapped the sausages seemed surprisingly feminine.

'Where's Carl?'

'Oh, getting something prepared at the office for tomorrow.'

'Working on a Sunday. That's no good.'

'Says you.'

Ralph smiled. 'Yes but then I'm not working five days a week on top.'

'True.' Natalie sighed, turning the sausages as they spat and sizzled. 'His latest promotion seems more like an additional ten hours a week.'

'Maybe it's just until he gets comfortable in the new role,' he offered.

'I doubt it.' She plucked some plates from the cupboard. 'Still, at least I've got you and Shelly.' She put the plates on the breakfast bar and squeezed his elbow. 'Friends are invaluable don't you think?' She paused, her eyes searching his. She was close enough for him to see the brown flecks in her iris. The lipstick was almost all gone. Ralph self-consciously licked his lips.

'Yes.'

The front door banged and the teenagers came noisily down the hallway, Natalie moved swiftly to the fridge and got the ketchup. She followed up with the hot sausages and some soft white rolls.

'Hi, Mr C.'

'Hey Troy. Good game? You two look like you've been working hard.' Ralph noted his son's ruddy cheeks, both in Tshirts despite the cool temperature outside.

'Not bad.'

'I trashed him,' Liam crowed, grabbing at the nearest roll and filling it with ketchup. Ralph reached out to give his son's shoulder a squeeze. Liam was caught by surprise and then grinned back. He turned to Troy. 'You were rubbish today.'

'I was not. You got lucky, my end was a muddy ice rink.'

'That's why we swapped, remember?' Liam stuffed a large mouthful in. Ralph prepared his own sausage in a roll.

'Yeah, after you'd stamped down all the grass.'

'Now, now boys.' Natalie stood between the two munching teenagers, she ruffled their hair, pausing to give Liam's cheek a squeeze. 'Well done,' she murmured.

Liam turned pink and mumbled, 'Thanks for the sausages.'

'Mmm.' Ralph joined in, they were tasty.

29

Halima – Lentil curry and stopped clocks

'Have you paid those bills yet?' Halima's mother frowned, sauce dribbling down her chin.

'Stop worrying, I've got a payment plan thingy.' Halima sighed, starting the lentil curry on her own plate.

'Well I do worry, you with that dreadful job, me not knowing where my next meal's coming from. And you're late. Spending all your time in that garden, no good will come of it. I've warned you, clay and cat shit, that's all you'll find out there.'

Halima took the remote and turned up the volume on the television. They ate in silence for a few minutes as a panel of guests discussed what to do with spiders in the bath. Mum's hacking cough drowned out the funny bit and Halima looked across at her. The coughing shook her body, making her straggly hair sway, one hand up to her mouth, revealing a hole at her elbow in the faded cardigan she wore. Halima swallowed her mouthful. The coughing stopped and they could hear the TV once more.

'What kind of curry is this anyway? Tastes like cat meat.'

'It's lentil, same as we always have.'

'Hmmmp. Don't suppose I'll ever get fine food again, not since you turned away that nice man from the station. He would of taken me out to dinner. Been a damn sight better than this.'

'Your nice man from the station never called, OK?' Halima stood up and took her empty plate back into the kitchen.

'Not surprised he hasn't called with you and your mouth, Halima Shah!'

Halima stood at the sink and stared out at the garden. At least some of her plants were growing. The buds were looking fatter although some of the leaves had holes where the slugs and caterpillars had eaten their fill. Soon there would be flowers, she was sure of it.

Halima put her plate in the sink and turned the kettle on. She waited for it to boil and then set about making their cups of tea. It was only when she'd finished stirring in the sugar that she noticed the stillness. An uncanny quiet that she couldn't remember hearing before. Odd, she could still hear the voices from the TV, but it felt as if the house had let out a sigh and stopped. Halima felt a prickle on her scalp and dashed into the lounge.

Her mother was still watching TV, her head cocked slightly to the left. Halima relaxed. But then she noticed the plate had slid on her mother's lap, and curry sauce was slowly leaking onto her trousers.

'Mum?'

Halima's hands shook as she bent to look at her mother properly. Her eyes were open, looking straight through Halima, but she wasn't sure if they were seeing anything. Her whole body seemed to be slumped to the side.

'Mum! For pity's sake, Mum!' Halima grabbed the plate and put it on the floor, then she picked up her mother's limp hands and shook them. It made her breasts wobble and her head slid further to the side. The prayer beads rattled from her lap and dropped onto the rug.

'Oh no.' Halima fiddled in her pocket and swore again then ran into the kitchen, searching for her mobile.

Halima saw the flashing lights through the net curtains and was at the door before they had turned the engine off. A man dressed in green walked quickly towards her carrying a bag.

'It's Mum, I don't know what happened. She was eating lentil curry, from the Co-op. It was the one I always get.'

The man smiled warmly. 'That's OK love, I'm Ralph, why don't you show me where she is?'

Halima went back to the lounge as Ralph followed her. She indicated her mother, still slumped in the chair with her eyes closed. Halima backed away towards the net curtains and then a lady, also dressed in green, walked through the lounge door.

'What's her name?'

'Mum, umm sorry, Kaneez. Kaneez Shah.'

The man was holding her mother's wrist with one hand while he pulled open one of her mother's eyelids with the other.

'Kaneez, can you hear me? I'm Ralph, I'm a medic and we're going to help you.'

'She can't hear you. I shouted, and she still didn't move.' Halima spoke quickly, trying to explain. She could see Ralph pulling up the frayed sleeve of her mother's cardigan to get a better grip on her wrist.

'I'm going to get a new one. The cardigan, it's old but she likes it, but I'm going to get a new one, they've opened a new charity shop on Battersea Park Road. I was going to have a look tomorrow.'

Ralph turned around. 'That's nice. Can you tell me how long your mother has been like this?'

'Since we ate the lentil curry,' said Halima. She clutched her hands together, trying to still the trembling.

'And when was that?'

'About, about, err ten, fifteen minutes ago?'

'OK. And what's your name?'

'Halima,' said Halima. Watching his calm face, she began to feel slightly easier. She'd done the right thing of course, called the ambulance, stayed with her mother. This man, Ralph, would make everything better.

'Well, Halima, it looks like your mother has suffered a stroke. I've got a reasonable heart beat and her breathing seems a little laboured. Does she have any chest problems?'

'She coughs. I mean like not just a little cough, she has medicine and stuff for it.' Halima didn't think Ralph would understand if she told him how the cough was a creature all its own that lived with them, nestled in Mum's chest. It had to be fed regularly with pills and when it wasn't tended it roared a hacking bray in protest.

Halima had barely noticed the lady medic, but now with a quick nod at Ralph she left the room.

'We're going to get your mother into hospital. She could still be bleeding, so we're going to be careful how we move her.'

Bleeding? Stroke? Halima's thoughts rolled around her head, not finding a place to go, or anything to connect with. She remembered the red petal on the white windowsill of Mrs Pease's flat. Like a drop of pure blood. But her mother wasn't bleeding, at least not that she could see. She'd just stopped. Like a clock. What did it all mean?

Suddenly there was the grey cat, peering around the door. On seeing Halima, it stalked in and rubbed against Ralph's bag on the floor.

'Hello kitty,' said Ralph, 'I'm afraid your mummy's not well.'

'No,' said Halima, 'I mean Smokey isn't Mum's, he's mine, well, not mine exactly.' She reached out and stroked Smokey's back, he purred and came to rub against her legs. She thought the name suited him. The soft fur was soothing, taking Halima away. Making her forget about her mother lying half dead in the chair and the nice man, Ralph. Halima liked the way Smokey's fur moved against her fingers as she stroked. He rubbed against her shin and then moved away. Smokey went towards the motionless body, briefly he crouched and then leapt straight onto Mum's lap. Her mother's eyes fluttered and she glared at the cat. Smokey leapt down and disappeared.

'Whoa full thek t. Mout. Funk.'

Halima stared at her mother, wondering if maybe her hearing had gone wrong.

Ralph took charge. 'Kaneez, it's all right, I need you to keep calm and still. You've had a stroke and we're going to get you to hospital.' Ralph held her mother's left hand which appeared to still be limp but she moved the right one, pulling her cardigan across her chest. Just then the lady in green pushed a wheel-chair awkwardly into the room.

'Hao th thek aw ewe?'

Halima couldn't help but stare at her mother. The tone was right, but Halima had no idea what she was trying to say. Ralph and the lady manhandled her mother into the wheelchair. Halima could see that half of her mother's body appeared to be operating but the other half was like it was still asleep. She caught her mother's eye, and recognised that she was frightened.

'It's OK Mum. Don't worry.' She grabbed the prayer beads off the floor and thrust them into her mum's working hand. Then she turned to Ralph. 'It wasn't the lentil curry was it?'

'No, no, definitely not the lentil curry.' He smiled at Halima. 'Relax, you've done nothing wrong. Is there anyone else? I mean who lives here, or maybe a friend you'd like to call?'

Halima shook her head as the lady swivelled her mother around. Mum's grey hair lay limply over the back of the chair.

'I was going to wash her hair tonight,' Halima said.

'I'm sure that can wait. Do you want to come in the ambulance with your mother?' Halima felt Ralph's hand gently touch her shoulder, his warm smile a caress against the craziness. She nodded mutely and went to get her coat.

'I think you should lock the back door before we go.' Ralph nodded towards the kitchen where Smokey sat in the open doorway washing himself.

After two more indecipherable outbursts, Kaneez Shah had stopped trying to speak. Halima thought that was a good idea, it was quite a novelty sitting next to her mute mother. She wasn't dead. No. And everything was going to be fine. Ralph would make it so. Halima had answered all his questions about Mum's health and past ailments, the medications she took. For once Halima was the important one, the person with the knowledge speaking clearly to Ralph without annoying interruptions or degrading comments.

The ambulance rounded a corner and Halima gripped the stiff sides of the seat.

'I'm going to attach this little gadget to your finger so I can watch your heart beat, OK Kaneez?' He put a strange clip on her mother's finger and then a beeping noise started and a red digital display showed some numbers. Halima allowed her gaze to roam around the ambulance. So many things, buttons, lines, compartments, gadgets. How did Ralph ever know how to use them all?

'So is lentil curry a favourite then?'

'Yes, well I like it,' Halima said and they both looked at her mother, who opened her mouth but then shut it again.

'Why don't you squeeze my hand, once for yes, twice for no,' said Ralph, he was holding her good hand where the prayer beads were threaded through her fingers.

Halima watched her mother's hand clench twice.

'And who does Smokey prefer? You or Halima? He seemed a very friendly cat.'

Her mother's hand was clenching again. It squeezed so many times that Halima gave up counting and Ralph let her hand go.

'So just the two of you at home then Halima?'

'Yes.' Halima sighed, waiting for her mother to add her bit about Halima being no good at anything and not taking care of her properly but she didn't speak, only scowled back.

'Yes,' said Halima again, emboldened, 'I'm a sole carer.'

'I see, I bet that can be tiring, hard on you both sometimes I expect.' He was analysing the digital display and writing something on his pad.

'Yes. Yes. My mum's not been very well lately.' Halima glanced briefly at her mother and saw her hand twitching. There was only the sound of the traffic and the siren somewhere above or in front of them. Halima continued, 'She doesn't go out any more, finds it difficult to move around. I help her have a bath, do the cooking, take care of her.'

'That's very noble of you.' Ralph was watching his patient and making more notes. He nodded at Halima. 'Do you get a chance to go out?'

'Well I work, early in the mornings, I'm a cleaner.'

'Aah I see. Well, you've certainly got your work cut out.'

Halima leaned back and folded her hands on her lap, she felt oddly triumphant; not wishing to spoil the moment, she cast her eyes over the gadgets again, deliberately avoiding her mother's gaze. She wanted Ralph to ask her more questions; she wanted to tell him about her garden.

'No children then?'

Her mother snorted loudly and Halima glared briefly at her. 'No. But I have a garden, I mean, I like to do gardening, I'm growing some flowers.' Halima paused realising how lame that sounded.

Ralph looked up from his notes. 'We're almost there, there will be a couple of bumps as we go over the speed humps.' He took her mother's hand again.

30

Ralph – Unravelling

'Why is your brother always late?' Shelly asked.

Their coffees were finished and the boys were arguing over the last piece of chocolate brownie.

'You know what he's like.' Ralph looked around the busy café and then pulled out his phone to check his texts.

Shelly huffed, 'I still need to go in Marks and you'd better take Liam into Sports Direct for those football socks.'

'Yeah all right, just give him another five minutes.'

'Uncle Dave.' Cameron suddenly leapt up from the table.

'Hey, it's Cam the cool dude.' Ralph's brother high-fived and then did a fist-bump with Liam. 'What's up?'

'Mum says you're late and Dad's moody,' Cameron said loudly.

Ralph stood up and gave his brother a brief man-hug.

'I'm not moody,' he said to Cameron.

'Hi Dave.' Shelly offered her cheek for a peck.

They all sat down again.

'Have you got us a present?' Cameron said.

Liam gave his brother a dig in the ribs.

'Cameron. Don't say things like that. It's not polite,' Shelly said.

'Actually.' Dave leaned in to the table grinning widely at the boys. Even Liam couldn't help smiling back.

'What, what?'

Dave pulled out an envelope from his inside pocket. He tapped it against the empty coffee cups. 'What have I got here?'

'Money.' Cameron tried to grab it but Dave was too quick.

'You've got tickets.' Liam was assessing the envelope, his eyes alight.

'Tickets for Arsenal in three weeks time.'

'Yey.' Cameron successfully grabbed the envelope and started opening it.

'Fucking A.'

'Liam. Language.'

Dave folded his arms looking self-satisfied. 'That's if Mum and Dad say you can go.'

Shelly smiled. 'Only if you've done all your homework and tidied your bedrooms.'

Liam rolled his eyes.

Ralph watched the boys eagerly tear open the envelope and spread the tickets on the table.

Dave nudged Ralph. 'Hey what's up with you, Mr Moody.'

Ralph sighed. 'I'm not moody.'

The boys were busy poring over the tickets.

'Hey, did you hear they're going to have some kind of memorial event at Clapham? Re-opening of platform nine.'

Ralph felt like his brother had just thumped him. Why did he have to bring that up?

'You might get on TV. Ralph Calder the hero.'

'I'm not a hero.'

'Is Dad famous?'

'No, I'm not.' Ralph checked his watch, they should get going.

'Course he is. He's the golden boy. Got that award hasn't he?' Dave kept on.

'He keeps it in the drawer.' Cameron said.

Shelly squeezed Ralph's thigh under the table and then said, 'Dave, it's terribly sweet of you to get the tickets but we need to get moving.'

'Uncle Dave can come back to our house and watch Game of Thrones. Heeyah.' Cameron sliced the air with his hand and sent a glass rolling to the edge. Shelly caught it.

'Cameron, that's enough.' Ralph said.

'Lighten up big bro' that's a cool show. Lots of heads getting hacked off.'

Shelly grimaced.

'Don't worry Mum, if Dad was in it, he'd be able to stick them back on again.'

'Cameron, stop being silly,' Shelly said.

'Well Gramps said that Dad puts people back together.'

'Well that is not what he meant.'

'But didn't he get the award for saving people?' Cameron asked.

Shelly looked across at Ralph. 'Yes,' she said. But Ralph couldn't hold her gaze and looked out of the window instead.

'Can we not talk about it?' Shelly started stacking the plates together and banging cups into an untidy pile.

'Why not Mum?' Cameron asked.

'Because it makes Dad drink.' Liam glanced at Ralph.

'That is quite enough boys.' Shelly stood up, gathering their bags together.

Ralph rubbed at the twitch in his eyebrow.

'Oh really? What does he drink?' Dave said.

'Don't encourage them.'

'Beer.'

'No, Dad likes wine.'

'But he mostly drinks beer.' Liam crossed his arms.

'Well actually I saw him drinking whiskey from the cabinet.'

Cameron stuck out his tongue at his brother.

'No you didn't.'

'Yes I did.'

'Cameron and Liam, stop it this instant or there'll be no TV for a week.' Shelly's face was bright red.

31

Adam - Suspicions

'I'll see you at the mosque Friday?' Adam asked.

'Yeah sure, and don't forget to email that stuff about getting through level ten on the Xbox. Tariq is going mental that he can't get past it.' Faizal grinned and put up his hand in farewell.

'Yeah sure.' Adam turned away and started heading home. It had been a good meeting, lots of discussion about the latest ISIS beheadings but also about the progress the UMIA was making across Europe. They'd secured a Muslim negotiation specialist to advise the French government and apparently they had an insider within the Syrian government. The British minister was proving a harder nut to crack but a Twitter campaign in Iraq had gone well and they had thousands of new subscribers to the new website. Adam was pleased with some of the design work he'd got involved in to make the website more youth friendly.

However, he'd heard nothing about any special operations. No secret contact and there had been too many people around to try and talk to Aisha about it. Of course, there was always the chance that he wouldn't be called upon. Adam remembered the Arab's comment, that he might not get contacted at all. Surely they had to give him a chance. Why give him an interview if they thought he was worthless? He'd been chosen, recommended by Aisha and then succeeded in the interview. At least, he presumed he had.

A disturbance on the street ahead brought Adam's attention back to where he was. Probably a domestic with the angry voices of a couple up ahead. Adam regarded the busy road, wondering if it might be easier to cross early, but there was too much traffic. It was only as he drew nearer that he recognised Aisha's tall outline and that dodgy guy who always wore a kufi. The man was holding Aisha's arm as she tried to pull away.

Adam pushed his wheels forwards faster.

'Hey,' Adam yelled, 'get your hands off her!'

The man turned around, his cheeks flushed. He let go and Aisha staggered back.

'This has got nothing to do with you.' The man faced Adam.

'You wanna bet?' Adam drove his wheelchair right up to the guy who trotted back a few steps to avoid Adam's footplate.

'Take it easy, you've got no idea.' The man had put out his hands as if to calm Adam or keep him back.

There was a screech of tyres and a white car pulled into the kerb ahead. Two men got out and went to Aisha.

'Now look what you've done,' the man in front of Adam said, his arms dropping to his sides. 'Aisha, wait!' he shouted, but he didn't move towards her.

One of the men had opened the back door, the other was guiding Aisha into the car. She glanced behind her at Adam and then stepped in. One of the men seemed familiar, could it be Jamaal? He hadn't seen him since that meeting at Subway.

'Who are they?' Adam said suddenly uncomfortable.

'Her cousins.'

Well that sounded OK. It wasn't like she'd resisted or shouted.

The kufi-wearer turned on Adam. 'See what you've done? You idiot, they're the enemy, not me.' He pointed at the car as it zoomed off again.

'What's that supposed to mean?'

The man simply shook his head.

Adam gripped the wheels tightly and jerked his chair forwards. 'Who are you? Are you with ISIS?'

'Me?' He stepped across the pavement away from Adam's chair. 'Are you crazy?' Then he laughed bitterly.

Adam struggled to make sense of what he'd just witnessed and what this man had said. 'I saw you at the march, near the petrol bomb.'

The man nodded slowly staring back at Adam. Then he pointed his finger at Adam's chest. 'I saw you there too. Near the petrol bomb.'

Adam gasped.

The man sneered, 'Been to any secret meetings recently?' And then he was off across the road dodging the traffic.

32

Halima – Home alone

It was late by the time Halima got home. Stepping into the dark hallway, she couldn't remember the last time she had entered when the house was so black. Normally there would be at least a light on in the lounge, or, if her mother had snoozed off, then the TV flickering away to itself. This evening it was like stepping into a power cut. Halima flicked on the hall light, half-expecting nothing to happen. The dull orange shade cast a glow across the floor.

It smelt different too, an unfamiliar chemical smell that reminded Halima of the hospital and she wondered if she'd brought it with her. She shut the door and the sound echoed through the silent house.

After several biscuits and a second cup of tea, Halima tried to settle in front of a documentary about the Indus river in Pakistan. It was the kind of thing her mother liked to watch. Half way through there was a mating scene and Halima automatically glanced across at her mother's empty chair. She wasn't here to make any sarcastic comments. In fact, she didn't even have to watch this, so she hopped channels and found a singing programme instead. The volume was too loud, normally to drown out her mother's comments. Halima turned it down, but then it was awfully quiet. Funny how she had learnt to ignore most of Mum's back-chat during the programmes they watched. It was only without her here that Halima noticed how strange it was to hear every single word from the TV without her constant comments.

Halima got bored, flicked around and gave up. She could have a long bath with a book, her mother would complain that it was too late, but Halima could do as she pleased. Glancing at her watch, she found it was already half ten, maybe she wouldn't have that bath, she should probably go to bed. There was work in the morning, or maybe she should call in sick. Was that allowed? Even though it was her mother that was sick? Cheryl might use it as an excuse to get rid of her, Halima couldn't afford to lose her job. There would be time to visit Mum after work.

At the top of the stairs, Halima walked into her mother's room to turn back the covers. Part way through she realised her mistake but decided to carry on anyway. It was strangely comforting to do the routine. However, she couldn't pretend to help her mother into bed. Turning off the light Halima went to her own bed and lay staring at the small triangular gap between the curtains. The street light had recently been changed from orange to a dull white. The cars continued outside, and an intermittent distant siren. The normal sounds of night-time on their street in their house, and yet, how different it seemed. Halima found herself becoming more sensitive to other noises. A flapping sound that could be something on the roof or that plastic bag still attached to the front hedge. There was an occasional drip from the bathroom sink and then a cat wailing at another outside. There would be no snores tonight. Halima wondered whether her mother would snore in hospital, would the nurses tell her off? Would they move her to a private room if she kept the other patients awake?

Halima sighed and turned over, looking at the patterns of shadows on her wall. One was like a witch with incredibly long fingers that waved and merged with the curtain edge. Her mother was being well looked after, they'd said so, said she should go home. But what if Mum couldn't sleep? What if the hospital beds were too hard instead of the soft bed she'd slept in for years? Would the nurses put a glass of water by her bed? Would they wake her if she had one of her noisy nightmares? Halima frowned at the wall. It was silly to think these things. The hospital was two bus rides away. There was nothing she could do about it now. Might as well enjoy the peace. Halima closed her eyes.

The tap dripped. Outside the cats yowled a new tune. A police car wailed along Battersea Rise. Halima pulled the quilt up over her ear and tried to imagine her garden in full bloom.

The wind made whatever it was flap and a car vroomed along the crescent.

How was it possible that sleep came so easily when Mum snored loudly in the room next door, and yet now, when it was quiet with just the faintest sounds, it was as if someone had turned up the loudspeaker and made all those small noises into a great percussion orchestra. Halima got out of bed and tightened the taps as hard as she could. Downstairs, she stuck her head out of the back door and called for 'Smokey' but there was no sign. Back upstairs, she checked that all the windows were closed and stared out onto the orange-lit street. A tall man was walking his dog slowly along the pavement. Halima pulled the curtains closer together in the middle. The house creaked and Halima spun around to see nothing but dim shadows. She clambered quickly into bed and pulled the covers up tight. She didn't think she'd ever been quite so alone. At least not since, not since her baby had been taken away. Halima discovered she was weeping, and now that she'd started, she couldn't stop.

33

Ralph – Falling apart

Ralph was getting tired, he paused as Cameron took the ball. It was a tough game; two on two made for a lot of running around. They had shortened the pitch to make it easier using Ralph's jumper and one of the kids' coats as goalposts.

'Go Cameron!' Natalie cheered from the sidelines. Ralph glanced over at her and smiled. He was hot and sweaty but the boys were showing no signs of letting up. They were up to eight goals each. Liam, as goalkeeper, scooped up the ball in his hands and tossed it to Troy. Ralph rushed to defend his own goal while Cameron ran forwards to tackle. There was a small skirmish and then Cameron was in the mud and Troy was dribbling straight at Ralph. He kicked the ball hard just as Cameron yelled 'Foul'. Instead of stopping the ball, Ralph's attention went to his son on the ground. The ball hit him squarely in the face and Ralph staggered backwards from the blow. For a moment, one half of his face went numb, he blinked, aware that sound had stopped and all the boys were staring at him. Then the feeling came back and it really stung.

'For fuck's sake,' said Ralph, holding his face. 'Alright, time out.' He held up his hand, jeez that boy could kick hard. Natalie came running over.

'Troy, what were you thinking?'

'I was only playing the game, I can't help it if Liam's dad put his face in the way.'

'Troy!' Natalie stared at her son until he lowered his eyes and slunk off to get the ball.

'It's fine Natalie, he's right, it's a hazard of the game,' Ralph declared, wishing that he felt stronger than he did. His face was on fire and he was utterly exhausted.

'Let's go back and I'll make us some lunch,' Natalie urged brightly. She put a hand to his face, it was warm and soft and Ralph wished he could melt into it. All the strains of the past few weeks, the row with Shelly that morning, the physical tiredness from running over this muddy pitch. Her hand was still there and Ralph pressed his burning skin into her palm.

'Dad?'

Ralph opened his eyes again. 'Yes Cameron?'

'It was a foul wasn't it?'

'No it wasn't,' Liam chimed in.

'I don't know,' Ralph sighed, shooing his son forwards so he could retrieve his clothes from the field. They started walking.

'But you saw!' Cameron pleaded.

'Not really, all I saw were you two, all legs and scuffling. I wasn't that close.' Ralph walked a little faster, all he wanted was to collapse into a sofa and close his eyes.

'Well?' Cameron had turned to Natalie, 'did you see what happened?'

'Me?' Natalie seemed surprised. 'Well it doesn't really matter now, does it? That was a good game boys. Don't forget your gloves Troy.'

Ralph walked across the field heading to the street that led to another that would take them back to Natalie's house. He could hear the boys behind him arguing about the game and Natalie trying to negotiate peace between them. Perhaps she would have something cool to press against his face, and maybe something cold to drink too. Something that would not only quench his thirst but also ease the tension in his mind. He could see Shelly's face, pinkly furious, as she had berated him that morning for forgetting that she was going away. The sting on his face could so easily have been her hand. But then she hadn't hit him, not physically anyway. His face continued to burn, and the noise behind from the arguing boys grew ever more irritating. Suddenly Ralph stopped walking and spun around.

'Look, I don't bloody well care if it was a foul or not. Shut the fuck up about it!' he yelled. A dog walker on the other side of the road stared at them. Ralph swallowed and noted the shocked faces of the three boys. Natalie was studying the pavement.

'Just stop bickering, OK?' he spoke more quietly. Turning his back he walked on, his shoulders heavy. Nothing was going right at the moment, and the weight of it all pressed down on him. Natalie brushed his side and kept pace next to him, silently, until she pulled out a key and unlocked the door.

'Why don't you relax and I'll find you a cool cloth, at least to get the mud off.' She smiled, wiping a finger under his eye and showing him the dirty smudge that had appeared on her fingertip.

In the kitchen Ralph sat at the table while Natalie whirled around putting together a sweet and sour stir fry, after having given him a cool white wine to drink and a damp cloth for his face. Ralph gazed at the expert way she chopped the vegetables and tossed them into the wok. It was soothing just to sit and watch while sipping the wine.

Lunch was noisy with the clanging of cutlery on plates and loud voices from the boys. As soon as they were finished, the boys disappeared upstairs to play computer games on Troy's Xbox, leaving Natalie and Ralph alone again.

'Let's take the coffee into the lounge.'

'Sure.' Ralph raised his mug, the coffee was rich and dark, made in the cafetiere, Natalie had even ground the beans beforehand, filling the kitchen with that slightly burnt smell of fresh coffee.

Natalie curled her legs up, nestling into the opposite end of the sofa. The coffee was a good idea. Over lunch he'd drunk too much and this would help sober him up. What with the wine and the tumbler of whiskey he'd gulped from Carl's cabinet. Ralph was fairly woozy, although, he had to admit to himself, it was better than the overwhelming exhaustion he'd been feeling earlier.

'So what time do you start tonight?' Natalie seemed relaxed too, she was burrowing her toes under the cushion near Ralph's elbow.

'Start?' Ralph frowned and through his foggy mind came a picture of the back of the ambulance, with its gurney, instruments and equipment. 'Eight.' The thought gave him a chill, and a drop of coffee slid down the side of his cup. 'Thanks again for having the boys overnight. Normally the Crinklies, I mean Mum and Dad can step in but they've got some show they're going to.'

'Oh, that's fine. Keeps Troy amused while Carl's away. They'll love it.' She smiled, her big toe resting against his thigh. Upstairs the boys laughed loudly and then the noise subsided again.

Natalie was looking at him intently. 'Where did you say Shelly was going?'

'Newquay, with a few girl-friends, apparently it's Helen's fortieth.'

'Oh.' Natalie bit her lip. 'I don't think I've met Helen.'

'Me neither.' Ralph was still convinced that it hadn't been on the calendar last week, that it wasn't him that was losing touch. However, Shelly had been adamant and told him in no uncertain terms that if he hadn't sorted out the right shifts at work, then that was his problem not hers. He didn't really want to go to work, wasn't looking forwards to the callouts, the pain, the needy patients with death always hovering in the background.

'Carl's trip was pretty last minute too, he didn't find out till Wednesday but apparently that's how it is in his new position.' Natalie sighed and sipped her coffee. Ralph felt her toe rub his thigh. 'Don't you think it a bit strange that Carl and Shelly are away on the same weekend?'

Ralph frowned. 'But Carl goes away a lot.'

'Yes.' Natalie looked sad for a moment. 'But Shelly doesn't.'

'No that's true. Just coincidence, I mean it's not like they went to the same place.'

'I suppose not.' Natalie seemed to be watching him. 'But then, Carl took the car, so I don't really know where he went.'

Ralph wasn't sure what she was getting at. 'Do you mean he might have lied to you?'

She gave a small chuckle. 'Wouldn't be the first time.'

'Natalie.'

Her eyes were glassy. Ralph reached for her hand and gave it a squeeze.

'I had no idea.'

'Do you know where Shelly is, for sure?' Natalie said softly.

Ralph pulled his hand back, startled. 'What are you saying? Shelly's not, I mean she doesn't, at least not that I'm aware of. No, Shelly would never-' He clenched his fist. Could she? Would she? Did he even know his own wife?

'I'm sorry.' Natalie had moved closer. 'You've been so tired lately, stressed, I wondered if you knew.'

'Knew what?' He stood up, putting his coffee on the table with rather too much force. 'Know what Natalie?' He was almost shouting.

'Ralph, please, I didn't mean to make you angry.' She stood up too, speaking gently to him, stepping closer.

Ralph was bewildered, what was he to think? What did all this mean? And in only a few hours he had to be back on shift, and then there would be tomorrow morning when he finally got to bed, alone, with the dead boy leaking blood onto the tracks running through his mind over and over. So many sleepless nights, and it would seem he didn't know the half of what was going wrong in his life.

Natalie spoke: 'Your eyebrow's twitching.'

Ralph dropped his head and noticed she was uncurling his fist, straightening out his fingers, she drew them to her chest and kissed the tips.

'I wish I could help,' she whispered. Her other hand came up to caress the side of his face. Her thumb smoothed over the twitch. Ralph closed his eyes, there was so much pain, so much suffering. He wanted her to take it all away, to make him whole again. Her lips on his, soft, damp, smelling slightly of coffee. Opening his mouth, their tongues met, and he put his arms around her pliant body.

It was the door slamming that startled them. The kiss brought to an abrupt end. They both stared at the lounge door, firmly shut in its frame. Ralph grabbed his jacket from the hallway and left.

*

Ralph checked-in late at five past eight, he was standing staring at the team board where his name appeared next to Ian's. The station controller told him Emma had called in with a sickness bug.

'When you're ready then, we're late.' Ian slapped him on the back and jangled the keys in front of him.

'Right.' Ralph took a deep breath, his palms were sweaty. It would be fine, he could do this, just put everything else out of his mind and concentrate on this moment. Check out the drugs bag, walk to the ambulance, give it the once over with Ian and then head to their callout position. Ralph was already walking towards the ambulance when he paused, what was their callout position? Ralph couldn't remember what it had said on the board only seconds ago. He kept moving; Ian had the keys, he would take them to the right place.

Ian unlocked the back doors and jumped in. 'Looks like it'll be a good sunset tonight, although I believe they said the temperature was going to drop. Shame, I've been enjoying the warmer weather for a change.'

Ralph nodded in response, he was checking the drugs bag before sliding it into the back.

Ian stepped back out of the ambulance. 'Looks like we're all set. I've replaced the oxygen, the last team didn't get a chance to refill it.' He closed the doors while Ralph double checked their paperwork.

'OK,' said Ralph.

'I'm sure it's all in order, already checked it, I'm on the ball, so to speak.' Ian glared pointedly at Ralph. 'Not half asleep, you get my drift?'

Ralph nodded in a vague way and went round to the driver's side, realised he didn't have the key and instead went to the passenger door.

'Are you all right?' Ian asked once they'd seated and belted themselves.

'Sure.'

'You seem a bit, I don't know, not quite here.'

Ralph breathed deeply, willing his body to relax, his mind to be still. That twitch in his eyebrow that wouldn't stop.

'I'm fine. Let's go.'

Ian started the engine and off they went. All Ralph wanted to do was go home, climb into bed and never speak to anyone again. The house would be empty with the boys over at Natalie's. He could simply forget the world existed, at least for a while. Ralph tried to relax with this in mind, but then he knew that bed was not the place where he felt rested these days. The dying boy invaded his dreams and kept him awake. Then he thought of the phone call and Shelly's anger, screaming at him only an hour ago. Ralph stared out of the window, actually maybe sitting here in the ambulance was the best place to be. Safe in the warm vehicle, protected from the outside, from the people he knew, from the people he didn't. For a few minutes Ralph felt the tension ease a little but it was Saturday night and they had barely set off when they were called to a code red, the results of a pub brawl.

As the night progressed so did the incidents. Ralph did his job, he'd been doing it so long that these Saturday nights rarely brought up anything new. There was little time for chit chat between Ian and himself which suited Ralph just fine. As each new patient appeared Ralph concentrated on the arm, the head, the cut, or whatever piece of equipment was required. He let Ian do the bedside manner bit, for Ralph it was simply medical. A wound that needed to be staunched, a body that needed transporting. Not people, just patients requiring attention. The hours tumbled by in a stream of sirens, hospitals, roads and dressings until at last Ralph was clocking off and saying bye to Ian.

'Well, I hope you've got more jokes for tomorrow.' Ian waved his arm, then shaking his head went to his car. Ralph watched him go, then turned wondering where he'd left his own vehicle.

On reaching his drive, he turned off the engine with no recollection of the journey he had just completed. Tired. So tired. The house stood bright and empty before him in the morning sunshine. Ralph dragged himself from the car, fumbled with his keys and let himself into the hollow corridor. He should eat, but the effort of putting together a meal was too much. Instead he went to the lounge, grabbed the bottle of Scotch and staggered upstairs.

34

Adam – Getting stuck in

A message popped up on Adam's computer screen. It was time for prayers. He'd scheduled them all in after he'd been shown how to use the Outlook Calendar. It was the perfect way to stop him being late or missing it altogether. Adam glanced up at the clock on the wall, it was getting close to one, he would need to go down and meet Zeeshan in his post room for Zuhr prayers. But before that he needed to wash. He would just finish this paragraph first.

'Thought you weren't coming.' Zeeshan smiled showing the gap where one of his incisors was missing. He already had his sign up in the window of the post room: *Quiet prayer in action.*

Adam thought it funny but he hadn't come up with anything better so that was how it was. Zeeshan already had his prayer mat unrolled and had removed the office chair so there was space for Adam to turn around. He positioned himself slightly behind and to the left of Zeeshan. In many ways Adam was glad to come here. The more he was learning about Islam and the more meetings Fazial took him to, the more right it all felt. Stephanie, the HR woman, had brought him down to meet Zeeshan on that first day and he didn't have a good reason not to join the older man.

In fact, Adam admitted, following Zeeshan in prayer was helpful, he knew so much more off by heart than Adam did. He could copy and follow Zeeshan, and even ask him questions afterwards.

Zeeshan was warm and kind and shared details about his family. He had grandchildren but his wife had died of cancer three years before. His face didn't falter when he told Adam this, instead his whole demeanour lightened.

'She was such a good woman.'

Adam nodded and tried to look sympathetic.

'Allah took the suffering away and so I am most grateful. If anyone deserves Allah's blessing on judgement day it is my Shahida.' He had a faraway look in his eyes.

Adam found Zeeshan's serene nature a comfort. He didn't judge Adam or ask him awkward questions. Their conversations were mostly about Islam or Zeeshan's grandchildren. He had several pictures up in the post room, bright daubs of paint that were out of place amongst the neat typewritten lists.

'Shabnam did that one at nursery. She painted it for her grandpapa,' he said proudly.

'And this one is me.' He pointed to a brown face with tiny

black eyes, black hair and a large mouth filled with white teeth, all except one where the child had painted a large black bit. It was a good likeness for a five year old.

'See?' Zeeshan put his face next to the painting and gave a big grin.

Adam laughed.

'I am blessed in so many ways. It is good to count one's blessings. Allah is generous.'

Adam wondered about that, about how Allah had taken Zeeshan's wife and yet it was seen as a blessing. It made Adam contemplate his own situation; his useless legs. Could he ever consider this wheelchair existence a blessing?

Zeeshan knelt down and Adam placed his hands in his lap to signify he was ready. Following the older man's lead, they started the rakah, Adam bending forwards as the old man knelt and placed his head on the floor. Adam got the sense that Zeeshan quite liked having him there. They murmured the prayers together. Adam felt the familiar peace flow through him. The restfulness and the clarity. At the end Zeeshan stood up and rolled up his mat. They shook hands and Adam went to leave.

'You are new to Islam,' Zeeshan suddenly said.

'Kind of,' Adam agreed.

'It is good that we pray together. It will help you.'

'Yes, thank you.' Adam was embarrassed.

'We can be our own Ummah here at Transport Rail.' Zeeshan smiled, showing off the black hole in his mouth. 'It is Allah's plan that we should pray together.'

Adam nodded, it wasn't like the Ummah of the United Muslims in Action but he was grateful to share his faith and have these calm moments with Zeeshan and their communion with Allah.

Adam pushed the rims of his wheels back towards the lift.

He stopped on the ground floor to get a sandwich from the small canteen and took it with him to his desk.

'I could have got that for you.' It was Melanie, the PA who sat opposite Adam.

'It's fine, I was passing anyway.'

'OK, well just shout if you want anything.'

Adam assured her he didn't. In the first few days, he'd appreciated the extra help, bringing him cups of water and offering to carry things or photocopy for him, but Adam was beginning to get irritated by it. The first couple of weeks had been hard, learning where everything was and spending long hours with Dave Calder as he explained the new asset management system to him. Melanie had been a huge help, but now that he could work the photocopier himself, and had his own sports bottle that he could refill and transport back to his desk without spilling it, her help was becoming an interference. It reminded him of the way his mum fussed around him sometimes.

He took a bite of his sandwich and started to input some of the data sheets Dave had given him. It was fairly dull matching up product numbers and sometimes it was difficult to read what the workmen had written. There were also order sheets that had to be inputted whenever a delivery was received on site, another piece of paper was generated and signed off and all the equipment had to be logged into the system. There was a backlog of paperwork through which Adam was slowly making his way. Dave had said soon the people on site would be able to do it themselves from handheld devices. The sooner the better as far as Adam was concerned. This was mind-numbingly boring.

'Hey, how are you getting on?' It was Dave Calder coming out of his office.

'Fine, I've almost finished the delivery sheets but there's loads more of the other ones."

'Good. Listen, I thought you might be ready to have a go at reports so we'll get together next Tuesday and I'll show you what to do. Are you any good with Excel?'

'It's been a while but I think I'll remember.'

'Good, 'cos that could be useful. It will take a lot more thinking power than this stuff.' Dave gave him a nod and dropped some papers on the desk. 'These are a few of the publications we've done internally over the last couple of months. I'd like you to try and write an article for the next one.'

He picked up the top piece of paper and leaned over the desk next to Adam's arm.

'See, I've already pulled the statistics for you on this one, so you could display them any way you want and write an article around those results. Take a look at the old ones to get an idea.'

'OK.'

'By Thursday?'

'Er, I'm not in on Thursday, it's my day at college.' Adam said.

'Of course, close of play on Friday then?'

'OK.'

'Great. If you get stuck, just come and ask.' Dave Calder gave Adam's shoulder a firm pat. 'Then once you've got a handle on reporting, you'll be able to pull the stats yourself.' He headed back into his office. They certainly kept him busy here. Adam picked up the papers and leafed through them, this was a 'real' piece of work, more interesting than data input. The first piece of work that wasn't just numbers in a computer system. Adam had better get it right. He put the papers down again and stared at the equipment entry screen he was completing.

35

Ralph – Broken down

Ralph was woken by the bright light swamping the bedroom. He shaded his eyes and through his fingers could see a figure standing in the doorway. It was Shelly: she didn't come in, her face cold and unyielding.

'It's six o'clock, dinner's ready,' she said and the door shut once more. Ralph turned to the bedside clock and picked it up. She was right. He lay back on the pillows staring at the thin line that ran most of the way across the ceiling. It couldn't be six already, in two hours he'd have to be back at work to attend to more injuries and illnesses with Ian. But Ralph was so tired, so very tired. He turned on his side and pulled Shelly's pillow over his head to block out the bright afternoon sunlight.

The next time he woke, it was to the door banging against the wall. Ralph flinched and put an arm protectively around the pillow over his head. He listened to Shelly's footsteps come to the side of the bed and then the pillow was wrenched from his hand.

'Get up. It's almost seven and you and I need to talk.' Her voice quavered slightly and Ralph opened his eyes to see Shelly barely containing her fury.

'OK, OK, I'm coming.'

Shelly threw the pillow back at him and stormed out slamming the door behind her. Ralph sighed and sat up; he felt a little shaky as if he'd been ill and not eaten for two days. In the bathroom he switched on the shower, but the noise and hiss was so nauseating that he turned it off and trudged downstairs in his dressing gown.

'Are you ill?' Shelly was sitting at the kitchen table, a glass of water in her hands and a plate of sausages and mash with beans looking cold and neglected. Food was the last thing he wanted.

'I don't think so, well, maybe, I feel a bit strange.'

'I'm not surprised, must feel really strange when your son walks in on your romantic liaison.' Her eyes were large dark pupils, small cannons that shot into him. Ralph turned away and went to switch the kettle on.

She hadn't finished. 'That and half a bloody bottle of Scotch, no wonder you're feeling like shit, well you're not the only one you bastard.'

Ralph kept his back to her, she was so loud, so angry. Like a vicious cat tied to the table spitting at him, straining at its leash which might break at any moment.

'Look at me!' she yelled.

Ralph closed his eyes, the kettle building up to a crescendo.

'Look at me you cowardly piece of shit!'

Ralph turned around. Her face was distorted, high points of pink on each cheek bone. Her hair was loose, tumbling in uncontrolled waves to her shoulders. She was a wild animal and he the cornered prey.

'Well?' she yelled, her mouth set in a grimace that showed her

216

shining teeth.

The kettle clicked off.

'I told you.' He was defeated before he'd even begun. 'It was one kiss, I promise.'

'Here.' She slid an orange and pale card towards him. He picked it up, it was a train ticket to Bristol.

'I thought you were going to Newquay?' Ralph stared back warily.

'I did you idiot, Bristol is where I met up with Rhianna and she drove from there. At least I've got evidence. In fact I don't even need evidence, me and Carl, how could you even think such a thing?' She slammed her hand onto the table. 'He's a conceited prick who thinks more of his job than he does of his family.'

'Where are the boys?'

'Oh, so now you're worried about the boys. It's fine for them to see you smooching with Natalie but not when you and I are having a discussion, is that it?' Ralph could see her white knuckles holding the water glass tightly.

'You're yelling,' he said.

'I know I'm yelling. What do you expect me to do when I go away for the first time in ages and get a phone call from my son to say his dad is having it off with his mate's mum? Jesus Ralph.' There were tears, not so much running as bursting from her eyes. Ralph stood motionless feeling cold and clammy.

'I trusted you, you stupid bastard. How can I be sure it was only one kiss? How do I know anything?' The anger was seeping away and the sobs taking hold. Ralph turned back to the kettle and went through the motions of making an instant cup of coffee with one sweetner. When it was ready, he picked it up and walked to the kitchen door. Shelly was sobbing into her hands on the table. She looked up as he passed.

'Where are you going?' she stammered.

'To bed. I don't feel well.'

'What do you mean? Why won't you talk to me?' Her voice had lowered, softened even.

'I have.'

'Ralph,' Shelly stood up, 'you're crying.'

'Am I?' Ralph put his free hand to his face, it came away wet.

'What's happening? You've been strange for weeks, you fidget in bed all night, forget appointments.' She paused. 'When Liam rang me, I thought it must all be because of your affair with Natalie.'

'I'm not having an affair,' Ralph wiped his eyes, 'I told you that.'

'Then what?' she pleaded, her palms open. Ralph saw her thin wrists, the faint blue lines of veins beneath the skin. It didn't seem possible to bleed to death by cutting such fine blood vessels. He saw the mother on the bed, the sequins twinkling at him from the duvet.

'Ralph!'

He looked at Shelly's face, wet with her own tears.

'I'm going to lie down now; will you call work for me?'

Shelly nodded her head slightly and he continued with his coffee, along the hall and up the stairs.

36

Adam – Worthy of a goddess?

'Hey look,' Adam pulled on Faizal's sleeve, 'it's her.'

A woman swished her way into the hall. Adam and Faizal were sitting to the side near the front. She was wearing a purple Niqab and dark gloves. Behind her another girl hurried in, wearing just a headscarf with jeans and a jumper. She turned and gave Adam a slight nod and a smile, it was Noor, following her sister. Then she tugged on the purple sleeve and her sister turned, Adam caught her eyes for the briefest second before she lowered hers and disappeared behind the screen where the women were grouped together out of sight.

'That was Aisha,' said Adam.

Faizal glanced across at the screen. 'How do you know? She was all covered up.'

'I saw her eyes.'

'So what, all the girls have brown eyes.'

Adam smiled to himself, not like hers, not with that slight greenish fleck. There was something about Aisha that sent tingles down his arms and elsewhere, and seeing only her eyes did nothing to quell his desire. She was as devout as he was and ready to take Islam fully into her life. If anything, he admired her even more. Adam caught Faizal staring at him and turned his attention back to the front where an Imam was taking the microphone.

Later they broke into small discussion groups. Adam was with Faizal and four other young men. Aisha and her sister were in the group next to them. Adam deliberately moved to the edge of his group, closest to Aisha, while everyone was still moving their seating. The topic under discussion was Jihad and what it meant. They were exploring the numerous references in the Qu'ran and the Hadiths. Each group had a kind of leader, usually an older more experienced member who invited questions. As the discussions got underway Adam's attention was drawn to Aisha's group, to her voice, clear and sweet above the general murmur of men.

'What about women and Jihad?'

'A good question sister, there are a number of references to this in the texts. For example in Khashshaf al-Qina, three fifty six, it tells us that women should not fight, women are generally weaker than men and we would not want our enemy to capture or do unto women what Allah has forbidden. Yet it is also clear that women can help in tending to the injured and in other ways.'

'So we cannot fight?'

Adam smiled at her determined confrontation.

'Actually that is not strictly true, you see at times such as when the enemy is seeking to invade a Muslim land, then it becomes an individual obligation - fard al'ayn - on every single Muslim who is able to fight, because Allah says "March forth, whether you are light," which means healthy and young, "or heavy," which means ill or old.'

'So we can fight.'

Adam detected a note of pride in her voice and marvelled at her confidence.

'Is Syria a Muslim country?' the leader continued.

'Yes,' Noor answered loudly.

'And is it under attack?'

This time there was a general murmur of assent.

'Then you have your answer sister.'

Was she really willing to fight? Would she find a way to get across to Syria and fight against ISIS with their Muslim brothers and sisters? A tingle of excitement rushed through him but it was quickly followed by deflation and that awful familiar sense of loss and defeat. If she went to Syria, he certainly wouldn't be going with her. Here she was with a willingness to fight for Islam, what on earth could Adam do?

He let his focus come back to his own group. Faizal was nodding as their leader talked about Jihad being a personal decision. As soon as there was a lull, Adam spoke up.

'What about me? I mean, what about disabled people and Jihad?'

One of the group members piped up, 'It's OK, you don't have to, because you are not physically sound.'

Adam turned angrily to the skinny youth. 'Bet I've got stronger arms than you.'

The leader held up a hand.

'Ah, but it is also said that Allah burdens not a person beyond his scope. Therefore if you continue to pray and keep Allah in your heart, I am sure there will be tasks that are aligned with our fight against the Kafirs that will be within your capability. There is a great deal that we are doing here in the UK to support the UMIA and our journey towards a united Islam. Be patient friend, Jihad may take many forms.'

Before they finished the session, tea was served and the groups began to break up. Some were standing and debating scripture, others sitting and catching up with friends. When he saw the women standing and about to depart, Adam grabbed his opportunity.

'Aisha.'

'Hey Adam, how are you?'

'Yeah, pretty good.' Adam gazed into her eyes, the only part of her that was uncovered, and they were electric. 'I like your-,' Adam paused wanting to say outfit but that sounded all wrong so instead he said, 'modesty.'

'You do?' There was a smile in her eyes and Adam grinned back.

'Absolutely, there's no doubt Allah will look on you favourably come judgement day.'

She laughed then with a musical lilt to her voice. 'I hardly think a Niqab is going to prove very much to Allah.'

'No, no, I...' Adam realised how childish and ignorant his remark was. What an idiot. Then he remembered the odd scene from the other week, when Aisha had been tussling with that kufi-wearer.

'Were you alright, the other week when-' Adam began.

'Aisha.' A tall man had returned and towered over Adam. 'Time to go.'

'Oh.' Aisha rose. 'This is Adam, we went to the same school.'

The man nodded briefly and made a come-on gesture towards Aisha. Adam stared, was this one of the men from the car?

'Don't be rude,' she hissed under her breath at the newcomer.

He rolled his eyes and glared down at Adam.

Adam stared back, smiled, trying to work out if he recognised him.

Suddenly the man thrust out his hand. 'Javed.'

'He's our cousin.' Noor had suddenly appeared from nowhere and looked with clear disdain at Javed.

'Nice to meet you,' Adam said uncertainly.

*

'Jeez, you don't really think you stand a chance with Aisha? She's probably already betrothed. Take my sister for example-'

'Shut up Faizal.'

'I'm only saying.'

'Well don't.' They were heading home on the tube and Adam realised he was digging his thumbnail into the edge of the tyre on

221

his wheelchair. Instead he clenched his hand shut and put it in his lap.

'I mean it's not like you can compete with a surgeon.'

'Who said she's marrying a surgeon?'

Faizal shrugged.

Adam glared out of the window.

'In fact what is your apprenticeship for? Train driver?'

'No.'

'The thing is, even if your legs still worked, didn't you say you'd been training to become a rugby star or something?'

'Football,' Adam said between clenched teeth.

'See, even that wouldn't top a surgeon, well I suppose it might, if you played for England. They earn millions right? Are there any Muslim football players?'

'Just shut up, all right?'

'But brother, there is good news, at least you'll get a chance to inherit the earth, you remember, the meek will inherit the earth and all that?'

'Faizal.'

Adam would show them all one of these days. Somehow he'd find his own Jihad and do something amazing. Be a Muslim man of whom Aisha would be proud. His opportunity would come. Inshallah.

37

Ralph – Lost in space and time

It wasn't the best room in the house, but the bed was comfortable and the curtains fairly thick. If he was going to have a refuge, then their bedroom would have to be it. Ralph kept the curtains closed and used the bedside lamp for soft lighting. The laptop was balanced at the end of the bed playing Ocean's Eleven, one of his favourite films.

Suddenly there were bangs and voices, Ralph studied the screen but it took him a few seconds to recognise the noises were not from the film but downstairs. He could hear Liam's voice goading Cameron and then Shelly telling them to be quiet.

'Ralph?' Her voice sailed up the stairs. Ralph noticed the DVDs strewn all over the duvet and the empty wine bottle on the bedside table. He quickly scooped up the DVDs, shut the lid of the laptop and put them neatly on the floor beside the bed. With the bottle, he raised it to his mouth to catch any final dribbles and then rolled it under the bed. He could hear her footsteps on the stairs.

'Ralph?' She had opened the door. He stayed motionless under the duvet. 'I'm going to cook supper, will you come down?'

Ralph clenched his hands under the duvet, he was asleep, couldn't she see that? He heard her sigh and then the bedroom door closed again and the boys' voices became muffled into the background once more. He just needed to rest for a while, that was all.

Part 2

1 week before the Clapham Junction Memorial

Tuesday
(1 week to go)

38

Adam – Secrets in the system

They were sitting in Dave's office. Adam was waiting patiently while Dave rifled through his bottom drawer. He leaned in close next to Adam's wheelchair, his deodorant strong in Adam's nose. Adam wondered if it was expensive and whether it had the desired effect on the women in the office.

'I've got some worksheets somewhere that we were given during the training. I seem to remember they were quite useful.' Dave dumped the stack of papers onto the side of his large desk and began sorting it. Adam watched him sling his tie over his shoulder out of the way.

'Here we are.' He pulled three pages from the pile. 'You'll have to ignore my scribbles.' He put the papers down beside Adam on the desk. 'Right, we'll use the test system.' He grabbed his office chair and pulled it out of the way, indicating that Adam should take the driving seat.

Once into the system Dave began telling him about how the reports tool worked. He showed him some examples and then Adam tried the first exercise on the worksheet.

'That's it, perfect. Well, you've got this quicker than Melanie did. Do you want to try the next one?'

'Yeah, OK.' Adam felt himself glowing, this was actually quite fun and it all made logical sense how to use the different operators and limiters. The next report was about finding out how many rails would need to be replaced in the next two years between Paddington and Reading. It didn't take long although Dave showed him a couple of shortcuts.

After about an hour, Dave picked up the papers and studied them. 'I don't think there's any more I need to show you. Just have a go at the rest of these and let me know if you get stuck. Then you could try some of your own. Maybe mimic some of the stats that are in those reports I gave you last week.'

'OK then.' Adam took the papers from his outstretched hand and placed them in the side pocket of his chair. He wheeled himself out from behind the desk and towards the door.

'Adam,' Dave said.

Adam had the door open and turned around to see what Dave had to say.

'You're doing well. Keep it up.'

Adam couldn't help smiling back. Maybe this job was going to be all right. If he could impress Dave then he must be doing OK. Melanie had said he was a hard manager to please, but so far Adam had received nothing but praise.

Back at his desk Adam logged onto the test system and got cracking on the other reports. They began to increase in complexity and a couple of times he had to break them down and do two smaller ones before working out how he could combine the information into one. It was almost four o'clock when he turned the page to the last sheet. There were just three more exercises and Adam got distracted by Dave's scribbled notes. He twisted the paper to try and see what he'd written. There was a date in May three years ago circled twice and then on the other side were the names of two stations, Queenstown Road and Clapham. Adam felt a shiver and his left hand automatically went to the rim of his wheel and squeezed hard. Lower down the page was scrawled, *pattern of failure* and lots of exclamation marks. Adam's breathing had quickened and he tried to calm it down. He read through the last three exercises and found the final one was just an open invitation to write your own report. Was that what Dave had been doing when he wrote these notes? Trying out his own report? And why for that date and between those stations?

Adam looked across towards the closed door of Dave's office. He'd said Adam could ask him anything, should he find out?

'Those reports are tricky aren't they?' Melanie was staring at him across the top of the divider. 'I mean I told them, pulling reports from this new system, well it's not in my job description is it? Besides it was like talking gobbledy-gook. Probably fine if you've got a degree in Maths but not me. I hate numbers. Do you need a hand? You never know, I might remember something.'

'No, no, it's fine.' Adam pulled the top two sheets back down over that last one. He licked his lips and stared at the screen. Did the system really hold equipment data right back to the date of the crash and beyond? What pattern of failure had Dave been looking for? Or had he found something?

Adam pushed up the sleeves of his shirt. He began to create a new report but wasn't sure where to start. Pattern of failure. The term rang loudly in his head like some kind of alarm. He thought about Vijay working on his basketball videos, creating patterns of failure for them to analyse. He needed to think like Vijay. Adam grabbed a folder from his desk and started flicking through back to the first few days he'd been here and Dave had given him some reference sheets. What if? Adam began to make a couple of notes. Could there have been an equipment failure? Adam suddenly felt chilled as his sweat cooled. He needed to run some more reports, take a proper look. Besides, that was what the last exercise encouraged him to do, try out his own report. Adam breathed out slowly and watched Melanie gather up her bag ready to go.

'I'll see you tomorrow then. Don't let him make you stay late.' She nodded towards Dave's office.

'I won't.' Adam could feel his dry lips, a cool drink was what he needed but this was more important. He set to work.

39

Halima – Secrets in the Tate

'What do you fancy?' Veronica asked.

They were standing staring at the information board in the Tate Modern. It had been Halima's idea after she'd seen an advert in the local paper. At the time, she'd been proud of coming up with somewhere new to go, but it turned out that Veronica had been here loads of times. Still, she was happy to come anyway which was nice. In fact everything about Veronica was nice. Like her kind questions about her mother and how she, Halima, was managing without her. She'd shared with Veronica about her mother's stroke and the hospital ward where she was under observation and even how lonely she felt without her mother at home. Veronica had been very sympathetic.

'Let's go down to the basement, they've got a special exhibition of masks.' Veronica indicated the place on the map. Halima hadn't really been reading the signs, they reminded her too much of those in the hospital with their great long lists of departments. Mum was on the Nell Gwynne ward, fourth floor.

'It's this way.' Veronica led them down the hall. Halima followed staring at the wooden floor, thinking of the vinyl at the hospital. She'd stared at it, then at the walls and then the other patients. The nurses coming and going, anywhere to look except at her mother. They'd sat mostly in silence. Halima had run out of things to say after the first five minutes and there was no response from her mother. She was propped up on the bed and her eyes roved around but Halima wasn't sure if she even understood anything. Halima had been embarrassed to leave too soon; she thought an hour might be acceptable. Eventually she picked up a newspaper that someone had left on another chair and started to read it. A nurse walked past.

'That's nice, are you reading to her?'

Halima glanced up, feeling caught out. She nodded. The nurse continued on to see to another patient that had been making noises further along the ward. Halima saw another visitor giving her a funny look. Maybe she should read to her mother.

At first it was awkward, Halima didn't do reading aloud, not normally. She was embarrassed to hear her own voice, and she still couldn't get used to the fact that Mum didn't interrupt. There were no opinions thrust at her, no derisory comments. Just silence. Halima wondered where her mother was, did she really still exist inside the collapsed body on the bed? Even the eyes didn't seem the same, not fixing her with that sharp glint but instead wandering around, never resting in one place for long. If they weren't moving, the eyes became still and glassy as if whoever had been operating them had left the control tower. Basically, this just didn't feel like Mum. Even her smell.

Halima stopped reading. She had never thought about her mother's smell before but, here in the bright hospital with its chemicals, she had lost even that. Maybe that was the strangest thing of all, no wonder Halima felt so empty coming here, this stranger in the bed that she didn't know.

She cleared her throat and resumed reading from the newspaper. Gradually it had become easier and she gained a sense of purpose. That perhaps this could be helping. Halima stole a glance at her mother and noticed her eyes had closed. Maybe she was asleep or maybe she had closed them to listen more carefully, either way Halima had a sense of responsibility. She swallowed and started on the next article about an honour killing in Birmingham and then she couldn't read any more. She had put the paper down, picked up her bag and left without a backward glance. That had been yesterday and now here she was in the Tate gallery with her friend Veronica. The time had come to share her secret, and Halima knew it.

'Oh my goodness, look at all those feathers.' They were standing by a glass case with an array of masks from Australia. The one that Veronica was pointing out was particularly magnificent. 'I could just imagine them dancing around a fire chanting and singing, can't you?'

Halima tried to smile. Lovely Veronica.

'Poor you.' Veronica slid her arm through Halima's and led her to the next glass box. 'She'll be all right.'

Halima nodded, but she was beginning to wonder if she, Halima, was going to be all right, let alone her mother. As they crossed the room together to the next cabinets, they passed a lady sat on a bench breast-feeding her infant. The woman smiled but Halima turned away embarrassed. It seemed everywhere she went these days there were babies. Pushchairs galore. Mothers everywhere. Even on her walk to work along the quiet dark streets of early morning, she had passed a house with a light on and a wailing sound coming from within.

'Don't you think it's interesting that so many cultures created such fantastic masks? As if they all wanted to act out or be somebody or something else. All cultures seem to have a story to tell. I think it's fascinating.'

Halima thought about who she'd rather be. How easy, if all you had to do was make a mask of someone and then wear it. You could be anyone you wanted. She thought about the people on TV that she might like to be and then Veronica. Lovely Veronica. What would it be like to be her friend? She could look back on her life in wonder. A husband, a family, two grown boys. Such a full life compared to Halima's own.

Veronica turned to face her friend. 'Are you still thinking about your mother?'

Halima shook her head.

'You look so glum, Halima.'

'Veronica?'

'Yes?'

'You remember I said I'd never had children?'

'Oh dear.' Veronica's face creased and she came to put an arm around Halima. 'Why don't I buy us a nice pot of tea to share and you can sit down.' Veronica guided Halima back the way they'd come and produced one of her neatly folded paper tissues for Halima to use.

Veronica misunderstood at first, started talking about miscarriages and then accidents but Halima put her straight. She explained about Nathaniel, about their love affair and her parents' reaction to the teenage pregnancy. Veronica took this all in her stride with sympathetic nodding and refills from the tea pot. But when she got to the part about death threats, Veronica's face changed.

'What?' It was almost a shout and a group of mothers at a nearby table looked their way. Veronica recovered herself. 'Sorry, I'm sorry.' She grasped Halima's hand across the table. 'Oh my god Halima. Your own father threatened to kill you?'

Veronica's hand was warm and comforting so Halima took a breath and continued with her story, explaining about culture and family. How important it was, back then, not to bring shame on your family. The hardest part for Halima to tell was the leaving. It was dark when her mother woke her up. Halima remembered being so incredibly tired, her parents had argued late and kept her awake. But her mother was whispering urgently.

'Get up Halima, get up.'

'What are you doing?'

'Sshh, put your things on quickly.'

There was a tension and earnestness in her mother's voice that she hadn't heard before. Halima dared not speak but hurriedly dressed. She followed her mother down the dark stairs; it wasn't completely black, dawn was beginning and a pale washed-out grey light filtered in through the window. When they reached the front door, Halima stopped, her mother's large suitcase was sitting on the floor. She was suddenly struck by the finality of everything.

'What about my things?' she whispered.

Her mother looked fearfully back at the stairs and shook her head defiantly.

'Come.' She opened the door gently and through they went out into the icy air of early morning. Halima was dragged along the street, almost losing a shoe as she tried to keep up. Frightened and staring around wide-eyed as if a gang might be approaching at any moment. The street was silent except for a car waiting on the corner, its headlights off.

'Mum, I don't want to go.' Halima pulled back frightened of who might be waiting in the car. She put a protective hand on her small bump.

'Come on.'

As they drew closer Halima recognised it was a taxi, the driver leaned forwards and nodded at them.

'What about Dad?' Halima could hear the panic in her voice.

'Get in.'

The taxi drove for hours and Halima fell asleep at some point in the back. She remembered being woken by her mother when they arrived at a terraced house.

'I've never been back to Birmingham.'

'Never?' Veronica was staring at her.

'No. We had to break all contact; it was the only way to be safe.'

'No wonder I haven't seen you in all these years. How awful for you, I couldn't even begin to imagine. But what about your father, didn't he come and find you?'

'No. Mum said we were better off without him, that she couldn't trust him.'

'But you're his daughter.'

Halima stirred sugar into her last cup of tea.

'I had no idea, I'm so sorry.'

Halima nodded and sipped the tea, although it was only lukewarm. It was good to let it out, like a big sigh to share the story of her life with Veronica. But Halima knew you could never really share one life with another, Veronica would never understand the yawning black hole of despair that Halima had fallen into shortly after their escape. Kept home alone while her pregnant belly bloomed. No Nathaniel, no friends, family, aunties, uncles, the whole lot gone as if they'd been through a holocaust and they'd all been wiped off the face of the planet. Halima and her mother left to survive alone in a small terraced house in the strange city of London.

Veronica squeezed Halima's hand. Then her thumb stroked the soft bit between thumb and first finger. It felt good to be touched. So good in fact that a sob caught in Halima's throat and she had to shield her face in case those mothers looked over again.

'Here, keep the packet.' Veronica passed over the remaining tissues.

'I'm sorry.'

'You have absolutely nothing to be sorry for. Nothing at all.'

'It's just you're so nice,' Halima sniffed loudly, 'nobody else is nice to me except Vincent.'

'Who's he again?'

'Oh, just the security guard where I work. He does the night shift.'

Veronica nodded and gave Halima's hand another pat. Halima finished wiping her eyes and drank the last of her tea. They were ready to go but Veronica was still looking at her curiously.

'Have I got a smear on my face?'

'No, no.' A smile crossed Veronica's features and then she was serious again. 'You didn't say what happened to the baby?'

Halima tidied the cups and saucers back onto the tray. There wasn't much to say about the baby.

'It was a boy.' Halima picked up the tray looking for one of those stands where you slot it in. Not wanting to share how beautiful her child had been. His smooth skin, the colour of milky coffee, lighter than her own. That one perfect night where he'd laid in her arms and she'd fallen deeply in love with his dark brown eyes and his smell. On the edge of his left ear a tiny imperfection that thrilled Halima as it matched her own oddly flattened bit. This beautiful baby was so assuredly hers. It was truly amazing that she had borne such a child into this world.

Veronica stopped her by clutching at her arm. 'But where is he now?'

'They took him away.' Halima spotted the rack and pulled her arm out of Veronica's grasp.

'Away where?'

'I don't know. Mum said he'd have a good family; that he'd be well-looked after.'

They walked out of the cafeteria and back into the hallway of the gallery.

'Haven't you tried to find out?'

Halima turned sharply towards Veronica's wide open eyes. 'No, of course not. Veronica I was fourteen.'

'Yes, but.'

'Where's the exit?.'

'It's that way.' Veronica pointed. Halima set off across the wide open space towards the stairs.

'I'm sorry, I didn't mean to upset you, I was just curious, I'm sorry.'

'You didn't upset me.'

Once outside, Halima gulped lungfuls of the fresh air. She kept walking towards the river, aware that Veronica was just a few steps behind. At the wall they stopped and Halima gazed out over the brown water as it surged past. A riverboat was coming from Blackfriars Bridge.

'Well, I guess I'd better be off then.' Veronica gave a quick smile.

Suddenly Halima felt bad for being so brusque, of course Veronica was curious, who wouldn't be?

'What ward did you say your mother was on? I'll try and visit on Friday, I've got the day off.'

Kind, lovely Veronica. 'Nell Gwynne, level four.'

'Right.'

'Wait.' Suddenly Halima felt bereft all over again as if the one thing she'd ever truly loved was about to be taken away. 'It's not possible to find out where he is, and it wouldn't do any good, would it?'

Veronica stared back. The water surged below them and the pedestrians streamed past. Halima felt suspended, frozen in time and space. As if all the successive years since his birth could be sucked into a hole. Her life rewound to that precious night with her baby boy, Rafiq.

'I don't know,' Veronica said, 'maybe we could find out.'

40

Ralph - Dregs

The phone was ringing, shrill and insistent. Why did they ever decide putting an extension in the bedroom was a good idea? Ralph glared at the lighted gadget on the chest of drawers, willing it to shut up. Eventually it did. Ralph picked up his half-eaten sandwich, grimaced at the plain contents and shoved it in his mouth anyway. He went to pick up his glass but found it was empty. Sighing, he climbed out of bed, shrugged on his dressing gown and trotted down to inspect the fridge. Ralph stood on the cold floor staring at the empty shelf. He went to check the cupboard under the stairs. That's odd. Had Shelly been having people round for dinner? They always had at least half a dozen bottles and usually more. Why hadn't she replaced them? For a moment Ralph contemplated getting dressed and going round to the local off licence. But then he spotted a half bottle of sherry tucked at the back behind the ironing board and there was still some port left over from Christmas. That would do, he could go out later perhaps.

Wednesday
(6 days to go)

41

Halima - On shaky ground

There was something wrong with Jessica's desk that morning. Halima set to work, tidying the normal mess, moving the fluffy pink pen. She couldn't quite put her finger on what it was, just a feeling that something was drastically wrong. Perhaps it was just the worry of her mother in hospital playing tricks on her. She pulled the chair out and picked up a paper from the floor and emptied the bin.

Once she was finished, she still couldn't pinpoint what was making her so uncomfortable. Sighing, she moved on to the next and finished three more desks. She turned the corner and glanced back across at Jessica fluffy-pink-pen's desk, and that's when it registered. The photograph was missing. Halima froze, her hands on the trolley. Where was the photograph? Maybe that man she'd met a couple of months back had really taken Jessica's place. But she didn't want that, she didn't want any more changes. Halima decided to go back and check the desk more thoroughly. Everything else seemed normal, even the pencil with the chewed end. Then, for the first time ever, she opened each of the three drawers, but it wasn't there. Suddenly she spotted the pale wooden edge, wedged between the back of the monitor and a red project file. She pulled it out, but as she did so, she saw Cheryl coming out of another of the managers' offices. Halima ducked down and then peeked between the curved boards that separated each quad of desks. Cheryl had something gripped in her hands and was looking about her. She hurried into the cleaner's room and shut the door behind her. Halima realised she still had the photograph in her hand. Quickly she pulled out the little triangle shape and stood it up in its normal position.

Satisfied, Halima went back to her trolley. When Cheryl came out of the cleaning room, she was facing Halima and seemed a little startled to see her.

'Where did you spring from?' she demanded.

'Nowhere.' Halima shrugged and kept pushing her trolley.

'You weren't here just now.' Cheryl looked around the room as if searching out a place where Halima might have hidden. 'I looked.'

'I was scrubbing at a mark under one of the desks, that's probably why.' Halima found the lie easily slipping out.

'Hm.' Cheryl pursed her lips and stormed off.

42

Adam- Sharing the secret

Cara plonked two plates on the table. 'Ere you go, I would 'ave made more if I'd known you were comin','

'Thanks, I didn't mean to put you out,' Adam said.

'Forget it, it's only spag bol.'

Vijay winked at Adam. 'Thank you Cara. Do you still want to get to that dance class?'

'Shit, I forgot all about that, what's the time?'

'I think you'll make it, now that Adam's here, you can go if you want.' Vijay gave Adam that quirky smile of his. What was that supposed to mean?

'Great, I'll just get changed then.' Cara disappeared.

Adam rolled up to the table to see what spag bowl was. It smelt funny.

'Is this meat halal?'

'Oh dear, not more of your religious indoctrination,' Vijay sighed, whirring his chair around to stop beside Adam.

'It's not indoctrination, it's shari'ah. You've no idea what a difference it's made to my life.'

'Do bore me with the details.'

Adam moved the pasta around on the plate. Just then Cara

reappeared in tight leggings and a T-shirt.

'Right, I'm off, you'll still be 'ere when I get back won't you Kiddo?'

'This isn't pork is it?'

'Go Cara, I'll be fine,' Vijay insisted, then turned to Adam. 'No, it's beef mince. What planet do you live on? See you Cara.'

Adam pushed the plate aside and noticed there was still more plain spaghetti in a colander over the pan that Cara had left on the table. Adam pulled it towards him and took a forkful of pasta, he was starving.

'So you were going to give me the details of your Islamic conversion.'

'Seriously Vijay, it's not a joke. I think this is what Allah wants me to do. Ever since I started praying things have been going right.'

'Like?'

Adam considered sharing about Aisha, but he didn't want Vijay to say anything sarcastic or rude about her. Besides, he'd probably point out the fact that cripples like him and Vijay never got the best girls. And then there was the elite group within the UMIA, he was bound to get contacted soon but he couldn't share that either.

'Well I got the job for starters.'

'The apprenticeship, which you didn't really want.'

'That's not the point, it's all in Allah's plan.'

'Really? Do you think providing me with some sustenance might be in his plan too?'

'What?' Adam looked at Vijay's untouched plate of spaghetti and sauce. 'Oh sorry. I forgot.' He took the fork that Cara had put on the table and scooped up some food guiding it carefully towards Vijay's mouth. 'No wonder you let Cara go out, so you could use me instead.'

Vijay chewed while Adam prepared another forkful, it wasn't easy at this angle and then he realised there was no reason for the plate to be in front of Vijay. Adam moved it so he could more easily cut up the spaghetti.

'There must be some retribution if I've got to listen to your religious fanaticism.'

'It's not fanaticism. It's true and real. The United Muslims in Action group is against fundamentalism. We're nothing like ISIS or Boko Haram. Seriously, it's like it's answered all my questions. I've never felt this good, at least not since the accident.'

Vijay coughed and a small piece of spaghetti dropped onto the table. Adam ignored it and put another mouthful in.

'I think Allah might be trying to show me something.'

'Like how to get brain-washed.'

'No Vijay, can you just be serious for once?'

'I haven't seen you in ages and then you turn up full of religious fervour, certainly looks like brain-washing from where I'm sat.'

'You spend all day in front of your computers doing finances for your dad's hotels, then you spend your evenings learning even more stuff about accounting and I don't know what, does that mean you've been brain-washed into money? Is that your religion?'

'Good point.' Vijay gave that quirky smile of his. 'Yes I guess I am a fervent believer in money. How to manipulate it, spend it, save it, distribute it. Hmmm. I like that.'

'See. It's not just me who's fanatical about something.'

'Actually, having you here is quite entertaining. You should come over more often. It can get quite dull talking to people from your own religion all the time.'

Finally Vijay opened his mouth again so that Adam could feed him some more instead of talking. He chewed slowly and then started speaking again.

'By the way, I meant to ask you. What exactly do you do in this new job of yours?'

Adam stopped with the fork part way to Vijay's lips.

'Actually that was what I wanted to talk to you about, I think that was part of His plan too.'

'You'd better tell me about this divine plan or I shall die of anticipation.'

Adam filled Vijay's mouth. 'OK, enough of the sarcasm. The thing is we've got this system at work.' Adam told Vijay all about the data management and the reports. About the kind of equipment and parts that it was designed to monitor. 'So maybe Allah put me there for a reason.' He paused, not sure quite how to go on. 'To make me take note of what the system could show me.'

'Which was?'

Adam took a breath, he wasn't certain yet, but he had to share it with someone. It felt as if the knowledge was burning his insides.

'I think I've found a reason for the Clapham Rail disaster.'

The room was silent, Adam could hear the clock on the wall ticking, they'd finished eating and the cutlery lay discarded on the plates. Some of the pasta and sauce was missing from his own plate and he couldn't be sure if he'd eaten it himself or fed it to Vijay. He hoped Allah would understand his slip in concentration.

'You did say this was test data?'

Adam's shoulders slumped. 'Yes, that's the problem, I don't know if they just made it all up or whether they got it from somewhere, that's where I thought you could help. You know all about corporate systems and stuff.'

'Hmmm, test data is usually an import from another system, their previous database perhaps. What did you say the software was called?'

'Rail Asset Management.'

'Do you know the name of the software company that built it?' Vijay reversed from the table. 'Or did they design it in-house?'

'Um, I think it was something like Tyre Data Enterprises, actually no, I think it started with T H.' Adam followed Vijay as he headed across the lounge and through the doorway that led to his office.

On the large desk running along one wall the three monitors were all displaying the same screen saver. Vijay lined himself up in front of the screen at the end.

'Can you plug me in?'

Adam found the thick black cable with one of those plugs full of tiny pins. He plugged it into the joystick box on Vijay's chair.

Suddenly all three screens came to life. Adam stared as Vijay expertly entered a password and began navigating on the internet. It was amazing what he could do with just a joystick and a few buttons.

It was difficult to keep up, Vijay seemed to be searching for something about the software but he was obviously quicker at scanning a page than Adam was. It was incredible how someone who couldn't even wipe their own arse could make Adam feel so inadequate.

'How about this one, Thyredata Enterprises, specialises in DBMS's.'

'What does that mean?' Adam stared at the screen but Vijay had already clicked.

'Database Management Systems.'

'Yes, that's the logo.'

'OK, we're getting somewhere.' Vijay hopped around the company website for a while.

Adam checked his watch. 'I need to go soon, I'm not sure when the last bus is.'

'Don't worry about that, Cara will drop you back.'

'Oh OK, thanks.' Adam was relieved. This had definitely been the right place to come, Vijay knew so much, he would be able to give Adam the next step. The next step in this new road he was following. Allah's path. In fact couldn't it be possible that Allah had introduced him to Vijay for just this purpose? It wasn't as if they had very much in common. Maybe everything had been leading up to this point, to help Adam discover the cause of the disaster that obliterated the use of his legs. That had killed and injured others too. Adam nodded to himself, he felt strong and excited. This was it. This was his purpose, to seek retribution for the wrongs that had been done to him and the other victims of the crash.

Vijay swivelled his chair from under the desk to face Adam.

'I'm assuming you did actually try your queries in the live system?'

'Err no. It only went live about six months ago, it's just recent stuff.'

'Try it anyway, just to make sure. Sometimes what someone says about the data doesn't match the reality. Check it for yourself,' Vijay instructed.

'OK.'

'There's more investigating you'll need to do. From what you've said about the data, you must cross-reference and tie the queries together. Triple-check your codes, you can't afford to make a mistake.'

Adam nodded and flexed his hands, then put them together in his lap. Thank you Allah.

'We also have to find the source of the test data to see if it's reliable. Your whole hypothesis hinges on that data being accurate. Find the implementation documentation and go through it with a fine-tooth comb. If any of it is held electronically then email it to me, but not to my normal account, I'll send you a different email address.'

Adam licked his lips, his mouth was dry. He'd never seen Vijay so serious.

'What if it is?'

'What do you mean?' Vijay gazed steadily at Adam.

'I mean, what if we find it's true, that the data is reliable like you say?' Adam swallowed.

'Let's not open that can of worms yet. One step at a time.'

They were silent for a moment and then Vijay said quietly, 'You might want to pray that your query was wrong.'

43

Ralph – Losing focus

The film had finished and Ralph was studying the thin line that ran across the ceiling. It stopped just short of the light fixture in the centre of the room. In some parts it was ruler straight, in others, tiny wiggles made an inaccurate line. Like when you cut wrapping paper, and some of it tears a bit but the rest is cut smoothly with the scissors. Suddenly there was noise, lots of noise and it wasn't behind a closed door. Ralph sat up in bed. Liam and Cameron stood in the doorway shoving each other, Cameron was holding some kind of toy gun.

'Dad,' Cameron shouted. 'This one's mine isn't it? Remember you put gaffer tape on the end when it broke.' Cameron was trying to show Ralph without Liam grabbing it out of his hand. The boys scuffled and swore.

'It's not yours, it's mine. Give it back you little squirt.' Liam shoved Cameron roughly against the door. 'Dad, tell him. His got thrown in the bin, it's mine!'

'Get off me.'

Ralph watched them struggle for a moment and then he let his head sink back into the pillow and his eyes rest on the thin line. The noise subsided and Ralph could hear their breathing.

'Are you going to marry Troy's mum?' a quiet voice enquired. It was Cameron. Ralph lifted his head again and frowned. The two boys were staring at him. Liam clipped Cameron on the side of his head with his hand.

'You idiot,' Liam shouted at his brother and dragged him out of the room. The door slammed shut.

Thursday
(5 days to go)

44

Austin - Taking the brakes off

It was almost lunch time and Austin thought it might be a nice change to walk outside instead of relying on the canteen. He shrugged on his jacket and headed down in the lift.

The sun was shining out in the street, a welcome surprise to the flat light intensity of the office. In fact it was too warm for this jacket but he'd already packed his lighter one ready for the move. He marched down past the Royal College of Art and crossed the road to a small deli. It was while he was waiting for his avocado and cream cheese that he noticed there was an envelope in his pocket. It was a letter he didn't remember, still unopened. Austin turned it over in his hands, he must have put it in his pocket the last time he wore this jacket, which was ages ago; he hoped he hadn't missed anything important.

It was rather heavy paper, the kind you expected solicitors to use. He tore it open and read the letter. It was an invitation. A memorial. He tried to breathe a little deeper, it felt like somebody was squeezing him too tight. A memorial event for the victims, friends and families of the Clapham rail disaster.

'Do you want anything else with that?' The lady behind the counter popped his sandwich neatly wrapped in paper onto the top of the counter.

'Um, an Appletise please.'

Austin paid and left.

'Your sandwich.'

'Oh, thanks.' He went back and picked up his drink and roll. Outside again, he suddenly didn't want to go straight back to the office, instead he went towards the Thames and walked along the side of the river towards Albert Bridge. Just beyond was the edge of Battersea Park. He took the pathway past trees and bushes. Tulips made a colourful array in one of the flower beds. It was too warm for his jacket so he took it off and sat down on one of the benches to face the river and re-read the invitation. Odd that he should read it just as he was putting the finishing touches on his new life. Perhaps Matt's parents would have received one too. Would they come in from Guildford to go? Probably. In fact, they might as well go together, mutual support and all that. Austin munched on the fresh bread, the avocado squashing between his teeth.

But what would he do about David? He disapproved of Austin's relationship with Pat and John or 'your dead boyfriend's parents' as David cruelly put it. And what would he say about a memorial event three years after Matt's death? David would say he shouldn't go, that looking back would just make him sad and perhaps he was right. Did Austin really want to visit the site where Matt was killed?

Austin had squeezed his sandwich so tight that a blob of cream cheese had dropped onto his knee. He scraped it off with his finger and licked it. Although he could feel the tension in his neck, he didn't feel like crying and that gave him a sense of relief. He thought back to those sessions with the counsellor when she'd talked about the five stages of grief and he'd thought she was mad, all there was was pain and more pain. Yet sitting here watching the Thames flow slowly past he recognised that he had far more good days than bad days. That he hadn't needed those pills for almost a year. Maybe he was finally getting to that last stage: acceptance. And maybe David had helped him with that. He was getting used to his large bulk in the bed which was now almost half the week. Soon he would be moving home, away from the memories of Matt, and David had encouraged him to put the photos and albums in a box in the bottom of the wardrobe. Now the only photo of Matt he had on display, was at work. The one on his desk.

Austin put the invitation back in his pocket. He had his new life. David. And soon the flat. There'd even been mention of a promotion at work. In fact it seemed so much had changed since

Matt had died. And actually that was OK. Austin screwed up the paper from his sandwich and headed back towards the office.

As he approached his desk, his mobile buzzed in his pocket. It was a message back from David.

V busy. Speak soon. See you later. XD

Austin grinned to himself, texted a reply and sat down at his desk. The photograph of Matt stared back at him: Austin picked it up and held it in his lap. He was sure he'd shoved it in with his folders the other day. Maybe David's approach was right, maybe he needed to put Matt away, to live in the moment. In this new life he had made for himself. What would he gain from going to the memorial? Austin slipped the photograph into his desk drawer, screwed up the invitation and chucked it towards the bin under his desk. Then, taking a breath, he opened up the testing document he was working on, but just as his fingers settled on the keys to type, the desk phone rang. He glanced at the grey display, it was an internal call.

'Hello, Austin Baker speaking.'

'Hi Austin, it's Tim. I've got some guy from Transport Rail on the phone.'

Austin immediately thought of David, but then he already knew Austin's direct number.

'He wants to find out some stuff about the implementation of the Rail Asset Management System. I'm supposed to be in a meeting, I wondered if you could speak to him instead. You know as much as I do.'

'OK, sure.' Austin wondered why on earth someone would be calling them now? They'd finished that project nine months ago.

'Hello?' A tentative young voice was put through.

'Hi, this is Austin Baker, how may I help?'

'Erm, well I was asking the other guy about the test system.'

'Yes? What would you like to know?'

'Well, um, where did the data come from? I mean, is it valid?'

Austin wondered why on earth an employee from Transport

Rail was asking him questions about their test system. Thyredata Enterprises were no longer responsible for it, they had completed the project successfully and the rail company had full ownership of it. As far as Austin remembered, they were going to keep the test system to use for training purposes, which made sense. He tried to think back to when they first populated some data. There had been several attempts to get it right which was quite normal with a system of that size. But each attempt had used the same source data from the company themselves.

'It was your own historical data from the obsolete database.'

'Oh right. So it was real data?'

Austin frowned. 'Well it was whatever data you had in the old system, I can't comment on that data.'

'No, no, OK, but it was our data, about our rail parts and everything.'

'Yes.' Austin paused considering the apparent naivety. 'Perhaps you'd be better talking to your own IT department about this. They will have all the project documentation.'

'Right, yes. So is it, well, will it tell me what data and when kind of thing.'

Austin was getting tired of this. 'It should detail the transfer and upload process in depth and give you the timestamps of those uploads, together with the errors.'

'Errors? What, errors in the data?'

'Not specifically, I mean it can appear as corrupt data but it's more to do with the mapping to specific fields. It can be difficult to get the mapping exact and this usually takes some working through. Do you know much about databases?'

'Um, I'm learning.'

Austin smiled to himself, at least the kid was honest. 'I suggest you talk to your IT department then, they'll be much more helpful than I can be. Also now that we've completed the project, if you need any consultancy work, we will have to charge you. Sorry about that.'

'Oh, OK. Thanks, you've been very helpful.'

'No problem, what did you say your name was?' Austin said.

But the phone connection had gone and Austin had too much

work to do. There was a reminder flashing on his screen for the project meeting that was starting in ten minutes.

45

Adam – Sitting on the evidence

Adam wiped a hand across his forehead, it came away damp. He swallowed the last of his water from his bottle. He just wanted to finish this last query. He'd done everything that Vijay had suggested and it was all tying together. The cross-referencing, the faulty parts. On his desk he had a series of printed tables of figures, the evidence to prove what he'd discovered. It was frightening. Around him the office was particularly tense that morning, as if the other employees were all waiting for something. The noise muted like a great blanket had been laid across the open plan room. Adam stole a glance around. Nobody seemed suspicious about what he was doing but it felt as if they were all watching.

'Hey, how's it going?' Dave stood right behind him.

There was no chance to change the screen or even shift papers under a folder. Adam's heart picked up speed.

'I forgot to mention, great job on that article last week. There was very little I had to change before passing it on. Good job.'

Adam nodded, not sure where to put his eyes. If he kept staring at the screen, Dave was sure to look. Instead he tried to normalise his features and voice. He turned his chair to face his boss.

'Thanks.'

'No problem, I've got some back-ups I'd like you to do and some complicated query that Neil wants. I thought you might like the challenge. I'll email them across to you.'

Adam nodded.

'Keep it up.' Dave gave his shoulder a pat and then he was gone, walking back across the office, stopping to talk to Melanie beside the photocopier as he went.

Adam exhaled slowly, a cold shiver running down his spine. Using the mouse he saved the current document to his personal work area and then collected up the papers and put them in a blank cardboard folder he had ready. He would take them to show Vijay tonight, he'd already sent some documentation electronically. Adam rubbed his face with his hands. He double-checked that everything was away before wheeling himself towards the water cooler. Glancing at his watch, he realised he'd better head straight down to see Zeeshan so they could pray together. Adam filled the cup twice, gulping down the cool liquid. He was wound so tight, like he was balancing on a wire and any small mistake could send him dropping off into the abyss. He pressed the button for the lift. Even being late for prayers could tip the balance, as if he didn't do exactly as he should then Allah would send him spinning. The doors closed and Adam descended. He closed his eyes for a moment, praying for Allah's guidance. The doors opened and it was immediately clear that there was a problem.

'You cannot put them there, that will never do.' It was Zeeshan.

Adam rolled out of the lift and headed across the tiled floor. A delivery man was placing a box onto a stack by the door of Zeeshan's little room.

'This is ridiculous. You'll only have to come back again.'

The delivery man was engrossed; ignoring Zeeshan's waving arms and heading back out to a waiting van. Zeeshan stormed into his post room, slammed the door behind him and picked up the phone. Adam watched him through the glass.

The delivery man was back with another box in his hands which he added to the stack. Zeeshan stuck his head out of the door. 'Stop, I tell you.'

The door slammed again and Zeeshan replaced the phone, then picked it up again and dialled another number. He was gesticulating wildly.

'Right, that's the lot.' The delivery man was back again, this time with a clipboard on top of the final box. 'Here, sign this.' He thrust the clipboard at Adam.

'Doesn't he have to sign?'

'Do you work here?'

'Yes.'

'Then you'll do.' He pointed out the line where a signature was needed. 'Listen, I've got a bunch more deliveries to do, I can't be hanging around here.'

'Don't sign that.' Zeeshan poked his head around the door, the phone lead stretched to breaking point.

Adam looked at his watch, they should be praying.

'Look, see here's the order note, ten boxes of three hundred gram headed paper.'

Adam stared at the invoice, it seemed correct.

'See, ten boxes.' The delivery man counted the two stacks of five aloud to make his point. 'If you need to return some, he knows the process.' He gestured a thumb towards the window where Zeeshan was still gesticulating wildly while talking on the phone. Adam checked his watch yet again. He signed the sheet and the delivery man doffed his cap and left.

'Where's he gone?' Zeeshan came storming out of the office.

'Here.' Adam held out the invoice.

'You signed it.' He glared. 'I can't believe it, this is crazy, what am I supposed to do with it all? Ten packets is all, not ten boxes of the stuff. Good grief, what am I supposed to do with that lot?' Zeeshan smacked his hand onto the top box which stood as tall as he did.

'Zeeshan. The time. We need to pray.' Adam was sweating again; the water he'd drunk already evaporating through his pores.

'Pray, you expect me to pray now with all of this? Are you crazy boy? You go pray if you want to and make sure you ask Allah to get these boxes out of here. Got it? I've got a crisis here. Give me that.' He snatched the invoice from Adam's hand and slammed the door behind him.

Adam sat motionless, a trickle of moisture slid down his neck in to the little hollow at the top of his chest. This wasn't how it was supposed to be. They always prayed together, Adam had come to rely on Zeeshan, his soft voice and gentle demeanour.

The way he guided them through the rakah each day. And today of all days, he needed that peace and tranquillity, that sense that Allah was with him, guiding him, supporting him.

Adam rolled his wheelchair closer to the window, but Zeeshan was back on the phone, red-faced. Joe the stores man was setting up a ladder near one of the high shelves and someone else was banging a trolley down the corridor. Where was he supposed to pray without Zeeshan? His little post room with its big window was their sanctuary, their private haven to faith. Adam felt sick. It wasn't an option today, to miss prayers. He had been so dedicated these last weeks, months. And now, more than ever, he really needed that peace. The path ahead terrified him.

Upstairs on his desk could be the reason behind the Clapham rail disaster which killed twenty-seven people and injured countless more. What could he possibly do without Allah's guidance? Especially now, especially with that information burning a hole into his desk. Had he put it in his desk drawer or left it out? Again he wiped a hand across his top lip, it came away wet. Adam swivelled around and headed back towards the lift.

46

Halima – Faulty records

Halima was watering the plants when the intruder appeared. It was a woman, short and dumpy in a navy coat. Halima stood rooted to the spot, trying to understand how the woman could be standing in her kitchen doorway looking out at her.

'Hello.' The woman smiled.

Halima hadn't left the front door open, she never did, not in this neighbourhood. Finally she found her voice, 'How, how did you get in?'

'I have a key.' She raised it up like some kind of talisman. 'From Mrs Shah. I did try the bell.' She beamed at her as if this explained everything. 'Are you the gardener?'

Halima stared. 'No.' She put the watering can down and stared at the stranger. 'What are you doing in my house?'

'Your house?' For a moment the woman seemed uncertain and then she recovered. 'This house is owned by the council and tenanted by Mrs Kaneez Shah.' She raised her other arm which was carrying a fairly heavy bag as if that was evidence. 'I should be asking what you're doing here?'

'I'm her daughter and I live here,' Halima asserted.

'Ah, that explains it then. We only have one tenant in our records, are you staying here while your mother is in hospital?' This woman seemed very sure of herself and was blocking the back door.

'No, I always live here. Have always lived here.' The woman seemed to be expecting more. 'I live here,' Halima added again.

'Hmm, well why don't you come in and we can sort it out. I have Kaneez's file with me.' The woman turned and marched through to the lounge. Halima couldn't think of anything better to do than follow. Who the hell was this woman?

'There that's better.' She sat down on the sofa, in Halima's spot and started to pull out cardboard files and papers from the heavy bag. She looked up. 'Won't you sit down?' She patted Halima's mother's chair. Halima scowled at the old armchair and frowned at the woman sat on the most comfy part of the sofa. She should ask this woman to leave, but then she had Mum's key, why was that?

'First things first. I'm Eve Springs from the council. And you are?'

'Halima,' said Halima as she slumped down into her mother's chair. 'Halima Shah.'

'So is it you who's been to visit Kaneez in hospital a couple of times?' she asked.

'I've been more than twice.'

'Hmm.' She busied herself with the papers.

Halima had never seen this woman before, how could she know when she'd been to see Mum?

'It's two bus rides away,' Halima said, 'and I work….and the buses aren't reliable.'

'You don't drive?' she inquired with a non-committal face.

'No.'

'Very wise, I'm sure.' She shuffled a few more papers and then settled on one. 'Right then, the tenancy was reviewed almost three years ago and at that time Mrs Shah said only she was living here, let me see, that you had recently left very suddenly.'

'What?' Halima was startled.

The woman kept reading from her paper. 'I believe Kaneez was quite upset at the time, the notes say you had gone to live with your boyfriend but she didn't have an address.'

'That's crazy. I don't have a boyfriend and I never moved out.'

'Hmm.' She paused as if to give Halima more time to explain. 'Are you saying that Kaneez was mistaken or that she lied?'

'I...errr...' Halima was at a loss, why would Mum say she had moved out? It didn't make sense. Three years ago?

'This is dated May the twenty-fourth.'

Halima stared, wondering why the date sounded so familiar. Of course, the invitation to the re-opening of platform 9 which lay on her chest of drawers upstairs, it was in just a few days. May the twenty-fourth three years ago was the day after the crash when she'd been kept in hospital over night. She remembered coming home, an argument with her mother about where she'd been over night and then her mother's tears of relief that Halima hadn't left her.

'Perhaps you have evidence that you've been living here?' the woman persisted. 'We would need to see a utility bill or something similar with your name on and this address.'

'But.'

'You see, Ms Shah, this property is in your mother's name and if you are not declared on the tenancy and you cannot prove that you have been living here then you will not be considered during my assessment.'

Halima was decidedly queasy. 'Assessment of what?'

'Of whether this is still suitable accommodation for Kaneez to live in, considering her recent illness.'

'But I pay the bills, I...I do everything.'

'Then you won't have a problem in showing me a utility bill?' The woman folded her hands on top of the papers expectantly.

Halima was about to go and get the latest bill sitting on the kitchen windowsill and then she remembered that no, the bills were not in her name, they had always been in her mother's name. Why change them? Halima racked her brain.

'What about a mobile phone bill?'

'I'm afraid we don't accept that as proof of address.' Her lips had drawn into a thin line. 'We need something official, a driver's licence-' Halima was sure she smirked then. '-or a passport, or a bank statement.'

'Bank statement.' Halima leapt on the words. Of course she could give them a bank statement. The woman didn't smile, she simply waited. Halima pushed herself out of the sagging chair and went upstairs. The bottom drawer of her chest was where she stuffed paperwork. She pulled out old bills, all addressed to Kaneez Shah, a mobile phone contract, a couple of old newspapers and the information about the sheltered housing. No bank statements. Damn. Halima scratched at the scar on her scalp. This was ridiculous. She yanked the drawer all the way out and tipped it onto the floor. She scattered the papers with her hands and heard a voice from below.

'Ms Shah!' It was that horrible woman sounding impatient.

The bank statements weren't here, impossible. Halima's shoulders sagged and she stood up, but there was a blue corner sticking out from under the chest of drawers. Back on her knees she peered in the gap where the drawer had been and saw a whole pile of more papers on the floor and at the back by the wall.

The council woman noted something down on her form as she analysed the statement carefully. 'You will need to send me a more up-to-date one, but I shall note this one to cover last December.'

Halima found she was scratching at her scar and tried to calm herself. 'OK.'

'However, I assume you've spoken with the hospital. Kaneez is unlikely to be coming back here. She's going to need a lot more care I'm afraid.'

'What do you mean? I've always looked after her. I only work in the morning.'

'That may be so, but she's going to need professional help. As you know, she can neither move around without assistance or eat. However, her condition has stabilised and people do recover from strokes.'

She was writing notes and then looking critically around the lounge. 'The council is short of housing. I need to go upstairs,' she announced. Before Halima could respond, she was on her feet and marching out of the room. Again Halima followed as she poked her nose into both bedrooms and the bathroom.

'In my opinion-' the woman was back on the sofa, '-this property is no longer suitable for Mrs Shah. I'll pass on the fact that you're living here to the housing department and they'll be in touch about alternative accommodation for you.'

'But-' Halima was at a loss.

'Unless you can afford round-the-clock care and put in a downstairs bathroom then this property will not be suitable for Mrs Shah.' She stared pointedly at Halima. As no response was forthcoming, she signed off the form she was filling in with a flourish and then fiddled around in her bag.

'Here.' She passed Halima several pages. 'Why don't you make a housing application for yourself, it could speed things along as I doubt very much that you'll be allowed to stay here.'

Halima took the sheets and stared at them blankly.

'I'll return the key to Mrs Shah.' The woman was on her feet and heading for the door. She pulled it open and then turned back towards Halima. 'I know this is a difficult time but I'm sure your mother would appreciate more regular visits.' And with that she was out and pulled the door shut behind her.

47

Adam - Hamster in the wheel

'Have you shared this with anyone else?' Vijay asked.

Adam shook his head. They were in Vijay's study in front of his bank of computer screens. Adam had pinned up the sheets onto a stand that Vijay used for reading. On two of the screens were the documents that Adam had emailed through.

'Well?' Adam asked.

Vijay didn't look at him, instead he left the office, his wheelchair whirring gently through the doorway and into the lounge. Adam followed.

'Cara my dear, could you get a couple of beers and give us some privacy?'

Cara glanced up from the Hello magazine she'd been reading on the sofa. She opened her mouth as if about to give her usual crass sarcasm but instead she looked from Vijay to Adam and back again.

'Sure,' she said and disappeared.

Vijay went towards the window staring out over the dockyard. It was a fabulous view, one for which he, or more likely his father, must have paid through the nose. Adam couldn't even guess at how much a pad like this would cost.

Cara returned with the beers, a straw in Vijay's. She popped it in the holder on his chair, offered the other to Adam.

'I don't drink,' he said.

'Of course. Allah dictates,' Vijay added.

'There's always milk in the fridge Kiddo.' Cara grinned and put the open beer bottle on the coffee table before leaving the room.

Adam was feeling sick. He knew part of it was because he hadn't eaten much today, he hadn't been able to face it with his churning stomach. His skin felt cold, he closed his eyes, and for a second wished that he was at home in bed. Wished that he still had the bedroom at the top of the house with his football posters on the walls. Wished that he was tired from a match in which they'd won. That tingling heaviness in his legs from overuse. Lying in bed wondering how long it would be till he hit the big time, before he became one of the England players.

'Don't underestimate the position you're in,' Vijay said.

Adam felt himself wrenched back into the room, into his wheelchair, his legs hanging numb. That wretched feeling in his stomach. There was no putting the clock back, no getting his legs back. This was now, this was the reality he had to face.

Vijay turned his chair to face Adam, 'You might not drink, but I need one.' His eyes went to the bottle in its holder. Adam shook his head.

'You're very stubborn, did you know that?' Vijay said.

'I'm a Muslim.'

Vijay smiled. 'Do you remember how we met?'

'What?'

'At the physio unit' - he turned his chair towards the window again - 'so stubborn and full of rage you were, it blinded you.'

Adam tried to recall the first time he'd met Vijay. There had been so many physio appointments after the initial recovery. Weeks, months and now years of physio. His mother and sometimes his father had helped enormously in the beginning, but as he'd developed more independence and movement, he didn't want them touching him. He didn't bother with the exercises any more. It didn't really matter, despite what the doctors said about the remote possibility of his being able to move his legs again, he didn't believe them. There had been nothing but ghostly feelings ever since the accident.

But in those early days, no one knew what was possible. Some days he'd spent hours in the physio area. It was a big room with all sorts of strange contraptions and equipment. Often there were other patients, one or two struggling to do some minor physical activity like raising a leg weight, or squeezing a hand press at the table. Adam didn't even notice who was there that day. He was focused on getting to the end of that walkway.

Adam lined himself up with the bars, he was sure that today would be it, he'd gained strength in his arms, had been practising several times a day lifting his body up a few inches from his seat with his arms on the sides of the chair, up and down, over and over. He leant forwards and grasped the shiny metal.

'Hold on, let me get around the front.' A physio with dark hair and big hands went to the far end.

Adam didn't want to wait, he heaved forwards and upwards, his arms shaking with the effort until he was able to lock his elbows straight. His legs were off the foot board of the wheelchair and on the floor, but one foot was twisted to the side.

'Hang on.' The physio bent down and set Adam's foot in line with the bars. The physio stood up in front of Adam, his hands grasping Adam's hips.

'Don't touch me.'

'Breathe for a moment, then when you're ready think about twisting and swinging those hips. Gently mind.'

Adam could see the physio's hands holding firmly.

'Let go.'

The hands loosened slightly.

'Get out of the fucking way.'

The physio shook his head. 'I can't let you fall.'

'It's my body, fuck off.'

Adam grunted staring at the far end of the bars, they were only three metres long but it seemed miles. He breathed short and sharp loudly through his mouth. With a jerk he twisted, almost lost his grip with his left hand but was able to edge it at least a few inches along the bar. His feet were still in line but a little further underneath him.

'Let me get you lined up again.'

'No.'

Adam clenched the bars tightly, he fixed his gaze on the end of the metal curve and heaved, this time attempting to swing slightly left to release his right hand to inch along the other bar. But something went wrong and he was pitching forwards, he gripped the bars and hung in a swing briefly before letting go and rolling down onto his chest, his chin connecting with the floor. He felt his teeth clunk together and the taste of blood in his mouth.

'Oh Jeez, Catherine, can you give me a hand?'

'Get off me.' Adam swung an arm thumping the physio on his blue-trousered leg.

'Woah, take it easy.'

'Fuck off, don't touch me. Leave me alone.'

'Adam we…'

'It's all right, leave him to cool down a moment. Let's move Vijay to another room.'

Adam shut his eyes tight, the tears squeezing out despite his attempt to keep them in. The floor was cold and hard under his cheek and smelt of bleach. If he wanted to, he could drag himself across the floor on his elbows, his useless legs trailing behind like some giant slug. But he didn't want to. He didn't want any of this. The constant failure, the falls. He hated all of it. Adam lashed out with his arm which connected with the upright part of the metal bar. It hurt. Adam rolled onto his back and shouted.

'I hate you. Fuck off, fuck off, fuck off, the lot of you.' He threw his arms around trying to grab anything within reach, he caught the end of a crutch that was leaning against the wall and flung it. It bounced and clanged out of view. He rolled over to see the side of a wheelchair and tried to shove it away from him but it didn't move and then he noticed there were feet sticking out of the front of it. He rolled over again and pushed himself up onto his elbows.

'Who are you?'

'I'm Vijay.'

The room was deserted save for all the specialist equipment. He and Vijay were the only ones left.

'I wanted to stay.'

'Good entertainment am I?' Adam considered grabbing the guy's leg and giving it a good jerk, maybe he could tip the smug bastard out of his chair.

There was a whirring sound and Vijay moved backwards out of reach. Adam snarled and started to crawl across the floor, his legs dragging, his elbows protesting against the hard vinyl. The electric chair continued to reverse out of reach.

'Chicken,' Adam said.

'Hamster.'

'What the fuck?'

'You know, they have those wheels, go round and round faster and faster using lots of energy, getting nowhere.'

'Come here.' Adam crawled faster but Vijay seemed to be able to turn and twist the electric chair with such ease. Adam's damn legs were slowing him down.

'They never get anywhere.'

Adam made an extra effort and caught hold of the rubber wheel at the back.

'Oh yeah?'

But the chair moved and Adam had to snatch his hand out of the way before it got caught under the wheel. Vijay was backed into a corner now beside a table and chair. Adam grinned and elbowed towards him. He grabbed the footplate and tried shaking. The chair hardly moved.

Vijay started laughing.

'It's not fucking funny.' Adam pulled himself closer, with both hands on the front bars that held the guy's legs in place, he shook the chair. It stayed stock still, it must be incredibly heavy.

Vijay was laughing harder. 'Nobody's every rattled my cage before.'

Adam struggled again, pushing and pulling, and the chair nudged backwards a few inches. The laughter bounced off the walls. Adam gritted his teeth, pulled himself to the side and then wrenched his weight backwards, the chair tipped, held for a second and just when Adam thought it was going to rock back again onto its wheels, Vijay swung his head to the side and laughed down at Adam. The chair came over and despite trying to push it away from him, he only succeeded in getting himself underneath the body that was falling out of the chair. There was a muffled thonk and then a heavy bang from the chair hitting the floor. Adam was squashed flat by the cripple above him. For a second there was silence and Adam suddenly feared he had damaged him, maybe hit the guy's head on the floor.

'Well, so the hamster thinks he's a horse.' Vijay burst out

laughing again, Adam could feel his body shuddering with guffaws above him. He tried to push up on his elbows but he was exhausted and this guy wasn't light.

'Uh-oh the prison guards are returning, come on Brown Beauty, let's go, giddy-up. If we're going to make a break for it, now's the time.' Adam felt something pinch his bottom.

'Giddy-up.'

Adam could do nothing, exhausted, he laid his head on the floor and closed his eyes, the sound of laughing and the body above him shaking. Slowly Adam felt his lips twisting. At least he hadn't killed the guy. He began to smile, and then the whole ridiculous situation ruffled through him and Adam began to laugh.

It took two physios, and a couple of nurses they dragged in from the corridor, to get Vijay back in his chair, then some more swearing and complaining as they got Adam back into his wheelchair. All the time he and Vijay laughed and whenever one of them began to slow down and regain their breath, the sight of the other would set them off again. Adam's chest ached and he wasn't sure if it was the flattening that Vijay had given him or the laughing which only made him laugh even more.

'Adam.'

'Huh?' Adam focused on Vijay's face. They were in the lounge at Vijay's penthouse, Adam immediately went forwards to give Vijay a sip of his beer, but Vijay shook his head.

'What now?' Adam said.

'Exactly.'

They sat in silence for a moment and Adam stared at the beer on the table. Wondering what it felt like to get completely hammered so you couldn't remember a thing. Obliterate the truth of his findings – the cause of the Clapham Rail disaster. But it wouldn't change anything come the morning. He had the evidence.

'I think you should speak to your boss.'

'Really? To Dave?'

Vijay nodded. 'If you're worried, speak to HR. They might even have an anonymous whistle-blowing number you can call.

Do that first.'

'If not?'

Vijay stared and said nothing.

'Shit.' The scrunching of his stomach was gone. He was cold and empty. The seriousness of the situation no longer felt crushing, it felt icy cold. 'Why did you ask about when we met?'

Vijay looked at him long and hard. 'Don't turn into a crazed hamster again OK? They're not going to take this information lying down.'

'What does that mean?'

Vijay simply raised and lowered his eyebrows in a quick gesture.

Adam tried to smile but it felt alien on his face. This was no laughing matter, not any more. But he had Allah with him now. Adam took a deep breath and silently prayed.

Friday
(4 days to go)

48

Halima - Accusations

Halima walked quickly along Falcon Road. She was late, had been finding it difficult to sleep and then struggling to get up in the mornings. There was just too much going on in her head. The strange woman in hospital who no longer resembled her mother. The fear about being turfed out of her home. Could her life get any worse? At least Smokey had been around for a soothing stroke and any day now the flowers in her garden would open. She clung to this thought as she crossed the road and hurried past the bus stop. The bud was purple and she wasn't sure which of the seeds had flourished but it was a good sign. The only good thing in her life. Yet even that was so fragile, what if the slugs came back and ate that bud before she got home. Then what?

Halima pushed open the door and Vincent glanced up from the reception desk. She entered the foyer and stopped. His expression was wrong, Vincent was coming out from behind the counter, his face registering concern.

'Halima,' he said.

Suddenly another man appeared from the corridor in a navy suit. 'Ah, Ms Shah I presume?'

Halima nodded looking between Vincent and the stranger. Vincent dropped his gaze, looked almost embarrassed.

'I'm Roger Knight, head of security here at Thyredata Enterprises. Could you come with me, we have a small matter that we need to sort out.' His smile touched the corners of his mouth but no further. He held out his arm as if to guide her along the corridor.

Halima stared at Vincent, who seemed worried, he didn't utter a word, yet something in his eyes confirmed that Halima should do what this man said. Vincent went back behind the counter.

'Ms Shah?'

Halima clutched her bag tighter and headed across the marble floor where the man indicated. He led her to a room half-way along. Inside was her boss Cheryl Phipps and a woman she didn't know.

'Obviously you know Cheryl and this is Leta Montero from HR.'

'Hi.' Leta leaned across and offered her hand, a broad smile of bright white teeth.

'Take a seat.' Roger said.

Halima slid into the nearest available chair and hugged her bag to her chest as a shield from these strangers. What could they possibly want with her?

'Unfortunately there isn't an easy way to say this but it has come to our attention that some things have been going missing on the fifth floor. Cheryl here has told us that you normally clean the main open-plan office and the other individual ones on that floor. Is that correct?'

Halima looked across at Cheryl but she was staring at a piece of paper on the desk, hadn't met her eye since Halima had walked in. No smiles, not even a pretend one.

'Is that correct?' Roger said.

Halima nodded.

'We have also been told that you have been seen opening a desk drawer. Is that correct?'

Halima turned to stare at Roger Knight and then quickly away again. Why would Cheryl tell them that? She still hadn't met her eye. Halima shook her head vigorously but then she suddenly thought about Miss pink-fluffy-pen's desk. How the photo of her beloved Matt hadn't been on the desk that day, how Halima had searched in the drawers but eventually found it behind the monitor.

'Well only once. I've never taken anything.'

Roger Knight and Leta Montero exchanged looks.

'Unfortunately due to the serious nature of the allegations, we are going to have to involve the police. We are not equipped to investigate this ourselves and as it is a criminal offence, we don't have an option.'

Halima stared at a piece of paper on the desk. Leta Montero pushed it towards her.

'This is a letter explaining your suspension pending investigation.'

Halima's chest was so tight she could hardly speak. 'For me?'

'Yes,' Roger continued, 'effective immediately.'

'But I didn't take anything. I've never stolen anything.'

'I'm sorry, I'm sure the police will get to the bottom of this matter and inform us of their findings. Until then-' Roger stood up and opened the door.

Halima stared at him in disbelief. She opened her mouth and closed it again.

'Your letter.' Leta held the paper for Halima.

Halima took it.

'I'll see you out.'

Halima followed Roger Knight back down the corridor. Ahead she could see Vincent coming out from behind his desk. She stared at the floor, shame and humiliation washing over her.

'We'll be in touch.' Roger Knight held the door for her.

Halima stepped out onto the street and the door sighed shut behind her. For a moment she stood frozen to the spot, the paper in her hand catching in the breeze and folding back against her skin. She turned to look back through the huge plate glass windows. Vincent was behind his desk watching her, his face sad, almost longing. Roger Knight had his back to her and was saying something to Vincent while pointing towards the door through which she had just come. Then Halima could see Vincent switch his gaze back to Mr Knight and his mouth move. Yes sir.

49

Adam - Whistleblowing

Adam wheeled himself to the door to HR. It was busy in there, four women working at their desks. He only knew one of them, Stephanie who'd been at his interview. If he went in, they'd all look up; all want to know what he wanted. Maybe he should phone instead. Adam rolled back down the corridor, through the door and into the open plan office to his desk. He turned on his computer and exchanged the usual pleasantries with Melanie. Maybe he should do a bit of work first, tackle those tricky queries that Dave had sent over for Neil. The trouble was his mind couldn't settle on anything. Eventually he picked up the phone and dialled HR.

'Hi, Jessie here.'

'Um, is Stephanie free?'

'She's on another line, can I help?'

'Um,' Adam paused.

'Shall I get her to call you back?'

'Yes please,' Adam said quickly.

'Adam on extension 3405, is that right?'

'Yes.' He was caught off guard. He'd forgotten that it showed up on the little telephone screen.

Adam put the receiver down and opened a new query on the database. He started typing away and then suddenly realised he was repeating the queries from yesterday, not doing the new ones at all, as if he wanted to triple check his findings. He stopped. Maybe he should get some water, try to relax a little. He looked at the phone, Stephanie hadn't called back yet. He couldn't leave his desk in case she phoned. Adam looked up, here was Dave walking fast towards him, a frown on his face. Adam felt his heartbeat quickening.

'Can you get those queries to Neil by lunchtime?'

Adam swallowed. 'I'll try.'

'Is there a problem?' Dave spoke sharply.

Adam shook his head.

With a curt nod, Dave was gone across the office, his tie flying over his shoulder. Adam breathed out. Why hadn't Stephanie called back? Maybe he should call again, but what if Jessie answered, then he'd feel stupid and she'd know it must be something important. With a heavy sigh, he opened up the database window and had another attempt at the first query required by Neil. It was complicated.

The next time Adam glanced at the clock, it was already eleven. Melanie had produced a tea for him and he'd finally got what was required for Neil. Stephanie still hadn't rung. Adam checked his emails again and discovered she'd sent him a message.

Adam
Sorry lots of meetings today, can you drop me a line instead?
Steph

He thought about what to write, about setting it all out in a document and attaching the spreadsheets he'd created. It was possible but he didn't think she'd understand. He needed to speak to her face to face, besides Vijay had talked about some anonymous way to do this. He had to find that out first, surely that would be the safest way. Adam wrote back and waited.

Adam
I've got a small window at 1- 1:30. Here's a link below to our policies if there's anything you need to look up, it might save time.
Steph

Adam clicked on the link, not because he needed to review policies, and certainly not about maternity or flexible working arrangements or pensions. He was hoping to find something on whistle-blowing. He tried a search on the company intranet with various key words but nothing looked hopeful. Perhaps those whistle-blowing numbers were just for high risk companies like hospitals. But then, this was about high risk, the highest kind.

Twenty-seven people had died in the crash and he was one of many injured. The enormity of his position was suffocating. He needed to get some air.

Adam took the lift downstairs and pushed himself out into the small rear car park. London air was rarely fresh but at least it felt less compressed here. The sky was overcast, the clouds overlapping in grey veils concealing all that might be above. He closed his eyes and prayed.

'I see.' Stephanie sat back, looking pale and tired.

Adam was almost panting. He knew he'd talked too fast, had zoomed through the documents as if they were running some kind of race where he had to impart the information in the shortest possible time. He removed his hand from one of the papers and saw he'd left a damp thumb print. He rubbed his hands on his trouser legs.

'Right.' Stephanie ran a hand through her long hair but it left her looking even more dishevelled. 'Can you wait here? I'm going to get a colleague who has more experience than me. This isn't a situation I've been in before. So if you could just stay here.'

She left the room.

Adam was exhausted. So it was out, the truth about the crash. He felt an enormous sense of relief and closed his eyes, he needed to give thanks. There was a knock at the door. A man's head poked round that Adam sort of recognised.

'We've booked this room.'

Adam looked up at the clock on the wall, it was half past one.

'I… Stephanie and I.. she told me to wait.'

'Typical.' The man turned back to some other people in the corridor. 'Even HR don't follow their own rules.' The door shut and Adam could see them in a huddle through the glass. The one that had opened the door headed off and another one from the group walked in the other direction. However, only a minute passed before the same guy was back again.

'I'm afraid you'll have to move, we've booked it and there's nothing else available. You tell Stephanie she needs to follow the rules.' He bore down on Adam who shrank in his chair. 'Here, do you want a hand with that?'

'No, no, it's fine.'

Adam cringed, he gathered up the papers before the man could touch them and thrust them into the folder. Sticking the cardboard envelope onto his lap, he twisted around and headed through the waiting group in the corridor amidst much sighing and tutting. What was he supposed to do now? Adam looked at his watch, it was twenty to two, he should be getting himself washed ready for prayers with Zeeshan. Adam set off down the corridor towards the disabled toilet.

It was during the second rakat that Adam noticed a group of people standing outside the post room staring at him. There was the HR manager, Sonia Greene, with her short-cropped blond hair, Dave, his boss, Stephanie and one of the security staff that worked on the front desk. Adam stared and the four people stared back. Zeeshan was leaning forwards again.

'Allahu Akbar.'

Adam joined in and bowed forwards in his chair forcing himself to look at Zeeshan's bent back down on the floor in front of him. Zeeshan started the next Sunnah. Adam took another quick glance to his right out of the window, they were still looking but the HR manager had broken away from the little group. Suddenly there was a knock at the door, Zeeshan didn't stop his recitation. The door opened and Adam locked eyes with the manager.

'I'm sorry to disturb you both, will you be long?'

Zeeshan leant forwards again.

'Allahu Akbar.'

Adam decided his safest bet was to follow Zeeshan's lead and leaned forwards himself. When he sat up again, she was still looking intently. Adam raised his hand to indicate five minutes. She nodded and shut the door. Outside the cubicle, he could hear their voices and then they left. Adam closed his eyes and tried to re-engage with the Arabic that Zeeshan was reciting but it was too difficult to concentrate. What on earth were they going to do? And why four of them? Adam squeezed his eyes and tried harder, attempting to say the words out loud following Zeeshan. Part of him wanted this to be over so he could find out what they all wanted from him. But the other part wanted to stay here, safe in Zeeshan's sanctuary, safe within their communion with Allah.

When they'd finished, Zeeshan stood up and rolled up his mat so that Adam could cross the floor and leave. Zeeshan opened the door for him but before he had a chance to go through he put his hand on Adam's shoulder.

'Are you in trouble son?'

'No.' Adam felt cold prickles down his back.

Zeeshan let go and Adam left without looking back, as he neared the lift he realised that not all four had left. There was the security guard walking towards him.

'Adam Rasheed?'

Adam nodded.

'Are those the reports?' He pointed to the folder in Adam's lap.

Adam nodded.

The security guard held out his hand and Adam handed him the brown file.

'We're going to meeting room five.'

It wasn't a question, it was an order. The security guard was tall and looked down on Adam as they waited for the whirring machinery. Adam shrank in his chair, the lift arrived and they went in. Adam's mouth was dry and he had that suffocating feeling again. He'd done the right thing, of course he had. Allah had led him along this path and it was righteous and he, Adam, was righteous and there was nothing he should feel guilty about. Over and over Adam tried to convince himself as the lift made its slow progress upwards. He followed the security guard down the corridor, left then right. At the door to meeting room five, it was clear that an argument was underway inside. The security guard knocked loudly and pushed the door open without any invitation. The argument stopped abruptly. The security guard held the door ajar for Adam to wheel himself through.

'Adam,' Sonia Greene, the HR manager, said. 'Thank you Brian.'

The security guard put the folder in front of the manager and left. Around the table sat Stephanie with a small notepad, her hair looking decidedly straggly, and Dave at one end, his face pink, a stern look directed straight at Adam.

'Right, well I think we have a way forwards, Adam.' She turned to face him. 'First of all, I would like to thank you for bringing this to the attention of the company. That was exactly the right thing to do. We will be treating your claim with the seriousness that it deserves. Dave here will go with you and you can demonstrate exactly what you have found within the system to him. This will verify your findings. Dave will then report back to us and we will take things to the next step if that is appropriate.' She nodded across at Dave. He responded with an acknowledging blink.

'May I make it absolutely clear that no information about the company can be taken outside of the company. As part of our contracts we have all signed a confidentiality agreement. Due to the severity of this claim, I must insist on absolute adherence to that policy. In fact I do not expect any information to be shared with any personnel beyond this room unless it is necessary for your investigations into the claim.'

She stared at each of them in turn and Adam felt like he was on trial.

'Seeing as we're half way through Friday already, we will meet again at nine o'clock sharp on Monday.'

'That's hardly any time at all.' Dave shot a look at Adam and back to Sonia Greene.

'Adam, how long do you expect it will take, to guide David through your findings within the system?'

'Err, maybe, umm,' Dave was glaring at him, 'a couple of hours or so?'

Dave slapped a hand to his forehead.

'Monday at nine then. And just to reiterate, this information is not to be shared, or discussed with colleagues, friends or family. We are on a strictly need to know basis until our next meeting. Is that clear?'

Dave nodded and so did Stephanie.

'Adam?'

'Yes,' his voice was barely above a whisper, his mouth so dry.

Dave removed his tie. 'What a fucking mess.'

They were in Dave's office and Adam wasn't sure what he was supposed to do. The HR manager had already handed the cardboard file over to Dave in the corridor on the way. Dave had thumbed through them but not in any detail. He was pacing alongside the window.

'What were you even thinking?' Dave stared across at Adam who sat near the closed door.

Adam said nothing.

'Why didn't you come to me first with this? If you've got an issue, or, or, something like this,' he slammed the cardboard folder onto the desk, 'you should come to me. I'm your line manager for fuck's sake.'

He put his hands on his hips, stopped pacing and stared out of the window. Finally he turned his back on the outside world and perched on the window ledge facing Adam.

Adam had to look away, down at his hands, at the clock on the wall and then through the narrow window in the door to the office beyond. He wanted to go back to his desk. Wanted to be out of here.

'Right.' Dave strode to the desk and yanked his chair out from behind it. 'You'd better sit here and show me what you've found. Build those queries from scratch.' He leaned over to the mouse. Adam wheeled cautiously nearer, Dave's emails were open on the screen.

'Damn. Did you send those queries to Neil?'

For a moment Adam thought he meant the incriminating ones but then he remembered.

'No, I er, I meant to, they're done, I just, well it was time for prayers.'

'Just fucking great. Are you deliberately trying to screw me over?'

Adam swallowed and shook his head.

'You do your stuff here. I'll be back.' Dave closed the emails and logged off, leaving the screen ready for Adam. He stormed around the other side of the desk, yanked the door open and slammed it behind him.

Adam drew up to the desk and started typing but his hands were freezing. If only Melanie would bring him a cup of tea. He daren't ask her, daren't leave this office even. Adam licked his lips, pulled out one of the sheets of paper from the file and started to rebuild the queries.

'Wait, hold on a mo, you've done all this in test. What about the live system?' Dave had pulled up his chair and sat close to Adam.

'The data doesn't go back that far.'

'You can't be telling me that you're basing your accusations on shit test data. You idiot.'

Adam felt his face getting hot. 'It's not shit data. I checked.'

'What do you mean?'

'The test data, it's real data from the legacy system you had before. I've checked the implementation schedule.'

'All right, so we used previous data but that's no guarantee that someone hasn't changed the data as part of testing or some jerk during training. This data can't be relied upon.' Dave was shaking his head.

'Vi-' Adam stopped himself in time. For a moment then he was going to mention Vijay. Then he would surely be in trouble sharing company information.

'What?'

'There are timestamps when this data is added or changed. I checked the timestamps. They all match the implementation date and time. Nothing has been changed.'

'Can you prove that?'

'I've got another report that shows them.'

'Print it, and these others. Wait for me to get to the printer, then print all these damn reports of yours.' Dave stood up suddenly and went to the door. The printers were situated in the middle of the open-plan office. Adam waited a moment and then sent the documents through. A few moments later Dave returned with a sheaf of papers. Adam noticed that he had undone two buttons on his shirt. The sleeves were rolled up to the elbow like someone who'd been doing some physical labour.

'So let me get this straight,' Dave slapped the sheaf of papers on one hand, 'these reports are all from the test system and not the live system.'

Adam nodded. 'But-'

Dave pointed the papers at Adam. 'The test data is from our legacy system and therefore you are assuming valid.'

'I spoke to someone at Thyredata Enterprises.'

'You did what?'

Adam thought for a moment that Dave might stride forwards and punch him. He kept his hands on the wheels of his chair in case he needed to move backwards quick. Not that he could possibly outmanoeuvre Dave in this small space. Instead Dave dumped the papers on the desk and strode to the window.

'Who did you speak to?' He turned to face Adam, his face more composed.

'I, um, I'm not sure.'

'So what did you ask them?'

'Just about the test data, where it had come from, that kind of thing.'

'And?'

'Well, it's kind of all in the implementation documentation.'

Dave was tapping his chin. 'They handed over responsibility for the test system a while ago,' he said.

'That's what he said.'

'Who?'

'The guy at Thyredata Enterprises.'

'Hmm.' Dave puffed out some air, staring at his shoes. Then he sighed. 'Why on earth would you be looking up stuff about Clapham anyway?'

Adam found himself startled at the question. Suddenly he was very aware of his body, of his tense shoulders and his hands clutching the rims of his wheels. The pressure on his back where the seat supported him. And below that, nothing at all. At least nothing that had feeling, only a weight and an annoyance of his useless legs. How could Dave ask about Clapham when the effects of that crash were staring him in the face? Adam's body was a living reminder of it every single second of every single day. Did the man have no empathy? No remorse? Adam clenched the wheels tighter feeling that he might explode. Dave's face had softened and he cocked his head, awaiting an answer. Only then did it dawn on Adam that Dave had no idea why Adam was in a wheelchair. The realisation was a wave of relief that swarmed over Adam's body, starting with his head and ending at the tips of his fingers which let go of the wheels. He didn't know. Of course he didn't. In the interview he'd merely mentioned it as an accident, not the details of that accident. HR hadn't asked, in fact everyone in this office, presumably out of politeness, had never asked the details of the accident that put him in a wheelchair. Instead some had gone out of their way to be over helpful, others had simply tried to ignore the fact that he sat about two foot lower than everyone else. Even Zeeshan hadn't troubled him with curiosity.

'Adam?'

'I..' where to begin? The realisation was a balm. Nobody at Transport Rail knew he'd been a victim of the disaster and that could be in his favour. Suddenly Adam was off the hook, the dreadful feeling that he was on trial ever since he'd rolled in that morning was gone. He could relax at last. His mind went dancing across to the queries he'd built, those first ones. He'd been using the sheets that Dave had given him.

'You'd written Clapham on one of the exercises. I was just building random reports, practising, that was all.'

Dave slapped his forehead. 'Oh Jeez.' He laughed with a sour look on his face. 'And you had time to play.'

'I was practising. You told me to.'

Dave's face had turned a deep raspberry but his words were controlled, forced even, 'OK. We can sort this. Leave it with me Adam. I'll see you at the meeting on Monday morning. And make sure you get those damn queries to Neil before you leave today.'

'OK.' Adam could feel relief creeping across his face. He was free, the jail door opened and Adam wheeled across the open-plan floor to his desk.

'Fancy a tea?' It was lovely Melanie.

50

Ralph – Everything's absolutely fine

Ralph became aware of somebody standing beside the bed. The sunlight shone through the curtains and lit the side of her face. Wrinkles with deep shadows, a pursed mouth and pale almost luminous hair. There was a sweet smell too, of lavender.

'Mum? What are you doing here?' Ralph noticed another figure standing in the doorway.

'Hello Ralph dear. Shelly gave me a key. How are you?' She perched on the edge of the bed and put a hand on his arm that rested on the duvet.

'I'm fine, just a little under the weather.'

'Under the weather my arse,' his father retorted, striding to the window and pulling back the curtains. Light streamed in and Ralph could see the concern etched on his mother's face. His father stood with arms crossed looking down at him.

'George, please,' his mother admonished. 'Now then Ralph, we've come to take you home, just while you get better.'

'What?' Ralph thought about the green front door of his childhood home, only a ten-minute drive from here. Cameron and Liam visited their grandparents a lot, it was still so familiar, but he didn't sleep there, didn't need to. 'I'll get better here, in my own home.'

'Well, it's been a long time now, and with Shelly working… we just thought that it might be better to come home, I can look after you, we can get Doctor Gerrard to come and see you.'

'I don't need to see Doctor Gerrard, it's just a cold or a touch of flu, I'll be better in a few days.' Ralph was sure it hadn't been more than a week. Wasn't it only a couple of days ago that he was checking equipment in the ambulance with Ian?

His mother persisted, 'Then why don't you spend those few days recovering with us?'

'Mum. I'm not a child, really I'm fine, I'd much rather stay here.'

'Shelly was right,' his father said sternly.

'About what?' Ralph looked between his parents.

His mother gave his arm a little squeeze, then her gaze wandered to the window and she took a breath.

'Maybe it's not a cold or flu, maybe it's something else.'

Ralph stared at his mother, unsure of what to say.

His mother continued, 'Shelly says you won't answer the phone or the door. You don't want to see anybody, not even Cameron and Liam.'

'I'm just a bit ill, that's all, nobody wants to have a social life when they're not well -' Ralph paused, '- when they're not feeling their best.'

'Ralph, I really think it would be a good idea. Please come with us.' Ralph studied his mother's face, then at his father who stared gruffly at him and nodded ever so slightly. Ralph looked up at the thin line on the ceiling.

'Well what about your brother? Perhaps you could stay with him instead?'

Ralph shook his head. 'You must be joking. That would never work. No. I'm staying here. This is my home, my family, this is where I belong. A couple of days and I'll be fine.'

There was silence for a moment while his mother stood up. Then his father spoke.

'You have responsibilities,' he said, 'to your family and not that other woman. Who did Shelly say it was?'

'Not now George,' his mother pleaded. 'Perhaps I could get Doctor Gerrard to come here?'

'I'm just a bit tired, that's all.' Ralph turned on his side away from them and stared at the bedside lamp. He heard his mother sigh, the rustling of clothes and the soft tread of shoes on the carpet. Then the door clicked shut.

51

Adam – Secret agent

Adam had reached level six in the game but kept messing up at the canyon battle. He was too tired, it had been a long day and he should probably have an early night. The stress of his findings and having to face Dave's wrath earlier in the day had left him feeling empty and exhausted. His phone buzzed on the desk and Adam flipped it open. It was Faizal.

'Hi mate,' Adam said.

'Salam bro.' Faizal's breath was loud.

'What's up?'

'I need to see you asap. I've got some news.' His voice was urgent.

'Listen, I've had a shit day at work.' Adam sighed at his computer screen as his character died yet again.

'Never mind, this is way more important than any of that. Seriously mate, I'm gonna explode if I don't talk to you.'

Adam rolled his eyes, as if anything could be more important than the day Adam had had. 'About what?'

'Shh, where are you, can you meet me outside Subway in ten minutes?'

'Faizal, I can't. I'm at home.'

'You must. I need your help.'

There was silence on the line while Adam digested the earnest plea in Faizal's voice.

'Can't it wait till tomorrow? I'm knackered.'

'Please mate, I really need to see you.'

'You could come here I suppose. But don't be long.'

Faizal was jigging from foot to foot like a junkie who needed a fix. It was making Adam dizzy.

'Sit down.' Adam indicated his bed behind Faizal.

'I don't know where to start.' Faizal licked his lips.

'Just cut to the chase, I've got a lot on my mind.' Adam sighed, turning to his computer and closing the game and the other windows he had open. Tomorrow he would go and see Vijay. Tell him what had happened at Transport Rail. He pictured Dave's angry face over the reports. Surely they were bound to confirm that Adam had discovered the truth about the crash. Monday's meeting would be about drafting a press release and finding out why the rail had failed and whose responsibility it was. Part of him was excited and the other part nervous as hell. Vijay would understand.

'Are you listening?'

'What?'

'I said, so who would you trust?'

Adam turned back to face Faizal who was looking hot and bothered.

'Weren't you even listening?' Faizal spread his hands, his voice loud. Then he looked towards the bedroom door and checked his watch. 'I have to go soon,' he said hurriedly and stared at Adam. After a few seconds, Faizal said.

'So Jamaal or that guy?'

'Jamaal?' Adam hadn't heard that name since he'd met him and Hakeem outside Subway to recruit him for the elite UMIA.

'That's what I thought. Jamaal.' Faizal sounded relieved.

'No wait, what other guy?' Adam said.

'You know the one, he always wears a kufi, hardly ever speaks. I don't even know his name.'

Adam looked across at Faizal, surprised. 'There's no way I'd trust him. You remember at the march when the petrol bomb went off. He was the one I saw standing near it.'

'Seriously?'

'Yeah, and another time after one of the meetings, he was trying to pull Aisha and shouting at her right in the middle of the street.' Adam thought about that strange encounter. Perhaps it had been Jamaal and Hakeem who had got out of that white car and helped Aisha.

'I knew it. Thanks for your help, Adam.' Faizal looked more relaxed but then he checked his watch again and worry registered on his face.

'What is it?'

'I have to go, shit, I can't mess this up.'

'Mess what up? What on earth are you on about?' Adam stared at his friend wondering why he needed to know who to trust.

'You won't be needing this then.' Faizal yanked an envelope from his pocket and started ripping it up.

'What is that?'

'Doesn't matter, kufi-man gave it to me. I knew something fishy was going on.' He dropped the bits in Adam's bin. 'He's just trying to ruin the operation.'

'What operation?

'I'll tell you everything when it's all over.' Faizal puffed out his chest then lowered his head secretively towards Adam. 'I've been chosen to deliver special information. Don't tell a soul.' He stood up again. 'See you later.' And with that he was off, leaving the bedroom door swinging.

Saturday
(3 days to go)

52

Austin – Time for change

'Why have you got a turkey baster in your bathroom cabinet?'

Austin looked up from the clothes he had laid out on his bed. Becky was standing in the doorway holding up the object.

'Err...' Austin thought quickly; some things you didn't share even with your best friend. 'Ear thing. I get wax sometimes, flush it out.' He shrugged, hoping he sounded convincing and then wondered what else she might find in there. 'Why don't I finish the bathroom and you can put these clothes in the suitcase?'

'No, I'm fine.' She grinned and disappeared back into the bathroom.

Austin went to empty the bedside table. There were several watches neatly lined up in their boxes, some condoms and a large purple dildo. He stuffed the latter amongst his jumper pile on the bed, maybe he was better off doing the bedroom packing after all. At the bottom of the sock drawer he found two pairs of Matt's. He paused, turning them over in his hands. They were black with a blue line around the ankle. The rest of Matt's clothes had been disposed of long ago.

'What time is David coming with the van?' Becky called out from the bathroom as bottles clinked into the plastic tub he'd given her to fill.

'About an hour ago.' Austin scrunched up the socks in his hand.

Becky appeared again in the doorway. 'Problems?'

Austin shrugged a response. He threw the socks towards the bin, one missed and landed on the floor. Why was this moving on so difficult? There were no guarantees that he'd be happy at the new place. Austin began to wonder why David had encouraged him to move. Surely you could still have a new relationship without having to move home? Austin shook his head and sat on the bed. He knew it made financial sense, but he felt like an emotional wreck.

'I'll stick this lot in the hall.' Becky walked through carrying a filled box. 'Hey, what's up, you need a break?'

'No, I'm fine.' He waved a hand at the neatly folded sections of clothes on the bed. 'I'll get a suitcase for this lot.' There was no point in getting morbid, he'd made the decision, given in his notice. There was no going back.

Once they'd finished the bedroom and bathroom, Becky said they deserved a treat and boiled the kettle for coffees, producing two pains-au-chocolat from her bag that she'd picked up from the bakery on her way over.

'Not like you to be devilish.' Austin pointed at the greasy looking pastry.

Becky handed one to Austin with a pretend kiss. They sat on the sofa, Austin sipping the strong espresso that Becky had made.

A loud honking from outside startled them both. Becky quickly stood up dabbing crumbs off her face and looked down through the window.

'He's here.'

Austin had stood up too, he should be happy, pleased that David had turned up with the van, but all he felt was dread.

Becky laughed at him.

'It's reinforcements, not the end of the world.' She chucked a toilet roll at him from the top of a box. 'You can do this,' she said and then disappeared out of the door.

Austin thrust a hand through his hair and peered out of the window to see, but it wasn't David who leapt down from the driver's side. It was somebody else, Reuben, or Rory or something like that. He seemed to remember meeting him with David one time in a bar. Becky appeared on the street below and introduced herself. Then she stood chatting, her hands on her hips, the tight T-shirt showing off her bust. Where the hell was David? Austin searched for his phone and found it in the kitchen.

The battery had died.

'Austin?' It was Becky's voice.

'Sorry.' He came out of the kitchen having plugged his phone in to charge.

'This is Ross. He's going to help, and drive the van of course.' Becky grinned.

'Hi.' Ross held out his hand and Austin leaned forwards. He would have to be civil at least, with Becky being so jolly. The trouble was he had a horrible feeling that Ross was an ex or maybe not even that. And his aftershave was far too strong.

'Dave sends his apologies. He's cashing in on a favour.'

'Oh?' Austin wondered what kind of favour.

Becky jumped in, 'Well it's really good of you to muscle in at the last minute, isn't it Austin?' she said, sending Austin a warning look.

'Yeah, thanks.'

Austin went back to his phone to see what messages he'd missed while Becky gave Ross an empty cardboard box and asked him to start on the bookshelf.

There were two missed calls and three messages. David was tied up at work, which had been his excuse for not coming over last night too. What on earth was he doing? He'd never worked at the weekend before. And why now, when it really mattered? What the hell did David think he was doing by sending his... Austin didn't know what to call Ross, was he an ex-lover, boyfriend, current lover, fuck buddy? For some reason they still hadn't had that conversation about whether they were a proper couple yet, the kind that didn't see other people. Austin kind of wished they had but then he was frightened of leaping on this relationship too heavily. Jeez, he didn't know if he was up or down.

'I know you're sad to see it go.' Becky had a hand on his shoulder. They were stood on the pavement and Austin was locking the door for the last time. He paused for a second. This had been their home.

Him and Matt.

Together.

Austin took a deep breath, he wasn't going to start crying again, especially not with Ross still hanging around. Besides, it wasn't their home any longer, hadn't been for over two years. But the thought didn't stop his chest from hurting.

'New start. Brush those cobwebs off.' Becky grinned, her arm wrapping around him.

'Where are we off to then?' Ross said, jangling the keys to the van.

'Listen, I have to go, I promised to meet Deana later.' Becky gave him a final squeeze.

Did he really have to get in that van with that awful grey shirt and the fumes of aftershave now mixed with sweat?

Austin held onto Becky's hand. 'We could drop you off somewhere.'

'I've got to get this van back by seven at the latest,' Ross said.

'You know it's in the opposite direction. Off you go. It'll be fine.'

'Sure.' Austin let go of her hand and gave Becky a hug. 'Thanks for everything.'

'No problem, see you later.' She pulled out her mobile. 'I've got the new address.' She gave him another squeeze and strode off down the street, her ginger hair flying in the light breeze. Beyond her figure he could see the park where he and Matt had so often run together on bright Sunday mornings. Never again.

It had clouded over and they would be hard-pressed to finish unloading in time. The new flat was on the top floor of a converted town house, a Victorian building that had been renovated and modernised with care. An original fireplace in his bedroom and stripped floors gave the flat a distinctive character and with the modern kitchen and bathroom it had all the mod cons that Austin preferred. His mood lightened as they began to fill the new space with his stuff. Maybe this had been the right thing to do after all. The curtains would have to go, of course, and he might get one of those stencils or perhaps wall stickers to make an impact on the end wall.

'Come on, I know you're tired but there's still more.' Ross bumped him with a box. The sofa was the most difficult and Austin found himself cursing and struggling until he swapped ends and Ross lifted up the lower side high enough to get it over the balustrade on the first floor.

'Well, I think we're good.' Ross was dusting off his hands. 'It's a nice flat. Mind you, so was the other one.'

'Yeah, but at least it's different.'

Austin had to admit that Ross had been a huge help despite the grey shirt and the aftershave that had finally worn off. Now he smelt like he'd been in the gym too long, so did Austin.

'I guess I'd better get going.'

Austin shrugged and nodded. 'I'd buy you a drink if you didn't have to get the van back.'

'That would be nice, maybe another time.' Ross paused appraising Austin. 'I'd like that.'

Austin felt suddenly embarrassed, that he hadn't appreciated Ross giving up his time and energy for a bloke he barely knew. He stepped closer. Ross had a nice smile, clean shaven. Austin was about to hold out his hand when Ross suddenly grabbed him by the shoulders and planted a hard kiss square on Austin's mouth.

'Definitely give me a call if you fancy that drink,' he said. 'And if things don't work out with you-know-who, then-' He shrugged, a cheeky grin on his face. And then he was gone, leaving Austin speechless and alone.

53

Adam – The chosen one

Adam manoeuvred out of his bedroom and into the kitchen. His mother was putting away some cutlery.

'Hello love. Are you looking for a snack before we go?'

Adam paused with his hand on the bread.

'Go where?'

'Auntie Nasreen's of course. We're going for lunch. A proper family get together.'

'But I've got plans.'

His mother gave him a steely look. 'If it's another of your religious meetings then perhaps you could put your family first for a change. Does it not say in the Quran that you should be dutiful and kind to your parents?'

'Mum.' Adam put a slice in the toaster.

'I told you on Thursday.'

'Did you?' Adam had no recollection of it.

'What is the matter?' She came over and put a hand on his forehead but he pushed it away. 'You've been acting a bit strange and quiet the last few days.'

'I'm fine.'

His father walked in. 'Of course he's fine, stop worrying woman.'

'Is it something at your new job?' she persisted.

Adam shook his head and stared at the way the wall rippled in the heat rising from the toaster.

'Make sure they are not taking advantage Adam,' his father said, rubbing at that flattened disc on his ear. 'I know these companies; they employ young people on less than the minimum wage and treat them like slaves.'

'It's fine. I'm fine.'

Adam knew they were both staring at him; he willed the gadget to fling up his toast so he would have something to do other than be tempted to share the astonishing and crushing findings at Transport Rail.

'Rafiq, he says he will not come to Auntie Nasreen's. Tell him Rafi.'

Adam could hear the sigh in his father's breath.

'Maybe he doesn't want to be surrounded by chattering women and eat Auntie's awful samosas.'

'Her cooking is perfectly edible.' His mother's voice was becoming more shrill. 'She's expecting all of us.'

'Yes all right, calm down woman. Adam she's right, it's family.'

'I made other plans.' Adam frowned at the toast he was

buttering. He reached for the jam jar and struggled with the lid.

'Then unmake them.'

Adam had planned to go and see Vijay, he wanted to tell him what had happened at Transport Rail. Tell him all the details about yesterday and Dave's reaction. The information was out. Surely the company would support his findings come Monday morning. But the last thing he wanted to do was share it with his parents. The event that had turned their lives upside-down didn't need to be revisited just now, it would only open up their raw emotions again. Besides he had signed that confidentiality document. He had to wait to see what happened on Monday.

Adam turned with the plate balanced on his lap, both his parents were staring at him, his mother in the doorway, her lips pressed tightly together.

'I have English homework to do, for college. The day release.' This at least was true.

His father nodded his head.

'I'm going round to Vijay's. He said he'd help me with it.'

'The boy is right, study is more important than gossiping with the whole of the Malik family in that tiny house.'

'It's a very nice house. Can't he do it another time?'

His father raised his eyebrows and put an arm across his wife's shoulders, leading her towards the lounge.

'I'm afraid that lunch at Auntie Nasreen's is not as important as Adam doing well in his next exams. You don't want him to be an apprentice forever do you woman?'

It seemed the one saving grace of Adam's apprenticeship, at least in his father's eyes, was the day release for college. For once he was on Adam's side. With relief, Adam sunk his teeth into the toast and escaped back to his bedroom. He checked his watch, he would have to leave soon if he wanted to get to Vijay's before Cara had to work on his friend's limbs. Adam chucked a couple of books in his backpack to at least make the lie look believable.

His parents were arguing in the hallway. The thought crossed Adam's mind that Allah might not look too kindly on him for this white lie to his parents, but wasn't he on the path of the greater good? Surely a small lie about homework could be overlooked and besides, wasn't Adam meant to find the shocking truth and share it with the world?

'I'm sure Nasreen will understand,' his father said, holding open the door.

'That's not the point,' his mother replied, folding her arms.

'Yes, yes, but it's not as important as Adam studying. He's lucky to have such a brainy friend.' He smiled as Adam rolled past. 'Make sure it counts,' his father said as Adam scooted down the ramp, 'you will need it to get a better job.'

Adam freewheeled onto the pavement and then set his arms pumping towards the main road.

Adam went into the tube station. He waited along with a couple of other passengers for the slow lift that would take him down to the platforms. The lift pinged and immediately Adam's phone started ringing. It was a private number. And there was a warning that his battery was low.

'Hello?' he said.

'Adam Rasheed.' The voice was clearly male and had an accent. One that Adam thought he recognised.

'Yes?'

'I understand you are a member of the United Muslims in Action group.'

Adam licked his lips and swallowed.

'Yes.'

Ahead of him people were coming out of the lift.

'Are you willing to help your Muslim brothers and sisters?'

Was this what had happened to Faizal? Last night when he'd been babbling about who to trust and secret information - was he involved in a secret UMIA operation? The man on the other end sounded older, foreign, a gravelly voice but again he couldn't think where he had heard it before.

Adam sat taller. 'Yes,' he said firmly.

'Good. One question before we go on -' the voice paused as if giving gravity to what he was about to say ' - I understand you went to school with one of our special members. Which class were you in together?'

Adam's eyes widened at the question. He'd been to school with Aisha. His mind filled with the events of last night, with Faizal agitated on the bed. Then after he'd gone when Adam had taken the ripped shreds of paper from the bin and put them back together. The envelope had simply said Adam. But inside didn't make sense at all, at least not till now. A short note,

Remember Computers J9.

It was a handwritten note in curly script, with the C and J standing out as if written over a couple of times. Handwriting that he recognised. He was convinced it was from Aisha and compared it to the note she had written for their meeting at Subway. It was certainly very similar but Faizal had said the kufi-wearer had given it to him. Why? And what did the message mean? But now with the mobile against his ear hearing the breathing of the man on the other end it all made sense.

'Which class?' the voice repeated. This was a test.

Adam took a breath. 'Geography.' They'd never been in computers together and definitely not in room J9.

'Perfect. In that case we can proceed.'

Adam silently congratulated himself. The kufi-wearer must have copied Aisha's handwriting and written that note. Faizal was right. Jamaal was the one to trust. Imagine if Faizal had given him the note, and he'd believed it to be an important message from Aisha. If he'd said Computers instead of Geography, the man on the phone would have put it down. Adam pressed the mobile hard against his ear, not wanting to miss a single word.

'Ibrahim Muhammad Sharif would like to meet you for tea at one o'clock today.'

The passengers had finished exiting the lift and there was tutting behind him, so he automatically rolled himself forwards with one hand into the metal cubicle.

'I must ask that you come alone and that you do not share Mr Sharif's address with anyone, he is a very private man.'

'Of course.'

Adam was facing the opposite doors now and the lift was filling up.

'The address-' the voice was drowned by beeping and an

electronic voice.

'*The doors are now closing. The doors are now closing.*'

'Wait,' Adam blurted into the phone and turned angrily as the doors started to slide; then he recognised his mistake. If the doors closed and they descended, he was bound to lose mobile signal and with hardly any battery life left he couldn't risk it. The panic rose up his chest.

'Wait. Stop the doors, I have to get out.'

He tried to turn but it was too crowded. There was nothing he could do as he stared over his shoulder at the doors as they continued to slide shut. At the last second a briefcase swung outwards and wedged in the metal clamp, preventing the phone connection from being severed. The doors opened again.

'Just a minute,' he said into his phone. The passengers shuffled around with some murmuring and further disgruntled comments allowing him to manoeuvre back into the station foyer.

Adam glanced at his phone to check it was still connected before putting it back to his ear.

'Sorry about that, I was stuck in a lift. You were saying about the address?'

There was silence on the line.

'Hello?'

Adam could detect a muffled voice talking in Arabic then it stopped abruptly. The gravelly voice returned and stated a London address. Adam listened intently.

'Mr Sharif has a tight schedule and he would appreciate your punctuality.'

'Absolutely.'

'Goodbye, Adam Rasheed.'

Adam exhaled loudly. His heartbeat was slowing down, as if he'd just raced across the basketball court. He closed his eyes for a brief moment. So this was it, this was the call. And a face to face meeting with Ibrahim Muhammad Sharif. The inspirational speaker who had come direct from Syria. And he wanted to meet Adam. A shiver ran up Adam's back as the sweat cooled. So maybe there was something that a Muslim cripple in a wheelchair could do for Islam. This could be his chance to make a difference, to shine the Muslim light. To show Aisha that he could be a hero too. Faizal hadn't been asked to meet the famous man, just given some supposedly secret information. Hardly exciting or world changing. But Ibrahim Muhammad Sharif wanted to meet Adam in person, now that was something.

All around him the weekend Londoners went about their business. Tourists queuing at the ticket counter. A bus with just a smattering of passengers sailed past and none of them could know how important this moment was. Only Adam knew. Only Adam had received the call. Now all he had to do was find that address before his phone died.

The location Adam had been given was in the heart of Kensington with grand houses and wide roads. He'd never been to this part of town before and was amazed at the size of these places. How could anyone afford a house this big in London? They must be worth millions. Adam rolled along the pavement, letting his hands gently skim the wheels as the slight gradient carried him down the avenue. Fortunately his phone had lasted long enough for Adam to memorise the last part of his journey, still it had taken longer than expected and he would only just be on time.

There were iron gates that blocked the entrance to a large house with many windows. On the gate post was a small electronic button which he pressed. There was a crackle and some Arabic which Adam couldn't hear clearly.

'It's Adam, I'm here to see-' But before he could finish, the electric gates hummed gently and began to open. Adam waited until there was enough space to easily wheel his chair through. There was a silver BMW parked at the side of the house, the forecourt was bare gravel with two trees in large pots either side of the front door. As Adam made his laboured way across the stone chippings, the door opened and a man in a suit stepped out. He carried a black briefcase with gold clasps. Without looking at Adam, or even acknowledging his presence, the man strode across the gravel and through the open gates.

The front door had closed again, but as he reached it and

searched for a bell it opened once more and a wiry man in white robes stood waiting on the threshold. He greeted Adam in Arabic and motioned for him to come inside. There was a deep stone step and then the lip of the door which Adam could easily negotiate. Inside was a large stone-tiled hallway with wide stairs sweeping up to his left and numerous doors, all closed.

'This way.' The wiry man led him to a wider wooden door and opened it to reveal an old-fashioned lift with a metal grill. He slid the metal to one side and Adam rolled in. It smelt musty and damp as if it had been shut up for a long time. As his escort entered the lift, his tunic flapped and Adam was startled to see the hilt of a knife. He glanced up at the man's face and found him staring intently at Adam. Without glancing away he smoothed his shirt down to hide the Janbiya. He said something in Arabic but the only words Adam recognised were apostates and infidels. Adam clutched the rims of his wheels tightly, the threatening tone was unmistakeable.

They went up two floors, Adam tried to remember how many rows of windows he'd seen outside, three but then hadn't there been a couple in the roof too? In the upper hallway was the giant, standing like a statue with his arms folded next to a stone urn.

Adam was relieved to see a familiar face. 'Hello again.'

The giant made no acknowledgement.

Adam smiled brightly and tried again, this time in Arabic.

The giant gave the perfunctory reply, his voice surprisingly soft in the empty hallway. He gave the briefest of nods and then the wiry man was leading him across the space to a door. It was disconcerting in the silence. Were they just servants? Adam felt his heart thumping. The man knocked.

'Udkul.'

Adam hesitated and then went through the opened door, relieved that the wiry man with his Janbiya didn't follow. Inside Ibrahim Muhammad Sharif was dressed in black like he had been the last time at the inspirational talk he'd given. Despite the fact that he was reclining on a plush sofa, he still exuded mastery with his solemn gaze. Opposite him was a low table and another matching sofa.

'Ah, Adam, welcome.' He rose and came to greet him. 'It is good to meet you at last my brother.'

He towered over Adam like some great black scarecrow and gripped Adam's hand in both of his.

'Well actually-' Adam had been about to explain that they'd met before, at the meeting a few weeks back, but Ibrahim Muhammad Sharif raised his hand and shook his head.

'So, we have tea and you and I can talk. Won't you be more comfortable on the sofa?'

'Oh no, thanks. I feel better in my chair.'

'Nonsense, you can relax here. We are cousins after all.'

'Really?'

'Gabir!'

Adam was pretty certain that he wasn't related to Ibrahim Muhammad Sharif. He was sure his mother had never mentioned the name nor had any of his aunties or uncles. Not that you can ever really know all your relations.

The giant suddenly appeared. So that was his name. Gabir.

'Adam would be more comfortable on the sofa, perhaps you could assist?'

The giant stood by the door a frown on his face.

'Gabir?'

The giant came towards him.

'No really, I'm fine.' Adam didn't want to repeat that embarrassing moment when he'd been carried into the meeting room like a babe in arms.

Ibrahim Muhammad Sharif had a fixed stern look. 'It's no trouble.'

Adam was confused, Ibrahim's tone was so warm and friendly and yet his eyes were not at all. Adam allowed himself to be lifted by Gabir and placed onto the deep sofa. He had to pull the rucksack off his back to stop the books digging in.

'Where is he taking my chair?'

'Oh, don't worry. We don't want that old thing here reminding us that you are different. This way we can be like brothers, don't you think? Cousins sharing tea.'

Gabir left with the wheelchair.

Adam was naked without it, powerless and vulnerable. The chair represented his independence. In the early days it had felt like a prison, an annoying contraption that he had to take with him everywhere. But somehow, and he wasn't sure exactly when, it had become an invaluable extension of his own body. Now, he couldn't do without it. He stared at the closed door. His body felt small and shrunken in the depths of the sofa.

'So, I understand that you didn't know we are second cousins twice removed on your mother's side.'

'We are?'

'Ah yes, you probably haven't met Malak Tiwana?'

'No, I don't think so.'

'So many relatives - difficult to keep track don't you think, brother?'

'Well, I guess so.'

'While I'm in London, I thought it might be nice to meet up with my cousins.'

'Oh?' Adam wasn't sure how to respond. Was he really related to this man? That would be amazing, Faizal would be livid. 'Perhaps I should have brought my mum and you could have met her too?'

'Oh, I'm not so sure she would want to meet me, family feuds Adam, they seem to last generations, I'm not even sure why our families don't talk any more. Silly really.'

'Well maybe Mum's forgotten by now, besides she's very nice, I'm sure she would forgive and forget.'

'Yes, your mother is a wonderful woman, I remember when she was very young, beautiful.'

'You knew her when she was young?'

Ibrahim Muhammad Sharif smiled. 'Is she still beautiful?'

Adam smiled too. Yes, he thought his mother was beautiful, also kind and always so generous. But the thoughts made him embarrassed.

Instead, he said, 'Dad thinks so.'

Ibrahim Muhammad Sharif laughed loudly.

'Let us have tea.' He turned towards the door and called out.

'Hasib, bring tea.'

The wiry man appeared holding open another door. Through the doorway came a tall woman carrying a tray. She was completely covered except for her eyes which were fixed on the floor. Adam was surprised, had they been waiting just the other side of the door all along? Or maybe it was just coincidence - after all, Adam had been invited for tea. The man stood close while she laid the tray on the table. An ornate tea pot and matching cups and saucers. There was also a plate of scones filled with jam.

The woman poured some milk and gave Adam a quick glance. With shock he recognised the green flash.

'Aisha.'

'Ah yes, of course, you knew each other at school, is that right?' Ibrahim said.

Adam nodded and smiled. 'Yes, in Geography.' Adam was nobody's fool. As if he would say computers. That kufi-wearer was the fool thinking he could trick Adam so easily. He watched Aisha, expecting her to confirm the answer, but she was busy with the teapot and strangely it looked like her hand was trembling.

Ibrahim Muhammad cleared his throat. 'Geography, that's right. Not a subject I was any good at I'm afraid.' He smiled benevolently and Adam relaxed again. This was where he should be, in the heart of the elite UMIA with Aisha and this inspiring man.

Aisha had finished pouring the tea. She looked at him once more, her eyes deep, staring as if trying to communicate something, but then she turned away heading for the doorway as the wiry man, Hasib, came across carrying what looked to be an iPad and sat on the sofa beside Adam. He was so close that the handle of the Janbiya under his tunic pressed against Adam's hip.

'Perfect,' Ibrahim said and nodded towards Hasib at Adam's side. Aisha closed the door quietly behind her. Adam felt suddenly ill at ease, pressed against the side of a man he didn't know. Hasib was holding the tablet for Adam to take. There was some large text on the screen.

'What's this?' Adam looked from the wiry man to Ibrahim Muhammad Sharif.

'What, these? They are my favourites; I do love the English scones and jam.'

Adam felt a prickle between his shoulder blades. Ibrahim Muhammad Sharif had clearly seen that Adam was referring to the tablet and yet he was talking about scones. Adam gripped the tablet tighter, was he really in the heart of the UMIA's elite group with Ibrahim as its leader? Surely that would make sense, what with Aisha here, and so Adam stared at the tablet and read the words.

Keep talking normally to Ibrahim Muhammad Sharif

There was a button that read next at the bottom.

'Would you like to try one? They were baked today.'

Adam looked up to find Ibrahim Muhammad Sharif staring directly at him, his voice was still warm and friendly but his eyes and his mouth were anything but. Adam suddenly felt very cold.

'Thank you,' he muttered. Ibrahim Muhammad Sharif gave a short nod with his head, gesturing for Adam to keep reading.

'And how do you take your tea? Milk, sugar, lemon perhaps?'

Adam glanced down at the screen and up again.

'Er, milk.' But Aisha had already poured it.

Hasib stood up and left the room. Adam breathed a sigh of relief.

'And one sugar.'

'Excellent.' Ibrahim Muhammad Sharif picked up a loaded scone, his eyes resting on Adam, waiting for him to keep reading.

Adam touched the next button on the screen.

You have been chosen.

Adam ought to have turned right outside the iron gates to get home, but downhill would get him away from there quicker. He turned left and his chair gathered speed. The faster he went, the more relief he felt. The speed cooled the sweat on his face. But then he was going too fast, much faster than normal, was it because the chair was heavier? Would that make it go faster? Ahead at the bottom of the road was the junction with Kensington High Street. He would need to slow down to make the corner, besides he could see people crossing the road. The pavement was likely to be busy.

Adam gradually squeezed the rims, attempting to slow his speed, but he was flying down the hill now. The wheels scorched his hands but there was no choice, he had to slow down. Although he was desperate to get away from the mansion, he couldn't risk a crash. Imagine the catastrophe. Adam gripped the wheels tighter, grimacing as the friction burned away the skin. A couple with a buggy appeared from the High Street. Adam felt sick, he couldn't yell out, couldn't draw attention to himself, couldn't crash. At the very last moment he leant to the right and brought the chair to a stop against a low wall. The jolt wasn't huge but he let out a gasp all the same. The couple turned, surprised, but continued walking.

Adam hugged his singed hands together, blowing on them and then gripping them together to stop the smarting. He had to take control, be normal, act normal. Just get on with getting home. Adam reversed out from the wall, the extra effort required surprised him. The additional weight under the seat was making it much more difficult to control and manoeuvre. He would have to take things slower, take his time, be extra careful. He turned around the bend and onto the high street, he'd been right; it was busy here. What if someone knocked the chair? Or somebody stopped him or it came undone somehow? Adam tried to quell the panic, he just needed to last fifteen hours, that was all. He checked his watch, OK, fourteen hours and fifty-one minutes, it would be fine, he could do this.

Was that girl staring at him? What about that man across the street looking his way. A small chihuahua with its head stuck out of a woman's handbag barked at him. Adam cringed, but the chihuahua was shushed and its owner disappeared into a boutique. The man across the road waved a taxi down and the girl smiled as she walked on past. Adam breathed deeply.

Everything was fine, he was fine, this was going to be OK. He wiped an arm across his face, he was sweating like a horse.

Breathe.

Adam rolled the wheelchair forwards, he could see the Underground sign ahead but he didn't know if it was a wheelchair friendly one. He'd never been to this part of London before and he'd arrived by bus. Keep breathing. Adam approached the pedestrian crossing where several people were waiting. It was OK. None of them knew what he was carrying under his chair. Even Adam didn't know, not for sure, but somehow it seemed obvious, and it scared him to death. Be calm, keep breathing. The lights changed and Adam joined the others, he tried to slow himself down, he didn't need to go so fast. Regular speed, except he didn't know what that was any more, didn't know even what expression to put on his face. Why did he feel so sick? The taste of scone and jam flooded his mouth and he swallowed it back down. He didn't think he'd ever be able to eat one again without thinking of Ibrahim Muhammad Sharif with his deadly eyes and his sickly-sweet words. Maybe he wasn't cut out to be in this elite group after all. Surely he couldn't fail during this, his first operation.

Adam was out of luck, there was no lift and no way he could get down to the platforms. Automatically he pulled out his phone but of course the battery had died hours ago. He shoved it back in his pocket. Checking carefully down both sides of the wheelchair, he suddenly remembered he should still have a step-free tube map in the rucksack strung on his back. He swivelled it round onto his lap and rummaged amongst the English books he'd thrown in earlier. He found it crumpled up in the zip pocket. The nearest tube he could use was Earl's Court. The trouble was, without his phone he didn't know which way to go.

Back out on the high street he found one of the tourist maps on a large post, he studied it for a while but his mind kept whizzing around. Ibrahim Muhammad's cold hard eyes. The giant's gentle arms as he was lifted back into his wheelchair. Aisha's green eyes staring at him. The instructions whirling across the tablet screen. He just wanted to get home and he needed to concentrate on the map. He blinked several times and stared hard.

Adam set off again in what he thought was the right direction. He passed an Asian woman in a green sari and it reminded him of Auntie Nasreen, she always wore bright colours. By the time he got home, Sully and his parents would be back from Auntie Nasreen's. His mother would be preparing dinner, a light meal as they would have eaten heavily at Auntie's. But she'd make a bit extra for Adam, just in case he hadn't eaten properly. The thought made Adam's throat constrict. He imagined arriving home and his mother dusting off her hands and coming to greet him, asking him how it had gone, her earlier disappointment forgotten. She'd ask about the English study with his friend. Except there hadn't been any studying. He would have to lie again. Would she notice the package under his chair? What if something went wrong? Sheer terror ripped through Adam and he stopped suddenly on the pavement as he imagined his house exploding, everyone inside blown apart. His father's favourite mug shattered, a torn piece of his mother's deep red blouse caught by the wind, its blackened edge twisting down Walton Road. And one of Sully's smart shoes lying at the bottom of the ramp with the foot still attached.

Adam gulped some air and started moving again. He couldn't go home, not with this under his chair. He couldn't risk his family, they didn't deserve that. Only he had signed up for this, for Allah's plan. He needed to reassure himself. Was this really what He wanted? Only days ago, hadn't Adam told Faizal that the UMIA was about peaceful protest? When did that change? Perhaps he should go to the police but what would they think? Turning up with a bomb under his chair trying to explain that he was a good Muslim who only wanted peaceful protest? They'd lock him up for terrorism right away. He'd never see his family again. Adam gasped in a breath like a drowning man briefly surfacing. No, he couldn't go to the police and he couldn't go home. But he didn't know it was a bomb, did he? Adam thought back to that interview when he'd been told they needed people they could trust, who could follow instructions. Who didn't go splashing information around. Hadn't they said that the operation at RAF Marham had been successful because everyone had followed their instructions to the letter? They obviously trusted Aisha and Faizal had been given secret information, surely Adam needed to prove they could trust him too. He'd already managed to avoid a red herring from the kufi-wearer.

Adam closed his eyes and sent up a silent prayer. If this was what He wanted, then Adam would pray for His strength. If this was right, and good, and it was going to help his Muslim brothers and sisters somehow then Allah would ensure he played his part. Allah was great and he would trust in Him even though Adam didn't know how, had no idea of the entire operation, only his small part. To transport this package. Wasn't that what the interviewer had said all those weeks ago? That he had to trust and do his part? That talk and sharing could be dangerous. He checked his watch. Fourteen hours and thirty-six minutes to go until he could rid himself of the package. Inshallah.

54

Halima - Lost and found

Halima stood outside the hospital watching the traffic crawl past. The evenings were so much lighter and despite it being almost eight the sky was still bright and the air warm. She didn't want to go home to her empty silent house. She was cut loose like a cotton thread hanging from her jumper. Cut and cast adrift to float on the breeze. There was no reason to go home, no reason to go anywhere. Her routine life had fallen apart.

She wondered how long she could stand here without someone bothering her or thinking it odd. A cyclist weaved through the cars and a suited man strode past. So many people, all with places to go and things to do. Halima stood as an island all her own. She blinked. If she disappeared in a puff of smoke, no one would notice. No one would care. Not even her mother. Least of all her mother.

On the ward, a kindly nurse had updated Halima and given her the doctor's phone number. He'd be back in on Monday and she could get the details from him about her mother's prognosis. Apparently she'd had two more smaller strokes while on the ward but they had her on some medication to thin the blood and it seemed to be working. Halima didn't really understand why her mother didn't or couldn't speak. She wasn't certain if a stroke could kill you or just paralyse you. It seemed to Halima that Mum had left, gone away somewhere, and only her body remained, despite what the nurse said about the possibility of her mother hearing and understanding. That woman from the council had been right, the nurse confirmed it, saying that her mother would need additional care, that she could no longer be considered independent. Going home was probably unlikely, at least not for a while, and then only if she made a dramatic recovery.

Halima felt helpless. Perhaps she should call Veronica then she remembered her friend was in Scotland visiting her son and his family for a week. Halima wished it was she who had grandchildren to visit. Anyone to visit besides her mother in the hospital behind her. Perhaps simply talking on the phone would help.

Halima took out her mobile and found the number but then she stopped. What she really wanted was some human contact, like when Veronica had rubbed the soft skin between her thumb and finger. Or maybe Vincent's smile as she walked into the marble reception at Thyredata Enterprises. Even Mum's ranting was better than nothing. But none of these were options for her now. Halima put her phone away. She watched the pedestrians crossing in front of her. A woman in jogging clothes talking on her mobile, two men chatting together. A youth, with his hands shoved deep in his pockets and shoulders hunched, loped by. Then a woman in a Burka, her eyes a flash of brilliant green glanced across at her.

'Hello,' Halima said.

The woman was momentarily surprised, then turned her eyes away, bowed her head and continued striding past in her pink pumps. Halima felt silly. What was she doing trying to talk to strangers? Then a woman of a similar age to Halima came past carrying two shopping bags and she smiled kindly.

Halima found herself following the lady. They went along the Fulham Road over the rail bridge and onwards. This was an area Halima wasn't familiar with but she didn't mind. Finally the woman stepped into the Fulham Broadway tube station and disappeared down the escalator. A lump rose up Halima's throat but she pushed it back down. She was tired and the light was beginning to dim. A tube ride would at least be relaxing. Halima got on the District Line heading west.

It was easy to change lines, travel in another direction, cross platforms and come back the other way. She wondered why more homeless people didn't do this, spending their day travelling under the streets of London. She took notice of the names of stations and wondered about their origins. She watched the other passengers and imagined lives for them like her office staff. There was Barry, a construction worker on his way home expecting tea on the table. Over there was Cassandra, annoyed that her husband had let the suitcases fall over. Standing up was Shabnam who'd spent the evening with her friends at a smart sushi restaurant.

The walls of the tunnels swished past in a blur along with the time. The passengers thinned out and Halima had fewer characters to choose from. The train stopped at Ealing Common and two young men in tight jeans got off. At the other end of the carriage was another lonely traveller, a young man in a wheelchair. He glanced her way as the doors beeped shut.

At Ealing Broadway, she had to get off; the train was terminating. She crossed over to the other platform and waited. There would be another train along in six minutes. On the opposite wall of the arched tunnel was a large poster advertising getaway breaks to the Maldives; she stared at the image. Halima supposed she could go to the Maldives if she really wanted to, now that Mum wasn't coming home. Now that the doctor and the social worker had made their decision, there didn't seem to be a choice in the matter. It was all very well making decisions about what was best for Mum but what about Halima? When did she ever matter to anyone? Now she had no family. Halima's grief washed over her and she gulped at the fetid underground air. A noise to her left reminded her she was in a public place. The Asian man in his wheelchair had reappeared, his strong arms thrusting the wheels forward. He stopped near the platform edge and glanced her way. Halima tried to smile.

She reminded herself that there were always people worse off than herself. For a moment she wondered how he'd ended up in a wheelchair. Diabetes could cause problems, but that was when you were older, surely he was too young for that. His upper body was strong and muscular, even his legs looked fine, just a bit thin.

The platform was eerily deserted and Halima couldn't help looking at the only other living body. She named him Nasir but it wasn't easy coming up with his story. Why was he travelling so late? Why had he come this far only to swap platforms and turn around? Surely he couldn't be homeless? His clothes were too clean for that.

The train arrived and Halima stepped on, taking a seat in the middle of a section. Further down she heard a clonk and saw Nasir manoeuvre himself with relative ease onto the train. Perhaps he was a Paralympian, his arms were remarkably strong. Maybe he'd been training all day, racing along a running track with his wheels and now he was tired and not thinking straight. He could have forgotten to get off at the right station.

At Acton Town two noisy men got on and sat close to Halima. They both had cans of beer and smelt of smoke. Halima clutched her bag tightly. She had been lulled into a sense of security on the tube but this was London and she never stayed out this late.

'Wanna sip luv?' One of the men lolled towards her offering his can.

Halima shook her head clutching her arms about her.

The other man stuck out his tongue and wiggled it suggestively. 'Do you fancy sum luv?'

Halima could feel panic constricting her chest, she looked

down the carriage towards Nasir and his strong arms. Suddenly she was on her feet and marching purposefully towards him. She dropped into a seat as close as she could get. Nasir looked up at her sharply and then at the men still laughing down the carriage. Nasir had sweat running down his face and seemed nervous.

Halima didn't dare look towards the men, she didn't want to encourage them any further. Instead she kept her eyes on the floor and occasionally checked Nasir. She could hear his heavy breathing. Although she could only see the side of his face, he appeared to have a perfect nose and flawless skin. His chin was covered by a neatly clipped beard. The sweat had given a sheen to his face and she wondered why he was so hot. Then she noticed his ear, and her hand flew to her chest, as if she could prevent her own heart from stopping.

At the next station the rowdy men got off and a mixed group of young people joined the carriage, chatting amiably. Halima couldn't stop staring at Nasir's ear, but of course he wasn't called Nasir, she didn't know him, did she? He rubbed the back of his hand across his forehead and glanced her way. He frowned and set his face towards the door.

'Your ear,' Halima whispered.

The young man's head shot round and he glared at her.

Halima put a hand to the side of her head but of course she was wearing her headscarf.

Nasir resumed his black stare out into the tunnel. A drop of sweat trickled down the side of his face past that perfect ear.

Halima fiddled with the hairclip that held the fabric in tight, her hand was trembling. She tugged at it until the clip pinged onto the floor and she yanked the material behind her ear.

At first the word didn't come out, Halima tried again. 'Look.'

The young man's jaw clenched and he darted a look at her and then he stopped, his lips parted and he stared at her ear. Confusion rippled across his face.

Halima's chest hurt, her heart swelled, thumping through her body making her dizzy. Could this really be? How many years had it been? She thought about Veronica's earnest face and her question:

306

'But where is he now?'

And Halima hadn't been able to answer. But here was her ear. His ear. Their ear with that strange flattened disc half-way down the curled edge.

He put a hand to his own ear, his eyes wide and then the train lurched as it slowed for the next station.

But he was too young, far too young, but look at his eyes, at that nose. He was still staring at her, looking her over and Halima reached out her hand.

The young man was startled and spoke too loudly. 'No, don't touch.'

The doors opened and he tipped back, balancing on the rear wheels as the front ones hovered over the edge and then he was out, his arms pumping the wheels along the platform.

Halima was on her feet, reaching out.

'Wait.' Her voice feeble. But she stumbled, almost lost a foot down the gap and she was only stopped from falling to the floor by a young Japanese girl.

'Steady, are you OK?'

Halima saw him turn his chair through the gap in the wall towards the exit and lost sight of him. It felt as if she'd lost control of her legs, but the girl was still holding on and guided her to a metal bench on the platform.

55

Adam – Safe haven

'Do you have any idea what time it is?' Cara glared down at Adam.

'Midnight?'

'Bloody 'ell.' Cara looked at her blank wrist. She was wearing a bright pink nightie that ended above her knees with a red dressing gown draped over her shoulders.

'Don't you go expecting me to get Vijay up. Ee's sound asleep and so woz I.'

Adam sagged in his chair and looked down at his feet. 'Sorry.'

'Mumblin's not going to 'elp is it? Look at the state of you.' She leaned down and grabbed his wrist, twisting his hand over. 'What the 'ell 'ave you been doin'?'

She stood back and held the door open. 'Get in.'

Adam wanted to cry with relief, he thought she'd been about to send him away. He fought back the tears and did as he was told.

Cara disappeared into the kitchen, swearing and complaining. Adam wheeled himself into the main lounge.

'I don't need anything,' he called out, worried by the cupboard doors banging.

'No of course not, we often get cripples 'ere turning up in the witchin' hour with their 'ands caked in dried blood and lookin' like death-' Cara replied, her voice loud from the kitchen, 'no you don't need anythin', all fine, just a normal night at Chez Vijay. I don't think!'

She stomped back into the room. In her hands she held a plastic bowl of steaming water and a cloth.

'I just need to crash, just until the morning.'

'Looks like you've already crashed.' She knelt on the floor and this time she didn't grab his wrist but held out her hand tenderly to take his. She squeezed the cloth in the water and gently wiped the palm of his hand where the skin was raw and the blood had dried into crusty bits around the edge. It stung and Adam flinched.

Cara shook her head, rinsed the cloth and cleaned around and between his fingers. Adam couldn't stop the tears, he stared at her soft hands doing the work. She had short red-painted nails and once she'd finished one hand, she took his other and began to bathe that one too. Adam tucked his chin in, not daring to look at Cara in case she saw his tears. He felt them roll down his cheeks. With his free hand he wiped his sleeve across his eyes and sniffed.

'Perhaps I could sleep on the sofa?'

'You don't 'ave any choice.' She rinsed the damp cloth. 'You think I'd send you 'ome at this time o' night? No chance buddy.

And I'm not givin' up my bed.' She finished rinsing the cloth and stood up.

'Thank you.'

'I'll wrap them.' She disappeared again, this time to the bathroom. She returned with bandages and a soft hand towel. Gently, just like before, she dabbed his hands dry.

'You don't have to.' Adam was embarrassed by all the attention.

'I'm not doin' it for you. Friction burns like these get all sticky with goo and I don't want you messin' up Vijay's sofa.'

She expertly laid pieces of lint across his palms and bound the soft cream bandages around his hands and fastened them with a bit of tape which she tore off with her teeth.

'Right. 'ot chocoloate and cookies next, and don't be expectin' anythin' more. I'm not about to start cookin' no fancy meal for you. You people think I'm only 'ere to serve and pander. An' at midnight too.' She walked off into the kitchen with the bowl and the cloth.

While she was gone, Adam took himself to the bathroom. In the mirror he saw his bedraggled hair, his tears had left clean lines down his face except where he'd smudged them. The goatee on his chin looked odd, as if he were a child pretending to be an adult. Adam looked at the bandages on his hands, he wanted to wash his face but he didn't dare get Cara's bandages wet. Instead he grabbed the hand towel, part-filled the sink and dipped in a corner which he used to wipe over his face. When he got back to the lounge there was a plate with two round cookies and a large steaming mug. On the sofa were blankets and a pillow. Cara appeared from the corridor that led to the bedrooms with a lamp in her hand. She plugged it in at the wall and then trailed it towards the sofa where she put it on the floor and switched it on.

'Right.' She stood with her hands on her hips.

'I'm sorry-' Adam started.

'Save it till the mornin'. I, for one, intend to get some sleep tonight. Do you need anythin' else?'

'No, no. Thanks Cara.'

She disappeared out of the room turning the main light off as she went. The room closed in around the sofa. Adam wheeled himself to the low table and ate the cookies in large mouthfuls, barely chewing before taking another bite. He gulped at the hot chocolate, burning his throat, and then set about getting his body onto the sofa and the blankets around him. His hands still hurt and he felt the skin crack where it had hardened. Finally he was lying down and it felt so good to be out of his chair and relaxing where it was safe. Adam leant down and switched off the lamp.

In the dark he lay with his eyes closed but then sat up and switched the light back on. He checked his watch and set the alarm for six. Only seven more hours to go and he would finally be free of the package. Adam lay down again and switched the light off. As his eyes became accustomed to the dark he could make out the bulk of the wheelchair at the end of the sofa. He was safe here. The package would be safe.

He'd spent a long time on the tube riding to the end of the District Line and back again like the homeless people. Nowhere seemed like the right place to go. But the trains didn't run all night, and he couldn't wander the streets of London. A wheelchair user at this time of night was an even more uncommon sight than in the day. He'd begun to feel more and more conspicuous. Finally the thought of being mugged and the package stolen, or worse, had driven him to seek refuge at Vijay's. Adam wondered why he hadn't come here earlier. He closed his eyes and tried to sleep.

Faizal was there sitting on the floor of Vijay's lounge. The bomb was laid out on the carpet, all wires and tubes. It was far bigger than could possibly fit under his chair.

'Look, I have the final piece.'

'Where did you get it?' Adam stared.

'It was my mission, to bring this.' He held up what looked like a child's bicycle bell with a red button on it. Dangling below was a long wire.

'Don't press it.' Adam was too hot.

'It's OK, I haven't attached it yet. That's your job.'

'Mine?'

'Sure. Hold on.'

Faizal shoved the end of the wire into the middle of the bomb. 'It's ready.'

Adam looked around. Cara and Vijay were nowhere to be seen.

Faizal's face was alight with excitement. 'You can blow them up.'

'Blow who up?'

'Transport Rail of course. It was all their fault, remember?'

Faizal was right. Of course, that was what he was supposed to do.

Now he was rolling in through the double doors into the foyer at work, the bomb safely stowed again under his chair. That security guard Brian glared at him but Adam ignored him and went straight up in the lift. He passed room J9 and stopped, pushed the door open and saw a room full of computers, but Aisha wasn't there. His fingers curled around the detonator. On the second floor he wheeled himself along to meeting room five. Inside, around the table, sat Dave, Sonia Greene and Stephanie. All talking ceased when he entered and they turned to stare at him. Before any of them could speak Faizal popped his head through the wall, his face beaming.

'In the name of Allah,' Faizal shouted.

Adam squeezed the detonator and the room trembled as the bomb exploded.

He was back at the train crash, the sound of metal groaning and sheering. Screams and a huge lurch as the train seemed to topple. Then excruciating pain and not being able to move, screams and cries all around him. A hot burning smell made his nasal hairs crackle. Adam felt himself panicking, he had to get out. To his left someone seemed to be hanging from the luggage rack, their head bleeding.

He was back at Transport Rail, meeting room five didn't exist any more. Below him was a huge hole where a large girder had crashed through and flattened the post room. There was a corner of Zeeshan's prayer rug sticking out from under the pile of broken debris. Adam cried out. Avoiding the hole, he wheeled himself along the corridor back to the open-plan office. The door swung open and the room was filled with flying papers, he could see his desk littered with plaster and glass. There was a pair of shoes next to the photocopier as if the person who'd worn them had simply vanished. They were Melanie's. The bomb must have vaporized her body. He imagined her little white dog, a Jack Russell that she'd talked about so often. Nobody would come home to it that night. It would sit, howling and scratching at the door of her flat. But nobody would come, the dog growing weaker, until finally it lay on its side by the front door, its eyes like pieces of brown glass.

Sunday
(2 days to go)

56

Adam - Revelations

Adam sat up bathed in sweat, his chest hammering. His eyes adjusted to the dark shadows of Vijay's lounge. Reaching down, he switched on the lamp. Letting his body fall back onto the sofa, he breathed a sigh of relief. But then he was up again and panicking about the package. He had to check, had to see for himself. The image of all the wires and tubes came back to him with Faizal's grinning face.

Adam shook his head and pulled the blankets off his legs. Carefully, he lowered himself to the floor and shuffled over to the wheelchair. Just one peek, he wouldn't damage anything, he'd take extra special care. He pulled the lamp closer. Using the ends of his fingers he cautiously felt around the box, there was a catch near the back of the seat, a simple swivel. Adam twisted it and the front of the box came loose. He lowered it carefully, it was hinged and hung downwards. Adam breathed out and then picked up the lamp to shine it into the box.

Three black round objects lay in a line, slightly rounded with sort-of nipples on the ends. Adam stared, there was something so familiar about them but his mind was struggling to make sense of it. It wasn't the image in his dream, that was for sure, but... Adam shone the light even closer, there was some liquid on the floor of the box and a drip hung from the middle object. He put his hand in, but what if it was corrosive? Instead he used the bandage on the edge of his hand to touch the liquid then pulled his hand out to analyse it. The bandage was fine, a little damp was all. Adam sniffed it, no smell but something smelled a bit strange in there. Adam tried desperately to think why these objects seemed familiar until finally he realised they looked exactly like the ends of sports drinks bottles. Feeling bolder, Adam put his hand in again and felt one of the ends. He tried to move it just a little, it slid with ease towards him, gently he pulled it out. Incredulous, Adam set the sports bottle down on the floor. He pulled out the next one. And the next. The last one seemed to be filled with a yellowish liquid. Adam sniffed again. It smelt of piss. What on earth?

This must be some kind of crazy joke. That bastard Ibrahim Muhammad Sharif had led him to believe, well what? The box under his chair had been referred to as the package and nothing more, it was Adam who had made all the assumptions. Relief washed over him until he felt quite delirious. Perhaps he really was his second cousin twice removed. Maybe this was why his mother never spoke about him, because he played evil practical jokes. Was that it? Adam remembered being led into the lift, but before the door was shut fully the giant Gabir, watching across the hall, had smiled. Had he known about the joke?

Adam contemplated the three bottles in the light of the lamp. One of piss, definitely not his, and two with water. He'd decided to taste the clear ones after pouring a little on the table and squashing a cookie crumb into it. A sudden noise made Adam look up towards the front door. A sliding, heavy kind of sound. Definitely not a sound for three o'clock in the morning. Adam felt his hairs rise and skin prickle.

CRASH.

The front door burst open and beams of light shone into Adam's eyes. Suddenly the room was filled with shouts and people and lights.

'Don't move.'

'Secure the area.'

'Bravo One, door left. Bravo two, door right.

'Put your hands up.'

Adam shielded his face from the glare.

'Hands up.' He heard a heavy click and keeping his eyes shut and his head down, Adam lifted his bandaged hands. Someone had turned the main light on.

There was a scream from the other room. The lounge was filled with black-uniformed men with guns. He cowered on the floor. There was the sound of feet and heavy movements.

'Clear,' someone shouted to his left.

'Female unarmed,' another called from a bedroom.

'Arms up!' a voice yelled, louder than the others.

'Don't touch 'im, don't you dare 'urt him,' Cara's voice shrill. 'Ee can't move 'is arms, for Christ's sake don't shoot a cripple stuck in 'is own fuckin' bed.'

'Get up.'

It took Adam a few seconds to realise the last command was aimed at him. He identified the one who'd spoken who was removing some kind of mask.

'I... I can't.'

'Are you hurt?' The man was holding a weapon in one hand which he kept pointed at Adam. He used the other to gesture at Adam's bandaged hands.

'I need the wheelchair.'

'This?'

Adam nodded.

'Stay there.' Without letting his eyes leave Adam, he commanded the others to bring their suspects into the lounge.

Cara arrived in just her nightie, looking wild-eyed with her hands behind her head.

'What do we do about the one in the bed?'

'Why can't he move?' the one in charge asked, addressing Cara.

'Motor Neurone disease.' Her voice was quiet and Adam could see her bottom lip tremble. Suddenly she bit it and she glanced down at Adam and then back to the officer. 'And why on earth you want to frighten us all to death, God only knows.'

'You two, start searching. Where's the dog?'

'Downstairs sir.'

'Well don't just stand there.'

Adam sat with his arms in the air. He was terrified, and he wasn't sure if his arms were shaking from fear or the effort of holding them up. So much for thinking this was a joke. Yesterday had been a long way from anything remotely funny and it wasn't finished yet. One of the men came over and roughly manhandled him, checking for objects. His house key was still buried in a pocket and the man pulled it out, then took Adam's phone and wallet from the coffee table and gave them to his boss.

A golden retriever arrived with its handler.

'Go ahead.'

The handler knelt down and spoke to the dog who was straining at his leash, tail wagging furiously. Suddenly it was off the lead, it sniffed around the wheels of Adam's wheelchair and then put its front paws up onto the seat, its nose probing into the corners. Next it bounded over to Adam and sniffed his trousers, stuck its snout right into Adam's face and then it was off, jumping up onto the sofa and making muffled noises into the seat cushions. The handler gave encouraging words and the dog jumped down and continued over to Cara.

'Nice dog,' Cara said.

Adam looked up surprised; she had her hands by her sides and was looking more composed.

'And what exactly are you expectin' to find in a disabled man's flat might I ask?'

'Shut up.'

'Polite too.'

'This isn't a social call,' the leader said. He shouldered his weapon and pulled out a walkie talkie. 'Bravo one, take over.' He nodded at one of the other men, then he went back out of the front door and Adam could hear his muffled voice speaking into the gadget. Several men were moving around the flat, he could hear one in the kitchen banging open drawers and cupboards. A couple more seemed to be in the bedrooms. More banging. Adam wondered about Vijay lying in his bed. He hadn't heard his voice. Was he all right? What had they done to him? Adam had a frightening vision of one of these uniformed men pressing a silencer against his head and firing. No, none of them had that kind of weapon. But what if they'd frightened him so badly he was having an attack of some kind? A fit maybe, where he couldn't breathe? Adam tried to calm himself down, surely one of them would have said if there was a problem.

The leader came back in and addressed Adam on the floor.

'Why were you down there when we arrived?'

Adam felt caught, the edge of the sofa was pressing into his back.

'I...'

Cara butted in, 'Well that's obvious in't it? He fell off the sofa.'

The leader ignored the comment and kept his focus on Adam.

'Have you been drinking?'

'I...no.'

Cara huffed loudly. 'If you 'ad legs that didn't work, you'd likely fall off sofas too. We were all just trying to get some sleep when you lot came bargin' in.'

'Listen lady, shut the fuck up until I ask you something OK?'

'Fine.' Cara crossed her arms over her bosom and made a loud 'Hmph,' noise. 'Don't suppose I could at least go and put a dressin' gown on?'

The leader rolled his eyes and nodded with his head for one of the others to escort Cara to the bedroom.

'Why thank you, so kind.'

Another man returned from the kitchen. 'Nothing boss.'

The leader sighed and shook his head.

With a bored expression he asked, 'Name?'

'Adam, Adam Rasheed.'

The leader undid a zip on his jacket and pulled out a small notepad.

'Who did you meet at Palace Green?'

Adam was cold almost to the point of shivering. Had they followed him ever since he left? How did they know he'd been there? Should he give them a false name of whom he went to visit? Adam hurriedly tried to remember all the instructions on that tablet. The text playing before his eyes, jumbling up and leaving him confused. He was certain it made no mention of needing to keep secret anything except the address where he had to deliver the package. The leader was staring at Adam.

'Er, Ibrahim Muhammad Sharif.'

'Why?'

'We, er, we had tea and scones with jam.' That taste swilled in

Adam's mouth again and he swallowed. 'It was blackcurrant jam not strawberry.'

'Do you really think I give a flying fuck what kind of jam you had?'

Adam looked down at the floor and noticed the three sports bottles still lined up in front of him.

'What are those?'

The leader leant down and picked up the one that was slightly yellow. He put it to his nose and retracted it again.

'What is it?'

Adam wanted to say 'piss' but it would sound as if he was being rude, and 'wee' was too childish. Finally he said, 'Urine.'

'What the hell have you got that for?' He plonked it on the table.

'Well that's obvious too.' Cara was back. 'Think about it, guy in a wheelchair, bottle of piss? Don't take a genius.'

The leader gave Cara a withering look but Adam suspected it would take more than that to stop her.

'The other two?'

'Water,' Adam said.

'Drink one, piss one, stands to reason,' Cara added.

The walkie talkie crackled and the leader pulled it out of his pocket and went back out to the landing. Adam couldn't hear exactly what he was saying, but he was getting the impression from the way the other men were standing and even sitting around that they didn't want to be there any more.

The golden retriever reappeared with its handler, back on its lead. They went out to the landing where Adam could see him talking to the leader, then he disappeared.

'OK lads, we'll make this quick, IDs and electricals including phones then we're out of here.'

'Can't the techie guys do that sir?'

'No. Do you have any idea how big this operation is?'

'No sir.'

'Right then.'

Adam stayed where he was, they took his student card from his wallet. Cara led two of them back to the bedrooms to provide passports.

'Ee's going to sue you.' Cara stood shaking her head as they filed out with computers and laptops from Vijay's office.

The uniformed men didn't seem too happy either. They grumbled as they went past the sofa.

'Bloody typical.'

'Waste of fucking time.'

'Intelligence my arse.'

'Have a good night.' The leader turned to leave.

'Just a minute.' Cara strode towards him. For a moment she was lost for words and then she said. 'What about the door?'

Adam could see the frame had splintered where the lock had been forced through the wood.

The leader sighed. 'Contact your local police station. You can file a claim.'

'And when will Vijay get 'is stuff back and my fuckin' phone?'

The leader shrugged. 'They've got a lot to get through. The tech guys will be in touch.'

After the police had left, Cara made tea and checked on Vijay, making sure he was comfortable before coming back to Adam. She stood with her hands on her hips staring at him.

'God only knows what you've got your sorry arse into but I ain't about to dig you out of it. Not at four o'clock in the bloody mornin'. I'm going back to bed. You can explain yourself to Vijay in the mornin'.'

With that she left him alone again in the dark. Adam climbed back onto the sofa and pulled the blankets over himself. But he didn't sleep. Instead he prayed long and hard. At first he gave thanks that he was still alive, that he had managed to get this far. Then he asked for Allah's guidance, for His strength to complete the task. Later as dawn approached Adam finished his Fajr prayers.

Now he was a lot calmer and in control of his life. Here he was in Vijay's flat and, despite the terror of yesterday and last night, everything was OK. It hadn't been a joke, the police raid was testament to that, it must have been a trial. This was the

319

practice run before the real thing. Adam was in the middle of the biggest challenge of his life. It was quarter to six, time for him to leave and deliver the package. He reloaded the bottles into the box under the wheelchair and twisted the catch to keep it closed. The blankets and pillow he laid neatly on the sofa and put his wallet and key back into his pockets.

In the kitchen, he had a quick drink of milk and then quietly pushed open the damaged front door before either Cara or Vijay awoke. Splinters of wood crunched under his wheels as he left.

He was nearing the address where he was supposed to deliver the package. The whole way he had been paranoid about being followed. He had deliberately gone back on himself and travelled an extra stop then back again to make absolutely sure. If he passed this test, they might give him something important. A part in the real plan. Something truly meaningful that would raise him up in the eyes of Allah and all his Muslim brothers and sisters. Adam was feeling quite exalted at having survived this test. The terror and confusion of last night was gone. Adam felt strong in his conviction; he had Allah on his side.

Ahead of him the street was untidy. Behind him, no one. There were cans on the pavement and an over-filled skip. Several of the houses were boarded up and the others were more like squats than actual homes. Window frames with cracked, peeling paint. An occasional piece of plywood in place of a windowpane. Numbers were intermittent, sometimes on the door or wall of a house. Sometimes not there at all. Number thirty-four had a metal sheet across the doorway. The name of a security firm warned that trespassers would be prosecuted and that the premises were monitored by CCTV. The ground floor windows were covered with the same metal sheeting, only the upstairs had normal windows looking blankly onto the street.

Adam's heart shrank. Nobody lived here, there wasn't even a usable entrance any more. He stopped his wheelchair on the pavement. A few cars were parked further up. Across the street someone had hung a sheet out the window that read 'Block the Development' in lurid spray-painted colours. Perhaps it was the wrong address, but Adam knew he'd got it right, there was no point in kidding himself. This was the correct place.

Small slivers of doubt were trying to push their way into his consciousness but he thrust them out. Perhaps someone was meant to meet him here in front of the house? Adam checked his watch, he still had ten minutes to go before eight o'clock. He would wait.

Someone was staring out of the house opposite, rubbing their eye and then scratching at their untidy hair. Adam averted his gaze. He felt conspicuous on the pavement, maybe he should go around the block and return. Down at the corner was a bus stop and he loitered there for a while, ignoring the bus that came trundling past. Another five minutes. Adam couldn't help checking his watch yet again. He would take himself back to the house for exactly eight o'clock. Surely someone would be there by then? Surely this whole nightmare hadn't been for nothing?

As he got closer to the house again, Adam found himself slowing down, still trying to contain the emotions that threatened to take over. He had been following Allah's plan, this was a test to see if he was good enough for the elite UMIA, wasn't it? He'd done everything right, he had. He *had*.

There was no one in front of the boarded-up house, no way in. Nobody even in sight. The figure at the window opposite had disappeared. The street was devoid of life. Doubts began to scramble at the edges of his mind, like so many little creatures of anger and humiliation, it made his face twitch and his hands clench. Adam flinched, he'd been gripping the wheels too tight and despite the bandages his hands still hurt. It had all been a waste of time. He was nothing to nobody. A carrier for someone's bottle of piss.

The shame and anger came flooding in. He was just some bit-part in a crazy hoax, a decoy in someone else's revenge or corrupted plan. Adam squeezed his hands harder till they stung. He wanted the pain, wanted the hurt to cover his shame.

Bastards.

It was five past eight. Of course no one was coming. Who on earth would want a package of three sports bottles, one of piss and two of water? He'd been played like the fool he was. Adam twisted in his chair and reached over the back. His fingertips swivelled the catch and the flap banged down. Leaning further he was able to grab the first bottle. In one swift movement he launched it at the metal casing on the door of the house. It clanged loudly and bounced down onto the path. Adam grabbed the next one and lobbed it at the downstairs windows, another clang and it ended in the bush. He pulled the last one out and he could see from the pale-yellow tinge that this one was the bottle full of piss. This time he made sure he was sitting squarely and used both hands in a basketball hold. With focused strength, Adam tipped backwards, his arms above his head and with a full body-thrust, the bottle went flying into the upstairs window.

'Bastards.'

The crash and tinkle of glass applauded his shout.

57

Austin – Eternal love revealed

By Sunday morning, Dave still hadn't arrived. There was another text message saying he hoped to see him that evening if everything went smoothly today. They hadn't spoken and Austin wasn't sure he wanted to. Anger bubbled up every time he thought about Ross jumping down from the van instead of David and there'd been that rude kiss too. Who did he think he was? The both of them were totally out of order. David certainly had some grovelling to do.

Austin ate some toast and then turned the music on loud as he set to work emptying the box of books onto a shelf. Half an hour later he went to check his phone again and his heart leapt when he saw he'd missed a call. Probably hadn't heard it through the thumping sound of Ed Sheeran. At last David had called to apologise. About time. But the missed call wasn't from David, it was from John, Matt's father. Austin paused, staring at his mobile. It must be to do with the memorial on Tuesday. They probably wanted to meet up. But he had decided hadn't he? That he shouldn't go, that living in the present was more important than raking over his relationship with Matt? Austin's thumb hovered over the screen. There was a text to say he had a voicemail message too. Perhaps that would be the apology from David. Austin listened to the message, but it wasn't what he expected.

'I'm sorry to take up your Sunday,' John apologised as he stood to let Austin take the other seat. He'd been here a while judging by the empty cold mug still on the table. Austin sat down with his own espresso.

'It's fine, I wasn't doing much.' Austin almost blurted out about David working all weekend and that he was sick of boxes, but he stopped himself in time. He still hadn't told them about David, wasn't sure how. Instead he asked, 'Where's Pat?' It was unusual to see Matt's father on his own without his wife.

'Oh... she-' John coughed slightly embarrassed. 'She wasn't feeling well.'

'Oh dear, I hope she's OK.'

'Yeah, I'm sure she will be, just a little blip.'

What kind of blip? Austin couldn't work John out, he seemed uncomfortable, shifting in his seat, raising his mug and putting it down again when he realised it was empty. And why the urgency?

'Nice shirt.' Austin attempted a smile at John's new crisp green shirt.

'Oh this?' John snuffed out air from his nose. 'Pat persuaded me.'

Austin took a sip of his espresso and wished he'd had a shot of something in it. He was beginning to recognise that something was terribly wrong.

'So, I may as well get straight to the point,' John said, clearing his throat.

Austin plonked his cup down a little too hard and the saucer rattled loudly. 'Sorry.'

'These two men came to see us,' John said.

'Two men?'

John raised his hand. 'Let me speak and then you can ask questions, OK?'

Austin hugged his arms, feeling embarrassed like he'd been reprimanded by that awful history teacher at school, Mr Dunston.

'I can't remember the name of the company but it doesn't matter. They had a package. They're working on behalf of the police.' John's words were tripping over themselves to get out but then he stopped, took a breath and continued in a more measured tone. 'Apparently after a disaster like the one Matt was in, they often have a lot of evidence and personal effects collected from the scene.' He paused again, staring into the bottom of his empty cup. 'Some of it is used as evidence, some not. Most of the personal effects are returned to the families if they're not needed. Sometimes there's quite a lot of stuff that goes unclaimed or they think might be useful but later is not required. Anyway, that's the way they explained it.'

Austin squeezed his arms, hugging his chest tighter. Where on earth was this heading?

'Apparently, it can be too time-consuming for the police to try and return or get rid of those items that get left over, so they draft in this company to sort it.'

Austin could see beads of sweat on John's forehead glistening in the sun coming through the window. Leftovers? What kind of leftovers? Surely they wouldn't still have preserved body parts? Austin shivered.

'They gave us this.' John pulled something from his trouser pocket and put it on the coffee table between them.

They stared at the small square box. It was navy with a neat gold line around the top edge. To one side were two tiny hinges and a line running around the centre of the box. Austin didn't want to open it. John leaned back letting out a heavy sigh. They exchanged a quick glance.

'We think it was meant for you,' John said.

Austin looked away, out of the window, the streets were quiet, a typical lazy Sunday. Opposite a couple were walking their dog. An open-topped car went past drifting music as it went. All so normal and relaxed, Austin wanted to walk out of there and join them.

'It's up to you what you want to do with it.' John had pushed his chair back from the table and was fiddling with his watch. 'Pat and I, we think you should have it. After all, I'm sure he would have given it to you if...' His voice cracked and he turned away.

Austin's mouth had that strange iron taste as if he'd been eating spinach. He just wanted to get up and leave, not look back, not deal with this new hurt.

'I'm sorry.' John looked down at his lap. 'We considered not telling you but I think honesty's the best policy and it really doesn't belong to us.'

The box was cursed and yet it surely contained a symbol of love. How many hundreds of years had such a gift signalled one's deepest desires for another and yet here, in this small coffee shop in Balham, it was breaking Austin's heart all over again.

58

Adam – Pawns and fools

Adam was woken by a loud knocking at the door. He turned to see his clock on the bedside table, it was quarter to twelve. Too early for lunch. Maybe if he ignored it, his mum would go away. Adam shut his eyes.

The knocking was louder, more insistent.

'Adam, it's me, Faizal.'

Adam propped himself up on his elbows, what on earth was he doing here?

'Come in.'

Faizal's face poked around the door and, instead of his beaming smile, he was frowning and appeared nervous.

'It's all right, come in.'

Faizal closed the door behind him and stood awkwardly between Adam's wheelchair and the desk.

'What's up?' Adam tried to wipe the tiredness from his eyes.

'Bro,' I've been texting and calling you.'

Adam glanced at his bedside table, only the clock and the lamp, then down at himself, he was still dressed and he automatically reached into his jeans pocket. But then he remembered and the recent events came smashing into his head. He didn't have his phone, the police did. He flopped back down onto his pillow.

'And what have you done to piss your parents off so much? They weren't gonna let me in, I had to use some major powers of persuasion.'

Adam stared at the ceiling, remembering the drinks bottles. He just wanted to sleep forever.

'So have you heard what's happened? Unbelievable, it's like totally out there.'

Faizal had plonked himself in the wheelchair and was trying to twist it by pushing one wheel forwards and the other backwards.

'Hey, this is quite fun,' he said as he spun around to face the desk and banged a wheel against the post at the end of Adam's bed.

'Quit messing about. Look, I didn't get much sleep last night.'

'You haven't heard have you?' Faizal's eyes widened. 'It's crazy, I don't know how it started but it's all gone tits up, I mean the bluebirds not-' he raised his eyes to the ceiling. 'Forgive me, Allah.'

'What are you talking about?' Adam said.

'ISIS and the UMIA of course. Didn't you read any of my texts?'

'I lost my phone.'

'Bummer.' Faizal shrugged. 'The word on the street is that ISIS has infiltrated the UMIA. They've been intercepting communications and I don't know what. And get this, Tariq, he got raided by the police last night. Thought he was some kind of terrorist. Course there was nothing there but apparently they saw him talking to some dodgy dude. His parents have gone ballistic, he's been grounded for a month. Anyway, early this morning, Twitter was going mad right. And they were saying anyone who'd had an unusual communication was to report it.'

Faizal paused to take a breath. 'Hey, are you all right dude, you're a bit of a weird colour.'

'I'm fine.' Adam was up on his elbows again. 'Keep talking.'

'So,' Faizal lifted his feet up onto the footplate of the wheelchair. 'Hey, this is a pretty cool chair.' He twisted it around and managed a complete 360.

'And what?'

'From what people have been posting this morning and what the police said, it seems ISIS is planning something big but they've set up all these dead ends.' Faizal shrugged. 'It seems like they're throwing out a blanket of misinformation, masses of false leads to cover their real target. It's chaos. Even some of the UMIA have been arrested but I'm sure that's because ISIS have tipped off the police or something like that.'

Adam was suddenly very thirsty.

'Could you get me a glass of water?'

'Seriously?' Faizal stood up. 'Only if you promise to take a shower, it kind of stinks in here brother.' He waved a hand in front of his face. 'And then you need to come with me to the mosque, there's a meeting after lunchtime prayers about what's happened. A UMIA official is going to be there to explain stuff.'

At the meeting, the speaker seemed to be trying to reassure them that the UMIA was a peaceful organisation and that anything they'd heard in the media to the contrary was false. He admitted that there was cause for concern that ISIS members had infiltrated the organisation but that it was unlikely to be local here in the west of London.

'However, there have been some rumours about an elite group of the UMIA which of course is absurd, there is no secret inner society. We have always been very clear about what our aims and campaigns are.'

'Oh fuck,' Faizal whispered harshly, clutching Adam's arm really tight.

'Ow.'

The speaker paused slightly and looked over at them. 'But if any of you have heard any of these rumours, do come and speak to me at the end.'

As soon as the meeting was over, the room of people broke up into groups chattering loudly.

'What have I done?' Faizal had his head in his hands.

Adam was feeling sick. If there wasn't an elite group of the UMIA then why had Ibrahim Muhammad Sharif invited Adam to his house?

'I'm such an idiot.' Faizal looked at Adam, his face pained.

Adam remembered Faizal talking about his secret information. 'What did you do?'

'There were these guys, Jamaal and Hakeem, they said I'd been chosen to join a special group.'

Adam could only nod his head, he felt so cold.

'And then I was given this supposedly secret number. I thought it was a special operation for the UMIA. What a complete dick I am.' Faizal was looking down at his knees, ashamed. 'I mean who in their right mind would think that one zero five three was important. I've been used by fucking ISIS.'

Adam didn't know what to think. A secret number sounded more credible than wandering around London with bottles of water and piss. If Faizal was a dick then Adam was way, way worse. The biggest fuckwit of all time.

An angry face suddenly appeared in front of Adam. 'Where is she?'

'What?' Adam gripped the rims of his wheels. It was the kufi-wearer.

He glared at Adam and demanded, 'Aisha? Where is she?'

Faizal jumped to his feet. 'Hey, you gave me that note. So who do you think you're working for hey?' Adam could see Faizal's face burning, the embarrassment being replaced by anger.

'It was from Aisha,' the kufi-wearer said, taking a step back from Faizal. He looked again at Adam. 'So where is she?'

'I don't know,' Adam said in a harsh whisper.

'What did she tell you in the note?'

Adam needed to get away, he wanted time to think, to work things out for himself.

'I ripped it up,' said Faizal hotly, 'I thought it was from you.'

The kufi-wearer turned on Faizal. 'You idiot, there's no telling what she risked to get that message to him.' He pointed straight at Adam.

The anger fizzled out of Faizal and his shoulders drooped. 'I...I didn't know it was from Aisha.'

'She and her sister have disappeared. They didn't come home last night and their passports are missing.' The angry man turned away from Faizal. 'So when did you last see Ibrahim Muhammed Sharif?' His bearded face jutted towards Adam.

'The guy from Syria?' Faizal asked.

Adam swallowed, his lips were dry but he didn't dare open his mouth. How did he know who to trust? This was the man who had been trying to drag Aisha away in the street. She had shouted at him, tried to pull away. Were they on the same side? Had that note really been from Aisha?

Faizal and the man both looked at Adam.

'I don't know where they are. It's got nothing to do with me.' Adam turned his chair around and started heading out of the room. He needed space and time to think.

'What happened to your hands?' They were following him.

Adam pushed the button for the lift several times.

'Too much rally driving.' Faizal attempted a laugh but the man didn't smile, he stared down at Adam.

Adam thumped the glowing button, willing the lift to hurry up.

'Where were you yesterday?' he persisted.

The lift doors finally shuddered open.

'Ease up brother,' Faizal said, 'he met me and then he went to see his mate Vijay. Didn't you?'

Adam hit the button for the ground floor. He ignored them both, staring only at his trainers on the foot plate.

'Adam?' Faizal said as the doors began to shut.

'Where is she?' A note of pleading had come into the man's voice. Only Adam got into the lift, it was such an old rickety thing that none of them trusted it.

The lift began to move and Adam tried to sort out the crazy thoughts in his head. If there wasn't an elite group of the UMIA did that mean that Jamaal and Hakeem were working for ISIS? And if that was true, did that mean that Ibrahim Muhammad Sharif was also with ISIS? Maybe he'd been given the package to deliberately divert the police attention away from some other part of an ISIS operation. What about Aisha? Was she also ISIS or was she being used by them too? What if Adam's desire to be a hero, to prove himself to Aisha, had blinded him to the truth? Perhaps his need to do something tremendous in the name of Allah had completely obliterated his moral compass. A braver man than him, a man certain of his place in the world, a moral man, would never have run around London like a headless chicken thinking he had a bomb under his wheelchair. A better man would have gone straight to the police, sought their help and protection or at the very least called a prominent member of the UMIA. No, Adam was a fool and a coward, and Aisha might be in serious danger.

59

Ralph – Head in the sand

Cameron was at the side of the bed, staring at him.

'What is it?' Ralph asked.

'Mum says you have to talk to him.' He held out his hand to show the black handset.

Ralph stared at the small electronic device but made no move to take it.

'Mum said!' Cameron implored, his eyes wide thrusting the phone at him.

Ralph took it and immediately Cameron ran out of the room slamming the door behind him.

'Hello?'

'There you are. Thought my nephew had played a trick and hidden the phone behind a cushion.'

'Oh, it's you.' Ralph blinked.

'Have you just woken up or something?'

'Um, sort of.' Ralph looked at the digital clock which read 16:10.

'It's all right for some, I'm still at work and before you start, yes I know it's a Sunday.'

'Is it?'

'I've got a few minutes while this process runs so what's going on with you? I've had umpteen texts from Shelly, and Mum and Dad have been on my case to come and see you.'

Ralph didn't say anything, there wasn't anything to say.

'So what's up? Cos I've still got stuff to do here and I want to finish before midnight.'

'Uh-huh.'

'What's that supposed to mean? Not sure what Mum expects me to do, she was going on about you needing counselling or something which just goes to show how much she's losing touch. I mean it's not like the golden boy needs any of that stuff is there?'

'No, I'm fine.'

'Exactly, that's what I told her. Oh by the way, you know Aunt Maureen's sixtieth, well get this, my invitation says plus one guest. Ridiculous. Can you imagine if I brought someone? Mum and Dad would have a heart attack.'

'No they wouldn't.' Ralph could see his mum's sister swimming into focus, her bright eyes and white curly hair looking all excited.

'Oh really! You have no idea how they'd react.'

Ralph sighed inwardly. 'Why do you think nobody knows?'

'OK, so they might have guessed by now, but it's a bit different to having it rubbed in your face at Auntie's party.'

'Suit yourself.'

'It's all right for you; married with two point four kids, you can't put a foot wrong. Well except for lying in bed too long.' There was a slight pause on the line. 'It's not anything serious, right?'

'No,' Ralph confirmed, 'just a bit tired, that's all.'

'Good. One last thing, would you mind me coming in on a present with you for Aunt Maureen? Shelly's much better at these things than I am. I'll throw in twenty quid, how's that?'

Ralph wasn't sure when Aunt Maureen's birthday was.

'Ralph?'

'Sure.'

'Looks like this data's almost done. I'll text you about coming over to take my nephews to the park or something, I promised Liam. And get out of bed, I'm sick of getting calls from Mum, I could do without the hassle.'

'I'll be fine in a couple of days.'

'Good. See ya.'

60

Austin – Raking over the past

'Hey.'

'Aaaahh,' screamed Austin flailing his arms as he lurched up from the sofa.

'Woah, you were really gone,' said David.

'That wasn't funny, what the hell is the time?' Austin blinked and widened his eyes, trying to be more awake. He focused on the clock on the wall. It was almost midnight. David was bending forwards to the coffee table and Austin thought he was reaching for the empty wine glass but David picked up something small.

'Give me that.'

David flicked open the box, the gleam of the gold bright for just a second before Austin snatched it back.

'It's not yours, I mean, it's not for you.'

David straightened and looked at Austin, his face suddenly incredibly tired. 'Of course not,' he said and turned away into the kitchen.

Austin clutched the box to his chest. Something was wrong, normally David would have spat back with some sarcastic quip or other, but that expression, so forlorn, defeated even.

'Can I have some of this?' David was taking some left overs out of the fridge.

'If you want.'

'Sorry I'm late.'

Austin stood in the doorway watching as David dug a spoon into the cold lasagne and slopped it onto his plate.

'What happened at work?'

David shook his head. 'Just some stuff I had to sort. It's been a nightmare.'

'What stuff?'

'You wouldn't understand,' David said.

'Oh really, except I helped build and test the flippin' system you use. Of course I wouldn't understand.'

'It's more about policy, company information. I can't share it, OK?' David was defeated, he glanced up at Austin, a sort of desperation in his eyes. 'Can we just drop it?'

Austin looked away from David's face to the plate of cold lasagne he was holding. 'There's salad,' he said, staring at the way it stayed in a solid lump, immobile on the plate.

'This is fine.' He stuck it in the microwave. 'What did you eat?'

Austin didn't remember eating anything, only getting a cool glass of wine out of the fridge when he got back from seeing John. It didn't matter, he wasn't hungry. They waited for the ping and David withdrew the hot plate.

They stood face to face, David holding the plate and Austin in the doorway. David's eyes glanced to his chest and back again, a frown on his face. Austin realised he was still clutching the jewellery box to his chest.

'It's...' Austin didn't know how to explain, so he stepped to the side to let David come back through into the lounge.

'A ring,' David finished.

'Yes.'

David's fork clinked on his plate as he started to eat. He nodded at the empty glass on the table.

'Any wine?'

'Err yes.' Austin hid in the kitchen, put the ring down while he opened the fridge and removed the empty bottle of white. No wonder he was so woozy, he'd drunk the entire bottle. Beside the cooker was the leftover red he'd bought to celebrate moving in.

333

A Merlot to go with the lasagne that he'd made yesterday, a meal that David never turned up for. Austin shook his head and unscrewed the lid. He pulled another glass from an open box on the floor.

'Thanks for this,' David said motioning towards his plate and the filled glass that Austin put on the table.

Neither of them spoke for a moment. The sound from the TV seemed unnaturally loud. Austin picked up the remote and pressed the mute button.

David had his head down, cutting the lasagne with the side of his fork and putting a huge piece in his mouth.

'It was nicer yesterday when you were supposed to come for dinner.'

'It's still nice.'

'If you'd been earlier, I could have cooked,' Austin said.

David shook his head.

Austin wanted some kind of retort, something for him to bat against but David just seemed resigned.

'You don't normally work weekends.'

'Mm.' Another forkful went in.

Austin had the jewellery box in his hand and he squeezed, feeling the corners dig into his palm.

'Don't you think it's a bit much turning up at midnight? I mean late's one thing, but this is beyond late. And you've only come for the lasagne.' Austin's emotions swelled in his chest.

David glanced up, his eyes heavy-lidded. He shook his head again and Austin saw his chest rise and fall with a sigh.

'Then you scare the living daylights out of me. Don't you even care?' Austin could hear his voice getting louder.

David put down the plate, only a smear of tomato sauce left. 'Well?'

David swallowed the last mouthful. 'Do you want me to leave?'

'Oh that's right, get your supper and then piss off again, lovely. Don't mind me, I'm just the local restaurant open all bloody hours. Just text a couple of messages and I'll be right at your service. Oh and don't even mention the fact that you couldn't be arsed to help with the move.'

David stood up slowly. 'Austin, I can't.'

'Can't what? Apologise? Give me some respect? Be on bloody time for a change?'

David put up his hands as if Austin had a gun. 'Look, I don't know what this is about, but I'm really tired, can we talk about this tomorrow?'

'And I'm not? You woke me up remember?'

'I'm sorry.'

'And I suppose that makes it all OK again. Why don't you go ahead, use my shower, make yourself comfortable in my bed. In fact just pretend this is a hotel why don't you?'

'Tell me about the ring,' David said quietly.

'This has got nothing to do with the damn ring.' Austin opened his palm revealing the jewellery box and then slung it across the room. 'It's not about the ring, it's about you and me.'

'Is it?'

'Yes!'

Austin stared at the jewellery box lying on its side on the floor, it had opened but the ring was still embedded in its pure white cushion. Had Matt really been on his way to propose to him that day? Austin covered his face with his hands; he couldn't stop the tears, or the sobs. He felt David's arms around him, gentle but firm, holding him, shushing him.

'It's not fair, why is my life such a mess?'

'Shh.'

The sobs began to subside, and Austin spoke into David's damp shoulder, 'I met John today. It was him that gave me the ring.'

'Who?' David's confusion was clear in his voice.

'Matt's dad. The police gave it to them, it's been sitting in some warehouse with other evidence from the crash and some company finally traced it back to the jewellery shop and then-' Austin hiccuped. 'It was Matt's.'

David's arms fell away and he stood back. 'And?'

'I think he was coming to propose to me that day.'

'The day of the crash.' David looked haggard, maybe he at last understood how Austin felt.

'Yes, it all makes sense, why he was on the train that day, where he was going.'

David blew air out of his mouth and then pushed a hand through his hair. 'Unbelievable.'

'But it's not, don't you see?'

'It's you who doesn't see.' David's face changed, his eyes began to flash dangerously. Austin stepped back.

'None of you seem to get it. Matt is dead. They're all dead. It's done, we can't turn back the clock and change what happened.'

Austin crossed his arms and hugged himself.

'There's no going back. What's done is done. We can't change things now. We just have to get on with the living.'

David grabbed Austin by the shoulders. 'I'm alive.' He shook Austin. 'This is your life now. I can't compete with a dead man.'

'I know,' Austin whispered.

David let go and started pacing across the room in the gangway between the boxes which Austin hadn't yet unpacked.

'Going back doesn't do anyone any favours. We have to move forwards, make sure nothing like this happens again.' He thumped the wall hard then he turned to face Austin again. 'See, you've proved my point, raking up the past just causes more pain, more trouble.'

Austin was uneasy, he had the distinct impression David was no longer talking about Matt or the ring or even their own relationship. He nodded briefly, hoping to placate him.

'Leave the past alone. John should never have given it to you.'

'But-' Austin felt suddenly empty.

'No buts. I'm right and you know it. It was an accident. I'm not going to open a whole heap of pain and regrets for anyone. Do you hear me?' David was shouting.

Austin flinched.

Monday
(1 day to go)

61

Adam – Wiped clean

On Monday morning Adam was sitting in meeting room five. He checked the clock. Two minutes to nine. He was the only one there and he was beginning to worry that he must have come to the wrong room. Perhaps he should head back to HR to check. But just as he started to turn his chair away from the table the door opened and there stood the HR manager, Sonia Greene, in a grey suit. She closed the door behind her and sat down.

'Thank you for being on time. I do appreciate punctuality.' She didn't have anything in her hands which she placed palms down onto the table. 'Right then.' She beamed at him.

'Where are the others?' Adam said.

'Not required.'

'But what about Dave?'

'Not required.'

'The IT guy?' Adam was beginning to feel incredibly uncomfortable.

'So let me explain. Several people worked very hard on Friday and over the weekend to ensure that your claim was thoroughly investigated. Dave Calder delivered that report to me this morning at eight o'clock. I've also spoken to Neil Rawlings, the IT director, and Nancy Fields, our senior systems analyst. They have both had input into the report and been involved in the investigation. As you can imagine, something of this type can't be left sitting and prompt action was the right thing to do.'

Adam felt cold as if they hadn't bothered to heat this meeting room.

'I'm pleased to say that no further action is required, the report is very clear and we can all relax knowing that a professional investigation took place. All that remains for me to say is that your ability with these queries is quite remarkable and I understand Neil Rawlings is very interested in you setting up some monthly reports for future analysis. Now that we have such a system, obviously it can play an important part in providing real-time data and can detect maintenance or repair issues ahead of time, making Transport Rail an even more efficient and effective company. You can play your part in that Adam, by setting up those new reports.'

Sonia Greene clasped her hands together and smiled at him. 'So I think that wraps it up.'

'No, wait. I don't understand.'

Sonia's face didn't change but her eyes grew cold. 'Which part?'

'I mean, the data was valid, I checked, it was real data and it hadn't been tampered with. There's clear evidence of equipment failure.'

'Ah. Perhaps I haven't made myself clear. You see Adam. We've had the head of IT examine this, and unfortunately, the test data is not validated, not by us nor by Thyredata Enterprises. Obviously looking forwards, then we have data for further analysis but I'm afraid historically this isn't possible. Actually to be fair, that isn't quite true. We do have six months worth of valid data since the system went live.'

'But the historical data-'

Sonia put up a hand like a stop sign.

'Adam, how long have you been with us?'

Adam was thrown, why was she asking that? 'Err,' he tried to think back to when he started. Five, six weeks ago maybe?

'A month or two,' he finally said.

'Five weeks to be precise.' She gave him a cool smile. 'Neil Rawlings has been with the company for thirteen years and was deeply involved in the project to install our new system. The thing is Adam, I wouldn't normally take time out of my busy schedule to sit here with one of our apprentices over a small data error. However, when you presented your claim on Friday, I took it seriously, you had attempted to provide evidence to the best of your ability and I respected that. To even insinuate that Transport Rail might, in any way, be culpable regarding the Clapham rail disaster is a matter I wasn't prepared to ignore. However, experience and qualified information has since proved to me that you made a mistake. If you'd like a copy of the report, just let me know.'

Sonia Greene stood up. 'If you'll excuse me, I think we both should be getting back to work.'

'But, you can't-' Adam paused, trying to find the words.

Sonia Greene raised an eyebrow.

'You can't pretend it's all right. That data is valid, I even spoke to someone at Thryredata and they said it was proper data too. You can't just wipe it out like it didn't exist.' He was panting now.

At that moment the meeting room door opened and the security guard stood there.

'Everything all right, Ms Greene?' His eyes shifted to Adam and back to Sonia.

'Yes, I think so Brian. We're almost done.'

Brian nodded curtly. 'I'll be just outside.'

The door shut.

Sonia Greene sat down again. Her eyes softened and a small smile crossed her lips.

'Why did you apply for an apprenticeship here at Transport Rail Adam?'

'Uh?'

She waited for a response, one eyebrow cocked, her hands neatly folded on the table.

'I, er, it seemed a good place to work.'

'No other motives?' The softness left her eyes and they glinted in the harsh light. 'Nothing related to your disability perhaps? A means to an end. A place to lay blame for your unfortunate circumstances perhaps?'

Adam shook his head as the room closed in around him, cornered and frightened. She was leaning in, her breath hot.

'I do hope there isn't a conflict of interest, Adam, between your work and your personal circumstances. Such a thing might create difficulties and assumptions of evidence where there is none.'

'But I-' Adam swallowed, his mouth had gone dry and the small amount of saliva stuck to the back of his throat.

'I think enough time has been wasted on this matter, don't you?' She stood up and without a backward glance she marched out of the room, the door closing solidly behind her with a thud. It was the sound of all hope being stamped out.

'Oh dear, don't look so glum, can't be all bad.' Melanie smiled. 'It's Kevin's birthday and he's bought doughnuts, shall I get you one? That'll cheer you up.' She bobbed up and trotted across the office.

Adam slunk into position at his desk and turned on the computer. He was numb.

'Here you go, they only had plain or jam left so I got you a scrummy jammy one.'

She'd brought it on a small saucer and placed it on his desk.

Adam looked at the sugary crystals and the dark purple spot on the side marked by the hidden jam. It made him think of the purplish rings under Sonia Greene's eyes. He thought about tea and scones at Ibrahim Muhammad Sharif's house and the blackcurrant jam. It made him want to retch.

'Shall I swap it for a plain one?' Melanie's face was crestfallen.

'No, thanks. It's fine. I'll eat it later.'

She nodded and returned to her desk.

Adam stared at the computer screen which awaited his login, he went through the motions and only when the system had loaded did his brain begin to wake up. He pulled his wheelchair closer into the desk. Hold on, Vijay had a copy of the reports. Adam went to pull his phone out of his pocket. Shit. He didn't have it. How many times was he going to forget that the police had taken his phone. With a groan Adam remembered they had Vijay's too and all his computer equipment. Slowly Adam's despair gained another few kilos. So wrapped up in his mission for Ibrahim Muhammad Sharif, he had naively assumed Transport Rail would support his findings, and he had no back-up plan. No insurance policy, as Vijay would call it.

Adam struck his fist on the desk.

Still, he could re-create those reports. If only he could get those reports to an outsider, someone who understood such things, someone who had links to the media. Hope bloomed and Adam began typing fast, pulling up the system and scanning through his saved queries. There they were, he hit the run button and waited. He glanced across the room at the closed door of Dave's office. After a few seconds an error appeared on the screen.

'What?'

Adam chose one of the others, the one that did the cross-referencing on timestamps. He drummed his fingers on the desk waiting for the results. Another error. It felt like someone had turned the heating up. Adam pulled up the third report, this time sending up a small prayer to Allah. A result. Adam scanned through, only five lines of data and all of them from the last month. This couldn't be right.

So that was it, either the system wasn't working or someone had deliberately fucked it up. But on Friday when he'd left, Dave had at least understood the reports that Adam had showed him and seemed to agree with his findings. What had happened over the weekend while he'd been played as Ibrahim's fool delivering piss? What had Dave done?

Adam went over to his manager's closed office door. Looking through the long thin window, he could see Dave sitting behind the desk talking into the phone with a frown on his face. He noticed Adam peering in and put one finger in the air nodding animatedly.

Adam turned to go back to his desk but he was only half-way there when he heard the door open.

'Adam, come on in.' Dave stood in a white shirt rolled-up at the sleeves with bags under his eyes.

Once inside, Dave closed the door and returned to the chair behind his desk.

'I assume you met with Sonia Greene this morning?'

Adam nodded.

'Well, it's good to have got it all sorted.' He puffed some air out, not looking at Adam. He fiddled with a piece of paper and then said, 'We'll need to schedule some time together to set up some queries to run on a monthly basis.'

Dave only glanced at Adam. 'Use your clever knowledge for these patterns of failure, be a great way to prevent any possible future issues, don't you think?'

Adam scowled. 'What's happened to the test system?'

'What?' Dave's surprise seemed false. 'It was working fine yesterday when I left.'

'You were working on Sunday?'

Dave nodded. 'We all took your...er...findings seriously.' He turned to his computer and tapped a few keys. 'It looks OK to me.'

'But none of my reports work.'

'Ah.' Dave kept his focus on the screen. 'What date range were you using?'

'The same as before.'

Dave nodded but still he wouldn't look at Adam. 'That figures, the test system was refreshed at the weekend.'

Adam's heart was thumping loudly. 'What do you mean, refreshed?'

'It's what happens with big systems like this, we refresh the test database every so often. Overwrite it from the live system.' Dave glanced at Adam and then quickly away again. 'Neil Rawlings signed off on it.'

'But you requested it?'

'Look, we should have updated it ages ago, probably ought to schedule it every two months. In fact I'll remind Neil about that.'

Adam's heart was hammering and he spoke loudly so he could hear himself above the thumping.

'You were covering up.'

Dave stood up suddenly, his face pink. 'It's not like that. Haven't you read the report Sonia Greene gave you?'

Adam said nothing.

'Well you should. It explains all the findings, it's an official document. It addresses everything you raised. It's finished Adam.'

'You lied. You knew those reports were valid.' Adam spoke

more quietly, his hands clenched tightly on the wheels.

Dave thrust a hand through his hair and marched to the window, then rounded on Adam.

'Listen, even if your reports were correct, and I'm not saying they were, but even if they were. What good would it have done? People died in the Clapham rail disaster, we can't bring them back. And their families, the people that loved them.' Dave appeared to be struggling to speak. 'Their partners, some of them are still only just getting over their loss. Do you really think it would be a good idea to open up all that pain again? We need to look forwards.'

Dave swung away from Adam and stared at the building across the street. 'We need to look to the future, make sure we've got a system that works, that can predict possible failures, possible faults.'

Adam stared down at his useless legs. When he looked up again Dave had slumped against the window ledge and had his hands thrust into his trouser pockets.

'The past matters,' Adam said.

'I realise that.' Dave let out a sigh. He seemed to be studying Adam.

After a pause Dave said, 'You're young, ambitious. You don't let your disability hold you back and I admire you for that. I admire your passion and your courage to try and do the right thing. Your work here has earned my respect. But you have to let this go. Think of your future.'

62

Ralph – Shut out

Ralph sat up, startled. Shelly was in the room and her mouth was moving quickly but no sound was coming out. She moved closer, her cheeks aflame. Gradually, as if turning on a radio and moving the dial slowly, her voice could be heard, softly at first and then louder and louder until Ralph had to put his hands over his ears.

'You even refused your parents' help,' she accused him. 'I can't take it any more Ralph. You won't talk to anyone, it's like you've fallen into a black hole.'

Ralph could still hear her through his hands so he dropped them back onto the quilt instead and watched her features bristling.

'Here.' She slung a black holdall onto the bed. 'I've packed you some things.' Her lips quivered.

'What things?' Ralph stared at the bag uncomprehendingly.

'Clothes, a toothbrush.' She waved her hand vaguely around the bedroom.

'But what for?'

She stared at him, amazement in her eyes, then they darkened. 'Because you're not here Ralph. You're not here with me or the boys. I don't know where you've gone, I can't help you. You won't talk, you won't let us in.' She pushed the bag towards him.

'You want me to leave?'

'Yes.' She dropped her head, her chest heaving in and out. 'You need to go. It's the only way I can think of to make you realise this is serious. Ralph, you need professional help.'

'But Shelly...' Ralph stopped, he was lost for words, lost because this room was his sanctuary, he couldn't leave. He stared up, looking for the thin line, but couldn't see it. He searched the ceiling but then his face swung sideways as Shelly slapped him.

'Stop staring into space. You need help, but you refuse it all. I can't support you if you won't even *try* to get help.' She glared at him. Ralph felt the sting on his cheek and his mind shot back to the playing fields and the muddy ball hurtling towards him. Was that when this had all started, all this pain, this suffering? But no, it wasn't then, it was before. It was the cool blue eyes imploring him from the track.

Ralph stood in the hallway, dressed and with the holdall at his feet. Shelly was propped against the kitchen doorway, a damp tissue clutched in her hand. There was steam rising behind her and pungent smells of something in the oven. Liam and Cameron were hovering at the bottom of the stairs, their eyes wide, waiting, watching. Ralph ought to say something, but what? They all looked expectantly at him but he had nothing to give them, only further pain and suffering. He turned away and opened the front door.

'Where's he going to go?' Liam's voice behind him as he picked up his bag.

'To his parents, if he has any sense,' Shelly responded.

'I know,' piped up Cameron, 'He'll stay at Troy's.' This statement was immediately followed by a scuffling sound.

'Ow, that hurt!'

Ralph pulled the door closed behind him.

63

Adam - Forgiveness

Adam was in the kitchen chopping onions. The knife was sharp, slicing through the purple skin easily. Adam pulled away the dry flaky layers to the moist flesh beneath. He sliced it evenly and then twisted the vegetable ninety degrees to slice again in the other direction. He scraped the onion to the edge of the board.

'I still don't see why your hands are such a mess,' his mother said, pouring rice into the pan.

'My hands are fine, I can still chop things.'

'You look tired.'

She didn't know the half of it, Adam was exhausted. He felt numb, his emotions all spent, ready to collapse into bed. He was only helping out so that dinner would be ready sooner and then he could go to his room and sleep without rousing more questions from his family. He just wanted to be left alone.

'How was your day?'

'Mum. You're right, I'm tired, can we just...'

'Oh love, you look terrible. Why don't I chop the pepper?'

'It's fine.' He took the green vegetable and sliced and diced it, the simple activity soothing and satisfying.

'What did you eat at Vijay's?'

'What?'

'On Saturday night?'

She was still angry about that, he could tell, the night he hadn't come home, hadn't even called. It seemed like a lifetime ago that he had turned up at Vijay's so late but Adam didn't want to think about that. He didn't want to think about anything. Especially not the fact that Aisha had disappeared off the face of the earth.

'Well?'

'I can't remember. What else shall I chop?'

She passed him another pepper from the fridge and some ginger root.

'I'm only interested that's all. Nasreen was very disappointed not to see you on Saturday.'

Sully walked in. 'Hey cook's boy.'

'Shut it.'

'What time will it be ready?'

'Soon. Get out of the way.' His mother shooed Sully away from the cooker.

Adam was thinking about Auntie Nasreen, about all those cousins and relations that spread wide and far.

Adam glanced at his brother and then his mum.

'Mum?' Adam said.

'Yes love?'

Adam pressed the vegetable knife against the board, he needed to be certain. 'Do you know someone called Ibrahim Muhammad Sharif?'

'Everyone knows that name by now,' Sully scoffed.

'What?' Adam's insides did a complete flip.

'The guy with a zillion dodgy mobile phones in his house? You've got to wonder about these people. The sooner they extradite him the better if you ask me.'

'What are you talking about?'

'The news, you idiot.' Sully pointed at the newspaper lying on the kitchen table next to Adam's chopping board.

Adam grabbed the paper, the article was on page four with a large photograph of Ibrahim Muhammad Sharif. Apparently the police had raided a house in Kensington and sources revealed they'd recovered more than twenty mobile phones, two illegal immigrants and twenty-six thousand pounds in cash. Suspected of affiliations with ISIS in the Middle East and Europe, Ibrahim Muhammad Sharif has been detained for questioning.

'What's up? Friend of yours?' Sully laughed at his own joke. 'Stupid fundamentalists, they give us a bad name.'

Adam held the newspaper in front of his face, he didn't want his mother or his brother to see how he felt. He tried to keep on breathing, to calm his nerves.

The doorbell rang and Sully left the room. Adam folded the paper back on itself and held it up.

'Mum, have you ever met this guy?' He just wanted to be absolutely sure.

His mother turned and squinted at the paper. She shook her head. 'Don't think so. Should I?' She went to the kitchen doorway to see who Sully was talking to.

Adam chucked the paper back onto the table. So it must be true, there was no elite UMIA, only ISIS bastards. Adam had been blind. Blind and stupid. He was utterly useless. He thought about the note in Aisha's curly script, could she have been trying to save Adam from making a fool of himself? That question on the phone before he'd been invited to tea with Ibrahim Muhammad Sharif, it had felt like a test. Which class? Adam thought he'd passed the test by answering with the truth but maybe Aisha had been trying to protect him, maybe she'd wanted him to say computers, then he would never have been invited to the house in Kensington, would never have thought he had a bomb under his chair. The police wouldn't have raided Vijay's house and he wouldn't have felt such a fool. What if she had meant to meet him at Subway that day but Jamaal and Hakeem found out and used him for their own ends instead? Were they controlling her? Where had they taken her?

'It's for you.' Sully was back holding a large square cardboard box. He dumped it on the table causing bits of pepper to cascade onto the floor.

'Sully!' His mother bent to pick up the vegetable pieces.

Adam stared at the box.

'Have you been ordering things on Amazon again?' she asked. Adam shook his head.

'Open it then,' Sully said.

Adam put his hands on the box, he lifted it cautiously, it was very light. There was one of those document holders stuck to the side with a folded piece of paper in it. He pulled it out, besides the address and company details, it stated one Spalding NBA Silver at £29.99. There was also a message at the bottom, it read.

I think we'd all be a lot happier if you went back to playing.
Vijay.

What did it mean? He hadn't spoken to Vijay or Cara since the police raid. Adam had been too ashamed to contact him, didn't even want to begin to explain or worse, lie his way out of it. Of course he had left early, hurried out of the apartment before the others had even lifted their heads. But what did Vijay mean? Playing what?

Adam picked up the long sharp vegetable knife and slid it under the flap. The box opened and he looked inside. He put his hands in and brought out the basketball. He placed it on the empty chopping board. Failure descended on him like an avalanche. He picked up the chopping knife and drove it into the ball. This was for Ibrahim Muhammad Sharif. He pulled the knife out but the rubber sucked on it tight. He changed grip, yanked it out and stabbed it in again, for Dave Calder and the wiped database, again for Sonia Greene and her cold eyes. Again and again for all the failure and torment he had suffered. His strong arms quivered delivering impact after impact, shredding the ball as the anger rippled through him.

Suddenly Adam's chair was yanked away from the table and the knife plunged through thin air. He only just stopped himself in time, the point nicking his jeans and pricking his thigh. He threw the knife to the floor.

'Have you gone crazy?' it was Sully yelling.

In the corner, his mother had her face in her hands and was crying loudly.

'Get off.' Adam twisted the wheels and felt Sully's hands release. He left the kitchen and zoomed down the hallway towards the front door just as it was opening. It was his father home from work. He stood in the doorway looking surprised and then frowned as he stood his ground. Adam stopped with the foot-plate creasing his dad's trousers.

With a pale face his father said, 'You're grounded, remember?'

Adam saw how small his father really was, just an old man in a crumpled suit. He was no match for Adam in his wheelchair. Using his strong arms, Adam could easily bowl him down the ramp.

'Stand aside.' Adam's voice boomed around the hallway and out into the evening. He was a man not a child and that power beat firmly within him.

Adam's father opened his mouth slightly and then closed it again, he rubbed briefly at his ear and then stepped out of the way.

*

There were just two pairs of shoes on the rack when Adam arrived at the mosque. He was between prayer times. Probably they belonged to the Imam and the office clerk or maybe the cleaner. Ignoring his own trainers, he went into the wash room and methodically went through the act of Wudu, taking time to cleanse himself thoroughly. Afterwards, he entered the silent prayer room and pushed himself across the deep red carpet to the front. Instead of stopping in the middle, he went to one side; it seemed presumptuous to take up the prime spot. With no sound except his own breathing, Adam closed his eyes. The anger had been spent and the power that had filled him earlier in the kitchen had been blown out against the basketball and his father. In here, in this quiet space, there was nothing to rail against, no judgement or failure, no expectations or fear. Adam could simply be. The peacefulness of the room descended on him and the tears started to fall.

A while later Adam felt a little easier. The weight of despair had lifted slightly. He had prayed quietly, asking for forgiveness, asking for acceptance and the safe return of Aisha and her sister. As peace and calm filled his heart, Adam felt ready to leave. He turned the wheelchair to find the Imam sat cross-legged a little way behind him. The Imam smiled warmly and stood up immediately.

'Adam.'

Adam gave a brief nod of his head.

'Come, let me get you a drink and I might have some biscuits left from the ladies' study meeting this morning.' He gave Adam a guilty smile and led him out of the prayer room and down the corridor to his office. It seemed rude not to comply. The Imam busied himself going to and fro to the kitchen, boiling the kettle and eventually returning with two teas and a plate with some broken cookies.

'Ginger creams are my favourite. If anyone brings them in, I hide them in my drawer just for me. Terrible. Even us Imams aren't perfect.'

Adam took a biscuit and sipped at the tea.

'You know that it's the Muslim community that decides if I should be their Imam or not?'

Adam nodded.

'So basically I'm employed by the community for the community. I'm here to serve in whatever way I can. Sometimes it's by being a listening ear, sometimes giving advice on personal problems, sometimes guidance on how to interpret the holy texts. Mrs Khan uses me to decide which colour scarves to display in her shop. I'm quite concerned that the people of Battersea are going to come banging on my door complaining that they look awful in turquoise.'

Adam smiled, he appreciated the Imam's effort.

'Life throws up all sorts of challenges,' he went on. 'I guess I'm just lucky that my difficulties aren't too burdensome like whether Mrs Quayyum's baby should be called Hassan or Habib or whether the UMIA should continue to use our upstairs meeting room.'

Adam looked up sharply.

The Imam didn't react, he simply carried on. 'What should I believe? That the UMIA and ISIS are in cahoots? Or are they opposed to each other and each is trying to undermine and infiltrate the other? How can I be sure which are the spies and which are the real members? Do I put special security men on the doors or do I ban all meetings just in case? In fact shouldn't I let the rooms out to ISIS as they are very clear on scripture, aren't they implementing a new caliphate in the name of Islam? If they are right then it is my duty to help them.'

'Are you serious?' Adam was incredulous at the Imam with his neatly groomed beard and kind eyes.

He smiled. 'The point I'm making is that sometimes life doesn't offer clear choices, sometimes it's more complicated than that and it can be difficult to see which is the right path. We are just men, we make mistakes. Only Allah knows best. Mashallah.'

Adam had to agree, he'd made a whole heap of mistakes, he was a walking disaster except he couldn't even walk. However, Adam thought the Imam was trying to allude to something more.

'But what are you saying?' Adam said.

The Imam gazed at him and munched on another half biscuit.

'Tell me, what would you do in my shoes? Allow the room to be used by whichever Muslim group requests it? Ignoring whether they claim to be UMIA or ISIS? Or should I have a vetting process or even security of some kind?'

'You're asking me?'

'Why not?' The Imam's voice was soft.

'But I'm...'

'A brother like me. And also like me, I think you believe in the one true God. '

'Yes but-'

'And like me, you pray and read the Quran?'

'Yes.'

'And like me, you feel it in your heart what is right and what is wrong.'

The Imam changed his tone and began to recite, 'So have they not travelled through the earth and have hearts by which to reason and ears by which to hear? For indeed, it is not eyes that are blinded, but blinded are the hearts which are within the breasts.

'We pray so that Allah may purify our hearts.'

At this point, Adam wasn't so ready to agree and yet when he'd sat on the sofa in Ibrahim Muhammad Sharif's house, it had felt horribly wrong. He had known in his heart that something was dreadfully amiss. He'd been scared. But he hadn't listened to his heart, he had listened to his head, the part that wanted to do something truly amazing, to be a hero amongst his friends and to impress Aisha.

The Imam was still watching Adam. 'So tell me, what should I do about the meeting room?'

Adam looked at the Imam, the thought of ISIS using the upstairs room to plan attacks and encourage young people to wage Jihad in such a violent manner was out of the question. Was it them who were holding Aisha?

'Not ISIS,' Adam said firmly.

'And the UMIA?'

Adam considered this, he thought about how he had been introduced to Ibrahim Muhammad Sharif, about the recent police arrests and the media coverage. It made him uncomfortable, not in the same way as ISIS, this was more a distrust. A concern that the UMIA was unable to prevent the fundamentalists from acting from within their own organisation. That their message was unclear and some of the members were not who they seemed.

'No,' Adam said, 'I think it would be wiser not to let the UMIA in either.'

The Imam smiled broadly. 'Exactly my thoughts. Both groups are highly politicized and at least one of them has a proven track record of extreme violence. In the current political climate and with my own knowledge and understanding of the holy texts I will not be promoting either organisation.'

The Imam scooped up the last crumbs from the plate.

'So there we are. You are capable of making good decisions that even your Imam finds tricky. Pray to Allah to keep your heart sound and then trust your heart, Adam, and never forget we are all simply men and Allah is the only one true God and He knows best. Mashallah.'

*

The leisure centre loomed large with its doors opened wide. Adam slowed down, a little nervous now that he was here. After leaving the mosque he had felt a little easier but he didn't want to go straight home. Noticing what time it was this Monday evening, he'd come here to the sports hall where the basketball team would be having their weekly practice. It smelled the same as always, that mixture of old sweat with the faintest overtone of cleaning fluid. Adam took a breath and went inside.

They were in mid-game, Stumpy had the ball but was cornered and needed to pass. Sophie put up her hand.

'Hey look, it's Adam,' she shouted. The ball hit her in the chest and she let out an 'Oof'.

'Shit, sorry Sophie.' Stumpy twisted around to stare with the others at Adam.

They came over then, to greet him.

'Good to see you.'

'You're looking well.'

'We've missed you.'

'Are you here to play?'

Stumpy said nothing but he was eyeing Adam with a slight grin.

Mikael the coach joined them. 'Take it easy with those hands if you're joining in.' He gestured at the thin bandages Adam's mum had used to re-dress the friction burns.

'No, I just came to watch for a bit,' Adam said.

'Like hell, come on.' Stumpy threw the ball at Adam who caught it easily.

Adam pressed his fingers against the nobbled surface of the basketball, he tossed it upwards and caught it again. The faces all around him were watching, smiling, encouraging. Maybe he would play.

Forty-five minutes later, Mikael called a halt and gathered in the balls. Adam was hot, sweaty and suitably tired; a good feeling. For a while then he had been lost in the game, totally focused on bouncing, passing and shooting. Playing the game with the others as if he'd never been away. Sophie came to give him a high five and the others said their farewells.

'That was great, I haven't worked that hard in ages.' Stumpy was grinning rolling up beside Adam as they headed towards the doors. 'You're a bit rusty though.'

'And you're not as fast as I remember.'

'That's because I've not had any decent competition for months. I've gotten lazy.'

They stopped near the doors where Stumpy's legs were leaning against the wall.

Adam said, 'What about the national team? I thought that you...'

Stumpy shrugged. 'They wanted me to practise with the Titans. It's the other side of London, I've got work, my girlfriend. This is meant to be my downtime, not more stress.'

Adam couldn't believe what he was hearing, 'But what about the Olympics?'

Stumpy laughed, 'I may be better than you but get real, I'm not going to devote my life to it. It's meant to be fun remember? And it's a much better game when you're here.'

Adam reached for one of Stumpy's prosthetic legs, it was surprisingly heavy and he handed it to Stumpy.

'Thanks.' He took the leg and began to attach it to the special sock with its small metal post. There was a rusty coloured smear on one side. Adam saw his right hand had soaked through the bandage.'

'Yuck, you need to sort those hands out.'

'Sorry about that.'

'I'll see you next week then?' Stumpy said wiping the smear off with his sleeve. 'You have to keep coming so you can beat me. I need the extra fun. Keep me on my toes.' He laughed as he stood up on the one leg and reached for the remaining limb.

64

Austin – A friend in need

Austin wiped the smeary glass of the window so he could see the darkly lit streets as the bus chugged forwards. He was beginning to sober up a bit having stood in the cool evening waiting by the bus stop. Still, it had been a good night. The sales and marketing lot were so much fun. They'd just won a big contract and invited Austin to join them. After the weekend he'd had, Austin had been only too happy when Becky met him in the corridor with a beaming smile. But now that he was alone on his way home, the light shower dampened his mood turning his thoughts to the row with David last night. It had been so horrible and then David had left. There had been a few texts today but David hadn't joined them at the pub, had made excuses and Austin wondered if maybe they were falling apart.

The bus slowed and stopped by a bench. Austin stared at the lighted windows of the gym he used. Only a couple more stops and he would be home. Then Austin narrowed his eyes, there was a man lying on the bench who had obviously had too much to drink. But it was the bag that the man's head rested on that had caught Austin's attention. It was a black holdall with a rounded end, and on that end was the face of a tiger. Ralph's bag. The bus started moving again and Austin pressed his face to the glass. It had to be Ralph's bag, the tiger was a big sticker his son had stuck on it ages ago. Austin remembered Ralph trying to pick it off when it had first appeared, they had laughed about it. But what was Ralph's bag doing under some tramp's head? Austin swivelled in his seat, looking backwards, trying to keep it in sight as long as possible. The man's head lifted slightly and he put an arm up and over his eyes.

No way.

The bus turned the corner and Austin looked forwards again. He replayed the movement in his mind, could it have been?

Really? He jumped out of his seat.

'Stop,' he shouted at the driver, hanging onto the rail by the closed door.

There was no immediate response from the driver, but after a pause a bored voice replied. 'You'll have to wait till the next stop.'

Austin gripped the rail tighter, what if it hadn't been Ralph? What if it was some violent man who had stolen Ralph's bag? He considered sitting down again, but then he couldn't forget Ralph's kindness when Matt had died. He was his gym buddy after all, and there was no way he should be lying on a bench at one in the morning. Austin made up his mind, he would go back and check.

The bus lurched to a stop and the door hissed open. Austin leapt out. He dug his hands deep into his pockets, hunched up his shoulders and walked quickly back along the road.

As Austin approached, he became more uncertain. The man had one arm across his head making it difficult to even guess his hair colour. At least the light from the gym splashing onto the pavement helped. Austin looked about, two guys on the opposite side of the road were chatting and walking, paying him no attention.

'Ralph?' Austin tried gently, standing a little way back from the bench by the lighted window. There was no response. He moved a step closer, swallowed and spoke a little louder.

'Ralph?' He could smell the man now, alcoholic fumes wafting off him. He was certainly the right kind of size and shape. The man murmured something indecipherable and the hand on his head fell down to his side. Austin cautiously went to the foot end of the bench so he could get a glimpse of the man's face. At that moment the man's head moved and his eyes locked onto Austin.

'Ralph!' Austin was so surprised he shouted the name. Ralph sat up unsteadily staring at Austin. His eyes wandered and then resettled on Austin's face.

'Hey.' Ralph raised his arm halfway and then let it drop.

'What are you doing?' Austin was alarmed. This wasn't right, not right at all, Austin had almost convinced himself that this must be some nasty drunken thief. Yet it was Ralph. A family man with kids, a wife, a paramedic, what on earth was he doing here, like this?

'Are you coming to the gym?' Ralph asked.

'The gym?' Austin looked at the firmly locked doors and the empty reception area beyond. 'It's the middle of the night.'

'Oh yeah,' Ralph nodded and then made to lie down again.

'Wait. Don't, I mean, what are you doing, why aren't you at home?' Austin was flustered, he didn't like it when things seemed so awry.

'I'm just going to have a little sleep.' Ralph lay down.

'No.' Austin grabbed his hand and pulled him into a sitting position again. 'You can't sleep here, look, come with me, it's not too far. You can have the sofa.' Ralph stared and said nothing. Austin thought for a moment maybe he had offered more than he could manage. Ralph was a big man, what if he was so drunk, he couldn't walk properly? He knew he wouldn't be strong enough to bear Ralph's weight. Still he had to at least try; it was the right thing to do.

'Come on.' Austin pulled on his sleeve. 'Stand up.' To his surprise, Ralph did. It was like leading a child, only one grown to giant size. 'Your bag.' Austin pointed and Ralph picked it up. After a few steps Austin let go of Ralph's sleeve and they walked together in silence. Occasionally Ralph would weave a bit, or stumble, but to Austin's relief, he didn't fall and only needed a guiding hand now and then.

Tuesday
(Clapham Junction Memorial Day)

65

Halima - Catching the right connections

Despite having no work to go to, Halima automatically awoke early. She lay in bed with the morning light filtering in. The sparrows had chosen the holly bush out the front to have their morning argument. It matched the thoughts clamouring in her head. Mum. Work. Veronica. Her baby. Housing. Halima tried to grab onto the one thing that made her glad, her friend Veronica. But the thought was slippery and she had to work hard to keep Veronica's smile and bright clothes at the forefront of her mind. They had chatted yesterday evening for over an hour on the phone. Halima had shared about her mother being moved to Barnet hospital where there was more specialist care. But Halima didn't want to think about Mum. She would be even further away. Her mother's illness was worsening and the distance between them growing. Their relationship was being stretched thinner and longer; eventually it would have to snap.

Halima sat up suddenly. She couldn't think like that. She rose and went through her normal routine, taking care to shut the bathroom door and wash quietly even though her mother wasn't asleep or even in the house. But habits were ingrained and Halima found a certain comfort in keeping some things the same.

Downstairs the early light was streaming in the kitchen window. She made just the one mug of tea and filled a bowl with cornflakes. If only her mother hadn't had a stroke, if only Cheryl Phipps, her boss, hadn't lied. There were so many what-ifs that Halima became overwhelmed, unable to even drink her tea because her whole life could have been different with what-ifs.

Smokey suddenly leapt onto the windowsill and meowed at her through the glass. He broke the spell; she felt a smile cross her face. There were some good changes too. She opened the back door to let him in. He rubbed against her legs as she poured a saucer of milk and placed it on the floor, then stroked his back while he lapped it up. Another new part of her routine was the radio, the sound connecting her with the wider world and other people. She turned it on and let the morning news fill up the silent kitchen. She poured the milk liberally on her cereal and took a mouthful looking out into the garden. Halima stopped chewing, down amongst the smattering of green shoots and buds that peppered the turned soil she noticed a bright spot of colour. Another new change? A good change? She hurriedly slipped on her shoes and went to investigate.

Kneeling on the ground, Halima marvelled at the perfect petals opening for the sun's early rays. The striking yellow colour reminded her of the lemon scarf and Halima had a sudden sense of her own vitality. Where there had only been weeds before, she had worked hard and now look at the miracle that had come. The lemon scarf too had been something that she, Halima, had bought and several people had complimented her on it since. Where had all this colour started? She thought about her friend Veronica and that first day when she'd arrived in her poppy-red skirt. How good it was to spend time with her doing new things. Today, on this sunny morning, perhaps Halima could actually create something good in her life. Something beautiful although achingly fragile.

Halima stared up at the pale blue of early morning sky thinking about the day ahead. It was Tuesday, the memorial day. She'd hoped to go with Veronica but she was still in Scotland and probably wouldn't want to come anyway, considering it marked the downfall of her marriage to Ian. But then, if the crash hadn't happened, and Ian hadn't met that woman, then Veronica wouldn't have been lonely and she wouldn't have taken the volunteer job and she would never have stood in her red skirt on Halima's doorstep. For the first time, Halima considered how what might first appear to be a terrible event might have unforeseen wonderful consequences.

Halima looked again at the open yellow flower, born from the earth and Halima's hard work. She smiled. Yes, she would go to the memorial today, and instead of doubt and misgivings, she thought it would be a wonderful way to give thanks for the good changes in her life. And what about that young man on the tube in his wheelchair, could she even dare to hope? The single flower beamed back at her. Halima leant in close, it even smelt beautiful. Today was going to be a good day.

<h2 style="text-align:center">66</h2>

Adam – Revenge or gratitude

Adam lay on his side, staring at the wall. It was dawn and time for prayers and despite not having his phone alarm to remind him, he'd woken anyway. It had become a habit, awaking early to pray. In a few moments he would go into the bathroom and wash, but for now he lay still. The window was open a fraction and he could hear the neighbour banging a tin for their cat to come in. The sound reminded him of the clang of the sports bottle hitting the metal shutter. Adam squeezed his eyes tight together. He didn't want to remember, didn't want to be reliving those scenes of failure. Would he ever see Aisha again?

The banging stopped and there was chirping as the sparrows that lived in the neighbour's bush were disturbed. Adam tried to ignore the images passing behind his eyelids, reliving the torture of the last three days, until he was forced to open them again. He turned over and stared at the light fitting hanging in the centre of the ceiling. There was nowhere for him to go, nowhere for his mind to run to and certainly not his body. He thought about the basketball lying in shreds on the kitchen table. His anger was spent. There was no point drowning in self-pity, he should get up and pray. Hang on to the one good thing in his life. Mashallah.

Feeling a little better after his prayers, Adam wheeled himself into the kitchen and put some bread in the toaster. He was hungry and took an apple from the bowl. The vegetable knife was in the block. Adam pulled it out, the sound of metal sliding on wood. He wondered if the attack on the basketball had blunted it. Adam took out the sharpener and glided the knife up and down the rough surface. The sound of the metal scraping was strangely satisfying. He thought about the day ahead at Transport Rail. Creating reports for Neil Rawlings, having dull conversations with Melanie about her Jack Russell, pretending that everything was fine. Pretending that Aisha was home safe and sound, and that he'd never been a pathetic pawn in Ibrahim Muhammad Sharif's grand scheme. Pretending that the train crash had never happened, that he'd never found evidence of its cause and that Dave had never wiped the database. Bastard. Adam jabbed forwards with the knife.

That was the root of all his problems. If there'd been no crash, there'd be no wheelchair. In fact he'd have been picked up for a professional football club. His whole life would have been different.

Adam's heart was beating hard as his thoughts hardened. He gritted his teeth, imagining Dave leaning back in the kitchen chair, one of those large charming smiles on his face, and then Adam was slashing at his soft belly. Ripping with the vegetable knife feeling the suck and tension as the knife ripped into his intestines, like the suck and pull when he had stabbed the basketball.

Suddenly there was a noise in the hallway and Adam froze. He dropped the knife into the side pocket of his chair and tried not to look guilty as his father walked in.

'Adam?'

Adam spun his chair around and got on with buttering his toast.

'So today's the big day,' his dad said as he took the kettle and started to fill it at the sink.

'What?' Adam watched his father set the kettle on its base. His checked pyjamas had been done up wrong, a button missed making the fabric poke out at his chest.

'It's the memorial day.' His father smiled reaching out and touching Adam on his shoulder. 'We said we'd all go together.'

'I have to go to work,' Adam stumbled over the words but

already something was draining out of him.

'You said you had the day off.' He squeezed Adam's shoulder. 'I know things have been difficult lately. It was your mother that reminded me about the anniversary of the crash coming up. It's not surprising that you've been a little crazy. But I thank God that I still have a son.' His father smiled and he let go of Adam's shoulder and went to rub that bit on his ear.

There was a bang from upstairs and Sully's voice singing a pop tune.

'You still have Sully,' Adam said staring past his father.

'Ah, but Sully doesn't have our wonky ear.' He twisted Adam's ear playfully. 'Nor our stubbornness huh? You proved that to me last night. I thought maybe you wouldn't come home again but I'm glad you did.' Then he crossed the kitchen to get some mugs. 'I'm going to make your mum a cup of tea, do you want one?'

Adam stared at his toast. His eyes heavy and tired.

Memorial day. He'd forgotten.

Dave had shown him the form he needed to fill in to request a day's leave. Adam had watched him sign it and then he'd taken it by hand to HR and given it to Stephanie. It felt like aeons ago but it had only been two weeks. Adam sagged in his chair. They wouldn't be expecting him in today. If he turned up, they'd think something was wrong. Adam imagined rolling into Dave's office, this time Dave's smile disappeared immediately and he swung his legs off the desk.

'What's up?'

Adam drove at him with the knife but Dave was on his feet in an instant and grappling Adam's arm with the lethal weapon.

'Get security,' Dave yelled as he forced Adam's hand against the door frame and the knife dropped onto the grey carpet.

Obviously Adam would never just glide into Dave's office and stab him to death. He didn't have it in him to murder someone, not in real life. Did he? What on earth was he thinking? The Imam had told him to follow his heart, but his heart was filled with hatred and revenge.

'I'll get Mum to do us some scrambled eggs before we go.' His father turned holding two mugs of tea. 'I've left yours on the

362

table.'

Adam watched his father walk back down the hallway, the smell of stale sweat followed him and a thread trailed from the frayed edge of his left pyjama leg. His steps steady up the stairs and then a thump as his father kicked the bathroom door.

'Hurry up Sully.'

Adam sighed, maybe going to the memorial was a good idea, at least he wouldn't have to go to work. There was some truth in what Dave had said yesterday, that they couldn't change the past. Maybe Adam needed to be grateful for his family, for the life he had now, even in a wheelchair. Adam clasped his hands together. Mashallah.

67

Ralph – Admitting to weakness

Ralph put the empty mug back on the table.

'Thanks, I needed that. And I'm really sorry, about the mess.'

'Are you sure you don't want a banana or something?' Austin asked picking up the mug and taking it to the sink.

'No really, you've been too kind already.'

'Well you don't have to go right away, I'm not expecting anyone and I don't have to go out until' -Austin checked his watch- 'well, around ten although I'm not sure I'll bother.'

Ralph stood up and picked up his black bag. He looked around for his shoes and saw them neatly by the door.

'I'm sorry you had to see me like this, I don't normally...' Ralph paused, not sure quite how to finish. No, he didn't normally get kicked out by his wife. Didn't normally drink to excess. Didn't normally sleep rough or throw up on other people's sofas. Didn't normally walk out on his family. So much that wasn't normal. And this hangover. Ralph felt the nausea beat inside his head.

'Are you OK, seriously, you can stay if you want to.'

'No, no.' Ralph fastened his trainers and prepared himself to open the door. He just had to figure out where he was going to go.

'What day is it?' Ralph asked, his hand on the door.

'Tuesday the twenty-third.'

'Tuesday.' Ralph nodded to himself, thinking about the boys in school and Shelly at work. 'Have I stopped you going to work today?' Ralph suddenly felt guilty.

'No, no, it's fine. I've got the day off, it's...' Austin didn't finish the sentence.

'Tuesday the twenty-third?'

Austin nodded briefly.

'The day of the memorial.' Ralph's insides did a slow turn. 'Excuse me.' He dashed past Austin and into the bathroom where he heaved over the toilet bowl. No wonder he'd gotten so terribly drunk last night.

'If you need to stay and sleep it off...' Austin stood holding a roll of kitchen towel. He ripped several sheets off and passed them to Ralph.

'Thanks, I'll be fine.'

'You don't look it.'

Ralph wiped his face and blew his nose. He did feel decidedly wobbly. He sat down again on the sofa. Just a few more minutes and he would be on his way. Leave poor Austin alone, he'd done enough.

Suddenly a musical tune started up and Austin disappeared into the bedroom, it sounded like he was talking on the phone. While he was gone, Ralph practised standing again and went over to the window, looking down along the street. It was a fine day, cloudy but bright. A good day for the memorial. This time his stomach only growled at him. Three years ago today. Ralph shook his head, what was he going to do?

'That was my-' Austin paused slightly, '-my boyfriend. He's going to come with me, so maybe I will go after all.'

'Oh?'

'To the memorial at Clapham Junction, I was in two minds.'

'You're going?'

Austin shrugged. 'Well, maybe I should.'

Ralph stared at Austin's expression. It was part sad, part

hopeful. He wished he hadn't drunk so much, it was difficult to make his brain work properly.

'Because of Matt.' Finally Ralph's brain clicked into place. 'Sorry, sorry, I wasn't thinking.'

'It's OK, I wasn't going to go, thought it might be easier not to, but well, that was David, he's going to come with me. He just got off the tube.'

'Right. I'd better go.'

'OK.'

'Thanks again Austin.' Ralph held out his hand and they shook.

The bright day made Ralph squint as he walked down the street. This road seemed familiar and he was pretty sure the gym wasn't far. At least they would have water there and a shower and he might even do a few weights. Move his body to give his mind a chance to work things out.

'Ralph.'

Ralph looked across the road towards the shout. 'Dave?'

Dave crossed over and frowned. 'What are you doing here? Shelly's been on the phone going ape trying to find out where you are.'

Ralph sighed. 'Well here I am.'

'You look like shit and you smell.'

'Thanks.'

'Jesus brother, what's going on?' Dave slung an arm around Ralph's shoulders and gave him a sideways hug.

'I messed up.' Ralph stared down at the pavement.

'What? The golden boy Ralph Calder isn't perfect?'

'Why do you always call me that, I was never the golden boy.' Ralph shrugged off his brother's arm.

'Oh really? The perfect son, winning all the medals, married with two point four kids. Too bloody perfect by far.'

'You have no idea.' Ralph rubbed at his eyebrow.

'So tell me? What could you possibly get so wrong?' Dave's voice jeered and it made Ralph clench his fist.

'You really want to know?' Ralph glared.

'Yes.' Dave opened his palms stepping slightly back. 'Try me.'

'Somebody died because of me,' Ralph struck a finger into his chest, then again, harder, 'and then because of that his mother committed suicide. That's two fucking people dead because of me. You think I'm perfect? Try living with that shit.'

Dave was shaking his head, then he said quietly, 'And how many people have you saved Ralph?'

'Oh shut up.' Ralph shoved past his brother and headed on, he didn't want to be sharing this crap with him.

'No, seriously.'

Ralph felt his arm grabbed and he stopped.

'How many people have you saved?'

Ralph spun around. 'That's not the point.'

'Yes it is, you twat. Just because you made a mistake doesn't turn you into a failure, it makes you human like the rest of us. Thank bloody Christ that you're not so perfect after all, now you know what it feels like to be me.'

Ralph stared at his brother turning over what he'd said in his mind.

Dave shoved his hands in his jeans pockets. 'You're not the only one that's guilty about things they have or haven't done.'

Ralph put down his bag and rubbed at his face. He felt lost. 'But what am I meant to do about it?'

'Call Shelly for starters, she's worried sick, thought you'd stayed the night with Mum and Dad or me. Now she's panicking.'

Ralph nodded, of course he was right, but what then? He looked up at the sky, the clouds were clearing and more blue was becoming visible. Down the street a couple of people were stood at the bus stop staring back at him. What was he even doing here? Then he turned back to his brother.

'What are *you* doing here? Shouldn't you be at work?' Ralph said.

Dave looked tired out, he glanced towards where Ralph had come from. 'I'm going to the Clapham Junction memorial, with a friend.'

Ralph looked behind him and then back at his brother. In a moment of clarity Ralph said, 'With Austin.'

'Yeah, how did you know?'

Ralph wondered why Austin called his brother David and not Dave like everyone else, he would have to ask him some time.

Dave was still looking at him quizzically.

Ralph's mind ticked over. Dave and Austin. The memorial event. The boy dead on the tracks.

'It was at the Clapham rail disaster that I let that kid die,' Ralph said quietly.

Dave stared back in surprise and then his face took on a pained expression, his eyes deeply sad.

Ralph had to look away.

Suddenly Dave's phone beeped angrily and he yanked it out of his pocket. 'It's him, Austin, I need to get moving or we'll be late.'

'Sure.' Ralph picked up his bag again ready to move on.

'Wait.' Dave put a hand on Ralph's shoulder. 'Maybe you should come with us.'

68

Adam – Follow your heart

'We didn't have to come,' said Adam's mother. They were on the train heading to Clapham.

'Yes we did,' his father said. 'It's the right thing to do. We should give thanks for our son.'

Adam glanced across and caught them both smiling at him. Sully was sitting opposite texting on his phone. Adam looked away out of the window at the backs of townhouses. A woman standing at a window stared back as the train rolled past. It was odd to be heading towards the site of the crash, to platform nine, Clapham Junction. The mayor of London was due to unveil a memorial plaque embedded into the new platform. A brass band and other dignitaries would be there. It seemed strange to be celebrating such a terrible event. Adam considered why his parents had been keen to come. Grateful, he supposed, that he'd been a survivor instead of the numbered dead. Sully had even given him a gift that morning. A crisp white shirt with thin yellow stripes, Adam hadn't been sure at first but when he tried it on, it looked and felt good. Better than the shirt he'd borrowed from Sully for his job interview. He was wearing it now.

The train slowed, drawing into Queenstown station. There were people standing on the platform and three men rising from a bench. Adam was startled and tried to look again but the train had already slid gently past, coming to a stop further along the platform. It had looked like Dave. Could it have been his boss? Adam rewound the image in his head, three men on a bench sitting close together like they knew each other. There had been a hand on Dave's knee, not his own. Adam dismissed the image. His boss would be at work. After the stress of the last few days, it was probably just his mind playing tricks. So many images swimming in his brain, hadn't he been imagining Dave's murder only a few hours ago? It seemed ludicrous now.

The sound of beeping and the doors opened. A few more people got on. Adam stared at the floor, a scuffed pair of brogues went past, some small green slip-ons and then a pair of faded blue trainers. Adam's eyes fixed on the trainers. One had a frayed white lace that was knotted after the first three holes. The trainers turned and stopped by a seat, just a short distance away. Only then did Adam glance up at the body and face. He immediately looked away again, staring at his parents instead.

'It's all right love, we're here with you.' His mother patted his knee.

Adam's stomach had knotted up tight. Those trainers, that face. He'd seen them before. Adam stared out of the opposite window away from the dark-skinned youth. He wondered if anyone else could hear his heartbeat, it was so loud. Adam breathed out. It was just coincidence; that was all. But Adam couldn't help a crawling sensation seeping up his arms, like ice chilling him. He tried to breathe normally, get interested in what was outside on the platform, the adverts on the billboards. The doors beeped again and hissed shut. Adam stole a quick glance across at the youth who was sitting with another Asian young man. The second one was whispering something. It was definitely him, no doubt about it. The shoes. The face. Adam shivered.

'Do you want your jacket on?' his mum asked.

'He's fine, it's not cold,' said his dad.

Adam stared hard at the billboard on the platform, wanting so much for the image of a new phone and its slogan 'you're more powerful than you think' to fill his mind, to block everything else out. Couldn't he just be one of these ignorant passengers blindly believing in advertising? The train started with a small jolt and the image was snatched away, leaving space for Adam's thoughts to come rushing in.

The face of Ibrahim Muhammad Sharif at one of the meetings staring intently at Adam, his finger pointing saying, 'We must give the British Government a strong message.' The next image was Faizal's energetic face, his eyes darting to and fro and his conspiratorial whisper.

'I've been chosen to deliver special information.'

What if Faizal had been given a real number? The media and police believed that somewhere amongst all the misinformation could be a real ISIS plot. Was that possible? As far as he knew, Aisha was still missing. He thought about Ibrahim Muhammed Sharif, his sweet words and sickly scones coupled with Hasib and the tablet of instructions. Yes, it was definitely possible.

Next he remembered the upstairs hallway of the tall terraced house. Lying in the giant's arms as they exited the toilet and came face to face with a youth wearing faded trainers and a broken lace knotted half way up. Adam willed himself not to look again, clenched his teeth and forced his gaze out of the window at the blurred buildings as the train gathered speed. But he couldn't stop himself; he glanced over again at the two young men. Adam wanted to doubt himself, find a fault in his logic. The youth was wearing a large denim jacket, too large for his skinny frame, and yet he wasn't skinny, at least not today. Adam tore his gaze away and let out a trembling sigh. Maybe it was his fat brother, or a cousin that looked really similar. Cold seeped along Adam's spine, spread tentacles into his body. No matter how much he wished, there was no changing the facts. It was the same guy and there was no way he could have put on thirty extra pounds. It had only been a few weeks since he'd been for that strange interview.

Adam closed his eyes shutting out the images but the sounds became intensified. The rattling of the metal train, somebody talking loudly on their mobile phone, another laughing at a joke, a zip being pulled and below all this clutter of noise was a quiet murmuring, warm and soothing. The lull and sway of the voice reminded Adam of Zeeshan saying his prayers. That same rhythm as they bowed together in the post room. It was the two Muslim young men.

A vision of Aisha's note leapt into Adam's mind. Remember Computers J9. The C and the J written in bold. Adam suddenly clenched his hands. J-block only had eight rooms not nine. Clapham Junction platform 9.

Adam opened his eyes, buildings flying past the window. Faizal leapt into his head again.

'One, zero, five, three.' That was the secret information Faizal had been given.

Adam checked his watch, it read 10:49.

A hot coal had deposited itself in the pit of Adam's stomach. It was growing hotter as if he'd eaten too many chillies and he was being warmed from the inside out. Memories swirled, snippets of conversations with Faizal and speeches at the meetings.

'It's easier to open an old wound than make a new one.'

'They won't use one of us, we're too westernised, they bring them in from Libya.'

Adam thought about the accented Arabic the youth had spoken in the oak hallway.

He thought about the memorial service they were racing towards. The new platform nine that would be opened at Clapham station and all the families and friends gathered to honour the dead and give thanks for the living. A wound that hadn't yet healed, Adam stared down at his useless legs.

The heat was intense, Adam flexed his hands, there was no pain, only a deep nervousness, a tenseness that he remembered before a basketball game started. His hands on the wheels ready for the whistle. He looked up at his parents; they were sitting close together, their hands clasped. They didn't deserve to die. The young woman tapping on her phone next to them. Those three men that had stood up from the bench as the train arrived. Even if it had been Dave, did they all deserve to die or, like him, become horribly maimed or scarred for life? Could this really be Allah's plan to wreak such pain and havoc? Again? Adam remembered lying in the hospital bed and his mother's tears soaking the sheet by his cheek.

Faizal's face was back, his eyes even more intense.

'One zero five three.'

Adam looked again at his watch.

10:50.

He was running out of time. Just three minutes until they arrived at Clapham Junction.

Now it was Vijay popping into his head, those steady eyes, his half-smile. They were outside the basketball court and Adam had just failed to get into the national team. All he wanted was to be left alone but still Vijay stung him with his words:

'Giving up is what everyone does, it's the ones that don't give in that get remembered.'

If he gave up now he'd just be the kid that was unlucky twice.

Adam wanted his life, useless legs and all, he wanted to be somebody and he wasn't going to let this foreign boy ruin his world. The heat boiled out of Adam. The youth with the trainers should never have come here, this wasn't his country, these were not his people. This fucked up place called London belonged to Adam and Adam belonged to it. He belonged to the basketball team and the community mosque, he was a member of his dear family and all the extended relations of aunties and uncles and maybe even that strange woman with the flattened ear on the tube the other night. This was where he belonged, these were his people, even on this train with so many strangers, they were Londoners like himself, they were the people that bound his world together. Adam wanted to be here in this body. He wasn't going to roll over and let someone else wipe him off the planet. It wasn't fear or hatred in his heart. This was love. A powerful love for all that meant something to him. He would fight, he would fight for all the people he might or might not know. For Aisha, wherever she was.

Adam had already assessed the space between himself and the bomber. The position of the pole that reached from floor to ceiling and the fact that his wheelchair would not pass beyond it. The space in which to turn and how much momentum could be gained in a short run. All these things came naturally from his basketball training and he was grateful for last night's practice. Now he was on the court ready for the goal of his life. In the side pocket he still had the vegetable knife, dropped in after his father had surprised him this morning.

There wasn't time to change his mind, to consider all the implications. As things stood his life would be over in just a couple of minutes. Unless he found the courage to make a difference. Perhaps this had been Allah's calling after all. The events in the last few months preparing him for this moment. The one true path, not in fear or hate, but out of love, here, now, on this train where people's lives mattered, where his life mattered.

Adam glanced one last time at his parents, the love filling him, making him even more powerful. Silently, without looking, he unclipped the belt that kept his legs in place, then slid his fingers into the side pocket, the palm of his hand curling comfortably around the handle of the vegetable knife. This was it.

He spun the wheelchair, pushed hard across the space by the train doors. The chair clanged into the pole giving his torso that extra momentum as he launched his entire body out of the wheelchair and onto the youth. In Adam's right hand, he had the vegetable knife grasped tight and as the youth jerked his head up in surprise, his smooth neck became an easy target. Adam struck hard and deep.

69

Ralph – The hero within

Ralph was on his feet looking back towards where the passengers were coming from.

'What the fuck? We should get off,' Dave said pulling Austin roughly to his feet.

'What's happened?' Ralph grabbed the arm of a suited man as he came tumbling past. He tried to pull away but Ralph held him fast. 'What's going on?'

'I don't know, there's blood everywhere. Let me go.'

Ralph released the man's arm.

'Let's get out of here.' Dave was already sliding out from behind the table pulling Austin with him.

But Ralph didn't move, he was staring at the doors through which the passengers were coming. It was the word blood that stopped him. Blood was what he dealt with. Blood was the life force of each and every one of them. A bleeding person could be a dying person. Somewhere beyond those doors was a person in need. Someone that Ralph could help. I'm a paramedic, he thought.

'Ralph, come on!' It was Dave, he was disappearing down the carriage with Austin just in front.

'I am a paramedic,' Ralph said and the words felt good in his mouth. They were substantial and true. He turned away from his brother and said the words again a little louder.

'I am a paramedic.'

The people were thinning out and Ralph started to make his way against the ebbing tide.

'Excuse me, paramedic coming through.'

A girl got in his way thrusting a phone in his face. He took hold of a bunch of fabric on her jacket, pulled her to him then turned and gently pushed her away towards where the other passengers had fled.

'Get out of here,' he said and marched on through the doors.

At first it looked like somebody had spray-painted the window and seat bright red. And for a brief second Ralph wondered if maybe it was a false alarm, some kid letting off a spray can. But there were two bodies on the floor, an over-turned wheelchair beyond them and a pool of the thick liquid by Ralph's shoe. It wasn't paint. And then the smell hit him. Blood and lots of it.

One dark-skinned man was lying on top of another. The one underneath was alive, his brown eyes, looking shocked, stared up at Ralph. It was difficult to know what injuries he was dealing with but he needed to move them apart at least. Standing astride the bodies, Ralph bent his knees and went to grasp the man on top but the brown face suddenly came vividly to life, shaking furiously.

'Don't. He's got a bomb.'

But Ralph already had his hands around the man and it felt all wrong like he was wearing some kind of hard box under the thin jacket. He paused staring back as the young man continued to shake his head vigorously. Then he saw the knife hanging at an angle out of the side of the upper man's neck.

'Jesus.' Ralph slowly released his fingers and stood back.

'Has Sully got my parents out?' The guy on the floor had tears in his eyes. Ralph surveyed the carriage, there were only three other people. One black lady sat stock still staring at nothing, another woman stood at the end of the corridor with her phone out and a man was leaning over a seat doing the same thing, only his phone made a clicking sound as he pointed it at the bodies on the floor. None of them looked like the young man's parents.

'Get out,' Ralph said.

He looked down again at the man pinned on the floor. 'They're not here.'

Cautiously Ralph put his fingers to the stabbed man's neck, on the side away from the knife. Of course there was nothing, no pulse, his body completely still. Gingerly Ralph lifted the back of the denim jacket, his own heart was pumping triple-time.

It was rather like the kind of black vest that armed police wore at the airport but it was too large, too boxy looking and it terrified Ralph. He let go of the fabric and staggered back, his foot sliding in the blood and suddenly his arms were pin wheeling. He hit the floor on his arse, hard.

'Jesus Christ.'

Ralph could see that the man with the phone was still there, the other two had gone.

'Get the hell out. Tell them there's a bomb.' Ralph was trembling and he deliberately squeezed his hands into fists and then yelled at the stupid guy with his phone.

'There's a fucking bomb!'

The guy scrambled off the seat and disappeared down the carriage and through the doors. Ralph shut his eyes for a moment and breathed out slowly. He was sitting on the floor by the legs of the two bodies. The wetness was seeping into the seat of his jeans. Something touched his arm and Ralph shrieked but it was only the youth reaching out his fingertips. His soft brown eyes were imploring him.

Ralph edged closer and grasped the man's hand tight, the brown fingers gripped him back.

'I know you,' Ralph said. That face, that strong hand grip. But he was older, more a man than a boy. 'You were on the train that day.'

Adam nodded. He was crying freely.

'It took six of us to get you out, I thought we might lose you, but you hung on. You survived.'

Adam nodded again, he was breathing shallowly then he licked his lips.

'Are we going to die?' Adam said.

Ralph didn't know. What could he possibly know about explosive devices? It could be on a timer or maybe the slightest wrong move from either of them could set it off. He squeezed Adam's hand a bit tighter.

'I don't know, but I'm going to stay here with you.'

70

Halima – Lost shoes

Halima stood amongst the crowd, a warm energy of kindness and welcome pervaded the audience. There were lots of smiles and plenty of people holding hands or clasping loved ones. They stood several rows deep all along platform nine at Clapham Junction. The chatter was loud but friendly and Halima let the noise wash over her. Despite not having anyone to speak to herself, she knew she belonged.

Suddenly there was a squeal of brakes and Halima turned sharply to see a train in the distance lurching to a stop. The crowd seemed to gasp as one. The train moved forwards slowly and then stopped again beyond the far end of the platform. As they watched they could hear noises, indistinct shouts. The crowd shuffled. What was warm before now felt sharp and tense as people elbowed to see what was happening. Then the loudspeaker came on and they were told to evacuate the platform.

Halima was thrust into a billboard as the crowd surged and the noise erupted. Gone was the friendly chatter, now the voices were rising in panic. Her feet moved as the sea enveloped her and carried her in its current.

People jostled around Halima as she tried to regain her thoughts. Where was she? The unfamiliar road junction was made more peculiar by the fact that no one was paying any heed to the traffic lights. People were running and walking in all directions across the roads; a steady stream still coming out of Clapham station and spreading out like a million ants from their nest.

'Move along love, we're clearing the area, there's been a bomb threat.' A policeman put a hand on her back.

She started walking, not knowing which direction or where she might go. It was all so confusing, so frightening. She stumbled a little off the kerb but kept her feet and was surprised to notice she didn't have her shoe on. She turned back, assuming it had come off as she stepped off the pavement but it wasn't there. Perhaps she'd lost it inside.

'Sorry love, not this way.' The same policeman prevented her from heading back.

'But my shoe,' she said.

He simply shook his head and motioned with his arm to move away. Confused, Halima crossed the road and tried to push open the door of a coffee shop but a staff member was locking it through the glass. Instead she followed some other people who were jogging along the pavement. Halima tried to go a bit faster but she was finding it difficult with only one shoe on. She paused and bent to take off the remaining one. It felt damp and when she looked at her hand there was a smudge of dark red. Horrified she dropped the shoe. She didn't think she was hurt. Putting her hands to her face, she found that was wet too. Slowly she pulled her hands away to see the blood, but there was none, only wetness. They must be tears or sweat, she didn't know which. Was she hurt? Standing still as others continued on, she clasped her arms.

Hadn't there been a bomb? Did it go off? Was she hit? Images pattered through her brain. The train stopping beyond the platform and then the side walls of the tunnel with masonry tumbled around her but that had been three years ago, not now. She thought about that strange evening a few nights ago when she'd travelled on countless tube trains back and forth.

'I have a grandson,' she suddenly said aloud. Two people ahead of her turned but didn't stop. Halima blinked wondering how it could be possible. She had no idea how to find him. She wanted to go home to her mother, but she wasn't there, had she died? Halima found herself walking along Falcon Road, a route she was familiar with. It felt right so she kept on going. She needed to find someone.

Veronica, that's who she needed but wasn't she still in Scotland? Or had she moved to Scotland? Halima felt like someone had taken out her brain, shaken it all up and shoved it

377

back in. Nothing seemed to make sense. Had there been a crash? A bomb? Halima kept going counting the steps as her socked feet slapped the pavement. It seemed the only safe thing to do. Walk. Count. Don't think.

At step three thousand and sixty four, Halima recognised the big glass doors of Thyredata Enterprises. With a huge sense of relief, Halima pushed through into the marble reception area. A strange man with white hair stood behind the desk staring at her.

'Where's Vincent?' she cried.

'Are you OK?' He immediately came around towards her.

'Vincent,' Halima said hearing the wobble in her voice.

'His shift finished at eight. I'm Barry. Do you want to sit down? Has something terrible happened?'

Halima burst into tears.

'There, let's get you a seat,' he led her to a side room that was small and had three monitors showing CCTV footage around the building. Halima sat in a brown swivel chair and Barry hurried off to get her a glass of water.

'Here you go.' He handed her the plastic cup and a bunch of tissues.

Halima took a sip and used the tissues to clean her face.

'Are you Miss Shah by any chance?' Barry said.

Halima gazed at his white bushy eyebrows and kindly smile. She nodded.

'Vincent's told me all about you, calls you his little rosebud. Why don't I call him, tell him you're here. Looks like you could do with a friend.'

'Rosebud?'

'Yeah,' Barry grinned broadly, 'reckon he can get you to flower. But I don't mean anything rude or nothing. Sorry, didn't mean to embarrass you, not my place, gob runs away with me sometimes. I'll go and give him a ring.' With that he disappeared and closed the door behind him.

Halima sat quite still looking at the damp tissue and down at her dirty socks. What had happened to her shoes?

Rosebud?

On one of the monitors she could see Barry talking into the

phone at reception, he was nodding vigorously and frowning. He said a few more words, smiled and then rang off.

Rosebud.

Halima felt a small knot of tension release somewhere in her belly and a tear rolled down her cheek.

2 weeks later

71

Austin - A new beginning

Finally the meeting was over and Austin dropped his empty cup into the bin on his way out. The project was going to be a big one, they might even need to recruit more staff which could mean a promotion.

'Exciting stuff huh? You were very vocal today.' It was Tim giving him a pat on the back as they stepped into the lift.

'Yeah, I'm up for a new challenge.'

Tim pressed the button for the fifth floor. They stood in silence for a moment and then Tim said, 'You seem very happy.'

'Yeah, I think I am.' Austin grinned.

'Good for you.'

The doors opened onto their large shared office. Across the room, he could see a gathering of people around his desk. What were they up to? It wasn't his birthday until next week.

'There he is.' Vincent, the security guard, pointed at Austin. From their faces Austin realised that this was no social visit. One of the senior managers, Mr Dhawan, was frowning and Vincent had a kind of desperate look in his eye. Between them stood a woman in a bright yellow headscarf, bowed over. She seemed upset.

'What's happened?' Austin said.

'Is this your desk Mr Baker sir?' Vincent spoke loudly.

'Yes?'

Mr Dhawan had his arms crossed and was staring at the woman's bowed head. 'Well, get on with it.'

The woman sniffled and looked up at Austin then dropped her gaze again. It was the cleaner he had seen a couple of times before.

'But that's not Jessica,' she whispered.

'Who?' said Austin.

'For pity's sake,' said the manager.

Vincent immediately put a hand on the woman's shoulder.

'Halima, we've talked about this,' Vincent said, 'there is no Jessica, this is Mr Baker's desk.'

Halima shook her head sadly and then she reached out a hand and picked up Austin's pen lying on the desk. She stroked the pink fluffy end, then replaced it into the pen pot.

'But it's Jessica's,' she said.

Mr Dhawan made an audible huff and said, 'Vincent, this is going nowhere, I think we should go back downstairs. I will not trail around the entire building looking for mythical people that may or may not have evidence.' He turned to Austin. 'I'm sorry we've had to bother you, Mr Baker.'

The room had grown remarkably quiet and Austin wondered what on earth was going on.

'Who's Jessica?' Austin said.

'We're sorry sir, it's just that Halima, well-' Vincent swallowed and glanced briefly at the manager then back to Halima. He seemed to rise up a little as if growing taller. 'Halima has been accused of theft and we are here to, to, show that Halima isn't a thief.'

'Well of course not.' Austin shrugged. Why would anyone think that?

'Please Halima,' Vincent said quietly.

Austin could feel Mr Dhawan's patience slipping away, his face getting pinker by the second.

'What is it you wanted to say?' said Austin to Halima.

Halima spoke tentatively, 'Where is the photo?'

'Photo?'

'Of Matt.'

Austin was momentarily surprised, then he pulled open the bottom drawer of the desk and rifled under the folders for the wooden frame. He pulled it out and handed it to Halima.

She clutched the picture tight against her bosom with what appeared to be relief and a small smile whispered across her lips.

'Yes, this is the desk,' she said.

'What on earth is going on now?' Mr Dhawan huffed.

Vincent said hurriedly, 'Um, there was a credit card, I mean, Halima said there was a credit card.'

'Yes,' Austin suddenly remembered. 'Tim!' He called out across the quiet office.

Tim stood up uncertainly, adjusting his glasses. Austin beckoned him over.

'Do you remember a few months ago, I gave you your credit card back?'

'Yes, I remember,' he nodded.

The manager butted in. 'Hold on a minute, let's get this clear from the start. What happened?'

'I came in to the office early,' Austin explained. 'There was Tim's credit card in the middle of my desk so I gave it back to Tim. I assumed the cleaner, I mean, Halima here, had put it there.'

Halima nodded vigorously.

'Is that correct?' The manager turned his attention to Tim.

'I guess so, Austin sent me an email and he gave it to me later that day,' Tim said.

'And was there anything missing from your bank account? Had the card been used?'

'No.' Tim shrugged. 'I think I probably dropped it under the desk or something.'

Again Halima nodded.

'I see.' The manager sighed. 'Right, we'll need you guys to put something in writing to that effect and email it through to me. Thank you, gentlemen.' He turned to Halima who immediately hid her eyes, still hugging the picture to her chest. 'Well you seem to have your evidence Miss Shah, I suggest we go back downstairs and you can put your version in writing too. Perhaps I need to follow up on your suggestion Vincent.'

'Yes sir, I do think Mrs Phipps should be investigated.' The two men started heading back towards the lifts.

Halima was still holding the photo frame. Austin stared at her and she stared back. He wondered why it seemed important to her. He smiled. Slowly she uncurled her arms and held the picture out for him.

Austin took it.

'He has a nice smile,' she said.

'Yes.' He paused, waiting to be overwhelmed by grief, but the feeling didn't come and he breathed a sigh of relief. 'He did. A lovely smile.' Austin opened the drawer and replaced the photo deep inside. When he straightened up, Halima had already left.

72

Adam - Home

Adam found his eyes were drooping; he was so, so tired. The first day had been bearable in the hospital but they soon discharged him into police custody. Since then, there had been nothing but questions interspersed with a hard bed, in a small concrete room, and sporadic meals. He had lived and breathed those same questions over and over until they swam in his dreams. The faces of the police officers and detectives asking him again and again was so constant that sometimes Adam wasn't sure if he was dreaming or awake. But finally he was nearly home. The police car turned the corner into Walton Road. Ahead there appeared to be a crowd of people. Adam rubbed his eyes and then stared between the front seats through the windscreen. There was a banner and people in the road.

'Don't worry son, we'll escort you inside,' the driver said. He had to honk his horn to get people to move and then the crowd were surrounding the car, cameras and faces staring in at him. There were a few he recognised like Auntie Sana but most he didn't, he assumed they were members of the press or maybe curious public.

'You wait here, keep the door shut. We'll make some space.' The two police officers got out and started moving the crowd, one of them shouting above the noise. Then the car door opened and one of the police officers had his wheelchair on the pavement. Adam tried to ignore the clamouring voices and the yelled questions.

'Are you glad to be home?'

'Was Ibrahim Muhammed Sharif behind the failed attack?'

'You're a hero Adam!'

'Do you think Marwan Al-Nasseri deserved to die?'

Adam stared at his chair. It was sitting waiting on the pavement, but the car seat was low and the pavement high. It would be difficult to get himself up and into it from this position. The last thing he wanted was to make a fool of himself in front of all of these people. He just wanted to be home.

'Come on then sir, let's get you inside.' The policeman holding the back of his wheelchair beckoned him out. Back at the police station it had all been on a level, no kerb and besides it was always easier moving from a higher seat into a lower one. Getting out was a whole different ball game.

'Let me through,' a familiar voice at last.

'Back off sir.'

'I'm his father, let me be.' Then his father's face was there, his eyebrows knit together. His face thrust in close and then he gently put his hand to Adam's cheek. 'Hello son.'

'Dad.' Adam couldn't say any more, the emotion stuck in his throat.

Adam wanted to drag his father into the car with him and shut the door. Maybe they could squeeze the whole family in and get out of there.

'Don't worry son, we'll sort this out.' Adam's father took on a determined look then pulled back out of the car. 'We need more space, move this chair back.' Adam could see him pull the wheelchair around until it faced the car a couple of feet further away, then he came back.

'You remember how we used to do this.' He smiled again and set his legs slightly apart with his knees bent.

Adam sighed, it wasn't the most elegant method but at least it would work and he shouldn't end up falling over. Adam lifted his legs and swivelled so he could plant them on the curb outside. Then he shuffled his bottom to the edge of the seat and wrapped his arms around his father's neck. Immediately his father straightened his legs. Adam could smell his father's sweat and feel his firm arms wrapped around his body for extra support. Now they were both standing up in a close hugging position. He was taller than his father, much taller and he worried that he might be too heavy. But the older man stood solidly and then they shuffled around and his father was bending his legs again and Adam put a hand behind him to guide his lower half into the waiting wheelchair. When he finally let go there was a round of applause and then the clamouring started again.

The police were moving people out of the way, providing a clear space for them to get through. Ahead his mother was stood in the doorway holding her scarf across her face, trying to hide the tears. Closer, Sully stood alongside the policemen with his arms out holding back a cameraman and a woman with a large microphone.

'Adam, what's your view of the UMIA?'

'Were you used by ISIS?'

'Do you still believe in God?'

Adam had his hands on the wheels and pushed himself forwards.

'Keep back,' his father shouted from behind, 'no comment.'

'Sir, do you think your son is a hero or a murderer?'

'What do you think?' said his father and then they were up the ramp and in the hallway and Sully came rushing in behind them and slammed the door shut.

6 weeks later

73

Ralph – A super man but not Superman

Ralph pushed open the door of the ambulance station. Inside looked just the same as it always had, two colleagues were refilling a drugs bag, another was at the board writing up some details about one of the vans. The difference was their reaction to his arrival. What started as a low murmur became a loud cheer and then a high-pitched squeal as Emma threw herself at him.

'Ralph!' She hugged him tight before letting go.

Ian came over and shook hands, giving him a firm pat on his shoulder. 'Good to have you back.'

Ralph swallowed, he hadn't expected this, he felt like he'd let them down. One of the managers was in there too and she came over smiling broadly.

'You're looking well Ralph. It can't be easy but we're here to support you. I've let control know that you're back today and they'll do their best to ease you in.'

Ian laughed loudly. 'Ease him in, what, in London? You've got to be joking. It's hell out there, like it always is.'

The manager didn't lose her smile. 'Well we'll do our best, if you need to call in at any time, ask for me. I'll be checking in with you throughout your shift anyway. You're on with Emma so that should suit.'

Emma winked at him.

Ralph breathed out heavily, maybe he'd be all right, he'd been dreading coming back, but now he was here amongst the welcoming paramedic family. He smiled back.

'So come on, let's get saving some lives,' Emma said. 'I've got the keys, you get the drugs and we'll be on our way.'

'Right.' Ralph took a breath and got going on the familiar routine. Checking the board, signing out the drugs bag. Just as he was heading out to the ambulance, Ian stopped him.

'Take care now lad, we've all been there and those of us that make it back, well, they need us out there in the jungle. They need you, Ralph.' He clapped him on the back. 'Be safe.'

Later they were sitting at the Farley Junction watching the drivers jump the lights as usual.

Ralph was watching Emma sip her coffee.

'I thought they had already posted you to a different area.'

'Not yet, my final exam isn't till next month.'

'You worried?'

'A bit,' she looked across at him, 'but I've got the perfect team mate to help me prepare.'

Ralph shook his head. 'I wouldn't be so sure about that.'

'Seriously, you're one of the best and believe me, I've worked with a lot of different paramedics.'

'You're just saying that cos it's my first day back.'

Now it was Emma's turn to shake her head. 'No, it's true. You have like this professional commitment, like it really matters. You care.'

'Too much and look where it got me.'

Emma looked out the windscreen again. 'I'd like to be as good as you one day Ralph.'

The side of her milky white neck looked vulnerable.

'You OK?' she asked.

'Yeah, I'm good.' And he was. Sometimes he still thought about that kid on the track, and the kid's mother, also about that bomber on the train but Ralph was reconciled with the fact that he wasn't Superman, nor Superdad. He was just Ralph, a paramedic, a husband, a regular father who tried to do his best. Emma and Shelly obviously thought that was good enough and maybe so should he.

The radio panel crackled to life and beeped at them loudly. Ralph hit the button and the display came up with an address. Control started to explain the emergency callout, a child at school with a severe asthma attack.

'Blue lights on, let's go,' said Ralph.

74

Austin – Family party

Austin paused on the pavement to tuck the edge of his shirt in a bit tighter.

'Will you just come on?' David stopped a few yards in front. They were nearly there. Bright sunshine glinted off the hanging pub sign.

'I just want to look my best. First impressions count.'

'Believe me, it won't be your clothes that'll blow them away.'

The pub was now only fifty yards. Austin stopped again.

'What's that supposed to mean?'

'It doesn't matter.' David sighed. 'Look, we don't have to go.'

'You don't really want me to meet your family do you?' Austin folded his arms.

'It's not that, it's just-' David huffed out some air and ran a hand through his fringe '- I don't normally take people to family occasions like this.'

'But *you* invited me to your Aunt Maureen's sixtieth.'

'I know.'

'So now you wish you hadn't, is that it?' Austin just couldn't work him out.

'It's complicated,' David said.

A bald man had appeared across the street and was waving enthusiastically. 'Ahoy, is that you Dave?' Next to him stood a lady with greying hair in a hideous pastel pink dress.

'Who's that?' asked Austin in a hushed voice.

'Fucking Uncle Robin.'

David walked a few steps away from Austin and called across, 'I'm just talking with a friend Robin, I'll see you in there.' He pointed at the pub.

The man across the road nodded and then crossed over.

'Fine,' Austin said, 'go on your own.'

'No, Austin wait.'

But Austin was already marching back the way they had come. Behind him he could hear loud Uncle Robin.

'I say, lover's tiff?'

Austin kept walking but within seconds David had caught up and grabbed his sleeve.

'No really, please come,' he said giving that sheepish grin of his.

Austin checked his appearance in the mirror and smoothed his hands down the front of the new shirt. He pulled down the cuffs a little and swivelled the cuff links so they were both the right way up. Actually being alone here in the toilet was a bit of a relief. It seemed all of David's relatives wanted to meet him and he'd had barely a moment to himself or with David. Austin gave himself one last appraisal in the mirror and then pulled open the toilet door.

Two boys stood side by side in the narrow pub corridor blocking his way. Austin thought they were a bit young to get heavy with him but it didn't stop his heart giving a slight skip.

'Sorry, were you waiting to go in?' Austin looked from one to the other.

They both shook their heads but neither made a move to let him pass. Then the older one remembered himself and stepped forwards, extending his hand.

'I'm Liam and this is my little brother Cameron.'

Austin shook the hand. 'Of course, you're David's nephews.'

They both nodded.

Austin was beginning to feel distinctly awkward, they obviously wanted something from him. They continued to stare, saying nothing. Austin tried to remember what David had said about them, if anything. He'd given a massive info dump on various people he should expect to meet at the party but Austin had forgotten most of it.

'Does one of you play football?'

'Yeah, me.'

'Him.'

'Great, it's a good game, do you play for a club?'

'I'm in the under fourteens,' Liam said cocking his head to one side and giving Austin an up and down gaze.

Cameron asked, 'What do you do?'

'Me? I work in computers, testing for a big software company. You probably haven't heard of it. Thyredata Enterprises.'

'I'm good at Maths.'

'That's a good subject. You can do a lot with Maths.'

Liam was staring critically at Austin's legs. 'Where did you get your jeans from?'

'Err, these ones I think came from Zara.'

Cameron sniggered and his brother elbowed him.

'They have a men's department,' Austin added, trying hard not to be embarrassed.

'Yeah, I knew that.' Liam said glancing towards his younger brother. 'He's too stupid.'

'No I'm not.'

'Yes you are.' There was another scuffle and Austin wondered how long they were going to keep him stuck in the corridor.

'Shall we go back in and join the party?' Austin said.

'Sure.' Liam led the way with Cameron following and Austin breathed a sigh of relief.

They went through the door into the garden and the hubbub of chatter. Cameron suddenly turned around and said, 'Josh in our class has got two dads. He calls one Dad and the other one Pops. What are your kids going to call you and Uncle Dave?'

'Cameron you idiot, you can't ask that!' Liam grabbed Cameron's arm and started dragging him away.

Just then Mrs Calder approached. 'I do hope my grandsons aren't being tiresome, they are rather lively sometimes.' She smiled at him. 'Why don't you come and meet Jack, he always likes to meet new people, he gets bored of all of us.' She slid her arm through Austin's and pulled him gently towards an elderly man sitting in a chair with a half pint of beer in his hand. Austin looked around in the vague hope of spotting David but instead Auntie Maureen stopped them.

'Now then Mary, it's my party.' She took Austin's other arm and steered him away. In a hushed voice she said, 'Jack's awfully boring I'm afraid. If I was polite, I'd tell you he had a heart of gold, except he doesn't. Right miserly old sod. Anyway, I'm glad I caught you. There's something I've been meaning to ask you about Dave.'

Austin sighed. Did he have to spell it out? 'The thing is, me and David, we're not just friends Maureen.'

'Oh goodness.' She waved her hand. 'I know all that, it's obvious. No, no, what I'm intrigued by is why on earth has Dave handed in his resignation at work?'

75

Halima – A new start

Halima tipped out the contents of her handbag all over the worktop, she could feel panic squeezing her chest as her fingers spread out the objects, searching for that piece of paper. She found it under a screwed up tissue and sighed with relief. She unfolded it and spread the newspaper photo out. She should leave it behind, stop carrying it around with her or it would end up disintegrating. The photograph showed a young man with short dark hair and a beard. Beneath the picture Halima had cut most of the words away and only his name remained in bold type. Adam Rasheed. She stared at it for a minute and then moved it to one side while she repacked her bag. Then she picked up the letter from the windowsill and slipped that into her bag too. She would show it to Veronica later when they were due to meet at a small gallery. She could share her triumph at getting her job back. The thought pleased Halima. But the photograph, she still hadn't decided what to do with it. Again she picked it up and studied that face with its slight smile and bright eyes.

There was no time, she needed to get going. She left the photograph on the counter where it wouldn't get lost and glanced through the window at her blooming garden. Outside the day looked like it might become warm and bright but she'd take an umbrella just in case.

It was an odd time to be walking to Thyredata Enterprises. Too late to be on her way to work and too early to be on her way home. The route familiar and yet changed by the time. More traffic, more pedestrians walking briskly along. A few of the shops were open and others were being unlocked, the shutters rolled up with a clatter. The morning sun was already warm and the traffic fumes hung heavy in the air. Ahead the tunnel under the railway loomed dark but a steady stream of cars and buses continued unperturbed. Halima braced herself and took a breath before she entered the gloom. She scratched at the scar on her scalp and thought about how next week she would be back to her normal routine. Early morning in the pale dawn, ready to clean those desks. Halima hurried on towards the light at the other end. Out into the sunshine again and she would be there in another ten minutes. Halima checked her watch, she didn't want to be early, nor late. Perhaps she should slow down slightly. After all, he would wait, wouldn't he?

Halima stared ahead past the marching city folk and thought she could see a figure standing still. Was that him? She hoped so. Her insides were getting all fluttery. Was this what it felt like? So long ago that it was difficult to remember.

As she got closer, she could see the shining glass windows of Thyredata Enterprises. The pedestrian in front was blocking her view of the pavement but then they suddenly darted away across the road and there he was in his smart black shoes waiting for her. She wanted to run into his arms. She was so happy to see him standing there, waiting for her. She clutched her bag tightly.

'Halima.' Vincent's face glowed.

'Hello.'

'I wasn't sure you'd come.'

'I said I would.'

'You're right. And I know you're to be trusted. I always knew you could be trusted.'

They were stood close now, close enough for her to see the speckles of stubble on his chin. She wanted to reach out and touch them, feel if they were rough or soft. She had never felt a man's stubble before. All those years ago, her lover had been too young for stubble, only some wisps on his top lip. Halima dropped her gaze embarrassed.

'I brought my flask and an extra cup,' Vincent said indicating the satchel at his side. 'We could walk by the river if you'd like.'

Halima nodded, realising she was still clutching her bag tightly. They set off walking slowly side by side. Gradually as they talked about the flowers, the river, living in the capital, she relaxed. Side by side, her arm swinging gently, until the backs of their fingers brushed against each other.

76

Adam – Friends together

Adam flattened the chapatti with his hands. 'You need to keep stirring that or it will catch on the bottom.'

'Keep your hair on brother.' Faizal held the pan and slopped the curry around. 'I know what I'm doing.'

'Have you chopped those peppers yet?'

'Shit.' Faizal left the curry and darted across to the worktop banging Adam's chair as he went. 'Ouch.'

'You're useless.' Adam shook his head.

Just then Vijay whirred into the kitchen doorway. 'I'd offer to help but-' He smiled. 'Are you sure you lads can handle it? I could ask Cara if she'll stay and help.'

Adam turned and looked at his friend. 'No, I've got this. We've only got one more curry to make and about a dozen more chapattis.'

'Just exactly how many Jihadists have you invited?'

'What?' Faizal jumped and half the pepper leapt onto the floor.

'You'll get used to his sense of humour after a while.' Adam tossed another chapatti into the hot pan. 'Stumpy's coming from basketball with a few others and then about five from the mosque.'

'Oh, I meant to say,' Faizal sounded guilty, 'I invited Hussein too.'

Adam looked across at Faizal, surprised, 'The guy with the kufi?'

'Yeah, you know he's actually an alright dude. You did know he was engaged to Aisha didn't you?'

Adam felt his shoulders tense at the mention of her name.

Faizal continued, 'Of course, he's not any more, not since they discovered she was being deported back from the Turkish border.'

'Great,' said Vijay from the doorway, 'Jihadist women too.'

'She won't be coming here, be arrested I suppose. Her cousins too. Tariq was saying-'

'Faizal, can you give it a rest? I need that pepper chopped.' Adam could only hope that the police believed his story about Aisha's note, about her attempts to keep him from being used like a fool and her code about Clapham Junction.

'Oh yeah, I was just going to say that my sister's bringing a couple of friends too.'

Vijay spoke up, 'Ah so we *will* have some Jihadist women after all.'

Faizal stopped chopping and spoke under his breath: 'He won't say any of that shit when they're here will he?'

Adam grinned to himself.

'Thirty minutes and counting,' Vijay said.

'Fuck, we'll never be ready. Women are much better at this shit than us.' Faizal stabbed at the green pepper. 'Let's get Cara to stay, she seems nice.'

'Stop panicking Faizal. It's *my* party and I'll do it how I want.' Adam tossed another chapatti in the pan. 'Why don't you sort the music Vijay?'

'Good thinking, now that's certainly something I *can* do.' Vijay backed out of the kitchen and disappeared.

'How do you even know this guy?' Faizal said in a hushed voice.

'Long story,' Adam said then he called out loudly, 'And none of that weird Indian ding-a-ling shit OK?'

Faizal finished the peppers and Adam added them to the curry at the back. He tasted each one carefully and demanded more coriander for one and ginger for another.

'Well, I'm off.' It was Cara this time, standing in the doorway in a tight vest top and hot-pants. Her thighs bulged and her breasts looked ready to take off. Adam averted his gaze.

'Remember, no coke, not too much alcohol and definitely no drugs, plays havoc with his medication. You know the score.'

'Sure, and thanks for doing the decorations Cara.'

'Well it ain't your birthday everyday now is it? That's your youth gone now. No more teenage angst just the midlife crisis to look forward to.' She paused. 'Looks like your friend here's still just a boy.'

Adam glanced over at Faizal, he was standing with his mouth hanging open staring at Cara's breasts. When he realised they were both watching him, he shut his mouth with a clomp. Cara blew him a kiss and disappeared.

Vijay called from the other room, 'Hey, send out the sous chef to move some of this furniture.'

'What's a Sue Shef?' Faizal whispered. 'You know your mate's really odd.'

'Totally,' Adam agreed. 'You want to watch out, if you don't do what he says, he's liable to fit, shake himself right out of that chair and without Cara here, it'll be you that'll have to pick him up.'

Faizal looked decidedly worried. 'Shit, really?'

'Best go move the furniture and keep him happy.'

'Yeah absolutely, no worries.'

Adam went back to his curries, tasting again just to be sure. They were good, maybe he should consider what Vijay had said about becoming an apprentice chef. Damn, surely Vijay couldn't be right *all* the time.

The End

Books by Sarah Bartrum

Keep Them Safe

Tracks

Acknowledgements

It would be impossible to get to the end of a novel without the help of my supporters. Huge thanks go to Tara Savage for never giving up on me, even when I give up on myself. Thanks to so many of you for your valuable feedback and encouragement including but not limited to: Nasreen Rafiq, Robert Joyce, Steven Petherick, Julie Holden, Gilly Goldsworthy, Wendy Smith, Bonita Porri, Peter Burton, Elizabeth Vousden.

Research is an important part of the groundwork and the internet can only take you so far. My huge thanks go to: Bex for sharing her paramedic knowledge and experience with me, Nas for her cultural insights, Steve Spilka and the Hereward Heat Wheelchair Basketball Club.

Thanks to Rendel Harris for his excellent copyediting, especially for catching my grammar and syntax errors.

Writing is hard and I spend hours locked away in my office. Thanks to my wonderful husband and two boys for giving me the time and space to get it done.

Printed in Great Britain
by Amazon